D1373609

"CAN'T MY BROTHER HARRY SATISFY YOU, MY DEAR?"

Kate's husband, Sir Derek Ravenshaw, believed her torrid affair with his younger brother Harry had never ended. It was easy to believe it since Harry lived with them in the same house, forming a cozy threesome.

But her husband's cruel accusations drove Kate from his room. She fled down the hallway—into Harry's arms. *He* would not refuse her love.

"I don't know where your loving husband is, nor do I care." Harry's voice was hoarse with emotion; his arms were like steel bands. "He already thinks you warm my bed—why prove him wrong?"

He picked her up and carried her into the bedroom —the one she'd shared with Derek. But Kate did not resist—she threw herself into their wild and uncontrolled lovemaking. And now she no longer cared about choosing between them—she was no longer sure which brother she really loved!

BRIDE OF FURY

RACHEL COSGROVE PAYES

PLAYBOY PRESS
PAPERBACKS

BRIDE OF FURY

Copyright © 1979 by Rachel Cosgrove Payes and Ron Goulart

Cover illustration by Elaine Duillo: Copyright © 1979 by PEI Books, Inc.

All rights reserved. No part of this book may be reproduced, stored in a retrieval system or transmitted in any form by an electronic, mechanical, photocopying, recording means or otherwise without prior written permission of the author.

Published simultaneously in the United States and Canada by Playboy Press Paperbacks, New York, New York. Printed in the United States of America. Library of Congress Catalog Card Number: 79-89322. First edition.

Books are available at quantity discounts for promotional and industrial use. For further information, write our sales promotion agency: Ventura Associates, 40 East 49th Street, New York, New York 10017.

ISBN: 0-872-16592-2

First published February 1980.

For
JACK THE BODICE RIPPER

PROLOGUE

November 30, 1888

Kate quickly stripped off her good clothing. The dark blue
merino suit jacket she hung carefully on one of the pegs
along the mildewed wall. The long, flowing skirt she folded
and laid on the narrow cot that nearly filled the dreary
little room off Fieldgate Street in the Whitechapel section
of London's East End. Her white blouse of weighted silk
with its full, cuffed sleeves trimmed with ruffles of French
lace followed, and it, too, she hung from a peg.

The room was a far cry from her suite at Scarlet Oaks,
but then that was the whole idea. If she were to lure the
Ripper to attack her, Kate knew that she must look the
part of one of the area prostitutes. Even her fine silk under-
wear must be shed, although it would not show under the
clothes she had bought from a second-hand clothing barrow
near Aldgate Station. No one was going to see her petticoats and her chemise, no one would know she was wearing fine silk hose rather than coarse ribbed woolen ones,
for her masquerade skirt would sweep the filthy pave-
ments; but Kate knew that in order to act the part of a
whore, she must be dressed from the skin out in suitable
attire. It all was necessary for her mental state—and from
that mental state would come, she hoped, the outward
appearance that would provoke the deadly Jack the Ripper
to pursue her.

As Kate unfastened her bustle, she stopped, her fingers
suddenly refusing to move. What was she doing here? She

7

was Lady Kate Ravenshaw, not one of the poor, sad victims of the Ripper's savage knife. She wasn't Emma Smith, nor Long Liz Stride. She wasn't even poor Monica Murphy. She was wife to a dedicated physician, Sir Derek Ravenshaw, Bart. She must be mad to be here in this horrid room that smelled of stale cabbage and drains, of mildew and rotted vegetables. She could be back in her lovely home, Scarlet Oaks, in little more than two hours if she so chose. No one here knew her true name, no one knew who she was. Why didn't she just give up this idea, go back to Aldgate Station of the Metropolitan, and then transfer at Paddington to the first train out of London for Essex?

Even as she thought this, Kate's fingers were once again working at the fastening of her bustle; but instead of closing it, she kept on opening the placket and stepped out of the garment. She had to know. She couldn't go on this way, not knowing, suspecting that the man she loved more dearly than life itself was the fiend who had been brutally murdering the low-class prostitutes who lived in Whitechapel—killing them and then mutilating their bodies hideously.

She donned a coarse cotton chemise and laced the plain stays, which pushed her firm, youthful breasts high. Next came white muslin petticoats and a cheap bustle tied around her waist. She kept right on dressing, pulling on the ribbed woolen hose, and finally adding a heavy black serge skirt, worn around the hem where it had dragged on the rough London streets. The blouse that went with it was of a finer cotton, white, with a bit of embroidery on the ruffled front; but the ruffles were mended, and the seams were worn.

There was no mirror in the grubby little room in this dilapidated rooming house. The landlady, an odious character out of one of the seedier of Mr. Dickens's novels, had been reluctant to take Kate in.

"Watcher want this room fer?" she had demanded, squinting at the elegant lady on her doorstep. "A fine lady likes of you don't want to take a room in Finster's Lane. You belong in the West End."

Lying with little skill, Kate had said the first thing that

came to her mind. "I am helping out at the chapel on Whitechapel. Sometimes I may have to stay late—perhaps too late to want to travel far to sleep." She produced twice the rent Mrs. Waterman was asking. "For two weeks," she added, holding out the money.

Mrs. Waterman took the money with alacrity, but she had the last word, twisting her doughy face into a travesty of a smile. "No entertaining of gentlemen. I keeps a decent house here, which is more than can be said about most in this neighborhood."

"You came highly recommended," Kate lied valiantly, taking possession of the brass key and feeling soiled all over as she completed the transaction.

"Front door's on the latch until eleven each night," the landlady said as she put the money Kate had given her into a commodious pocket concealed in the seam of her shabby green wool skirt. "Can't leave it open later, 'cause of that wicked man, the Ripper, cutting up women. No better than they should be, you understand; but he has no call to kill them." Her eyes gleamed avidly, belying her words.

"It's a terrible thing. I hope the police—"

"Hoo! 'The police,' the lady says. Little good they do, you know. He slits their throats and slashes them open with a constable standing almost on top of him." She leaned closer, her rotted teeth showing as she smiled a dreadful smile. "There's them as says the Ripper is a toff, ma'am. The police know who he is. But he's so well placed they daren't touch him. People have seen well-set-up men talking to those poor, unfortunate women he killed. Gentlemanly, not the likes of the men you'd usually find roaming the streets of Whitechapel."

Kate was unable to suppress an involuntary shudder. This was one of the most horrendous rumors afloat: that the dreaded Ripper was of the upper class, not some dissolute, deranged denizen of Whitechapel. It was this fact that drove Kate to do what she planned to do.

She had not seen Mrs. Waterman, the landlady, since the night she had paid her the rent on this rat's nest. No doubt Mrs. Waterman wouldn't be in evidence again until it was time to pay more rent. Well, by that time Kate would be long gone.

Kate's trembling fingers finished fastening the neck of the shabby white blouse. Next she picked up a short, fitted black jacket from the bed. It was a poor grade of wool with a ratty fur collar, but it would frame her pale face and set off the red of her hair. Part of her hair she covered with a sleazy, black straw bonnet, which sported a be-draggled white feather on one side where the brim curled up to show one delicate ear. She tied the wide black ribbons under her chin and then slipped her feet into low-heeled shoes of cracked black leather. From her own bag of fine Spanish leather, Kate pulled out a small hand mirror, viewing herself with distaste. She felt so grubby, even though she knew that the clothes were clean, having seen to that herself after carrying them home secretly to Scarlet Oaks.

She had a beautiful little fob watch, which her love had given to her for her twenty-first birthday. It was one of Kate's prize possessions, and she was reluctant to leave it here in the rooming house. Finally Kate decided to pin the watch to her chemise, under the white blouse, where it could not possibly be seen by anyone. She didn't want to be hit over the head and robbed of the lovely piece of jewelry. After securing the watch to her undergarment, she resumed dressing in the masquerade costume she had chosen for herself.

It was a far cry from anything she had worn to a masquerade ball in Essex. For the first time in her life, Kate was wearing cheap, coarse clothing, which was the normal attire for thousands of unfortunate women in London's East End. It brought home a basic truth to her: Clothes were the woman! Once she had shed her own expensive garb and put on this cheap attire, Kate felt a dropping of spirits, a kind of hopelessness, that was not her normal self. Even with her desperate worries these last weeks, Kate had not felt so low.

It was nine o'clock. She dreaded going out into the cold and dark world that lurked outside. But if she fled back to Essex this would leave her with all her fears and suspicions unresolved. No, she had to find out. But how? She couldn't go about asking for him by name. She decided she would just walk the streets as if looking for customers—though she didn't know what she would do if some man accosted her. She would have to discourage them, although there was some evidence that the Ripper sometimes engaged his victims in conversation before he lured them to a dark, lonely corner and slit their throats. Dare she talk to any man who approached her? No, Kate knew she would be terrified of such an encounter. All she wanted to do was to make herself available, so that if the Ripper was in the vicinity, he would follow her.

I must see his face, she thought. I must. Only then will I know any peace.

Lest she waver in her resolve, Kate left the room, locking it behind her and hanging the key around her neck on a narrow ribbon, tucking it into the deep cleft between her breasts. "Mounds of exquisite delight," he called them. Her heart beat faster just thinking about how lovingly passionate he was.

Perhaps she thought she was well disguised. But one look at her lovely face—its classic oval of the palest fair skin, with the faintest dusting of freckles over the bridge of her straight classic nose; the noble brow, the delicately arched eyebrows of dark red, almost mahogany; the dark lashes masking her sparkling green eyes—and anyone but a fool would know that she had aristocratic blood in her veins, that she no more belonged here in Whitechapel than a diamond belonged in a heap of garbage.

Outside, the air was raw, with the first wisps of fog curling opaque tendrils around the gas streetlamp on the corner of Finster Lane and Fieldgate Street. Kate turned right, consciously going away from Whitechapel, where the chapel was located. She meant to stroll along; but the damp, cold air bit through the cheap jacket, and Kate found herself hurrying, one hand clutching the mangy fur collar up around her throat in an effort to keep warm. Was it also a subconscious gesture to ward off the Ripper's knife? There were plenty of people on the streets of Whitechapel at this hour, many reeling along, drunk on cheap gin. She passed several common lodging houses where there were huge rooms full of beds—sometimes more than fifty to a room—that rented by the night for fourpence, or eight-pence for a double. Kate had heard of the brutalizing conditions in these houses from the Reverend Mr. Fiddler and his upright wife. Was it any wonder that women in these slum areas of London turned to prostitution as a way of life?

One man accosted Kate as she came near the end of Fieldgate, a sailor by his looks, who lurched in front of her and asked baldly, "How much?" He put his hand on her shoulder, more to steady himself than for the sake of intimacy, for he was glassy-eyed with drink. They were in front of the Pig's Whistle, a local pub, and the light from the gas lamps lighted up his flat blue eyes.

Murmuring, "I'm meeting my husband," Kate fled from his beery breath, clutching the collar even closer to her face. Then she forced herself to slow down, tried to saunter as she'd seen some of the prostitutes do when she'd gone to the chapel to help them. The corner of Greenfield was coming up, and she turned there, planning to make a circle back to her rooming house.

There were still plenty of people around. Perhaps she was making a mistake, staying on some of the wider streets in this warren of narrow streets, alleys, and cul de sacs. Kate paused at the opening into one of these alleys, but it was so dark, so malodorous, that she was afraid to step into its gloom. Instead she hurried on down Greenfield. She had nearly gotten to the intersection with Coke, where she would turn right to circle back to Fieldgate, when Kate realized that the fog had thickened. The gas light ahead now was only a fuzzy glow, and the street on which she walked was darker and more difficult to follow. She didn't want to get caught in this section of Whitechapel in a typical London pea-soup fog. She might not be able to find her way back to Finster Lane if the mist closed in too densely.

She hurried, and from being on a well-populated street with people jostling each other in their haste to get from one pub to another, she found herself virtually alone, as if the lowering fog had blotted out everyone except herself with its thickening opacity. The streetlamp now was only a faint gleam ahead, even though she was closer to it than

before. Sounds took on a muffled quality, and she had difficulty in determining from what direction they came. She
wasn't lost. She knew that if she turned right at the corner,
Coke would lead her back to Plummer, which in turn
would take her on a long leg of the rectangle to Fieldgate.
If she didn't turn down Plummer, she would come to Mulberry—but in order to get back to her room that way, she
would eventually have to pass by the clinic on Union Row.

That would be a foolish move on her part. She might
be seen and recognized. She must stay away from the
clinic. Only if her disguise was successful could she hope
to learn the truth about the man she loved yet feared so
desperately.

It was then that Kate first heard the footsteps behind
her, footsteps that she thought might only be echoes of her
own, caused by the tricks a heavy fog made with sound.
Unconsciously she walked a little faster, although by now
it was difficult to see where she was walking. One moment
she could see vague outlines of the houses that lined Greenfield Street, and the next, everything was gone, as if a wet
sponge had been wiped across a picture drawn on a slate
board, obliterating it.

The feeling of blindness brought on by the fog made
Kate stop momentarily. Whoever was walking, following
her, now stopped, as she had done. There was a waiting quality in the fog, a sinister feel to it, that hadn't been
there before.

Thoroughly frightened now, Kate picked up her skirts
and began to tiptoe along toward Coke, but in the obscur-
ing fog, she kicked into something that made a rattling
sound. Immediately she heard the footsteps start up behind
her again. For a moment Kate could hear nothing but the
thudding of her heart, the pulsing of blood in her ears.
She was trembling, both from cold, for the damp chill of
the fog penetrated through the cheap clothing to her skin,
and from throat-tightening fear. Was it Jack the Ripper
who even now was closing in on her?

She tried to hold her breath, listening. Yes, there were
steps, coming inexorably behind her, heavy steps, a man's
tread. Surrounded by the thick mist, Kate knew she must
find some point of reference. She moved to the right, one

hand extended as if she were blind, feeling for a building so that she could once again have some sense of proportion, could guess where the edge of the pavement was. If she felt a door, she might pound on it, scream, beg for help. She found, though, that fright had paralyzed her throat. Kate couldn't squeak, let alone scream.

Terrified now, she kept moving to the right but had no way of knowing if she was actually headed toward the buildings along the street. She might be going sideways along Greenfield now, so complete was her disorientation.

The footsteps kept following. Were they closer? She couldn't tell. It was a nightmare, trying to find her way blind, trying to escape from whoever was following her. Try as she might, Kate was unable to move in complete silence. Her foot would strike an uneven place, she'd lurch, there would be the sound of leather on brick, and the following footsteps would home in on her once again.

Just then Kate's extended hand hit against brick. She was at the edge of the street; she had found a way to orient herself. Now she could move more quickly, for she could guide herself, even in this blinding fog, by letting her hand move along the face of the buiding to her right.

She took courage, picked up speed, but the steps behind her matched her rhythm.

Although she had found the houses along Greenfield, the fog was so thick that she could see nothing, not even the looming shape of buildings towering over her. No lights shone from windows, no streetlamps glowed ahead to guide her. She moved, blind in a sightless world.

Then Kate stumbled over a step leading into the building her fingers had been caressing so avidly, and she fell heavily to her knees, bruising them and crying out from the pain. She clapped her hand over her mouth to still the involuntary sound, but it was too late. There was a rush of footsteps and a voice saying in little more than a menacing whisper, "Whore!"

Kate scrambled to her feet and tried to run, the follower so close to her that she could hear him breathing.

"You can't escape me, whore!" he said, his voice full of triumph. "I must rid all London of such as you."

Then hands came out of the fog, unseen hands, that

fumbled and then clutched at her, imprisoning Kate in a grasp of iron. The man behind her, pulling her tight against him, had one hard hand fastened over her mouth so that she couldn't scream, the other around her waist as he hauled her to her feet from the kneeling position in which she'd fallen.

"Whore, whore, whore!" he hissed. "I'm down on whores! You'll join the others, you rotten whore, you."

He'd quit whispering now, and the words echoed in Kate's ears, driving all the fright from her. She knew that voice, dear God, how she knew that voice! She'd heard it in anger, she'd heard it in love. She'd heard it murmur, "Kate, my beloved Kate," at the height of passion. She'd heard it cold and remorseless. All of her suspicions, all her nightmares and terrors, were realized in that moment. Her beloved was the Ripper, and she was slated to be his next victim.

Part of Kate died then, with the knowledge that her beloved was a brutal, mad killer, a fiend, a mutilator of helpless women. She wanted to die too. If only he'd take his bruising hand away from her mouth so that she could say something to him, she'd beg him to kill her quickly; for without him, life was meaningless. She struggled, straining to move her face to one side to escape the silencing hand; but he only clutched her more closely to him, in an embrace so far removed from their usual embrace of love and passion that Kate almost fainted—almost but not quite. She was not the fainting kind. Instead, when he held her even more tightly, even though she thought she couldn't live now, with the awful knowledge she had, Kate was instinctively fighting. She lashed out behind her with one heavy shoe, catching him in the shin with the sharp edge of the heel. With a muttered oath he eased his grip momentarily, giving her a chance to wrench her head away from his hand. She cried out then, not too loudly, for her lips were bruised and her mouth dry from the harsh treatment he'd already given her. But she did manage to cry twice, "Help! Help!"

Jack the Ripper gave her no further chance. This time his powerful hand was around her slender throat, thumb digging in under one ear, fingers under the other. The pressure increased unbearably and Kate felt herself falling into a deep, dark well. The fog followed her in her descent, closing in on her inexorably. Then as she slumped in his arms, just before she lost consciousness, Kate felt the cold steel of something sharp at her throat.

CHAPTER 1

Thursday, December 15, 1887

The huntsman's horn sounded above the baying of the
hounds, and immediately the Chipping Ongar Hunt was in
motion, a few scarlet coats punctuating the field of black
velvet jackets. Kate Kingsley, jaunty black top hat anchored
firmly on her dark red hair, put her gray mare to a gallop
and rode hard toward the patch of woodland where the
hounds were drawing the covert. She was trying to keep
apace of Harry Ravenshaw, whose big bay hunter had a
distance-eating stride. Close behind her rode the Honorable
Pamela Oldham and Viscount Alfred Cabot, known to his
friends as Alfie. All told, there were about twenty in the
hunt, as well as the master in his scarlet coat and black
velvet cap, the huntsman with his copper horn, and two
whippers-in.

There was a low hawthorn hedge between the hunt and
the hounds. Kate put her mare over it easily, reveling in
the crisp air, the excitement of the hunt, the pounding of
horses' hooves. She hadn't a care in the world. Well, she
did care about Harry, of course; but Kate felt that she
could conquer the younger Ravenshaw without any trouble. She'd seen that look in his gray eyes.

Now they were into the beech woods, and Kate had to
rein in her mare so that she could pick her dainty way
through the trees. Harry pulled up the bay and waited for
Kate to catch up with him. The hounds were baying frantically off to the right.

17

"Hurry up, Kate," Harry called impatiently. His horse danced a bit as if reflecting its master's mood. "We want to be in on the kill."

Actually that was the one part of a fox hunt that Kate didn't enjoy, but she wasn't going to say this to Harry Ravenshaw, not when she was trying her best to attract him. She could close her eyes at the dreadful moment of death. Kate touched the gray's flank with her whip, and the little mare responded immediately. Behind them, Pam and Alfie came along, and the four young people rode on in the direction of the deep baying of the hounds.

They came out into an open glade and saw the terrier men just loosing the small black-and-white dogs.

"Gone to earth!" Harry exclaimed. "We're too late!"

"Maybe the terriers will flush him yet," Alfie said in his bluff, hearty manner.

"Last time it happened too," Harry grumbled to Kate. "I think the master should give his earth stoppers a good talking to. They leave entirely too many holes for the fox to escape into."

Kate was secretly pleased that the fox had escaped. They waited around for a while, but the dogged little terriers had to give up, backing out of the burrow, shaking the dirt from their coats. Their keepers caged them and loaded them onto the back of a horse. Then, mounting, they led away the horse with the terriers.

"We might as well ride back to Fairlawn," Kate suggested. "I doubt if they'll raise another fox this morning."

The hunt breakfast was at her home today, so the four of them cantered along through the winter fields toward the Tudor manor house set in a lovely park laid out in the previous century by the famous Capability Brown. They rode through a tunnel of ancient elms lining the driveway. Through the end of this tunnel of overhanging branches, the gleaming white and black of the half-timbered house was beautifully framed. Fairlawn had been in the Kingsley family for generations. Although Kate's father had no title, he was a wealthy landowner, a well-respected figure in the Chelmsford area of Essex. Kate, motherless since birth, had never known a moment's poverty or care. Life to her was one endless round of parties, balls, hunts, and flirtations. Now that she was twenty, Kate knew she must soon marry. And the man who had caught her fancy, the man she loved dearly, was Harry Ravenshaw—handsome, witty, exciting Harry.

A groom was waiting to help the ladies dismount, but but Harry, gallant as always, was off his bay and beside Kate before the groom had a chance to help her.

As Kate kicked loose from the stirrups, Harry reached up and plucked her from the sidesaddle, strong hands almost spanning her tiny waist. His touch set her pulses racing. When he put her down, Harry held onto her waist just a moment longer than necessary, and Kate allowed herself to sway toward him ever so slightly, looking up at him coquettishly, her green eyes sparkling with mischief.

"You are a tempting morsel, dear Kate," Harry murmured. "Someday soon I mean to feast on your charms."

She tapped his shoulder lightly with her riding crop. "Behave yourself, Harry, or I may make you starve. Would you fast for me?"

Alfie, Lord Cabot, who had dismounted, heard only the last words. "Who's fast?" he asked eagerly, ready to relish any bit of gossip Kate might dispense. The viscount was short and stocky, with straight brown hair and hazel eyes. He was twenty-two, two years older than Kate, and a childhood friend.

"I didn't say anyone was fast, Alfie."

"You should have my dear brother, Derek, examine your ears, if he can find them under that shock of hair. Who is your barber, Alfie?"

The young man smiled good-naturedly. "Let Derek use his professional skills on those wretches he treats in his clinic."

Pamela Oldham, who had been assisted by a groom to dismount from her rangy hunter, now looped up the long skirt of her riding habit, fastening the hem at the waist of her riding skirt under the flaring hem of her snugly fitted black jacket. The Honorable Pamela Oldham was a tall, willowy ash blonde with cool gray eyes. The only daughter of Baron Oldham of Trinley, Pam had everything money could buy, for the baron dealt in wines and spirits and was as wealthy as any merchant in Chelmsford. Pam's father had been in the business of importing spirits since he had inherited the family business from his father. The original Baron Oldham had started as a smuggler, or so the story went, but had been given his title for service to the government at a time in England's history when pirates were brave men—if they were English! There were some of the nobility who looked down on Oldham because they said he was "in trade," but the baron smiled slyly and went right on making money.

"However does your brother bear working with those people in the East End?" Pam asked, wrinkling her straight English nose as if she could smell the foul odors of London in the clean, clear air of the Essex countryside.

"I am sure they need the services of a physician too," Kate said with some asperity. There were times when Pamela could be incredibly snobbish.

Pam tucked a gloved hand in the crook of Alfie's arm. "Why bother with them? They'll just contract some horrid disease. You know how loose their morals are, Kate. Look at what happened to Monica."

"Now Pam, I told you that was just a rumor," Alfie said, chiding his lovely, patrician companion.

"Monica Murphy?" Harry asked, all ears.

They moved toward the heavy oak door leading into Fairlawn. Kate picked up her riding skirt, purposely holding it a few inches higher than necessary, to show a flash of sleekly booted ankle until she was sure that Harry had noticed.

Harry's attention was divided between the titillating glimpse of ankle and Pamela's equally titillating gossip.

"What's this about the captivating Monica?" he asked. "She used to be one of Derek's lady loves, you know."

Ignoring Alfie's attempts to quiet her, Pam, assured of an avid audience, said, "I heard that Monica was walking the streets of London's East End, a common whore."

Harry's black wings of eyebrows rose, giving his long, devilishly handsome face a wicked look. "Somehow, it seems improbable that Monica the Exciting could be a common anything."

Pamela's lips were prim as a chapel cleric's wife's. "You know what happens when you are as indiscreet as Monica was," she said prissily. "Once your reputation is gone, there is nowhere to go but down."

Harry grinned and squeezed Kate's hand, which he had captured and tucked in the crook of his arm. "Are you saying that stodgy Derek, the esteemed Sir Derek Ravenshaw, Baronet, ruined poor, voluptuous Monica and sent her skidding to the depths of degradation in Whitechapel? Really, Pam, you don't know my prig of a brother if you think that!"

Crossly Pam said, "I didn't say it was Derek who ruined her. The way I heard it, she was loose with every man in the Chelmsford area. All of the men in the Chipping Ongar Hunt—" Then, realizing she was talking with two of these men, she had the grace to flush. "Not you two—she's much older," she added quickly. "Nearer Derek's age."

"A veritable old hag, I dare say," Alfie laughed.

Just then there was the sound of horses' hooves coming nearer, and Kate remembered her duties as hostess to the hunt breakfast.

"Daddy will be furious with me if he finds me out here chatting instead of making sure that everything is ready for the hunt," she said, tugging at Harry's arm. "Come along. I must make sure that Vinton has everything in order."

"Don't let him hear that," Alfie joked. "You'll be looking for a new butler. With all these factories offering such splendid pay, its hard to keep servants these days."

"Who'd want to work fourteen hours a day in a horrid, noisy factory when he can work in such lovely surroundings as Fairlawn?" Pam asked innocently, never considering for a moment the long hours that servants worked for their meager wages.

Inside, Kate went immediately to the formal dining room, where a sumptuous buffet was laid. The massive walnut sideboard was so crowded with dishes that it looked like a booth at a country fair. There were chafing dishes with spirit lamps keeping hot the kidneys, kippers, and eggs. Silver platters of ham stood next to ornate covered dishes of hot buns. There was also an abundance of fowl—woodcock, pheasant, and even guinea hen—on a long refectory table that graced the paneled dining room at Fairlawn. At either end of the table stood an ornate silver epergne, the graceful bowl filled to overflowing with polished red apples, rich oranges and lemons, with bunches of grapes hanging enticingly over the rim. There were fresh flowers from the conservatory, giving the impression that it was midsummer instead of mid-December. Tall, white French tapers rose from the curved candle-holders that grew from the fluted base of the epergne. There was a baked ham and a joint of beef, as well as decanters of whiskey, rum, and gin. In the center of the table stood a massive crystal punch bowl filled to the brim with a rosy liquid. Floating on this delicious lake was a swan carved from ice.

"Who did the ice swan?" Pam asked her hostess.

"Vinton says that one of the underfootmen is quite skilled at the art of ice sculpture."

"I wish someone at Trinley was that clever," Pam said enviously. "You wouldn't—"

"No," Kate laughed, "I'm quite sure Vinton wouldn't want to give notice to such an accomplished footman." But Kate fumed inwardly. She wouldn't put it past Pamela to try to hire the footman away from them. With the baron's money, she could lure away almost any servant in the country if she tried.

Soon the rest of the hunt arrived, noisy and hungry after their ride in the brisk winter weather. They crowded around the groaning board.

Kate saw her father across the room talking with Arthur Mansfield, and she thought her father seemed worried about something. Now that she thought about it, Father had been rather subdued recently, as if something might be wrong. She hoped he wasn't ill. Well, he could always have Derek check him over, bleed him if he needed it, or give him some pills or elixirs. Kate put it out of her mind immediately. She was twenty and in love. Although she was very fond of her father, his problems were not hers. All she had to worry about was attracting Harry Raven-shaw. She knew that if she married him she'd never have a title—Derek, as elder son, had inherited the hereditary baronetcy. But Kate didn't mind. Harry was handsome and exciting; he set her senses to singing when he touched her, and she was wild to become his wife and be truly his. It didn't seem fair that his rather quiet older brother should get everything—the title, the money, and Scarlet Oaks—but the lot of younger sons in Victorian England was unenviable. Everything went to keep the estate intact and preserve the inheritance for the title. The younger sons were hard pressed to find funds to pay their tailors and their gambling debts, yet it was frowned on to go into trade.

Kate's eyes again strayed to her father and Mansfield. The man was obviously pressuring her father about something. Mansfield's sleek, corpulent body was clad in an expensively tailored coat of scarlet, proof of his influence in Essex, for only a few of the men in the Chipping Ongar Hunt rated scarlet coats. Mansfield had long, gray, greasy locks, which just cleared his coat collar His face was pasty—nearly the color of the white stock at the nape of his neck. Even as Kate looked at him, he turned so that his cold blue eyes locked with hers. A smile twisted his thin lips, and he bowed slightly, forcing Kate to acknowledge his greeting with a formal little bow of her own.

"Looks like he'd like to eat you for breakfast, m'dear," wheezed a voice in Kate's ear, startling her. She turned to find the Duchess of Dorminster behind her, plate loaded to overflowing with viands from the sumptuous board. The duchess was a character known throughout the area. Tall, stork-thin, she painted her face with some ghastly cosmetic that made it a saffron yellow. Her cheeks were rouged to bright red spots like a clown in a Punch and Judy show, and long, improbable curls of an unnatural gold hung about her bony shoulders. She was gotten up in an outrageous riding habit of mauve with orange piping, and orange veiling hung from a man's black felt derby, which she wore pinned high on top of her flowing mass of hair. Her eyes were a deep and surprisingly lovely violet. The duchess was a true eccentric, but Kate had known her all her life and was used to the woman's extravagances.

"Bad 'un," the duchess went on, not trying to keep her voice down. "Rich upstart. Makes his money off the blood of the poor." She turned to a tubby little man who had moved to join the two ladies. "Right, Wimbley?"

Lord Wimbley stared about frantically with his pop

eyes, then mumbled, "Eh?" He scratched up under a full, powdered periwig with a long, ivory scratcher. His rotund body was clad in the court costume of the past century: knee breeches and clocked hose, long embroidered waistcoat of robin's-egg-blue satin, and skirted coat of a deeper teal-blue with huge cuffs and deep pockets laced in gold.

"Mansfield, there. A rotter."

Lord Wimbley nodded sagely. "Ah!"

"Dare say he's got his hooks into your pater, Kate. Do you think that's possible, Wimbley?"

On a down note, Wimbley intoned, "Oh."

Kate had known Lord Wimbley since childhood, and it was the joke of their set that he'd never been heard to utter any sounds other than "Eh," "Ah," and "Oh." But he was a member of the establishment and, like the duchess, accepted.

"I must warn Freddy," the duchess went on, referring to Kate's father. "Should stay away from Arthur Mansfield. Tainted meat, that one. Slumlord. Owns half of Whitechapel from what the Reverend Mr. Fiddler tells me."

"Eh?"

"Helping in their mission," she went on. "Saving the souls of the poor, Fiddler and his good wife—but sometimes I think they ought to think of their bodies too."

Wimbley nodded sagely. "Ah."

"Tell your pater to stay away from Mansfield," the duchess told Kate, mumbling around an enormous bite of roast duck she had stuffed into her mouth. "He's a bad 'un."

Kate agreed wholeheartedly with the eccentric woman, but as her father's hostess, she could scarcely gossip about one guest with another. She could still feel those cold blue eyes on her, and she glanced again in her father's direction. Sure enough, Mansfield was looking at her, his eyes magnetic in their intensity. To her dismay, her father motioned for her to come to join them.

"Please excuse me," she murmured, and made her way through the swirl of riding skirts and boots to the other side of the room.

Mansfield bowed and caught her hand, carrying it to his

lips. Bestowing a moist kiss on it, he murmured, "Miss Kate, you are a delight to these old eyes."

Had it been anyone else who had been so gallant, Kate would have responded with coquetry. With Mansfield, though, instead of saying, "Sir, your eyes are very young, indeed," she only murmured "Thank you" and carefully extracted her hand from his eager grasp.

"Such a charming hostess," Manfield went on. "And so lovely a lady to grace such an elegant home. Been in your family for generations, Fairlawn, has it now?"

"Yes."

Kate was surprised at her father's short answer. Usually Frederick Kingsley was graciousness itself to his guests. He was tall, slender, and distinguished-looking, his hair still retaining a bit of the ginger color it had had in his youth. Kate had his green eyes but her dead mother's features.

Kate chatted with Mansfield for a few moments but kept her eyes on the other guests, hoping for an opportunity to escape from his unwelcome presence. In the back of her mind she was a bit worried about her father, for Kingsley's color was poor, and there was a faint blue cast to his lips that didn't seem healthy. But Kate, with the exuberance of youth, put it down to a chill from the dampness this morning and thought no more about it.

Finally she escaped and was making her way back to the buffet when she heard a man saying, "Ah, there you are, Kate." She turned to see who it was and found that she was looking at Harry's older brother, Derek.

"Derek! How nice to see you," she said in her social voice.

"And I am delighted to see you, particularly as my brother isn't occupying all your attention."

Kate was surprised, as she'd never paid much attention to Sir Derek Ravenshaw, Bart., having eyes only for his younger, more handsome, more glamorous brother. Not that Derek was homely—far from it. As tall as Harry, Derek was heavier by ten or fifteen pounds, which weight he carried well on his big frame. He, too, had black hair; but his was only slightly wavy, where Harry's hair fell in curls across his forehead, as if inviting Kate's hand to smooth them back. Derek had dark, velvety brown eyes instead of the light gray eyes that were so startling in Harry's dark countenance. Still, he was an older man—eight years or so older than his brother—and to Kate, Derek was stodgy and dull, a poor second to his mercurial and flamboyant brother.

On impulse Kate said, "Derek, do you think Father looks well? I'm a bit worried about him. He hasn't seemed quite himself lately."

He gave Kate a very quick, sharp look, then turned to peer about the crowded room, looking for her father.

"He's over near the window—talking with Mr. Mansfield."

"If I'd known Arthur Mansfield was here, I'd not have come, Kate. Our paths cross all to often in Whitechapel."

"Is it true that he's one of the slumlords we hear about? The Duchess of Dorminster was saying horrid things about him just a little while ago. She says she's been doing some sort of good works in the East End and swears Mr. Mansfield is horrid."

Derek grinned, shedding years from his looks in the process. "For once the dear duchess is right, Kate."

"Well, just stay on this side of the room," Kate said, so slyly that Derek looked closely at her to see if she was joking, "and you won't have to speak to Mr. Mansfield." Then she added, "I didn't see you at the hunt."

"One of my grooms was kicked by a horse just as I was ready to ride off to Chipping Ongar. I had to see to him."

Then Kate led Derek to the groaning table and left him to the tender mercies of Vinton, the butler, and his ranks of footmen and maids. Now, however, she couldn't find Harry; and when she looked around, her father, too, seemed to have disappeared. Unfortunately Mansfield hadn't.

"Ah, my dear Kate, I consider it an honor to be in your presence," he went on in that oily manner he had that quite turned Kate against him. "You make a charming hostess. I wish I had one half as lovely as you to help me entertain at Bassett Abbey."

Mansfield was a bachelor who entertained lavishly. Ordinarily Kate might have said, "Sir, you are too modest. I am sure that all of the young ladies for miles around are vying for the honor of being your hostess." To anyone else, she'd have said it, but not to Mansfield, whom she found odious.

Mansfield, though, was not so easily discouraged. He smiled at Kate and said, "I have been discussing your future with your father."

This startled Kate so that she exclaimed, "My future?"

"You should be married, my dear Kate—one so lovely as you, with so much to offer a man."

His unctuous voice quite put her off. She felt as if his cold blue eyes were stripping her stark naked. Kate wasn't prudish—there were some old biddies in their group who had even told her, subtly, that they felt she was lacking in maidenly modesty—but being mentally unclothed by the likes of Mansfield made Kate feel queasy.

"I'm in no hurry to wed, Mr. Mansfield. Marriage is forever. I'm not ready yet for such a long-time commitment." Except with Harry, she added mentally. For him she'd give up her unmarried state with alacrity.

Finally she managed to get Mansfield to the buffet and was able to slip away from him while he was heaping a plate with jellied ham, breast of pheasant, and other choice tidbits. With Mansfield busy, she could look for Harry, but he was no place to be seen. Her father wasn't there either. Strange. Could they be together? Then her heart missed a beat. Could Harry be asking for her hand in marriage? He had never asked her to marry him, but he might feel that was much too forward until after he had spoken to her father. That had to be it! There was no other reason for Harry and her father to be closeted together, particularly when she and father were hosting the hunt breakfast. Kate went around, performing her duties as hostess in a lovely haze, sure that she soon would be announcing her betrothal to Harry Ravenshaw.

It was Derek Ravenshaw, though, who captured her attention.

"You are looking particularly well, Kate."

She smiled prettily at him. She could afford to be kind to Harry's older brother. Soon he would be part of the family.

"Are you speaking as a physician, Derek? Is my color healthy?"

She realized immediately that she had offended Derek, for his lips tightened momentarily, and there was the hint of a frown above his black brows, so like Harry's.

"I am not here professionally," Derek said rather shortly.

Sorry that he had taken her jest seriously, Kate laid a hand lightly on his arm. "Now, Derek, you know I'm joking. And thank you for the pretty compliment."

"I'm sure you hear them all day long, from much more gallant young men than I." He still was a trifle stiff.

"Heavens, you make me sound like the worst flirt in Essex. Don't let Father hear you, or he'll lock me up."

"Maybe that would be wise of him," Derek said. His words were so somber that it put a blight on Kate's exuberance. Why did Derek have to be so stodgy? He wasn't a bit like dear, fun-loving Harry.

Deciding that it was altogether too dreary chatting with Derek when he was in such a mood, Kate looked about for an excuse to leave him to his scarcely touched plate of food.

"Where's Harry?" his brother asked abruptly. "Is he with your father?"

There was something in Derek's attitude that worried Kate and puzzled her. Why would Derek care who talked with her father?

"I'm not sure—they may be together. They both seemed to disappear at about the same time. Father was talking with that horrid Mr. Mansfield, and then he was gone. And so is Harry. If you were a writer, Derek, instead of a doctor, you could make up quite a mystery plot from those few facts."

"Harry's no mystery to me," he said obliquely.

Kate sensed that all wasn't right between the two Ravenshaw men. Well, Derek probably was jealous of his younger, more handsome brother. And Harry, she knew, chafed at being the younger son, dependent on Derek's largesse for his living. Harry had gone off to medical school at Derek's urging, but he hadn't lasted even the term. He'd told Kate that carving up cadavers wasn't for him. "Although old Derek seemed to enjoy it," he'd added. Kate had shuddered at the thought. It seemed utterly ghoulish.

Derek broke in on her thoughts. "Ah, there Harry is."

She turned, radiant, to see Harry and her father coming back into the dining room. They still were deep in conversation. Somehow, though, it didn't seem the kind of thing she'd hoped for. Her father seemed worried, not happy. He had put out a detaining hand on Harry's arm, and was talking urgently.

"Now what's he up to?" Derek muttered. "I hope your father has more sense than to—" Then, as if just realizing what he was saying, Derek broke off and flushed. "Sorry, Kate. I shouldn't have said—"

"I don't know what you're talking about, Derek." Her voice was cool. She didn't know what was going on, but Derek's attitude plainly said that Harry was doing something of which Derek disapproved.

"Never mind, Kate. I'll talk with Harry later."

Taking this opportunity to leave Derek, she made her way toward Harry and her father; but by the time she had crossed the room, Harry was gone.

"What were you and Harry talking about?" she asked brightly, still hoping that Harry might have been asking leave to court her formally.

"It was nothing, Kate. Nothing. Just business."

Hoping to get her father to tell her more, Kate said, "I thought maybe Harry was talking to you about me."

The response she elicited from her father startled Kate. His glance sharpened, and his green eyes, usually so kind and warm, were hard and glittering like polished stones.

"Why would Harry Ravenshaw talk to me about you?" Kingsley demanded. "Kate, I want you to stay away from young Ravenshaw. He's—unstable. An adventurer. Not steady like Derek."

Kate pouted. "Derek's such a bore."

"Just do as I say. I wish you'd go over and talk to Arthur Mansfield, be pleasant."

"But Father, he's so—"

Again that strange hardness in her father's manner, so

unlike him. "Do as I say, Kate. And don't be snippy with him. He's—important—influential."

Her green eyes widened with shock. Since when had Frederick Kingsley of Fairlawn been worried about who was influential in the area? And Mansfield of all people.

"You don't even like him," she said rebelliously. "Why do you want me to be nice to him? He's odious."

"I—please, Kate, just do as I say." A pleading note had come into her father's voice, and she could see that something had worried him. He was troubled. Once again she noticed how poor his color was, the blue-tinged lips. She really must urge him to go to Derek and let him prescribe a tonic, something to make him feel better.

Worried now, she said, "Oh, very well, Father, I'll be pleasant to Mr. Mansfield. But I don't like him."

Reluctantly she worked her way through the guests toward the hateful man. As she skirted a group of younger members, including Pamela and Alfie, she found that the Ravenshaws were off to one side, standing almost hidden by a large china closet full of elegant Wedgwood.

Derek was saying, his voice low and full of fury, "What are you up to now, Harry? I warn you, I won't have you fouling the nest. Keep your sharp practices for your London cronies. Don't bring them here to Chelmsford. I saw you with Kingsley."

And Harry said insolently, "You're not my master, Derek. Keep your orders for the grooms at Scarlet Oaks—or for your whores in Whitechapel. But stay out of my affairs."

Journal entry. December 15, 1887.

Kate was ravishing today, her cheeks rosy from the brisk open air, her lovely green eyes sparkling. I must have her! And I shall have her, for my very own.

Kingsley doesn't look at all well. Suspiciously blue about the lips. But it isn't for me to say anything to him, although he's obviously worried. If what I suspect is true, worry won't do him any good.

Would that life were simpler, but it becomes increasingly complex. And the added factor of my beloved Kate is sure to make things even more com-

plicated. How I long for her, how hotly I desire her. I dream of her each night, I hold her in my arms, I have her in my bed; but when I wake, my bed and my arms are empty.

If Kingsley is in difficulties, it might work to my advantage. I might be able to appear as a knight in shining armor in his eyes, and he could give me his wildly desirable daughter as my prize for rescuing him.

I would like to lock her away, keep her out of sight of every other man in the world. Just seeing her flirt with the men at the hunt breakfast—and how prettily she does it, what a coquette she is—drives me almost wild. She needs taming, my Kate, like that famous Kate in Mr. Shakespeare's drama I watched at Sadler's Wells.

And I shall tame her when I possess her.

CHAPTER 2

Monday, December 19, 1887

"I promised to meet Pamela Oldham in Chelmsford for lunch," Kate said, almost in tears. "I'll be ever so careful driving back alone, Father."

She dabbed daintily at the corner of one green eye, trying to judge just how far she could go without making her father irritable. There was a very fine line these days with Frederick Kingsley, as well his daughter knew. Father had changed in this past year. Maybe he was just getting old. He'd soon be fifty, and to Kate, at a glowing twenty, that was ancient. She thought he might be having some problem with his health, but when Kate tried to quiz her father, he became very taciturn.

"Oh, very well," he agreed reluctantly. "I must catch that train to London at eleven. If you'll be cautious—"

She stood on tiptoe to kiss his pale cheek. "The soul of caution," she promised.

Kingsley smiled then, a bit absently, and patted his daughter's cheek. "The Duchess of Dorminster said she'd seen you racing down the road in the tilbury last week," he said, "as if you were being pursued by a gang of thieves."

"Now, Father, you know how she exaggerates everything. And she drives along with those pokey old horses of hers, so that anyone driving at more than a slow crawl breezes past her as if she were standing still."

Kate remembered the occasion all too well. She'd bet

Alfie Cabot tuppence that she could get from Yew House, his father's ancestral estate just this side of Chelmsford, to Fairlawn before he could. She'd won, but she almost tipped over the tilbury coming around the sharp bend near Scarlet Oaks. She'd been driving with great style then, hoping that Harry might see her as she careened past the gates; but he'd been nowhere in sight. If Father ever found out she'd been racing, he'd forbid her taking out a coach ever again.

"I shall be the soul of propriety," she promised her father, smiling up at him most beguilingly. Her mother had died when she was born, and from the earliest recollections of her father, Kate had been able to wind him around her little finger with ease. She was his darling, and she knew it. Today she would be more sedate. Actually it had frightened her somewhat last week when the tilbury tilted up on the right wheel, and left one a foot off the ground and spinning wildly. Kate had flung herself to the left side of the seat, and her weight was enough to right the gig; but it had been a close call. Afterward she was glad Harry hadn't seen that maneuver, for he was such a superb driver that he'd have been amused at her inept handling of the light coach.

Her father kept the roan gelding stepping along as they drove to the railroad station in Chelmsford, covering the two miles in quite a respectable time. Normally he did not drive so fast, but he explained that he had an important luncheon appointment in the city at one, and he mustn't be late for the eleven o'clock train.

"Have a pleasant lunch with Pamela," he said, kissing her on the forehead. "And drive home carefully."

"Of course, Father. Have a pleasant trip. When shall I send the coach for you?"

He frowned in thought. "About seven, I'd guess. If I'm not here, the groom will just have to wait for me."

Kate was meeting Pamela at a cozy confectioner's not too far from the railroad station. As she walked the short block to meet her friend, Kate was well aware that the men were all eyeing her appreciatively. She was wearing the new suit in the Black Watch plaid, which suited her red hair and green eyes admirably. It was cut severely, al-

most man-tailored, with the jacket fitted snugly over her
full, high bosom, which she'd pushed even higher with
her stays, insisting that her ladies' maid, Vera, pull the
laces even tighter than usual. You never knew whom
you might see in Chelmsford. Kate wanted to look her
ravishing best. The sleeves had a little lift, not a full puff,
and fitted snugly to the wrist. The skirt was cut severely,
only full enough in the back to fit over a medium-sized
bustle. Under the plaid jacket she wore a white lawn
shirtwaist with a tucked bib, the small white collar just
high enough to come out over the collar of the suit jacket.
With it she wore a small black felt bowler, which was
quite fetching on her red hair, the narrow brim rolling
up on the sides. Her shoes were high black kid, with
small heels and jet buttons up the sides, and her gloves
of Moroccan leather flared at the wrist. They, too, had
black jet buttons.

Pamela Oldham was in the confectioner's, waiting for
her at a small table in one corner. She rose gracefully
and bent to kiss Kate on the cheek.

"How smart you look, Kate. Here, do sit down so we
can have a good gossip."

Pam was wearing a beautiful overdress of grape velvet,
with embroidery of rose-pink flowers twined with green
leaves down the front fastening and on the sleeves and
the sides of the draped skirt. The purple overskirt was
pulled back and draped up over a bustle so that the pleated
pink silk underskirt showed. Her bonnet was of the same
velvet.

"I love your bonnet," Kate said, eyeing it appreciatively.
"Are those pink ostrich feathers?"

Pam lifted a slender hand to the tall oval brim with its
bow of pink ribbon. "I think so. Although," and she
laughed, "I dare say the ostrich fell into a dye vat first."

The two young women had only a small luncheon of six
courses, as they were dining alone, without masculine
companions. As they ate the sweet, Pam asked, "Have
you heard about the man who escaped from the jail in
Colchester? Tip Jones."

Sensing something juicy, Kate leaned nearer to her
friend. "No! Is he dangerous, this Jones fellow?"

Pam's gray eyes went from side to side to make sure they couldn't be overheard. Then, dropping her voice to a confidential murmur, she said, "He's a rapist!"

Kate's green eyes widened. "Are you sure?"

Pam nodded, the fringe of blond curls bouncing on her forehead. "I heard Father telling Mother when he thought I'd gone out. They think the man might be headed for London."

"But—Chelmseford's right on the way," Kate said, pleasantly titillated by this exciting bit of gossip. "What if he should stop near here. We'd none of us be safe!"

"I know. Aren't you afraid to drive home alone?"

A little thrill ran through Kate, then she grinned. "Let him try to catch me in the tilbury!"

"Alfie told me about the race. What did your father say when he heard about it?"

Kate sipped daintily at her tea, looking over the rim of the china cup at her friend. "He doesn't know. And I hope he never finds out, or he won't let me drive alone ever again!"

"Kate, you are so reckless!" There was rank envy in Pam's voice. She hadn't the daring to do such things. Then she added smugly, "But be careful, or you'll come to a bad end."

"But not, I dare say, at the hands of the Chelmsford rapist."

When the young women left the confectioner's, Kate was dismayed to find that the day had clouded over and it was beginning to spit rain. Pamela, who was carrying a tightly rolled gray silk umbrella, quickly opened it.

"I'll have to ask the man at the livery stable to put up the hood of the tilbury," Kate said, exasperated. "I hate to drive in the rain."

"Perhaps it's only a shower," Pam said encouragingly, holding the umbrella so that both of them could walk under it. "Don't you have a robe to put over your lap? With the hood up, and a lap robe, you shouldn't get too wet." They picked their dainty way along the cobbled pavement. "Unless you want to stay with me for a while to see if it clears."

Kate was tempted, but she knew how the time flew

when she was with Pamela. "It gets dark so early. And if Father gets back from London and the groom isn't waiting for him at the station with the tilbury—"

"You could meet the train," Pamela suggested.

"Father would be furious. Then I wouldn't get to go anywhere alone. I think that the Duchess of Dorminster has been telling him that a young lady shouldn't be out alone."

"Alfie calls her the Duchess of Scarecrow." Both young women giggled at this, earning the interested looks of several young men who were walking toward the station.

Kate found that the man at the livery stable had anticipated her request.

"Figured you'd want the hood up, miss, bein' it's rainin'."

She paid him, adding a small tip for his extra work.

"Shall I drop you somewhere, Pamela?"

"No. There's a hansom cab here. It's out of your way to drive me home."

Covering her lap carefully with a heavy woolen robe to keep her skirt dry, Kate took off her thin kid gloves and drew on a pair of driving gloves she had tucked in under the seat cushion of the tilbury. She flicked the whip, touching the roan gelding on one flank. Soon she was driving through the outskirts of Chelmsford, on the road to Fairlawn. It was raining steadily, a sullen drizzle that dampened Kate's spirits. By the time she neared the old ruined abbey, about halfway home, the drizzle had become a downpour. It had also gotten quite dark, although it wasn't more than four. If it hadn't been pouring, it wouldn't seem so late.

The horse shied at something that darted across the road—a stoat, perhaps, or a rat; and before she realized what was happening, the tilbury was in the ditch, tilted precariously, while she clung to the hood frame to keep from being dumped unceremoniously into the mud.

Sawing on the reins, which she still clutched in one hand, Kate finally managed to quiet the roan; but strain as he might, the horse was not able to pull the gig out of the ditch. The right wheel was mired almost to the hub.

"Whoa!" Kate said, pulling on the reins. Now what?

There were no houses nearby where she might get someone to help haul the tilbury out of the ditch. As the small coach was tilted far over to one side, the raised hood now did little to protect her from the downpour. She'd be drenched.

A movement in the ruins of the old gray stone abbey caught Kate's eye. Someone was there, sheltering from the rain in a protected corner. Probably one of the local farmers on his way home from market.

"Hello, there!" she called, waving frantically. "Could you help me? I'm stuck in the mud."

At first she thought the man was going to ignore her call for help. Perhaps he didn't hear her, for the rain now was beating down noisily, and the wind had come up, driving the cold drops against her face and chilling her to the bone. She supposed she might, alone, get the roan unharnessed from the listing tilbury; but Kate knew she couldn't ride a carriage horse without a saddle. It was ridiculous even to consider such a solution to a very wet problem. Her high-button shoes were not made for tramping along wet, muddy dirt roads, or she might walk home, although a mile in this downpour wasn't inviting.

Once again she peered through the rapidly deepening dusk and the rain to the ruined abbey with its empty Gothic windows and its uneven stone walls, which towered there gloomily.

Was there someone there? She was sure she'd seen a man in the shadows of the decaying building, but now she wasn't so positive. Once again Kate called for help. This time she saw a man leave the shelter of the old abbey and scurry through the rain toward the road.

He was thoroughly soaked and not very prepossessing in appearance when he got close enough to Kate for her to see him properly. He was a stranger. She didn't know all of the locals, of course, but she did usually recognize them. This man was no one she'd ever seen before. He wasn't so tall, but he was powerfully built, the bulging muscles of his arms and shoulders almost splitting the fabric of the old tweed coat he wore. He had the collar turned up about his neck to try to keep out the rain, but as his head was bare, it didn't do much good. His hair

was cropped very short and was so wet she couldn't tell
what color it was. Probably a light brown. He had odd,
very light-colored eyes, almost like a cat's yellow eyes, and
there was a week's stubble on his face, making him look
like a desperado. His trousers didn't match the jacket, and
his shoes were heavy workingmen's shoes, now covered
with mud.

"Oh, thank you for coming to my rescue," Kate said,
forcing a smile, for she wasn't sure she liked the looks of
her knight errant. "The gig went in the ditch, and the
horse can't pull it out."

He pushed at the wheel, but it didn't budge.

"Think you'll have to get out, miss; make the gig
lighter. Here, I'll help you." He reached up a grubby hand;
but when Kate reached for it with one hand, gathering
up her skirts with the other, the man lifted up both hands,
caught her roughly around the waist, and picked her bodily
from the slanting seat of the tilbury.

She was too startled to object, but when he set her feet
down on the muddy verge, he didn't let go of her.

Summoning all her aplomb, Kate said, forcing her voice
to be calm and not to shake, "Thank you, sir. Now, if
you can just get the wheel out of the mud . . ."

Instead of letting her go, the man slid one brawny
arm around her waist, pulling her to him with a grip of
iron.

"Let go of me!" she gasped. "This instant."

"Gimme a little kiss," he said roughly, moving his other
hand so that it caught the back of Kate's head. Forcing
her face toward his, he laughed, deep in his throat. "Been
a long time, girlie," he said. Then his lips were on hers
in a brutal kiss that left Kate almost unable to breathe.

Frightened now, but furious with the boor, she beat
on him with her gloved fists, landing at least one blow on
his ear, which must have hurt him, for he grunted. Then
his fingers twisted into her hair, knocking the stylish
bowler off into the mud, and he pulled her hair so that she
yelped with pain.

"Hit Tip Jones, will you?" he snarled, his ugly face thrust
close to hers. "I don't like that, I don't."

At the name Tip Jones, Kate nearly fainted from terror.

This was the escaped rapist Pamela had talked about. He'd made his way from Colchester just in time to take advantage of her mishap.

"Let go of me," she gritted, "or I shall scream."

He held her even tighter, crushing her against his burly chest so that her ribs felt as if they might crack. His breath was foul, making Kate feel like gagging. She opened her mouth to scream, but immediately his mouth was on hers in a cruel, lip-bruising kiss. Then he picked her up bodily, pushing her face into the coarse tweed of his filthy coat so that she could scarcely breathe, let alone call for help, and strode through the rain toward the gray ruins of the abbey. She struggled in vain, for he was strong, and he had her pinioned skillfully.

Now that she knew who her assailant was, Kate was terrified. Sex was a mystery to her, although she and Pamela had endless discussions about it. She knew, though, that whatever sex might be like with a man she loved, a man like Harry Ravenshaw, it was going to be ghastly with this degenerate.

At the moment, because he had her so immobilized she could scarcely move, Kate was helpless; but she knew she might have a chance to escape when he put her down. If only someone would come along the road, they would see her plight. Unfortunately the road was empty in both directions. Still, Kate didn't intend to allow this villain to have his way with her without a fight. For the moment she slumped, making herself a dead weight in his arms so that it was more difficult to carry her. Once, Jones slipped in the mud, but he didn't loose his grip on her while he regained his footing.

Now the crumbling walls of gray towered over them. Kate knew these ruins well, having explored them many times as a child. It was one of the favorite places of the youngsters in the area, although their parents deplored it as a playground, seeing the decaying stones as hazardous. There was one small section on the west front that was still partially roofed, and it was toward this shelter that Jones was carrying her. She presumed that even rapists preferred to do their raping out of the beating rain.

Her dark red hair had come loose when the criminal

had twisted his fingers in it, and now it streamed down, a heavy, wet torrent of color on this bleak day.

Once Jones carried her into the roofed corner of the old abbey, they were in almost complete darkness. It frightened Kate not to be able to see her molester, for she might get clues to his intent from watching his expression and be able to anticipate him and protect her virtue. On the other hand, he couldn't see her well either, which might work to her advantage in thwarting him. Unfortunately, she did not anticipate her treatment when Jones got her into the sheltered corner of the old abbey. With a vicious oath, he threw Kate down onto the pile of dead leaves and refuse which littered the ancient stones of the floor. The sudden impact stunned her momentarily, giving the rapist time to fall on her and begin clawing savagely at her clothing. Before she recovered her senses, he had ripped open her jacket, scattering the jet buttons so that they flew in all directions, falling like scattershot on the gray stones.

Kate was fighting him now, gasping with outrage and pain as his brutal fingers tore at the dainty white shirt-waist she wore, ripping it like paper; but his superior strength was difficult for her to combat. So intent was Jones on freeing her proud, young, full breasts from their confining corset cover of tucked lace that he forgot he was no longer covering Kate's mouth. As he made horrid animal noises deep in his throat while he pawed at her naked breasts, Kate took a deep breath and screamed at the top of her lungs.

"Help! Help! Please, someone help—"

He raised up off of her then just enough to hit her a vicious blow in the face.

"Shut up, you little trollop!" he snarled. "I'll choke you if you dare yell again." To show her he meant business, his ham-sized hands closed around her slender throat. The pressure was unbearable. Desperately Kate fought him, tearing at his throttling hands; but because she still wore her driving gloves, she couldn't claw him with her fingernails. Just as everything became a red blur, and Kate felt herself slipping into unconsciousness, Tip Jones loosed his hold on her throat and resumed ripping off her clothes.

Gagging from the choking, scarcely aware of what was

happening, Kate still fought him blindly, battering him with her clenched fists. She heard her skirt rip as he pulled at it. She tried to kick him but only earned herself another clout from Jones. As he tore at her ruffled drawers, Kate knew that in moments the unthinkable was going to happen. This animal would force her, and there was little she could do to stop him, for his superior strength would subdue her. If only she had some kind of weapon, but her hands were empty. She didn't even have a hatpin with which to try to blind him. Her hairpins had been scattered all over the mud of the Chelmsford road—or had they? Thrashing about as much as she could, which was little, for most of Jones's weight was now on her, Kate felt frantically through her hair for stray hairpins. Ready to give up in despair, for her wet hair was now matted with rotting leaves from the abbey floor, her scrabbling fingers finally touched one curved pin that still clung to her dark red locks. Pulling it out with care, Kate realized that she now possessed a formidable weapon. The pin was an heirloom—a long, harpoon-shaped metal pin with an extra barb on one end, and at the other end of the curved metal, a filigree butterfly. It was this butterfly that had caught in her hair when the other regular pins had fallen into the mud outside. As Tip Jones forced her thighs apart, Kate grasped the long hairpin in her fist and swung it forward with all her strength, aiming at the rapist's face. She felt the impact, felt a spurt of warm, sticky blood on her face as Jones gave a horrible scream and fell away from her.

"Me eye! Me eye! Little bitch, you've blinded me," he moaned.

Kate didn't wait for him to recover. Pushing herself up off the pile of dirty leaves and twigs, she fled toward the doorway. Behind her she heard Jones, still moaning and scrabbling on the littered floor, trying to get to his feet to pursue her. Terror gave wings to her feet. She, too, was sobbing and moaning. If Jones caught her now, he'd kill her.

She burst from the shelter of the ruins into almost complete darkness, stumbling through the mud and weeds, rushing toward her wrecked tilbury.

It was then that she saw the coach, righted and out of the ditch, the roan standing patiently, head drooping in the slashing rain. Behind her, Kate heard stumbling footsteps. Tip Jones was hardier than she had expected, or perhaps the wound she had inflicted was superficial. She raced for the tilbury and safety. Just as she reached the side of the road, her feet slipped on a particularly slippery patch of wet clay, and Kate fell flat, knocking the breath from her lungs.

As she lay there desperately trying to breathe again, she saw a man step out from behind the tilbury where he had been hidden from view. It was Harry Ravenshaw, an avenging angel with the whip from the gig in his hand. Behind her Kate heard the rapist's footsteps come to a halt, then recede as he turned and ran toward the abbey ruins. Harry didn't pursue the escaped criminal. Instead he was on his knees in the mud, ruining the exquisitely cut and tailored tweed trousers he wore under a plain shooting jacket.

"Good God! Kate, are you all right?"

Without waiting for an answer, Harry scooped her up in his powerful arms and carried her the few steps to the tilbury. He lifted her onto the seat and took the muddied lap robe to wrap about her to keep off the rain and to hide her nakedness.

It was only as he tenderly pulled the folds of wool around her bare shoulders that Kate realized the extent to which Jones had torn her clothing. One breast was completely bare, and as Harry pulled the blanket forward to cover her, his hand brushed accidentally against her nude bosom, sending a tingle through her that shocked her with its intensity. Harry had once or twice stolen kisses from Kate, but that had been the extent of intimacy between them.

As if unaware of what he had done, of the effect his touch had on her, Harry said, "I have my own horse tethered across the road. I'll tie the rein to the back of the gig and lead him with us. You are in no shape to drive."

Reaction was now setting in. By the time Harry climbed up beside her, Kate was shivering uncontrollably. Realizing her condition, Harry said, "I'm taking you to the closest shelter, our hunting lodge. I can have the fire going in moments. And I'm sure there's some brandy there."

Not a word about the man who had attacked her, nothing except concern for her immediate comfort. He cracked the whip, and the roan started off at a glood clip, with Harry's rangy hunter clattering along behind them. He soon turned off the main road onto a narrow lane and they drove between bare, dripping hedgerows so high they seemed to be in a tunnel. Out of the gloom, the hunting lodge soon came into view. It was very old, Tudor in style, the oak beams dark against panels of whitewashed wattle and daub. The lodge was empty, with no lights showing; but Harry didn't waste time going in to light a gas light before he carried Kate into the main lounge, putting her on a large sofa in front of the huge stone fireplace. A fire was laid in readiness, needing only a match to get it going. In moments orange flames were licking at the logs, and the small kindling twigs crackled and popped.

"Now, brandy."

Kate hated brandy; but she obediently sipped the fiery liquid, cupping her chilled hands around the snifter as if it would provide warmth in itself.

Harry poured himself a drink, then pulled a small chair close to the sofa. Sitting down, he looked at her with such intensity that Kate was almost frightened.

"Are you all right, Kate?" he asked, finally, his voice rough, harsher than she'd ever heard it.

She nodded, still not sure her teeth wouldn't chatter if she tried to talk. Reaction had set in, and she was very glad to be lying there, sipping brandy, cosseted, protected by the man she loved.

"He didn't—" Harry stopped short, not saying the words.

Kate shook her head. Then, voice low, she said, "I— I fought him off, Harry. Truly. I stabbed him in the face with a sharp hairpin I'd used to decorate the back of my French roll." She shivered, remembering that horrible moment, the ghastly sound Tip Jones had made when she jabbed him in the eye. Then she remembered. "Harry!

you have to get in touch with the police! That is the man who escaped from jail in Colchester—the rapist, Tip Jones."

Harry's gray eyes widened. "How do you know this?" he demanded, his voice stiff and cold.

"Harry, you don't think—Pamela told me about this man at lunch—we had lunch in Chelmsford, after I—she said a man, a horrible rapist, had escaped from jail—and that his name was Jones, Tip Jones." Kate was babbling, shocked that Harry might doubt her, that he might think she had lured that horrible man—unthinkable! "He told me his name. He was angry with me when I fought him, and he said, 'Hit Tip Jones, will you?' That's how I know it was the escapee."

The cold look left Harry's handsome face, and he smiled at Kate, a slow, indolent smile that left her weak and breathless.

"Some women invite a man's advances, Kate."

Indignant, she said, "Well, I certainly didn't invite his! Oh, Harry, he was—was—" Then the tears came, tears she'd kept bottled up until now. But the warmth from the fire, the heat of the brandy, helped relax Kate; and the fright she'd had, the close escape, now brought a flood of tears. She sobbed, and then Harry was beside her, taking the brandy glass from her hands, gathering her close and comforting her. He ran his fingers through her hair and murmured endearments as his lips traced the line of her brow. Then he was kissing her, not the quick kisses he'd stolen at balls and parties but slow, lingering, passionate kisses. Kate's senses, heightened by her terrifying experience at the old abbey, now exploded. She found such sensuous delight as his lips demanded more and more from hers that her senses reeled. She wound her arms about Harry's neck, letting the blanket slip from her shoulders, forgetting completely that she was nearly nude without its protection. Harry's hand moved to her exposed breast, and Kate gasped at the sensation that raced through her body, intoxicating her more than brandy ever could.

"No, no, you mustn't," she moaned as his skillful fingers moved over her eager flesh. "Please, Harry, don't."

He stopped her protests by kissing her lips again, and her own lips parted for his exploring tongue. Then his lips slid down the soft curve of her throat, and he kissed her in the hollow where throat met swelling breast. Kate was now so aroused that she scarcely knew what she was doing. All she knew was the pulse-pounding delight of her awakened young body. When Harry's lips moved to her bare breast, she moaned and fastened her fingers in the thick curls of his hair, almost swooning from passion.

Before she realized what was happening, Harry had taken off the little clothing that Tip Jones had left intact, and Kate lay there, her beautiful young body inviting him to take her and make her truly his.

Harry tore off his own clothes, tossing them onto the floor, and then he was lying with her, his hands almost as rough and demanding as Jones's had been. This was different, though, for Kate loved this man, and he had roused her to an incandescent level, so that she ached for his body to merge with her own. Kate cried out as he entered her, but she learned the lessons of love very quickly, matching his rhythm with her own eager demands, until she reached a climax so intense that she bit his shoulder and clung to him until he, too, had his pleasure.

Spent, sated, they lay there in each other's arms and dozed off before the blazing fire. When they woke, Kate found that Harry was ready for more love, and again she submitted to him, this time more quietly, more slowly, so that the sensuous delight was prolonged until she thought she must surely die from love.

"Do you love me, Harry?" she begged him, for he had not said once that he did.

His hand traced the curve of her hip, found the hollow of her tiny waist, then cupped her breast.

"What a silly question to ask me, Kate," he said. "You delight me. You are all mine, and I shall lock you in a tower and love you to death." As he said this, his fingers tightened on her breast until she gasped from pain.

"Harry, you're hurting me!"

His fingers tightened convulsively, then loosed their painful grip. "Sorry, love," he said, kissing away the pain. "But remember, you are mine—all mine."

"Yes, Harry, all yours," she repeated blissfully.

It was only then that she remembered her assailant.

"We should have notified the police about Tip Jones!"

"Are you out of your mind, lovely Kate? Do you want the whole county of Essex to know that this man tried to rape you—that I found you with the clothes ripped from your lovely, ripe body? Think, Kate, think what it would do to your poor father. The shock might kill him. He's not looking too well these days. And you'd be whispered about forever. There'd be plenty who would say that Jones did rape you. There'd be others who might hint that you had invited his attentions—you know how people gossip."

Kate was appalled at the prospects sketched by Harry. Still, it bothered her that nothing would be done to capture this man who would go on preying on women.

"He might attack someone else, Harry."

"The police will get him, Kate. Don't worry your pretty head about him. I don't want you thinking about any man but me." And he bent to kiss her passionately.

Finally, much later, Kate murmured, "I must get home. But how can I go in with my clothes in shreds? The servants will gossip. You know they will."

"I'll ride to Fairlawn and tell your maid that you've had a minor spill from the tilbury—and that you've gotten all torn and muddied. She can give me dry clothes for you."

Kate sighed. "Father won't let me drive alone for a year when he hears about this."

"But you can always go riding," Harry murmured, smiling at her. "And Derek scarcely ever uses the lodge these days. He's too busy doing good works for the whores in Whitechapel. We can meet here whenever we wish." He gathered her into a farewell embrace. "Do you wish, Kate?"

Heart pounding, senses inflamed, she murmured, "Oh, yes, Harry, yes—I wish!"

INTERLUDE 1

Friday, December 23, 1887

He took the first underground train out of Paddington Station and huddled in the dark, dirty carriage, his nostrils assailed by the stench of unwashed bodies, the fumes from the guttering gas jets, the miasma common to the area. A man across from him had lighted a candle and stuck it to the wall of the carriage with melted wax. By its light he read a book, turning the pages eagerly.

He peered across at the reader, but he couldn't see the title of the book. Perhaps he was reading that new story by Conan Doyle, *A Study in Scarlet*. Ah, what a story, gory, full of violence and blood, terror and revenge. He'd liked it; it had made his own blood run fast and hot. How he'd like revenge against his hated rival.

When the train reached Whitechapel Station, he rose, settled the deerstalker hat on his head, and went up to Whitechapel road. He'd worn an old, brown tweed suit with a rather shabby greatcoat of a darker brown over it. If he was to mingle with the denizens of this area of East London, then he must look the part.

He turned right on Whitechapel Road, moving with the teeming mass of humanity that crowded East London. Most of the people were grindingly poor. He regarded them as animals, vermin, no better than rats. As they ducked into dark alleyways, the illusion grew. Rats popping into ratholes. Rats to be exterminated.

He moved closer to a grimy brick building to avoid a

47

drunk who staggered by, smelling of cheap gin. A door opened at his side, and a blowsy woman looked out. She stretched out one hand and caught at the sleeve of his coat.

"Like some fun, dearie? Any way you want it, love."

"Damn you, take your filthy hand off me," he snarled. "Whore! Rotten whore!"

"Oh, touchy, ain't we?" Her beetling black brows pulled together over a drink-mottled nose. Several of her front teeth were missing, and her black serge dress was rusty and pulled at the seams.

He took a threatening step toward her. Something in his face frightened her, for she stepped back quickly, switching her skirt out of the way with a practiced hand. Then she slammed the door in his face.

"Whore!" he muttered, walking on. 'I'm down on whores."

A drunken sailor heard him and crowed, "Thas what I wanna be down on—a whore!" The sailor clapped him on the shoulder, leaning heavily, so drunk he could scarcely stand.

The man shrugged off the sailor and hurried on, careful now not to vocalize his hatred of the prostitutes who prowled the area looking for customers so that they'd earn the fourpence needed for a night's lodging at one of the common lodging houses.

All women were whores! If only he could rid London of every one of them. The man in the Conan Doyle story —what was his name?—Hope. Jefferson Hope. He'd had the right idea—kill with a knife. How he'd like to sink a knife into a whore's guts and rip her open. His breath quickened, his heart pounded in his ears as he hurried along. Mustn't go too near the clinic. Mustn't let anyone who might know him see him there. Stay on the streets away from Union Row.

Ahead, incongruous in the rabble sounds of the slums, came the wheezy tones of a harmonium, and the ragged notes of "Sinners, turn; why will ye die?" He was coming to Salvation Chapel, so he crossed the street. It wouldn't do for that fanatical cleric, the Reverend Mr. Fiddler, to see him wandering through the area. The sound of the hymn followed until he turned the corner, leaving salvation to Fiddler and his skinny wife. Trying to bring whores to salvation. What a laugh.

The stench of the abattoir drew him as it drew the swarms of flies that battened on the blood of the slain cattle. He'd watched the butchers at work, had seen the flash of long, gleaming knives that came away dripping blood. He was drawn to scenes of violence, tableaux of death. As the men at the slaughterhouse slashed expertly at the carcasses, so he might someday slash and slash. Would he need one of the leather aprons the butchers wore, their protection against the blood that gushed from their victims?

His pulses raced, his heart pounded, he was nearly sick from the excitement that such thoughts always brought on him. His hands trembled, but if he held a long, sharp knife, he knew his hands would be steady as a rock.

CHAPTER 3

Saturday, December 24, 1887

"Let's go to see the Duchess of Dorminster," Pamela Oldham suggested. "Her wassail bowl is always filled with well-spiced ale." She giggled and snuggled down into her furs. "I could do with a cup from that bowl. It's cold in this carriage, Alfie. Maybe the bricks were hot when we started out, but my feet are freezing now."

Kate didn't know whether it was hot or cold, day or night. She was so besotted with Harry Ravenshaw that she went about in a rosy haze, noticing nothing. Pam suspected something, Kate was sure; but she hadn't asked any direct questions. Well, Kate had no intention of gossiping to Pam about her beloved Harry. If Pam wanted to know about the joys of a physical relationship with a man, let her take Alfie to bed. Kate felt wrapped in a cocoon of love, isolated from the rest of the world. It was a heavenly sensation, one she wasn't about to share with anyone, even Pamela Oldham.

Harry's arm was around her now. "Just to keep Kate warm," he'd said to Alfie and Pam. "Pam's right, Alfie," Harry added. "It's nice and cold in your brougham. Gives me such a marvelous excuse to put my arm around Kate."

"Harry, you are wicked," Pam chided.

Kate thought she detected a note of envy in the other young woman's voice. Alfie hadn't been so bold as Harry. He'd kept his hands to himself. Kate slid one gloved hand out of the sealskin muff and slipped it into Harry's hand.

50

Just being here with him, his arm tight around her, was so exciting that Kate had difficulty in keeping track of the light-hearted conversation.

"Well, shall we go see the duchess?" Pam asked. "Kate?"

"The duchess?" Kate asked stupidly, not having been paying attention to Pam's chatter.

Harry leaned close, so that she could feel his hot breath on her ear. "The Duchess of Dorminster," he whispered. Then he kissed her ear, sending shock waves of sensation through her. Kate still marveled at the effect of his touch on her, the almost overpowering desire he could rouse in her by the mere touch of his lips, a hidden caress of his hand. It turned her bones to water, made her feel she was melting. All she wanted to do was to be alone with Harry so that they could make passionate love again and again. She had been riding out every day this week, meeting him secretly in the hunting lodge, lying there with him before the fire, giving herself to him with abandon.

"The duchess is always good for a laugh," Alfie said.

"And Pam's right, her wassail bowl will be tasty," Kate agreed, finally catching up with the conversation. She kept wondering if there would be any opportunity for her to be with Harry tonight. She rarely saw him except in the afternoon. He didn't come to her house to court her formally. At times she wondered why Harry wasn't at Fairlawn, begging her father for her hand in marriage; but her infatuation was so great that she drifted with the tide, assuming that they would soon be wed.

Alfie rapped sharply on the roof of the brougham and told the coachman, "Harcourt." Soon the carriage turned off the road into the driveway of the Duchess of Dorminster's house, windows ablaze with light in the Palladian mansion. The drive circled in front of the double steps leading up to the salon floor, and by now the graveled circle was full of tilburys, broughams, landaus, and berlins, with guests leaving and arriving in a steady stream. The duchess might be eccentric, but she was a lavish hostess.

The four young people went up the marble steps, shivering slightly in the sharp wind. Kate was wearing a dress of dark green taffeta, the overskirt pulled back and draped

over a large bustle. The underskirt was of a paler green
satin, flounced the entire length, each flounce edged with
narrow dark red velvet ribbon. She was wearing a short
coat of black wool trimmed with marten fur at neck and
cuff, the fur dyed to match her sealskin muff. Her bonnet
was trimmed with fur also, a fetching style with turned-
back brim and satin ribbons tied under her softly rounded
chin.

Pam was muffled in a flowing cape of sable with a
hood to pull up over her blond hair to keep her warm.
As she lifted the edge of the cloak, her gown of silver
tissue showed beneath the edge of the fur, a lavish flounce
that caught the light of the outside lamps in the metallic
threads.

Inside, the rooms were full of light and sound. Although Harcourt now had gas lights, for such festive occasions as this Christmas Eve party the duchess had the
rooms lit with French wax tapers, the hundreds of dancing
flames casting a beautiful soft glow over the guests. Can-
dlelight was much more becoming to a young woman's
complexion than the harsher light from gas lamps. Kate,
her coat left in the ladies' boudoir, glanced at her reflection in one of the full-length mirrors before she joined
Harry and the others. The green gown set off her red
hair to perfection. The décolletage was low, her creamy
white bosom scarcely covered. She'd had Vera lace her
extra tightly so that her breasts would stand up high, for
she knew what the sight of them did to Harry.

"Mooning over Harry Ravenshaw?" Pam asked a bit
sharply. Her reflection joined Kate's in the large mirror.
She was taller than Kate, and tonight she had her blond
hair piled high with a pronounced pompadour that made
her seem regal. Her figure was slender, and Kate un-
charitably thought that sometimes Pam wore ruffles under
the neckline of her gowns to add fullness to her bustline,
something Kate never had to worry about.

"Don't concern yourself about Harry, Pam. Just concen-
trate on Alfie Cabot. Has he proposed yet?"

"Not yet, but he will. His intentions are honorable."

"And you think Harry's aren't?" Kate asked, her voice
snappish. She could see that smug look on Pamela's face.

"Has he asked your father for your hand in marriage yet?"

"They had a long, private discussion the morning of the Chipping Ongar Hunt." Kate didn't add that she had no idea what that discussion was about. Harry had never mentioned it to her, nor had her father. She was sure it was not about marriage. She also was sure that her father did not approve of Harry Ravenshaw, although he had not forbidden her to see Harry. If he did, she'd slip out and meet her lover. Nothing her father could do or say would keep them apart.

Kate was pleased to see that Pamela was chastened by her statement about the private chat between her father and Harry. Sometimes Pam could be insufferable. Right now, Kate felt very smug about her friend—poor Pam, not knowing the bliss of a truly complete relationship with a man. No doubt Alfie planted chaste kisses on Pam's cheek. But Kate was sure that nothing else had ever happened between them. Pamela still had that ignorant, innocent manner, which meant that she was unschooled in love between a man and woman. Poor Pam! Lucky Kate!

The Duchess of Dorminster had outdone herself both in her lavish hospitality and in her own toilette. Tonight she was garbed in flowing panels of chiffon, lime green and yellow, both colors extremely unbecoming to her sallow complexion. Her violently yellow hair was dressed in a towering arrangement full of tortoise-shell combs and jeweled hairpins. The coiffure wobbled and tottered, constantly on the verge of coming down, never actually losing even a hairpin. As usual the duchess was painted like the clowns in a traveling circus, her hollow cheeks rouged in bright disks, her eyes completely circled with kohl. Her long, bony fingers were filled with a variety of rings, and a blazing diamond necklace covered the crepy skin of her throat.

"Still with that young Ravenshaw scamp, I see," she muttered to Kate when she maneuvered her away from Harry. "Ought to look at his half brother, m'dear. More stable. Better blood. Blood counts. Harry's mother was a trollop. Wound up in a house of ill fame in Manchester, I understand."

Kate was seething. "Harry can't be blamed for what his mother did, milady. He's charming and good company —his brother is a stodgy stick."

"Now, now, don't sell Derek short, m'dear. Fine man. Works hard in his clinic down there in Whitechapel. Horrid place. I'm trying to get classes started for those poor, unfortunate women of the streets, the ones Derek treats. The Fiddlers want to save their souls, but I think they'd do better to educate the women so they could do something other than sell their bodies for a few pence."

"Sounds exciting, milady." It was Harry, a devilish gleam in his gray eyes. Kate was overwhelmed by his good looks. Harry was impeccably dressed, as usual, his evening clothes the finest cut, the latest style. Rebelliously, she thought that Harry should be the baronet, not Derek; Harry was cut out for greater things than being a second son, always having to scramble for a living while Derek got everything. It wasn't fair.

The Duchess of Dorminster wasn't at all impressed with Harry's dashing good looks nor with his jokes about the whores of Whitechapel. "Poor women, no chance. Don't mock them, Harry. They are forced into the life they live."

Harry's voice hardened. "Whores do it by choice, my dear duchess. Don't feel sorry for them. They like being in the gutter." He took Kate's arm and drew her away from their hostess.

"Harry, you shouldn't say such things to the duchess," Kate whispered. "It's her party."

"She has no business talking about such things to you. Next thing you know, she'll be trying to get you down to the East End to help her with her charitable work—a waste of time and energy. She can't help those women. They like the life they lead. A different man every night, a few pence for gin, that's all they're interested in, Kate. Don't feel sorry for them. Leave all that sordid business to Derek."

He led Kate toward the salon, where the refreshments were laid out on two long tables, which groaned with the weight of the repast. Each table had, at either end, an enormous silver bowl: a matching set with curved handles and engraved scenes from mythology around the rims. The footmen were busy ladling out the spiced ale from the wassail bowls or filling plates with paté, slices of roast pheasant, delicately seasoned ham, or hearty roast beef. There were candied fruits colored in a most unnatural manner, and a staggering array of good English cheeses to please the palate. All, of course, to be washed down with innumerable cups from the wassail bowls.

There was a crush of guests. Kate thought that the duchess must have invited everyone in Essex. Somehow she got separated from Harry, and, being so short, she couldn't seem to find him. Instead, she discovered that her hostess was there beside her again, talking quietly to her.

"My dear, I do hope you aren't letting that young Ravenshaw scamp turn your head," the duchess said. "Really, I don't understand Frederick. Allowing you to see so much of Harry. Not good, you know. Unstable. Lives by his wits."

Annoyed, Kate said frigidly, "Derek holds the purse-strings. Harry is hard pressed to manage on his minuscule allowance."

The duchess gave her a sudden hard, shrewd look. "I understand Harry sails quite close to the wind sometimes, Kate. He's into some rather shady undertakings. I thought I saw him talking with Frederick at the hunt breakfast."

How well Kate remembered that, thinking that Harry was formally asking her father's permission to pay court to her.

"I'm sure Harry chatted with Father."

The duchess laid a long, bony hand on Kate's soft, rounded arm. "I hope Frederick has more sense than to get involved with Harry and his schemes."

Kate was enraged, but as the duchess was her hostess, she could not vent her anger. Horrid old hag, suggesting that Harry might be doing something that wasn't ethical. Just because he tried to make a little extra pocket money for himself. Kate herself wasn't sure just what it was that Harry did. She'd asked him once, but he'd only laughed and told her not to worry her pretty head about men's affairs. Business was not for her. And she'd not pressed him, not being overly interested in dull old investments or real estate or whatever it was Harry dealt in.

"Frederick ought to marry you off to someone solid," the duchess went on. "Derek, for instance. A baronet. A fine physician. Not flighty, like Harry. Harry takes after that trollop mother of his. Letitia never could control Harry. Told me the boy was a young scamp. Derek no trouble."

Incensed, Kate protested, "Lady Letitia Zangwill was Derek's mother's sister. Harry's not a blood relative. She's always favored Derek. Harry says—"

The duchess sighed. "So it's that way, is it? Kate, Kate, you are heading for heartache."

Kate, so madly in love that she could scarcely bear for Harry to be out of her sight, was glad when the duchess went off to see to her other guests. Poor misunderstood Harry. They were jealous of him, that was it. He was handsome and dashing. Of course his hateful Aunt Letitia didn't like him. Of course she favored her blood nephew, Derek. Kate wondered if the dried-up old lady was here tonight. No doubt, if she was, Derek was dancing attendance.

Kate heard the musicians tuning up. Where was Harry? Then, directly behind her, she heard him asking, formally, "My dear Kate, may I have the pleasure of this dance?"

She turned eagerly to him, a smile on her face, only to find that she was looking not at her beloved Harry but at Derek.

"Derek! I thought you were Harry. Your voices are so alike."

A bit ruefully the older man said, "Sometimes I wish that I were Harry. But at least I can dance with you now."

Kate was dismayed that Harry was not here for the first dance. Yet there was little she could do except agree to dance with Derek. He signaled for one of the uniformed maids to take her plate and cup, then he led her into the next room, the main ballroom, where dancing was to take place. It was a beautiful room, high ceilinged, with marble columns along each side. The ornate ceiling was beautifully done with oblongs, crosses, octagons, and ovals and decorated with urns, bows, festoons, acanthus, rosettes, and honeysuckle. Set into the ceiling at spaced intervals were a dozen paintings by one of the Italian painters of the eighteenth century, depicting the labors of Hercules. There were tall mirrors between the windows, so that the room took on a bewildering depth, with the dancers reflected in such multiplicity that it seemed at first glance that the duchess had invited all of London to her Christmas Eve fete. There were elegant torchères to hold the silver candelabra blazing with light. Portraits of the dukes of Dorminster and their wives hung prominently, including one of the present duchess that was more than kind to that eccentric lady.

At one end of the room a small platform had been set up, and the orchestra sat there, just starting their first dance number, a popular galop.

Derek caught Kate about the waist in a surprisingly close embrace and moved into the steps with superb grace, to her amazement. She had never danced with Derek Ravenshaw before, as he was older and often not at the parties she attended. Kate found it oddly disturbing to be held so close by Harry's older brother. Derek, not so flamboyant as Harry, still was very masculine. How was it possible for her senses to be stirred by him when she loved his brother so passionately? They whirled about the dance floor, which now was filled with women in colorful gowns and men in their black dress suits. Where was Harry? Just as the galop came to an end, Kate saw him at the edge of the dance floor, scanning the crowd. No doubt he was looking for her—and just then he saw her. Instead of smiling, he scowled blackly, turned on his heel, and stalked away into the other room.

"I must come more often to these affairs," Derek said, smiling at her, "so that I can have the pleasure of dancing with you. I'm lucky to get you away from Harry," he added.

Feeling distressed and not knowing what to do, Kate told him, "Harry is very annoyed with me. I'm sure he expected to have the first dance with me."

Derek grinned triumphantly. "I'm sure he did—it isn't often that I best Harry with the ladies. But when I saw you come in, I was determined to have this first galop with you, Kate."

She smiled, a nervous little social smile. Harry was furious that she'd danced with Derek, Kate knew. She'd have to make amends. Unfortunately, there was no way that she could make the kind of amends she longed to—there was no possibility of going to bed with Harry tonight. By the time the party was over it would be much too late for the two of them to have a passionate interlude in the hunting lodge. Now she heartily wished she'd not agreed to come with Pam and Alfie. If she and Harry had come alone, they might have been able to slip away unnoticed to their trysting place. Kate didn't dare risk it, though, for Pam was a sly puss who kept her eyes open. And she wasn't above some gossip if she thought that Kate and Harry were having an affair. If word should get to her father, Kate dreaded to think of the consequences. Why didn't Harry declare his intentions? Then she could see him more openly, without all this hiding and secrecy.

Kate was just ready to desert Derek and go hunting for Harry when the Duchess of Dorminster swooped down on them, her chiffon panels floating behind her like some bilious, exotic orchid.

"Ah, my dear doctor!" she cried, clasping Derek's hand with one bony claw and fastening the other on Kate's arm so she couldn't gracefully escape. "How good to see you together. Been telling Kate about your clinic. Ought to get her to help you out sometimes."

"Whitechapel is no place for a decent young woman." His tone was so short it just missed being rude. "I wouldn't want her in that rotten area, your grace."

"Tut, young man. Kate is a sensible young woman. She wouldn't faint at the sight of some unwashed bodies. And she might do some good there."

"It's too dangerous." He turned to Kate, urgency in his voice. "Don't let the duchess lure you there with her tales of doing good. It's a horrible place, and I wouldn't want you there, Kate."

"Don't worry," she said. "I have no desire to wallow in the filth of the East End."

The duchess looked disgusted; but she loosed her hold on Kate, who immediately escaped, hurrying into the dining room to try to find Harry. After a frantic five minutes, Kate found him sulking in a corner, a large cup of the ale from the wassail bowl rapidly disappearing down his throat.

"So you've decided to give me a few moments," he said angrily before Kate had a chance to say anything. "Can my dear brother spare you, Kate?"

"Oh, Harry, don't be that way," she pleaded, one hand on his wrist, begging as she'd never begged a man in her life. "He just—just carried me off. I couldn't find you, and I danced with him rather than be a wallflower. Listen, they're playing a waltz now. Come dance with me, dearest Harry."

For a moment Kate thought he was going to sulk, refuse to dance with her; but with a lightning change of mood, he said gaily, "Very well, waltz we shall, my lovely." He set the wassail cup on a marble-topped table with gilt legs ending in lions claws and led Kate to the dance floor.

It was heaven to be in his arms as they whirled about the polished dance floor, dipping and swaying to the strains of the latest Strauss waltz. Harry bent his handsome head and whispered, "I'd rather be dancing with you in bed, my lovely Kate."

"Shh! Someone will hear you." But the very words were so exciting that Kate wondered how she would be able to finish this dance. She, too, longed to lie with him, flesh against flesh, with Harry's loving hands caressing her, rousing her to such heights of passion that the very thought made her feel faint.

"We could find an unused bedchamber upstairs," he continued.

"Harry! We can't! Someone would know! I'd be ruined!"

He laughed then, a deep, throaty laugh; and his arm around her waist tightened, pulling her close against his body. "You're ruined already, delicious, passionate Kate. Do you mind?"

"Harry, don't joke with me about love," she implored, almost wishing the waltz were over, the violins silent. It was torture to be here in his arms, with no possibility of fulfilling her intense desire for him.

"I don't want to see you dancing with Derek again," he ordered, the change in his voice almost frightening; for it went from tender and teasing to cold and forbidding.

"Then you must dance every dance with me," Kate told him coquettishly. "You can't expect me to stand alone while the music plays, can you? Besides, our dear hostess is working hard at matchmaking—trying to pair me with Derek."

The oath Harry muttered under his breath shocked Kate.

"Old hag. They're all against me, Kate, because I had the misfortune to be born second, not first. If I'd been heir to the baronetcy, if Scarlet Oaks were mine, not Derek's, you'd see all the old biddies fluttering around me, trying to marry off eligible daughters or nieces or nubile neighbors."

"Well, you and Derek agree on one thing," Kate said as the music ended, and Harry escorted her back toward the dining room. "Neither of you thinks I should set foot in East London."

"Good God! How did that come up with Derek?"

"The duchess thinks I should go to Whitechapel and help her perform good works, or whatever it is that she does there."

"I'll tell you what she does: She meddles in things that are not her concern. Do-gooders usually do more harm than otherwise, Kate. I'll take a strap to you if you so much as show your face east of Mansion House."

Kate smiled a secret little smile. It was wonderful to be loved—and surprisingly interesting to have both Harry and his brother, Derek, so concerned with her welfare. Perhaps it wasn't going to be so grim to have Derek as a brother-in-law after all. If only she could find a wife for him. The prospects of playing matchmaker intrigued Kate and made her feel like a proper married lady.

The evening passed in fun and gaiety, with Kate a sought-after partner for the dancing. Every time she danced with another of the young men, Harry glowered jealous-

ly. Kate carefully avoided Derek, though, for she knew
that only Derek could raise real anger in Harry. Even the
fusty old Lord Wimbley claimed Kate for a sedate waltz.
Tonight he wore a full periwig of an outrageous chestnut
color, and his bulging body was stuffed into a lavender
silk coat, the skirt so long it came almost to his knobby
knees, which were much in evidence as he wore knee
breeches of fawn silk with a matching waistcoat embroidered in gold threads. His white hose had lavender and
gold clocks worked up the side, and his shoes had gold
buckles. The frills at his wrist were so long that they
tickled Kate's wrist.

"Lovely party," Kate said as they turned solemnly
about the floor.

"Ah!"

"Will it end at the stroke of midnight?"

"Eh?"

Stifling the impulse to burst into giggles, Kate left off
questioning Lord Wimbley, for she couldn't think of a
single question that would elicit his third response, "Oh."

But there was no chance for Kate and Harry to be alone,
no opportunity for lovemaking, to her sorrow.

Journal entry. December 25, 1887.

*Happy Christmas to me! At least I got to hold my
lovely, desirable Kate in my arms while we danced.
Not enough! The only place I want her is in my bed.
How frustrating to be able to hold her only on the
dance floor watched by the hordes the duchess invited.*

*The duchess can be a nuisance—and worse—urging
Kate to go to the East End to do good works. The
horrors of Whitechapel are not for my lovely Kate.
I don't want her exposed to the whores and their degraded lives.*

*The worst part of the evening was having to watch
my darling in the arms of my hated brother. I know
she danced with other men, but the only one I count
as a threat is my brother, who is truly my rival.*

*I swear it! Kate shall be mine, not his, to have
forever. I don't care what I have to do to get her. I*

shall go to any lengths just so that she is finally and completely mine, with no threat from my brother to dim my joy of possession.

The clock is striking two A.M. By this time next year, Kate shall be legally, eternally mine.

CHAPTER 4

December 26, 1887

"Spend New Year's Day at Bassett Abbey, Father?" Kate
was dismayed. She'd hoped to spend that holiday with
Harry, although they'd made no firm plans yet. This afternoon when she met him at the hunting lodge for their
tryst, Kate had expected to pin Harry down about New
Year's Day. Sometimes he refused to plan ahead, laughing at her, teasing her by telling her that he might be
seeing some other delectable young lady on the date in
question. Kate pretended not to mind, but it hurt her
terribly when Harry joked about other women. Surely she
was the only one in his life now. No doubt there had
been other women before her. After all, Harry was a man
with a man's appetites. Kate was well aware of Harry's
appetites! But now she hoped she was satisfying him, so
that he had no need nor desire to turn to other women for
gratification. So, to hear her father ruin all of her hoped-
for plans to spend New Year's Day with Harry was intolerable.

To her surprise, Frederick Kingsley frowned at her, an
almost unheard of occurrence in her young life. "My dear,
I don't know why you seem to have developed such an
antipathy to Mr. Mansfield. He is a very eligible bachelor,
well-to-do, owner of a lovely home, which he hints needs
a hostess. I want you to be your charming best when we
dine with him Sunday."

"But Father—"

"I have already accepted Mr. Mansfield's invitation."

There was a steely quality in his voice that disturbed Kate. What had happened to her father of late? He had become increasingly short with her. With a flash of concern, a kind of intuition, she asked, "Father, are you feeling well?"

"I'm fine." The answer was so short that it bordered on rudeness. This from a heretofore doting only parent set Kate's world completely out of kilter. She took a good look at her father. It came as a shock to the young woman to see new lines on his face, lines she'd not noticed before. His mouth had a grim set so far removed from the pleasant expression she'd known all her life that it frightened her. Was he ill? Was Father worrying about his health, wondering what would happen to his only child if he fell ill or, heaven forbid, died? The prospects were appalling. Perhaps this explained his sudden interest in Arthur Mansfield. She felt ill herself. Surely her father wasn't planning to marry her off to that slimy creature? To her father, perhaps, Mansfield was a good catch—a suitable husband to care for his darling child; but to Kate, the very thought of marriage to Mansfield was repulsive. He was of her father's generation, not her own. She was madly in love with a virile young man only a few years older than she, certainly a more suitable match for a passionate young woman than a man her father's age—and such a disagreeable man to boot.

"Father, I find Mr. Mansfield very unattractive." Kate could be very stubborn when she set her mind to it. She was not going to be bundled off into marriage with the likes of Arthur Mansfield, no matter what her father thought. Boldly she added, "I thought you didn't care for him, either. The day of the Chipping Ongar Hunt, I thought you were unhappy with the fact that he was here at Fairlawn."

"I was much more annoyed with that young scalawag, Harry Ravenshaw. I only hope I—" Then he stopped short, compressing his lips into a thin line as if to stop the flow of injudicious words from his mouth.

Kate laid an imploring hand on his arm and was shocked to feel how thin it was. Father was losing flesh.

He'd never been the burly, robust type. He was tall, thin, and elegant. Now, however, Kate saw that the bones of his face stood out starkly, and under her own gentle hand, his was skeletal. He must be ill. She'd have to lure him into seeing Derek. Examining his familiar face with eyes that now saw what was there, instead of what they were used to seeing and so thought they still saw, Kate felt dismay at the color of her father's skin: a pasty gray instead of the healthy glow she was so used to. His lips had that blue look again, and frown lines creased his forehead. Father looked old, a stunning insight that frightened her.

Then she was comforted by thoughts of Harry. They'd soon marry, and her father would no longer have to worry about her future. Now, however, at least for a short time, Kate realized that she must humor her father. As ill as he appeared to be, worry was not what he needed. He'd been good to her for her entire life. Now was the time to be good to him.

"Very well, Father, we'll go to Bassett Abbey for dinner come New Year's Day. And I shall smile sweetly at Mr. Mansfield, although I find him quite odious. The Duchess of Dorminster says that he—"

"The duchess is mad," her father cut in angrily. "You should know that. Don't pay any attention to her nonsense."

Kate knew that the duchess was a true eccentric, but mad? Somehow she didn't think so. Oh, they all joked about the duchess, laughed at the dreadful outfits she wore, made sly remarks about that hideous head of yellow hair; but with it all, the duchess, for all her oddities, had a solid core of common sense. She might speak abruptly—bluntly, at times—but what she said was all too often disconcertingly true.

That afternoon when Kate had the groom saddle Lady, her gray mare, she was apprehensive about the coming tryst with her darling Harry. If he wanted to spend New Year's Day with her, what would she say to him? He'd be enraged to find that she was going to Bassett Abbey.

Kate had chosen her most fetching riding habit today, as a kind of ammunition against Harry's anger. She knew that the dark green cord was vastly becoming to her complexion, setting off her dark red hair to perfection. The habit was severe in cut, snuggly fitted to her lush figure. It fastened up the front of the jacket with tiny gold buttons. If Harry wanted her today, he'd have to work hard unbuttoning that nicely cut jacket. Then, underneath, she was wearing a shirtwaist of finest Indian muslin. It buttoned up the back. Vera had spent fully five minutes just doing up the shirt. The full riding skirt was draped over a very small bustle, and Kate had the skirt fastened up to the waist at the moment. Her boots were of the best English leather, polished to a high gloss. Today she wore a top hat of black silk, with a length of light green chiffon tied about it so that it floated gracefully in the slightest breeze. Her dressmaker assured her that all of the ladies who rode in Rotten Row in London wore just such habits, and it pleased Kate to be stylish.

She rode along toward Scarlet Oaks, reining in Lady just before they came to the narrow lane leading to the lodge. It wouldn't do for anyone to see her ride in here. There could be gossip that might reach her father's ears. Kate sighed before tapping Lady with the whip to start her up the lane. Why didn't Harry speak formally for her hand in marriage? Then they could meet quite openly. Kate did realize, though, that once engaged, they might have more difficulty in slipping away by themselves than they did now. Once the engagement became official, she'd be chaperoned by every older lady in Essex county. They'd all fasten their gimlet eyes on Kate to make sure that her conduct was completely virtuous. Maybe they should elope. Otherwise, a long formal engagement might be more than she could bear. Once wakened, her sexual impulses would not go quietly back to sleep. Her desire mounted as each day passed. The hours spent with Harry were utter bliss; the longer hours spent away from him were torture.

Kate had heard plenty of whispers about your "duty" to your husband, of having to "submit" to his animal nature, loathing this coarse side of marriage all the while. She laughed aloud as Lady picked her dainty way along to the lodge. Surely the women must be joking. Love with Harry was the most wonderful thing in the world. Submit? That was scarcely the proper word. Kate entered into their lovemaking with enthusiasm, so that Harry called her—tender-ly—his wanton. If that was what it meant to be wanton, then Kate welcomed the name. She felt sorry for every un-fulfilled woman she knew. The nearest she ever hoped to get to heaven was in bed with Harry, while he made passionate love to her, caressing her eager, willing flesh to such heights of rapture that thinking about it made her faint with desire.

Lady moved her ears forward and gave a little whicker. Kate knew this meant that Harry was already inside the lodge, his chestnut hunter tethered outside. He was watch-ing for her and raced to meet her, lifting his strong arms up to take her from the saddle. He crushed her to him, kissing her ardently, until Kate nearly swooned from the surge of emotion his kisses generated.

"Harry," she protested, "we must go inside. Someone might ride by and see us. I'd be ruined."

He laughed his devil-may-care laugh and held her even closer. "Dearest Kate, you are ruined already. Nothing can change that. Why worry what people say?"

Harry tethered Lady beside his own mount, then swung Kate up into his arms and carried her into the lodge where the fire was blazing hotly and one oil lamp burned with a soft, yellow glow.

"All these buttons," he complained. "I should just rip the jacket off and let the buttons fall where they may."

"Don't say that, Harry!" It reminded Kate too forcefully of that dreadful experience with Tip Jones when he had torn her clothes from her and had almost succeeded in forcing her. She'd never heard whether or not he was apprehended by the police. Occasionally Kate had night-mares about stabbing him in the eye with her hairpin.

Harry seemed not to realize what was bothering her now. When he did get her jacket unbuttoned and off, he swore loudly to find more buttons on her shirtwaist.

"I sometimes think, Kate, that you deliberately wear the most time-consuming clothing to remove that you possess when you come to meet me. Now, if all you were wearing was a lovely nightgown—or a silk negligee—I wouldn't have to play ladies' maid to undress you." He now had her blouse off, and he slid his hands around her shoulders and down to her breasts. "Get those damned stays off, Kate, or I swear I shall get a hunting knife from that case against the wall and cut the laces."

She melted back against him delirious with longing for him, her fingers shaking as she fumbled with the laces. The stays were tossed on a chair with abandon, for now Harry's eager hands had slipped the straps of her corset cover off her shoulders as he caressed her smooth flesh. Soon they lay together in front of the fire, and Kate moaned with delight as her lover entered her. She was carried away on a tide of sensual delight, crying out "Harry!" as she reached her climax. Later, lying there with her beloved in her arms, she traced the strong muscles of his shoulders with her fingers, feeling the sweat their passion had produced as an evidence of the love they had for each other.

"Harry, I do love you so," she breathed. "Do you love me as much as I love you?"

"Silly goose, haven't I just demonstrated to you how much I love you?"

Kate smiled and kissed him sweetly. Should she tell him now about New Year's Day, or would it be better to wait for a little while?

"Kate."

"Ummm?"

"I have to go away for a while. Business."

She wanted to cry, no, no! But Harry might not like it if she were too possessive. So all Kate asked was, "When? And for how long?"

"For a week, or perhaps longer. I hate this, Kate. I won't be with you to welcome in the New Year."

Although she was desolated that he would be gone so long—a week! How would she bear not seeing him, not loving him, for so long?—still, it solved her problem neatly. There was no need now to tell Harry about the invitation to Bassett Abbey. No danger of incurring his anger when he learned that she would celebrate the New Year with Arthur Mansfield instead of with him.

"How will I know when you've come back home, Harry?"

"I'll ride over to Fairlawn," he promised. "Miss me," he ordered. "Miss me every moment I'm away, Kate."

"I shall, Harry," she promised, "I shall."

Then they made love again before the dying fire.

When Kate left the lodge, she was shocked to find that it was nearly dark. "Father will be furious with me, Harry. I had no idea it was so late."

"Tell him you met a handsome prince," Harry suggested.

It was true, but Kate knew that her father wouldn't appreciate such an explanation. "Well, if he tells me I can't go riding for a week, at least I won't miss seeing you."

Harry lifted her up onto her gray mare. Then she leaned down to give him one last kiss.

"Will you miss me, Kate?" he demanded.

"Terribly, Harry." Her lips parted in a final kiss. Then she urged Lady along the lane, hoping that it wasn't so dark that the mare would stumble and throw her. That's all she would need. Father would keep her locked up forever.

When she got home, her father was waiting for her in the drawing room. As she hurried past the door, hoping to get upstairs and out of her riding habit before he saw her, Kate heard him call her name.

With a little sigh, she went into the drawing room with its familiar, homey look. The furniture here was massive and ornate, and the room was cluttered with ornaments of all sorts. Kate had furnished it in the latest style, and she was quite proud of the two pictures she'd found at a grubby little second-hand shop in Chelmsford. One was a dramatic picture of a dying child, with the mourning parents hovering over the cot. The other was of a small child with his arm about a large, shaggy dog.

Kate had little time, though, to admire her good taste in art. Her father looked at her and frowned.

"Kate, it's dark. Surely you weren't riding at this hour?" Disapproval made his voice stiff and cold.

Rapidly she ran a list of excuses through her mind. "Truly I didn't mean to be so late, Father," she said breathlessly. "I thought that Lady had thrown a shoe, and I didn't want to ride too fast for fear she'd go lame."

"Where were you riding so late?" he insisted.

"Oh—no place in particular," she said airily, meanwhile watching him covertly to test his reactions. Kate, although much indulged, had learned that there were lines with her father over which she could not step with impunity. "I just get restless sometimes, here by myself. I thought about riding in to Chelmsford to see Pamela Oldham, but I decided that it was too late for that. Dark comes so early at this time of year."

"The Duchess of Dorminster says she sees you out riding alone quite often. I thought you always took a groom with you when you went riding."

Kate sighed as if greatly put upon. "It is so—so dull, riding with a groom, Father. And if I meet some of my friends, I feel as if you don't trust me, sending me out like an infant with a nursemaid."

"I don't want you to get the reputation of being loose. It will ruin your chances for a good marriage, Kate. Surely you realize that. A man wants a chaste, modest, quiet wife, not some hoyden who goes racing about alone on horseback." She could see the disapproval on his face. "There was a young woman from Colchester who went tearing about the county wearing her brother's riding breeches. Father can't find her a husband now for love nor money."

"Well, you needn't worry that I'd do anything so stupid as that." She didn't want ever to be mistaken for a man. Being a woman was much too delightful.

Then Kate realized that her father was holding what looked like an invitation card in his hand.

As if realizing she'd seen it, he said, "Sir Derek Ravenshaw has invited us for New Year's Day. I was just getting ready to pen our regrets. There've been times recently when I thought perhaps young Ravenshaw was going to ask for your hand in marriage . . ." His voice drifted off to silence.

Kate's heart leaped with joy. So Harry had approached her father, at least obliquely. "Harry Ravenshaw wants to marry me?" she asked eagerly.

"Harry? Good God, no!"

"But, you said—"

"Derek, my dear child. Derek. The baronet. Not his

younger brother! No prospects. None at all. Don't ever marry a younger brother. But now, with Mansfield showing interest in you . . ."

Kate was appalled. "Don't I have anything to say about the man who'll be my husband?"

Frederick Kingsley looked genuinely surprised. "What do you know about men, Kate? It's my duty to select a good husband for you. Someone suitable, a man of substance, who can keep you in luxury. Of course Ravenshaw fits those criteria—but I must keep Mansfield—" Then he stopped short, as if he'd had his tongue cut out of his head.

Kate, confused at this turn of the conversation, laid a gloved hand on her father's arm. "Father, is something bothering you?" she asked gently.

"Bothering me?" he blustered. "No, why would anything bother me—except that I think you are not always as decorous as I might wish. You should have had a mother to raise you, my dearest Kate. If my wife had lived . . ."

Kate squeezed his arm. "You've done a wonderful job of bringing me up, Father. You've been mother, father, and friend to me."

"I only hope I've not made a mistake." There was concern in his kind green eyes.

"Mistake, Father? About what?"

"Nothing, Kate. It's nothing for you to be concerned about." Then, tapping the invitation from Derek, he added, "I must write a refusal and send one of the grooms to Scarlet Oaks with it tonight."

How Kate longed to say she'd ride over with the note. She might see Harry one last time before he left for his business trip. She'd forgotten to ask him where he was going. But she knew that her father wouldn't think of letting her go out now, to run a servant's errand, with full dark fallen.

It was going to be a long, boring week without Harry. How would she manage?

CHAPTER 5

January 1, 1888

Kate and her father traveled the two miles to Bassett Abbey in the victoria, hot bricks at their feet to warm them, and heavy lap robes to ward off the cold, for it was a raw, nasty day with a mixture of snow and rain falling. As they passed the gates to Scarlet Oaks, the Duchess of Dorminster's carriage was just turning into the grounds, and Kate got a glimpse of a landau farther up the driveway. Derek must be having quite a party. With Harry away, she didn't mind too terribly not being able to go to Derek's dinner; but the alternative, the day spent with the odious Mr. Mansfield, was helping to make her feel chilled to the bone.

A bit petulantly, she said, "If you hadn't told Mr. Mansfield that we could dine with him today, we might have gone to Scarlet Oaks too. I think it will be a famous party." She didn't think anything of the kind. Without Harry, the dinner would be a bore. Derek couldn't hold a candle to his younger brother.

"I don't want such an attitude to show when we reach Bassett Abbey," her father snapped. Father was getting very crochety of late. If he didn't improve soon, he'd be as cross as Harry's Aunt Letitia, who was, according to all reports, a real termagant. Harry hated her, and she hated him in return.

"What's so wonderful about Mr. Mansfield?" Kate asked, not making any effort to quell the rebellion in her voice. "I find him distasteful and think it quite mean of you to insist that I come along with you today. I could have dined with my friends at Scarlet Oaks while you went alone to the Abbey, if you are so interested in being friendly with Mr. Mansfield." She paused, seeing her father's temper rise, then added spitefully, "I thought you found him a boor."

He turned to face her, green eyes blazing with anger. "You are much too young to understand such things, Kate. I insist that you trust me—trust my judgment. I am doing this for your sake, not mine."

"My sake? Father, you have to be joking. You know I can't abide the man."

She saw the stubborn lines settle on his aristocratic features, stubborn lines she recognized, for she sometimes saw them on her own face when she looked into the mirror.

"Kate, you don't understand such business affairs as I am—involved in—with Mr. Mansfield." Was there fear on his face for a moment, or was it a trick of the light coming in through the rain-spattered windows of their victoria? "As to why you are going—the invitation was expressly to you." He gave a wry laugh. "I am functioning only as a chaperone today. Mr. Mansfield is much too correct to expect a young woman of refinement to dine alone with him in his home."

"Father, you aren't arranging a marriage for me with him, are you?" She could hear the panic in her own voice, could hear it rise almost an octave, at such a prospect.

"Early days for such talk, Kate."

No denial, no reassurance. No matter that the bricks beneath her dainty boots were still hot, her feet felt like lumps of ice, and another huge chunk of ice lay in her stomach and froze her heart.

"Father, no!" It was more a whimper than a refusal. "You wouldn't—you couldn't marry me to such a horrid man as Mr. Mansfield. His money is tainted, and he battens himself on the poor of Whitechapel. The Duchess of Dorminster—"

"I've told you I am not interested in her crazy ideas."

"Derek Ravenshaw thinks Mr. Mansfield is terrible too."

"I may have been misjudging him. I've always thought Ravenshaw had some sense. But now that he's opened this clinic in Whitechapel for treating wh— low-class women, he's turned almost as peculiar as the duchess. Plenty of work for a good doctor here in Essex, caring for the old families of the area. Why go to London several days a week and waste his talents on the likes of those who live there? Degenerates. Low types of every variety."

Kate, who had never concerned herself with the poor, suddenly found herself defending Derek. "He has compassion for those poor unfortunates, Father. They live in poverty because the slumlords like Mr. Mansfield take advantage of them."

"That's enough!" Kingsley thundered. "I won't have my own daughter talking such radical rot. I forbid you to mention such sentiments today. Mansfield might not take kindly to being called a—slumlord."

Kate was stunned into silence by the vehemence of her father's words. What had gotten into him? He never used to be like this. Then she noticed that he had put a gloved fist to his chest, and his face twisted as if he were in pain.

"Are you all right, Father?"

"Just indigestion. I think the pheasant I had for a late supper last night was a bit too high." He took a deep, almost cautious breath. "I'm fine now."

He didn't return to his talk of Mansfield, nor did Kate mention it again. She had too much to think about. It was obvious to her that her father was indeed thinking of the dreadful Mr. Mansfield as a husband for her. How could he? The man was her father's age, an old man, surely fifty if he was a day. Married to him—she knew too well what that would mean. It made Kate feel queasy to think of being bedded by such a revolting man as Mansfield, with his overfed body, his greasy hair, his cold blue eyes that disrobed her every time he saw her. Could Father's mind be going?

She'd seen trained bears at the fair, animals tethered on a long chain, poor beasts that paced back and forth, around and around, never able to escape their bonds. This was just how Kate felt now, with the prospect of Mr. Mansfield for her husband. She would have to tell Harry, as soon as he got back to Scarlet Oaks. Kate smiled a scarlet little smile. That should wake him up! He'd propose marriage at once when he learned that Mansfield wanted her for his wife.

Soon the coachman was turning off the highway into the driveway that led to Bassett Abbey. In spite of her loathing for its owner, Kate couldn't help being excited about a visit here. The Abbey had been considered a showplace for years. Mr. Mansfield had bought it about three years ago. Where he came from, no one seemed to know; but he was so obviously rich that he was accepted into the county society in short order.

She was learning that money counted more than family these days. Look at poor Harry, the second son, penniless because everything had gone to Derek when their father died. Perhaps this trip Harry was on now was something that would make him rich. Then there'd be no problems. He could ask Father for her hand, they'd be wed and live graciously in a home of their own. Perhaps someplace as grand as Bassett Abbey.

The house now came into view as they drove out from a double row of plane trees that almost met overhead. The original structure went back hundreds of years, but the successive owners had rebuilt and made so many changes that little remained of the old Cistercian abbey. The same gray limestone as the original had been used by builders through the years, so the basic structure had a unity. The style now was much more ornate than the abbey had been, with porches, parapets, and towers added. There were formal gardens, drab now in the depth of winter, although Kate caught a glimpse of one lone red rose still bravely blooming in a sheltered nook. The abbey was large, easily as big a house as Scarlet Oaks, and much bigger than Fairlawn, which was only modest in size.

"I understand that Mansfield has added that turret." Her father pointed to the south wing, where a high tower with a conical roof reached for the sullen sky.

"It's not very cheerful, is it?" Kate felt oppressed by the towering gray stone walls, as gloomy as the day.

"It's the weather, Kate. Bassett Abbey is a fine house, one of the finest in Essex. And Mansfield seems to have all the money he needs to keep it up. It takes a small army of servants to keep a place this large in order."

The first of that army appeared out of the drizzle, a wizened little man who held the lead horse's head while the coachman dismounted and opened the door of the victoria for them. A second man appeared as if he'd been conjured up by magic, and he opened a large black umbrella so that they wouldn't get wet from the rain that was now coming down steadily.

They entered the abbey through an ornate, columned porch that was two stories high. Huge double oak doors, carved with fanciful religious scenes, opened as Kate neared them, and an elderly butler bowed in greeting.

"Mr. Mansfield is in the small salon."

He took her father's coat, hat, and stick, while a dumpy little maid in prim black, with white ruffled cap and white apron, took Kate's long, fur-trimmed coat, her fur muff, and her velvet bonnet.

The entrance hall was a huge, rather austere room, two stories high, with a screened balcony at one end, possibly once a minstrel's gallery. The floor was of polished gray slate, and Mansfield had several Oriental rugs scattered about on it, their rich, muted colors helping a little to dispel the gloom of the high-ceilinged room. A fire blazed in a large fireplace that was at the end of the hall opposite the gallery, and Kate longed to go toast her cold feet in front of it. Anything to put off meeting their host. The butler, though, was leading them through a doorway toward another wing of the building, and Kate had no choice but to follow him, with her father at her side.

In the hallway, dark portraits hung along the walls; but whether they were of Mr. Mansfield's ancestors, or whether he had bought them with the house, Kate couldn't tell. The butler stopped at a door, knocked once, opened it, and announced, "Miss Kingsley and Mr. Kingsley." He stood aside and gestured for them to enter the salon.

Mr. Mansfield was waiting for them before the fire. "Happy New Year," he greeted them, his voice treacly. He moved forward, took Kate's hand, and bowed over it, kissing it like a Frenchman.

It took great restraint on her part not to rub the back

of her hand along the satin of her skirt to wipe off the kiss.

Mansfield rang for the butler, who served them sherry from a cut-glass decanter. Kate sipped daintily, trying to take in the room without being too obvious about her interest. She didn't like Mansfield, but she had to admit that this small salon was decorated in the latest style. One entire wall was covered to the wainscoting with porcelain plates.

Seeing Kate's interest in the china, Mansfield said with considerable pride, "I've been collecting porcelain as an investment. Most of it is our own English china. That plate is Minton, the design by Pugin. This Staffordshire is, of course, a snapdragon design. You've played the game, I'm sure, Miss Kate."

"And burned my fingers trying to get those flaming raisins and almonds off the plate," she said ruefully.

"Ah, what a pity to scorch such lovely fingers." Before she could retreat, Mansfield had caught her hand and kissed it again.

Kate repressed a shudder. If a mere kiss on her hand could be so revolting, how could she bear to submit to the kind of intimacies she enjoyed with Harry?

Her father, oblivious to Kate's feelings, was examining Mansfield's porcelain collection as if he were a true connoisseur. Kate knew that her father didn't know Wedgwood from German Meissen. His interest was frightening, for she recognized it as an attempt to ingratiate himself with Mansfield. Frederick Kingsley of Fairlawn fawning over such an upstart as this *nouveau riche* slumlord made Kate feel ill.

"Ah, scenes from the Great Exposition," Kingsley exclaimed, seeing something familiar.

"Bat-printed," Mansfield said, not bothering to explain what bat-printing was. Kingsley nodded sagely, as if bestowing his approval on the collection.

Kate saw one porcelain object that was unusual enough to catch her attention. It was a thermometer stand, very ornate, with an arch of leaves around the thermometer. The temperature-measuring device was interesting in itself, for although the degrees were shown on one side of the ruling, on the other were such quaint designations as Summer Heat, Blood Heat, and Fever Heat.

"With such a thermometer, one doesn't need a doctor," Mansfield joked.

Kate pasted on a polite social smile, feeling as if her face might crack in the process, but her father laughed immoderately.

It was all very disturbing. Did Arthur Mansfield have some kind of hold over her father? Kate knew nothing of her father's business affairs. She'd been raised to think that there was always an abundance of money for anything she wanted. Poverty was an abstraction she did not comprehend. She'd heard gossip of aristocrats who lost their fortunes. Sometimes these men took the gentleman's way out, putting bullets through their heads. There was even talk that part of Monica Murphy's fall from grace could be blamed on the fact that her father, Major Murphy, had lost all of his money gambling and had then committed suicide, leaving his only child to fend for herself in a world which was completely alien to her. There were plenty of stories about Monica, juicy tidbits chewed over whenever the elite gathered. Now Kate became aware of what might have happened to the young woman, accustomed to luxury, when she suddenly found herself penniless.

Marrying for money was common. Kate knew of various young ladies whose family fortunes had dwindled, and their fathers had been glad enough to marry them off to rich men with less than impeccable social backgrounds. Could this be her father's problem? Kate knew he'd been worried lately. Were they on the verge of bankruptcy? If so, she'd have little choice if her father arranged a lucrative marriage for her; yet she was determined not to be sold off to this Mansfield creature as if she were a prize sheep. She'd elope with Harry first. Surely, with a wife to support, Harry could count on more money from his brother the baronet.

While her father admired some salt-glazed jugs of Doulton's Lambeth stoneware, Kate looked more closely at the other furnishings of the room.

"Ah, I see that you are admiring my chairs," Mansfield

said, noticing that Kate had drifted away from the wall of porcelain. "Perhaps I could interest you in some piquet later."

He didn't even bother to include her father in the invitation.

"I'm not a very good card player," she said ungraciously, earning herself a frown from her father.

Gallantly Mansfield assured her, "With such an attractive opponent as you, my mind would not be on the cards. You would win easily. But then"—and he gave that oily smile that disgusted her so—"my only wish is for you always to win."

Kingsley was looking daggers at her, but Kate was determined not to play the coquette with Mansfield. She'd give him no encouragement whatsoever. Her heart—and her body—belonged to Harry Ravenshaw. She would not allow her father to make a match for her with this boor, no matter that he was on his good behavior today.

The butler reappeared to announce dinner, and Mansfield offered his arm to Kate. She had worn a brown satin dress today, one with a high neck and long, fitted sleeves. Kate's feeling about Mansfield was that she wanted to be covered up as much as possible so he couldn't ogle her flesh.

As Mansfield escorted Kate to dinner, he murmured, "How charming you look today, my dear. So maidenly. Some young women these days dress like strumpets. I admire modesty in a woman."

Kate wished she'd known this. She'd have worn her most daring gown, which was cut so low that she was almost afraid to breathe when she wore it for fear her bosom would escape from the neckline. And it bared her arms completely, making up for the lack of fabric at the top of the gown with a long train which always made her feel very elegant.

Modest! What would dear Mr. Mansfield say if he knew how wanton she was when she met Harry in the hunting lodge? If Father did try to arrange a marriage with Mansfield, Kate swore to herself that she'd tell the man she wasn't a virgin. That should put paid to any marriage contract. She was sure he'd not want some other man's leavings. The thought pleased her so that she smiled, which caused Mansfield to lay his free hand over hers, which was tucked into his arm.

There was little conversation at the dinner table. Mansfield was a trencherman who took his food seriously, but Kate ate sparingly. She was determined to keep her slender figure so that she would resemble the women in the fashion plates rather than the older women she knew. Alfie's grandmother, the dowager Countess of Morganton, was so enormously heavy that it took two sturdy footmen to heave her out of a chair and to her feet. And she was no exception. Most of the older women of Kate's acquaintance were built along the lines of the famous English beef cattle rather than their equally famous race horses.

Normally, after dessert Kate would have retired to the drawing room with the ladies, but as there were only three for dinner, Mansfield suggested to her father that they all take their port in the drawing room.

"Perhaps Miss Kate will honor us by playing selections on my newest acquisition, a grand piano."

And grand it was, enameled a cream color, with intricate inlays of ivory, tortoise shell, and mother of pearl. Kate played reasonably well, having been trained in piano at Miss Forbes's Select School. Mansfield stood beside her to turn the pages of the music. He had chosen a group of old English folk songs, and when Kate began to sing the familiar words in a light, clear soprano, he joined in with a surprisingly good baritone. If it had been anyone other than Mansfield, Kate might have enjoyed the musical evening.

Later, after politely refusing coffee and further refreshment, the Kingsleys made ready to return to Fairlawn.

"Miss Kate, your father has given me permission to call on you," Mansfield said, a possessive note in his voice as if he thought he owned her already, that marriage was certain. "Perhaps we can go riding tomorrow."

Kate, determined not to go out alone with Mansfield, made the first excuse that came into her head, earning a scowl of disapproval from her father. "I'm sorry, sir, but I have promised the Duchess of Dorminster that I would help her tomorrow with some of her London charitable endeavors."

"The depths of degradation in the East End aren't for you, my dear." Mansfield said at his unctuous best.

With spirit Kate retorted, "The duchess says a lot of the problem is caused by slumlords who herd the people into rat-infested firetraps, extorting exorbitant rents from them. She insists that this forces the women into lives of prostitution."

"Kate!" Her father was shocked and angry. In apology to their host he said, "I sometimes despair, Mansfield. This younger generation—I don't know what they're coming to. If only my dear wife had lived—I'm sure she didn't even know such words as those Kate is using so glibly."

"What Kate needs is a husband with a firm hand," Mansfield said darkly.

It took no imagination on her part to know who that husband would be if Arthur Mansfield had anything to say about it. Fortunately though, perhaps as a result of the flurry caused by her words, Mansfield, put off about riding tomorrow, had not pressed for another engagement. If only Harry would come back. It was going to be difficult to keep from seeing Mansfield for an entire week with Harry gone. If he were here, she could always plead another engagement. And when she and Harry were together, she was truly engaged in their passionate lovemaking. The thought of having to go to bed with this sleek, pompous upstart sickened Kate.

INTERLUDE 2

Tuesday, January 3, 1888

This time he had put on a false moustache, bought at a theatrical supply house, and he wore a shabby bowler instead of the deerstalker hat. He was drawn to the night streets of Whitechapel as a moth to a candle flame; but he knew that he must use caution in his prowlings. There were people in the East End who might recognize him and wonder at his disguise.

He walked purposefully down Whitechapel. Ahead of him was a young woman in tawdry clothes, walking with a drunken gait, catching at the arms of the men who hurried past.

As he came abreast of her, she caught at his sleeve. "Care to 'ave a bit uh fun?" she cajoled, leering at him, lips pulled back from rotten teeth.

"Get your filthy hands off me," he snarled.

"Oh, ain't we the prissy one! Plenty of men like Polly." She staggered away, accosting the next man who came along.

He turned into Great Garden Street from Whitechapel. Ahead, only dimly seen in the light from a streetlamp, was a tall, gaunt, familiar figure. He was lurking in the doorway of one of the squalid houses. It was the Reverend Mr. Fiddler, pastor of Salvation Chapel. What was he doing lurking around here? Fiddler was up to something, and it wasn't saving the souls of the damned whores who polluted the East End. One of the rotten women stopped beside Fiddler, trying to solicit his trade. What would he do?—Exhort her?—Try to win her to the Lord?—Preach a sermon to her? None of these. Fiddler took the woman's arm and they disapeared into one of the narrow alleys leading off Great Garden.

He hurried forward, stopped, held his breath listening. To his right, just inside the fenced alley, were the unmistakable sounds of lust. He could picture it in his mind: the whore, leaning against the rough board fence, her skirt pulled up around her waist; the man, brutish in his desire; the final exchange of a few coppers. What would the zealous Mrs. Fiddler do if she knew her husband was out whoring instead of evangelizing? Leave him? More probably she'd pray for his damned soul. The Reverend Mr. Fiddler could stand watching. There was a chance to pick up a bit of money by blackmailing the holy lecher.

CHAPTER 6

Friday, January 6, 1888

"That's a more appropriate outfit for the East End, Kate," the Duchess of Dorminster said approvingly. "The lovely blue taffeta you wore Tuesday was too fancy for our work. Don't want to make the poor women envious, do we? They've enough troubles without our adding to them."

Kate herself had realized she was overdressed on that first trip to Whitechapel with the duchess. Today she'd chosen a subdued suit of brown wool, very plain, the skirt only full enough to fit over a small bustle. The jacket buttoned to the neck with plain buttons, the sleeves were plain with little lift. The high-necked white shirtwaist made a pretty frill under her chin, but that was the only ornament. Her bonnet was of matching wool, tied with brown satin ribbons. The coat she wore over the suit was three-quarter length, also of brown, but the fabric was a deep plush, with some fringe trim at the bottom.

The hansom cab was rattling down Whitechapel Road. Kate wished they'd taken the Metro; but the duchess didn't like the underground railroad.

"Dirty. Smelly. And I always feel it's going to cave in, trapping me. Much better to go by cab, my dear."

On Tuesday, Kate had accompanied the duchess just to defy her father and Mr. Mansfield. They'd gone direct to the Salvation Chapel, where a small group of local drabs had gathered to be taught to read by the duchess. Mrs. Fiddler, the parson's wife, clearly at odds with the eccentric duchess, had spent her time exhorting the women to leave their sinful ways and be converted to Christ.

On the way home by train that afternoon, the duchess had said, "Abby Fiddler is a fool. Those women need jobs, not religion. Be grateful you're not one of them, Kate."

Kate shuddered, remembering the depths of poverty she'd witnessed. She'd known there were poor people in London, desperately poor souls; but she'd not realized, until she saw them for herself, how terrible was their lot.

When the duchess had sent a message to Fairlawn asking if she'd go along today to the chapel, Kate had first thought she couldn't bear to face that degradation again. Then she remembered that Mansfield might well call on her, so she had agreed to go.

The duchess, adhering to her own eccentric style, yet also following her admonition to Kate not to dress too richly, was wearing a tattered Empire gown of gray, which might have been sewn from faded drapes. Her yellow hair was up in a chignon, a bit less wild than usual, and she'd covered the entire outfit, hair and all, with a flowing cape complete with hood of rusty black. Kate thought her companion looked like a witch. She hoped no one who knew her saw them together.

Kate had learned last Tuesday that, despite her appearance, the duchess was very practical about some matters and truly Christian in her attitude toward the prostitutes in her class.

"Teach them to read, they may be able to get jobs. Haven't a chance now. Born poor, live poor, will die poor. Nothing to look forward to except grinding poverty. And men like that rotten Mansfield batten off their troubles."

Today the duchess insisted, "You must help with the class, Kate. We'll divide the women into two groups."

Kate was terror-stricken. "I know nothing about teaching!" she protested.

"More than they do, my girl, more than they do." The duchess's voice was inexorable.

"Why can't Mrs. Fiddler help? Tuesday all she did was interrupt your lessons every chance she had so that she could preach to them about sin."

"Wouldn't mind gagging Abby," the duchess said fiercely. "Sometimes I think that she and that beanpole husband of hers do more harm than good with their psalm singing and their preaching. Derek Ravenshaw does a lot more good for those poor, benighted women than both the Fiddlers put together."

Mention of Derek made Kate think of Harry. What would he say if he knew she was here in Whitechapel again, after he'd told her to stay away from East London? On that all of the men she knew were in accord: Derek, Harry, even Mr. Mansfield, all had told her to stay out of this sink of degradation.

"And speaking of Sir Derek—I haven't seen you riding past Harcourt with that young scamp brother of his this week. Had a spat with him, I hope."

"Harry's away on business," Kate said with all the dignity she could muster. Just when she thought she'd misjudged the duchess, the old witch had to go sticking her nose into Kate's affairs.

The duchess's laugh was raucous. "Any business Harry Ravenshaw conducts is apt to be funny business, my girl. No good. I told you that. Wouldn't trust him with tuppence of my money." Then, her eyes glittering shrewdly, she asked, "Has your Pa bought any of those shares of stock Harry's been peddling on the sly?"

"I—I have no idea. I told you Father doesn't discuss business with me."

"Well, I do hope Frederick is too smart to be taken in by Harry. I've heard rumors . . . ."

She didn't go into what she'd heard, though, for she suddenly leaned forward, peering from the cab window. Catching up her umbrella, the duchess pounded on the roof of the cab until the little door opened and the cabby peered down at them.

"Stop here, my man."

Before the man had pulled up his horse, the duchess had opened the door on her side and called out, "Monica! Monica Murphy! Come here!"

Kate was so embarrassed she wished she could sink into the cushions of the cab and become invisible. After the gossip she'd heard about Monica—now this incredible woman was going to invite her into the cab with them? Obviously that was exactly what the duchess intended, for she said, "More over, Kate, there's a good girl," and then called out again, "Plenty of room with us, Monica," even though the cab sat only two comfortably.

Kate hoped that Monica would refuse; but to her chagrin, the woman climbed into the cab saying, "It beats walking in the cold. How are you, duchess? And—Kate Kingsley, isn't it?"

The faint aura of unwashed flesh battled with the stink of cheap scent as Monica Murphy settled herself into the seat with a sigh. If Kate had met her on the street, she might not have recognized her. It had been months—maybe a year—since she'd seen the older woman. Although she knew Monica casually, they have never traveled in the same group, Monica being some years older than Kate. She remembered her as exotic-looking rather than beautiful, her Irish features a bit too sharp for conventional beauty, her glossy hair so black that some whispered she must dye it. Her eyes were tilted ever so slightly over high cheekbones, giving a quality to her face that was almost Oriental. Now Monica was gaunt, cheeks hollow, blue eyes bloodshot and deeply shadowed. Two bright red spots glowed on her cheeks, whether from fever or rouge Kate couldn't decide. Monica was dressed in what had once been a stylish dress; but now it was dirty and there were rips in the skirt that hadn't been mended. The color might have been blue at one time. Now it was so dirty that it was hard to tell what color it was.

Monica coughed: a deep, choking sound.

Kate saw the quick look that the duchess gave Monica. "Bad cough you have there, my girl. Catarrh?"

"I guess so," Monica muttered.

"Ask Derek to prescribe a syrup for you."

Monica laughed bitterly. "Medicines cost money."

"I'll pay." The duchess was brusque, perhaps to hide her pity. "Just tell Derek to bill me for whatever you need."

Monica had another coughing spell, which left her gasping. When she could talk once again, she said, "And what do I do in exchange, your grace? I have learned that we get nothing free in this life."

"Come to my classes at the Salvation Chapel. I'm trying to teach some of the women how to read."

"I'm quite capable of reading without any instruction." Monica's voice was sharp with annoyance.

"I want you to help with the teaching. Today I've drafted Kate, but you could be there every day, living as you do in the area."

Monica laughed a wild, hysterical laugh. This set her to coughing, and before the paroxysm had passed, the hansom cab came to a halt.

"Oh, we're here at the chapel. Come along, young ladies. We have work to do."

The coachman had opened the doors with the lever he controlled from his high perch behind the body of the cab. The duchess passed up his pay to him, then herded Kate and Monica ahead of her toward the dirty brick front of the small chapel.

"Sorry. I'm not playing teacher for anyone," Monica said, her voice surly now. "Give it up, your grace. You are wasting your time. All the women want is gin to dull their misery. And the way they get money for gin is the way I do: I sell myself to any man who has a pocket full of pounds." She turned to Kate. "Go home. You aren't the type to be a do-gooder."

"Now, Monica," the duchess admonished. "If you spent more time here at the chapel than—"

"With that old lecher! My dear duchess, you amaze me. I had thought that you were sensible. Don't you know that your precious Mr. Fiddler, that upright man of God, is the most notorious whore-chaser in Whitechapel?" Again she addressed herself to Kate. "Watch his hands, Kate. They'll be all over you, if you give him half a chance." She laughed bitterly. "Instead of taking lessons, I should be giving them to that pillar of rectitude and frigidity, Mrs. Fiddler." Her laugh was lewd. "Oh, I could teach her how to keep her reverend husband so busy that he'd have no time to chase other women!"

"Fie! Enough of such talk!" the duchess chided. "What will Kate think of you, Monica?"

Monica gave a defiant look at Kate. "If she doesn't know by now what I am, she's stupid. What do my dear friends in Essex say about me, Kate? I'm sure I'm one of their juicier morsels of gossip."

Kate felt she should protest, insist that she'd heard nothing about Monica from her friends; but she waited too long to disclaim knowledge of Monica's present situation.

Monica gave a lopsided grin. "See?" she said to the duchess. "Kate won't lie. I've embarrassed her. Kate, remember well, it's not a man who brought me to this sorry pass. I did it to myself. I always thought that all of the prim and prissy women of the community were full of nonsense. What harm could come to me if I allowed myself to have the same pleasure from a man that a man would get from me? Well, to my everlasting sorrow, I've learned. It is a man's world, Kate, and don't forget it. Men can be rakes if they wish, and no one thinks any worse of them; but let a woman act with anything but modesty, and the whole of society turns on her."

"Monica, stop such maundering and come inside to help with the reading class," the duchess commanded, imperious despite her scarecrow clothing.

Monica shook her head. "Sorry, your grace. I have more pressing things to do. I have to earn enough so that I'll have a bed for the night."

With a vast wealth of pity and compassion in her voice, the duchess suggested, "You could come home with me, Monica. I could give you work to do."

"No." Sadly the woman shook her head. Then a paroxysm of coughing shook her. When she'd recovered her voice, she continued, "I can't come back to Essex, your grace. It would never work."

Kate saw acceptance on the duchess's face. "Go see Derek though. And remember—tell him I'll pay for whatever medicines you need." She turned toward the door of the Salvation Chapel. "Come along, Kate. The women may be waiting for us."

Kate turned to follow the duchess, but Monica laid a detaining hand on her arm. Speaking softly so that only Kate could hear, Monica said, "Get rid of him, Kate. It will only lead to heartbreak. Look at me."

"I don't know what you mean." Kate wanted to pull away from Monica's not-too-clean hand.

Monica's mouth twisted in a wry smile. "Oh, you know exactly, Kate. I can tell. You have that look. You know all about loving a man, lying with him. You are sure you're in love with him, whoever he is. Let me tell you something, dear Kate. That's what I thought at first. You think he'll marry you, don't you?" Her fingers tightened painfully on Kate's arm. "He won't. They never do. They use you, they enjoy your body—but when they marry, they look for sweet virgins. Escape while you still can, Kate. Maybe no one will find out. Meet some decent man who doesn't know what you've done—never, for God's sake, tell him —and marry him."

Kate, smug in her knowledge of Harry's love for her, said heartlessly, "Just because that happened to you, Monica, doesn't mean it will happen to me."

Monica, feeling Kate's instinctive withdrawal, let go of her arm. "Someday, when it's too late, you'll remember what I've told you. Oh, Kate, I hope you don't come to the same end I have." Her eyes filled with tears. "It's hell, being here in Whitechapel. And it's too late for me to leave." She was seized with that terrible cough again. This time, when she wiped her lips on a tattered, soiled kerchief, Kate could see bright flecks of blood on the cloth. "I know what I have. Consumption. 'Get out in the country, Monica,' Derek insists. 'You need fresh vegetables, milks, eggs.' Dear God, Derek, of all people, should know that it's too late for me. Hopeless. I'm already coughing up my lungs. Go back home, Kate, back to the safety of Essex. Get rid of the man. Wait for marriage. It's the only security for a woman."

From the doorway to the chapel, the duchess called, "Kate!"

"Coming, your grace."

In the moment she turned away from Monica, the woman hurried away, her ragged gown, a legacy from better days, brushing the filthy streets.

With a shudder of distaste, Kate turned away from Monica's retreating figure. Monica had been spouting nonsense. She was understandably bitter, because a man had betrayed her. Kate, though, knew her Harry. There'd be no such treatment from him. Soon they'd be wed. Monica just wanted to make her unhappy, because she herself had fallen on such desolate times.

INTERLUDE 3

Friday, January 6, 1888

He saw a whore coming toward him. There was something familiar about her walk, something that alerted him; so he ducked into a malodorous alleyway until she passed. From his place of concealment he peered out cautiously to see who she was. Monica! It was lucky for him that he'd spied her before she saw him. How could he hope to explain his presence here in Whitechapel dressed as he was? If he'd been wearing his usual clothes, it would have caused no comment, even if she were sober enough to recognize him. It was his subtle disguise which would have been impossible to justify.

A hansom cab clattered by, then pulled up beside Monica. A well-known voice carried over the noises of Whitechapel Road. The Duchess of Dorminster, that busybody, was calling to the Murphy woman. He watched the whore get into the cab. How low Monica Murphy had fallen! A fit one for the clinic—but he mustn't think about the clinic now. And he had to stay away from Union Row. He watched the hansom cab pull in to the curb further up Whitechapel Road, in front of the Salvation Chapel. He laughed out loud.

"What's so funny, ducky?" one of the Whitechapel regulars asked, giving him a toothless smile. "Want a bit of fun?"

"On your way, you rotten whore!"

She raised one eyebrow. "Slummin', eh? Go back to

your fancy ladies, then." She spat so accurately that only by dancing back a step did he keep from having his boots soiled.

Moving on toward Salvation Chapel, he saw Monica Murphy walking away from the duchess, who seemed to be exhorting her, although they now were far enough away that he couldn't hear what that scatty old woman was saying.

Then to his horror and great consternation, Kate stepped daintily down from the cab. Kate! Here! He wanted to rush to her, force her back into the cab, have the cabby drive with all haste to the nearest train station. Kate had no business here amidst all this filth and degradation. He knew, though, that he must not let Kate glimpse him, even momentarily. If he couldn't explain his apparel to Monica Murphy, how could he ever explain it to Kate?

CHAPTER 7

Friday, January 6, 1888

The reading class was held in the chapel proper, a bleak room so cold that the chill ate into Kate's bones. There was an iron stove in one corner, but the fire in it was so small as to be almost nonexistent. The fires of hell weren't burning very brightly in Salvation Chapel!

There were only two women in the room, both huddled near the stove, trying to draw a little heat into their bodies. The women were middle-aged and alike in one respect: both were exceptionally unattractive. One, tall and bony, with a long horse face and straggly gray hair creeping out from under her black straw bonnet, looked around at them, but gave no greeting. The other, a woman almost as broad as she was long, her head reaching only to the other woman's shoulder, smiled a toothless smile at the duchess and muttered something which might have been "Good afternoon." She wore a green tartan skirt over a bustle, and the top of her costume seemed to consist of a variety of old woolen scarves wound about her mammoth torso. Her hair was a faded ginger.

"Ladies, where are the others?" the duchess demanded.

The shorter woman kept smiling, but didn't answer. Finally the tall prostitute muttered, "Got better things to do than learn to read 'dog' and 'cat,' they have. Should be out on the streets meself. Gotta earn my night's lodging."

"Now, Elizabeth, this will help you in the long run."

"I live for the short run, milady." The answer was short, blunt, and very revealing.

Kate thought the duchess was out of her depth. Did she honestly think she could do anything for these women? No doubt every penny they made from their customers went for gin and lodging in one of the common lodging houses where they paid for a bed by the night. Kate was sorry she'd let the duchess talk her into coming here again today. Monday she'd come only to have an excuse not to go riding with Mansfield. Why was she here again? Monday's session had been a fiasco. There had been six women, these two plus four equally unfortunate types. The duchess had tried to teach them their letters; but as at least three had been drunk on cheap gin, she had accomplished little.

"Very well, as there are only two today, we may be able to accomplish more. Miss Kingsley has kindly agreed to help again today. Kate, my dear, you work with Molly while I teach Elizabeth."

Molly, the short, fat woman, gave a sudden wild giggle. "Elizabeth! Imagine being called that, Liz." Again she cackled. "Long Liz they call her on the street. Tall as a man, she is."

"Belt up. It's the gin talking," the woman muttered, tone vicious. "Belt up or I'll cram one of those scarves down your gin-soaked throat."

"Violence in the house of God! Fall on your knees, woman! Beg God's forgiveness for your sins."

Kate couldn't suppress a little gasp, she was so startled by the words delivered in sepulchral tones, seemingly from out of the air in the chapel. She saw an expression of exasperation cross the painted face of the duchess, whose eyes went to a point behind Kate.

"Oh, Mr. Fiddler." The duchess's manner was unenthusiastic in the extreme. "I didn't know you were about."

Kate turned and saw that a man had entered the bleak room of the chapel through a door in the back. Having read Washington Irving's droll tale of the headless horseman, all she could think of was Ichabod Crane. The Reverend Mr. Fiddler was at least six feet tall; but his frame was spare to the point of emaciation, and the tall, black, stovepipe hat he wore set squarely over his fanatic's face made him seem even taller. He was dressed all in black, except for the dingy white collar of his shirt which showed above the worn lapels of the coat buttoned almost to his scrawny neck. He advanced on the luckless Elizabeth like some strange waterbird, stalking down the aisle between the hard, backless benches.

"We must pray for your immortal soul, Elizabeth. You must not threaten violence here in Salvation Chapel." He turned to the Duchess of Dorminster. "Where is my good wife? It was the agreement, when I allowed you to organize these classes, that if I could not be in attendance, you would see to it that my good wife was present. Where is Mrs. Fiddler?"

The duchess was brusque with him. "We just arrived. I haven't had a chance to find your wife."

"I think today's session might be better spent in prayer than in trying to give these sinful women airs. Reading! I can read the Scriptures for them and interpret their mysteries. What need have such as these to read?"

"They just might be better-equipped to earn a decent living than to go on whoring," was the duchess's blunt answer. "Pray over them on Sunday, reverend sir. Let me work with them through the week."

It was the wrong thing to say. Kate saw fire in his eyes, and he thundered, "God works seven days a week, your grace. These poor, fallen creatures need to petition his mercy seat constantly. They go about their wicked ways, selling their bodies to men for sinful purposes, every day of the week. I must save their souls."

He fell to his knees there in the aisle, and prayed in a loud voice, after taking off his hat and laying it carefully on a bench beside him. Kate noticed that his scant hair was oiled and combed carefully to hide the bald spot on his skull.

Not being used to this kind of evangelism, Kate wondered what she should do. As it seemed the preacher would pray for hours, she finally sat down quietly on one of the benches. Not feeling at all religious at that moment, Kate covertly watched the others. The two prostitutes finally did as she had done and sat down on a bench, one at either end, and glared at each other. Kate felt that had the preacher not come in just when he did, the two might have gotten into a hair-pulling match. The duchess stood there, obviously disgusted. Kate realized that her friend from Essex had no great love for Mr. Fiddler. Having spent her life commanding people, the duchess was using the minister only because he could provide a place for her own private charity.

During the interminable prayer, Kate looked carefully at the fervent man. Monica Murphy had said flatly that he himself, for all his godly pretense, patronized the local whores. Did the two women on the bench know this? If so, they must be laughing to themselves to hear his exhortations. He was no less a sinner than they.

When he finally did get up off his knees, he turned abruptly to Kate and asked, "And who are you, young woman? Are you here to help the duchess with her wild scheme?"

There was something about those dark, burning eyes that made Kate feel uneasy. She'd never known anyone who was mad, but the look he gave her made her think of madness. It was as if there were another man inside him, fighting to get out, a man the opposite of the man of God he professed to be. He'd not been here Monday, although his wife had been present to play the harmonium for hymns, to the disgust of the duchess.

"This is Miss Kate Kingsley, a neighbor in Essex, who is kind enough to help me with my little school."

"And what do you think of these sinners, eh, Miss Kingsley?" he demanded. "Whores. What's worse, unrepentant whores. They'll leave these sanctified walls and go out onto the streets to solicit men, to sell their bodies to satisfy the lust of any and all."

Elizabeth stood up and yelled, "Don't call me filthy names, Parson, or I might call you a few. I keep myself out of the workhouse."

Molly cackled in delight. "You tell 'im, Liz. Proper prig he is, prayin' over us." She turned to the Reverend Mr. Fiddler, her broad face spiteful. "Better pray for yourself, Parson. I've heard—"

"Silence, you Jezebel!" he shouted, the cords on his long neck standing out like ropes.

Kate was afraid he'd have apoplexy if he didn't calm himself. How could such a man do any good in a place like East London?

"I don't take such names from anyone," Elizabeth announced belligerently. "Come along, Molly. We needn't listen to the preacher."

"Now, now, you've not had your lesson yet," the duchess protested. She rounded on Fiddler, "I can't teach them unless you leave us alone." Then, smiling slightly, she added, "I can always hire other quarters. I thought you could use the added income for Salvation Chapel."

Kate hadn't realized that the duchess was paying rent from her own pocket to use this mean, cold room.

"No need to be hasty, dear lady." The change in Fiddler's manner was laughable. He even smiled a toothy smile at the duchess. "I am so fired with my zeal to win these poor souls for Christ that I get carried away at times."

"You tend to their souls, but let me tend to their temporal problems, Mr. Fiddler." The duchess knew she'd won, so she could afford to be friendly. "Come, ladies, time for your lesson."

The moment was gone though. The two prostitutes said they'd come some other day, when the others were there too. Then they made their escape from Salvation Chapel. As they went out the door, Kate heard Molly say something about looking for someone who'd buy her a bit of gin.

"See, they are unteachable," Fiddler said smugly.

"You turned them off their lessons today." The reprimand was sharp and swift. "Save their souls some other time after this. Come, Kate, there's no point in staying today."

"You did use the chapel. I shall expect my rent for today," Fiddler said.

"You'll be paid in good time. Come along, Kate." Then, as if Fiddler were one of her servants at Harcourt, she ordered, "Find us a hansom cab, there's a good fellow."

Fiddler shot her a look of pure venom, but the duchess either didn't see it, or pretended she didn't.

After the parson stalked out of the chapel, the duchess said, "It may have been a mistake, setting up my school here. Fiddler is so intent on saving their souls that he interferes with my efforts."

Personally, Kate thought that there was no hope for the poor drabs the duchess had lured to her reading class. No doubt they came only to get in out of the cold briefly, although with the minuscule fire that Mr. Fiddler kept going in the stove, they'd probably be warmer in the local grogshop.

"Do you truly think it will help them to learn to read, your grace?"

"Probably not," the duchess said with honesty. "But I must try. Something has to be done about East London, or one day the whole area will explode in revolution. Can't have that, you know, Kate. Would mean the end of the kind of life we're used to. So I try to do my bit. Just as Derek does his." She slipped an arm through Kate's companionably and drew her toward the door. "Hopefully Fiddler will have found us a cab by now." They went out into the street to find that Mr. Fiddler was in the road, waving his long arms to attract a cab. "Looks like a windmill, doesn't he?"

Kate had to laugh at the duchess's uncharitable comment, for it was very true. Just then the parson managed to wave down a cab, and he helped the two ladies into it.

"I shall return on Tuesday," the duchess told him. "Do try to have a bit more coal on the fire. That place would chill the soul of the Devil himself." Then, imperiously, before Fiddler could do more than splutter, she called, "Drive on, cabby."

Once they were clopping along Whitechapel Road, the cabby opened the little door in the roof of the hansom and asked, "Where to, milady?"

"Union Row." To Kate she said, "I think I want to see Derek Ravenshaw before we go back home. Just to make sure he's doing everything he can for poor Monica. Pity that she fell so low. Might have made a good wife if she'd kept her skirts down. Always was a wild one. Let it be a lesson to you, Kate." She took hold of Kate's hand in a harsh grip. "Don't let your heart rule your head, my dear. I'm not stupid. See you riding off alone, know you meet Harry Ravenshaw on the sly. Remember, Kate. When a man's intentions are honorable, he presents himself to a young woman's father and declares himself. Has Harry done that—hmmm?" Before Kate had a chance to protest, the duchess exclaimed, "Speak of the Devil! I do believe that's Harry Ravenshaw walking—"

"Where?" Kate leaned across the duchess, trying to see out of the far cab window. She was startled to hear that Harry might be in Whitechapel.

"No, guess I was mistaken. Turned down Osborne, you can't see him now."

"I'm sure you must have been mistaken," Kate said, "as Harry's away on business." She didn't add that he'd been gone longer than she'd expected. How she longed for him. It was torture to go to sleep so unfulfilled, full of desire, wanting Harry's arms around her. Maybe when she got home today, he'd be there at Fairlawn, waiting for her. Impatient now to get back to Essex, Kate resented this stop at Derek's clinic.

"Where on Union Row, milady?" the cabby inquired.

"About midway. There's a clinic—do you know it?"

"Yes'm. My wife goes regular. Fine doctor—not stuck up, even if he is a baronet. Don't charge an arm and a leg. Within my means. Hear he treats some free, them that can't pay."

The scene from the cab window was even more depressing than it was on Whitechapel Road. At least the street there was wider, with the trolley tracks running along it. Here on the narrow side streets the rickety old buildings sagged tiredly, their brick fronts blackened from years of accumulation of London smoke. Dustbins had ill-fitting tops or no tops at all. Stray dogs and mangy cats rummaged in the garbage for bits of food.

Kate pressed a perfumed handkerchief to her nose to shut out the stench of rotting vegetables, stuffed sewers, and urban decay.

"Mighty depressing sight," the duchess said. "Better off in cottages with a bit of ground to grow peas and cabbages. Filthy place, city slums. And men like Mansfield make it worse by building unsightly tenements three and four stories high to crowd even more poor folk into any given area. If it wouldn't cause so much hardship, better London had another Great Fire to clean out these warrens."

The cab pulled over the pavement, and the cabby opened the doors to let them out. "Pick us up in half an hour, my good man. Take us to Paddington."

The duchess paid, and then she and Kate picked their way past piles of garbage to a brick building like all the rest of the row, except that the sidewalk directly in front of it looked scrubbed. The steps leading up to the door were also relatively clean. On this door was a small sign: UNION ROW CLINIC, with surgery hours posted.

Inside was a small, gloomy room crowded with people, the dregs of the East End. The smell of unwashed bodies was almost overpowering. Kate thought she might faint, so she quickly pressed her handkerchief against her nose again.

In the crowd one old crone cackled, "Lookee the fancy lady. Finks we stink!" and a titter went through the room.

The duchess, oblivious to everything except her own purpose, pushed through to a small table and chair near an inner door. A harried young woman in a neat, clean skirt of dark blue with a plain white shirtwaist looked up and peered myopically at them.

"Yes'm? Doctor's very busy today."

"I haven't come here for treatment," the duchess said drily. "Just want a few minutes of his time. Tell him it is the Duchess of Dorminster."

"Yes'm—milady. As soon as he's through with the patient inside." Officiously, she ordered two elderly men, "Give the ladies seats, Alf—Davie."

Muttering, the two men rose reluctantly. Kate felt she should say she'd stand; but she felt faint from the overpowering effluvium, so she dropped into the hard wooden chair gratefully. She wondered what dreadful diseases were contained in the mean little room. Why didn't Derek finish with that patient, so that the duchess could see him and they could leave?

The young woman in charge of the waiting room murmured, "Doctor was delayed today and got here late. Usually the crowd has thinned out a bit by this time."

The wait seemed interminable. Kate kept glancing at the watch that she had pinned on her lapel; but it was an old one, which had belonged to her mother, and it didn't keep accurate time. Finally an old crone dressed in a tattered gown that must have been someone's ball dress came out of the inner room, and the young helper slipped inside, closing the door after her. Kate hoped that they'd be able to see Derek soon, so that they could leave. It was exceedingly depressing. The people crowded in here were so obviously ill, so dirty, so hopeless, that she wanted to hide her eyes. It was a whole new world, one which Kate, in the company of the duchess, had only learned of this week. She was appalled at the squalor of these people's lives; yet what could she do about it? As for the duchess, Kate thought her a female Don Quixote, battling with windmills. There was nothing anyone could do to alleviate the lot of these poor, distressed people.

The helper came out of the inner room and nodded to the duchess. "You may go in now, milady."

" 'Ere, now, we was afore 'er!" someone protested.

The duchess was either deaf or impervious to that kind of thing. Saying, "Come along, Kate," she swept into the inner office.

Derek Ravenshaw's face went white when he saw Kate. He might have been staring at a ghost. Then his face darkened, and he turned to the duchess, demanding, "What is Kate doing here in Whitechapel? It's no fit place for a decent young woman. It's bad enough that you come here—but to bring her along!" He rounded on Kate, dark eyes flashing with rage. "What's wrong with your father that he allows you to come to such a place as this?"

"Tut, Derek!" The duchess was unimpressed with his display of temper. "It's time Kate woke up to the reality of the world around her. The poor live in such abysmal circumstances. You know this—you're here helping them."

"I'm a man—and a physician."

Kate, tired of being discussed as if she were some half-wit child, spoke up, "Derek, it's really no concern of yours what I do." Annoyance with him and his ridiculous, overprotective attitude toward her made Kate rash. "I'm helping the duchess with her reading classes for the women of this area."

"I forbid it!" he thundered.

"You forbid it! You have nothing to say about it," Kate lashed back. "You aren't my keeper, Derek."

"Obviously you need one."

"Derek! Kate! That's enough nonsense. I came here for a reason, which didn't include wasting Derek's valuable time with such a squabble. Kate's a capable young woman, Derek, and I'm delighted to have her help with my little school. But I came to make sure you were looking after Monica Murphy. Has consumption, hasn't she?"

Derek sighed. "Yes, unfortunately. There's little hope for her. I tried to get her to come back to Essex—even offered her a place at Scarlet Oaks—but she just laughed and said it was too late to go back."

"Keep track of what her medicine costs. I'll pay."

"No need of that, Duchess."

"I'll pay, Derek. I insist. See to her—do what you can. She's right, of course. I could take her to Harcourt; but unfortunately it's much too late for poor Monica."

Journal entry. January 7,1888.

It is two A.M. *I have not been able to sleep for thinking about my beautiful Kate. To see her in the midst of all that degradation in Whitechapel was too much for me. The Duchess of Dorminster must be mad to take such a delicate flower into the slums of East London. Teaching classes to the whores to try to get them off the streets! Insanity. I suppose the duchess means well; but she is as ineffectual in her aims as is the Reverend Mr. Fiddler, who wants to save their souls.*

Fiddler. I think someone should pray for him! I wonder if his austere, upright wife knows what her husband does when he prowls the back alleys of the area? His name is a joke amongst the whores. They know. Ah, how well they know. And the duchess, for all her seeming worldliness, is blind to what this man really is.

Kate must be kept away from Fiddler, and away from the East End. Should I warn Kingsley? Or is he so enmeshed in his financial problems that he doesn't pay any attention to his greatest asset, his daughter? My Kate.

CHAPTER 8

Sunday, January 8, 1888

Kate and her father drove in the victoria to the church of St. Michael-in-the-Dell in the local village, rather than ride all the way to Chelmsford on such a cold, blustery day. They clattered over a narrow hump-backed bridge of yellow brick that took them across the village pond. In summer swans floated on the still water, but today it was gray and cold. The church was very old, with a squat tower of flint and stone ringed with crenelations. Rising from the top of the tower was a square, white frame spire topped with a tall metal cross. The bells were pealing as they drove up to the church that lay on one side of a triangular village green.

Kate would rather have stayed home, hoping against hope that Harry would come calling. It had been nearly two weeks since she'd last seen him, lain in his arms, made love to him. Where was he? What business could take him away for this long? He'd said a week or a bit longer. Had something happened to him? She wished she'd asked Derek yesterday if Harry was back; but she thought it might be wise not to advertise the fact that he was her lover. Derek was so unpredictable. You'd have thought that *he* was her lover, not Harry, the way he'd gone on about her being in Whitechapel. She wondered if Derek had any idea that she and Harry were lovers—not that it was any concern of his. Would her marriage to his younger brother make Derek more generous to Harry?

Kate knew little of the business world. She had no idea what it was that Harry did, nor whether or not he could support a bride on his income. She daydreamed of living with him in a picturesque cottage with thatch on the roof and a rose twining over the doorway. The fact that she'd never lived in such a place didn't bother Kate. It would be their own little love nest. They could shut out the world and exist only for each other.

Her fantasy was shattered by her father's words. "I do believe there's young Ravenshaw. Don't see him at church very often."

"Where?" Kate craned her neck, trying to see Harry from the window of the victoria.

"Pulled his gig around the side of the church."

Kate could scarcely wait for the coachman to open the door and help her down to the ground. She picked up the skirt of her mauve taffeta gown to keep the hem from being mired with mud from the churchyard. She saw the Duchess of Dorminster, clad in a flowing costume of bright orange, going in through the Norman arch with its zigzag molding. Behind her was Lord Wimbley, his head covered with a full periwig of henna red, topped with an enormous tricorne of black with a cockade of peacock feathers on one side. She couldn't see the rest of his costume, for he was swathed in a long black cloak that came to his heels. Kate suppressed a smile. Perhaps it would be less distracting at morning prayer if the man left on his cloak. The costumes he wore belonged at a masquerade ball, not at divine worship.

She looked around for Harry, but didn't see him anywhere. Derek was there, though, rather resplendent in a fine black overcoat with velvet collar and lapels. He'd been almost shabby yesterday in that grubby little clinic on Union Row. Kate had remarked on it to the duchess as they traveled back to Chelmsford on the train.

"Does it on purpose, same as I do. Same reason I told you to wear something plain. Don't want the poor souls to be completely envious of us, do we? Doesn't do them any good to see us in our fancy silks and furs when they've little to wear to keep out the cold and damp."

Now Kate wondered if she should ask Derek where

Harry had gotten to. Her father had seen him. That thought was rudely shattered, though, by her father's next remark.

"Ah, there's Ravenshaw—headed our way too. I do think he has his eye on you, my dear. First time I've seen him at St. Michael's in ages."

"Oh, it was Derek you saw drive in?"

"Who did you think—not that brother of his. Harry at church? The chancel arch would collapse." He took Kate's arm. "Come along, it's cold out here. Hopefully, the verger will have the church warm. The cold gets to me these days."

Again Kate noticed the blue color in her father's lips. As raw and cold as it was out here, her lips were probably bluish too.

As they went into the old Norman church, Kate couldn't keep from asking, "Has Harry gotten home yet?"

There was such a look of hate and anger on Derek's face that she wished she'd kept quiet.

"Oh, he's home, all right. Came in about two this morning, not even pretending to be quiet. Getting his beauty sleep this morning. One of these days, I'm going to throw him out of Scarlet Oaks. If what I think he's been doing . . ."

Derek stopped and looked at Kingsley. "Are you all right, sir?" They had come to the back pews. "Here, sit down."

"All right," Kate's father said. "Touch of indigestion."

Unobtrusively Derek took the older man's wrist, feeling for the pulse.

Kingsley pulled away muttering, "I'm all right, I say."

It was time for the service to begin, so Kate slipped into the pew with her father, making room for Derek, who kept glancing at Kingsley throughout morning prayer.

As they were leaving the church, with Derek hovering over them to Kingsley's annoyance, her father said, "Tell that young pup of a brother to come see me this afternoon."

Kate didn't understand the look of utter dismay on Derek's face. Surely he knew that she'd been seeing Harry. Kate was very excited over her father's request to see Harry. It must be about her. Why else would he want to see the younger Ravenshaw?

As they headed for their victoria, Derek drew Kate aside when Kingsley stopped to chat for a moment with Lord Wimbley.

"Try to persuade your father to see a doctor—not necessarily me. And don't let him overdo things. He's not as young as he used to be." Kate could see deep concern in Derek's dark eyes, and again that flare of worry hit her.

"Is he seriously ill, Derek? You must tell me."

Derek hesitated. "I haven't examined him recently, Kate. I don't like his color." Then, as if realizing that he'd caused her worry, he added with forced cheerfulness, "Probably he's just run down. A tonic—a bit more rest—and no worry. That's very important, Kate. No worry for your father for a while."

"What would he worry about?" she asked innocently. Derek sighed. "I just hope he hasn't—"

"Hasn't what, Derek?"

The doctor shook his head. "Nothing, Kate. Don't concern yourself. I'm just projecting my own worries on your father."

Then Kingsley looked around and beckoned for Kate to get in the carriage with him. Just before they drove off, he called out to Derek, "Remember what I said. Tell Harry I must see him today."

As they drove out of the churchyard, Kate asked, "What do you want with Harry, Father?"

"Business." His tone was so curt that she didn't dare ask further questions. Oh, well, she'd see Harry this afternoon when he came to see Father.

All the way home to Fairlawn, Kate wrapped herself in her expectations. Harry and Father would transact whatever business it was—Whatever could it be?—and then she and Harry . . . but where? She could scarcely take him up to her bedchamber and lie with him on her own canopied bed. No place in the house would be safe. The servants had an uncanny knack of being at the wrong place at the wrong time. She'd have to plan to ride back with him. As she thought this, there was a dash of rain on the victoria's windows. By the time they reached Fairlawn, it was a downpour. She'd not be able to go riding with Harry in the rain. Even her maid would know something was going on if she asked to be dressed in her riding habit on such a day as this.

Maybe it would be better not to be here when Harry arrived. She could tell her father that she was going to call on the duchess—or even tell him she might pay her respects to Lady Zangwill, Harry's hated aunt, who presided over Scarlet Oaks like a horrid spider over its web. Then the two of them could meet at the hunting lodge. She ached to feel his hard, muscular body pressed against hers, to feel his hands caress her, rousing her to heights of passion that would leave her sated and spent. Not that it would take much rousing. It had been nearly two weeks since they'd made passionate love. Kate was tormented by desire; she longed to be with Harry intimately and wondered how she could possibly wait until this afternoon to know his passion and love.

As they drove under the porte-cochere that her father had added to their Tudor house just that summer, Kate smiled a secret smile of love. What would dear Father think if he knew what a wanton puss his darling daughter had become? What would stodgy Derek say if she told him that she knew all of the joys of physical love between man and woman, thanks to the exciting tutelage of his younger brother? Poor Derek. She wondered if he had any love life. Or did he spend all of his energy taking care of those horrid, drab people she saw last Friday at the clinic on Union Row?

Kate noticed that her father ate very little of the good Sunday dinner cook had prepared. Vinton kept urging dishes on his master, but Kingsley waved them away impatiently.

"I must have a touch of the grippe, Vinton," was his excuse for eating so little.

The butler carried the stewed hare back to the kitchen, and after serving Kate a small portion of the home-cured ham, took it away too. Kate was too excited to eat. She was going to see Harry again, after ages apart from him. She drank more wine than was her custom, and ate a portion of an elaborate molded custard, but other than that, she wasn't hungry.

"Why don't you lie down for a while, Father, if you

feel ill?" she suggested. Father did look bad, with that gray color she'd noticed several times before. She hoped he didn't have something serious.

"I must see young Ravenshaw first."

"You could send a message for him to come later in the week." Then, ingeniously, she added, "I was thinking of calling on Lady Letitia this afternoon. If you like, I could carry word to Harry from you."

"No, no, I must see him today." He winced as if in pain.

"Shall I stay here, then?"

He looked at her as if he didn't know her. "Stay here? Whatever for, Kate? I have private business with Ravenshaw. Run along, do your visiting." Then, remembering, "But isn't it raining?"

"I'll have the groom put up the top on the tilbury, and I'll spread a lap robe over me. I shan't get wet. It's much too gloomy a day to spend moping about the house. I may be late," she added, hoping that she and Harry could have a tryst later. "Don't worry about me. Maybe the duchess will invite me to sup with her."

"I don't like for you to drive about after dark, Kate."

"It's such a short distance, and the lamps on the tilbury will be lighted. Don't worry about me so much, Father. I'm a woman now. I'm quite able to take care of myself."

"I suppose so," he said absently. He kissed her on the forehead. "Run along, then. Give my regards to the duchess."

As Kate dressed for her outing, Vera said, "Oh, miss, you'll be soaked. It's raining that hard now."

"I'm not made of spun sugar, Vera. I'll scarcely melt in a bit of rain. Hurry now. The green gown, I think."

"The velvet will spot if it gets rained on."

"I'm going to wear that old traveling cloak, Vera. I'll be covered from the top of my bonnet to the tips of my shoes. I don't know why everyone is worrying about me today. You'd think it never rained in England."

As Kate drove along the road to Harcourt, she kept her eyes open for Harry. She thought he'd probably be in a light carriage, rather than on horseback, because of the weather. Sure enough, just before she got to the entrance to the Dorminster estate, she saw another tilbury racing toward her as if the fiends of hell were in pursuit. Harry always drove that way. Leaning forward, she waved frantically with her white lace handkerchief to attract his attention. At first Kate thought he was going to race right past her; but at the last moment, Harry reined in so sharply that the horse reared in the traces, almost giving her heart failure.

He walked the horse until the two light coaches were side by side on the road. "Kate! I thought I'd find you at Fairlawn. Derek said he'd seen you at church with your father, and when I got the message to call this afternoon . . ."

She pouted prettily. "I'm not interested in twiddling my thumbs while you and Father talk business. What business do you have with him, anyway, Harry?"

"Men's business." His voice was surprisingly curt. "Don't trouble your head about it. But if you knew I would be there, why are you out driving in this downpour?"

"Oh, Harry, I've missed you so desperately."

"And I you. I thought I'd have a chance to be with you today, and you're running away from me."

"How could we have any privacy at Fairlawn? But if just by chance you happen to stop by the hunting lodge after you see my father—and I just happen to be passing there after a brief call on the Duchess of Dorminster . . ." She smiled at him.

"Ah, Kate, you are a clever one, aren't you. Well, my business with your father shouldn't take more than an hour. If you get to the lodge first, you'll find the key under one of the ornamental urns beside the door. The fire will be laid—it needs only a match touched to it. And they are in a silver matchbox on the mantelpiece."

"I'll manage." She blew him a kiss. "Hurry, hurry!" Then, remembering, "But don't let Father get worked up or upset, Harry. He's not feeling too well. Derek said that he should try to be as calm as possible until he recovers."

"Now, why would I say anything to make your father ill?" he joked. "Don't let the duchess keep you too long. She loves to talk—and drink innumerable cups of tea. Tell her that you are eloping with the village idiot and must not linger."

"She might believe me! Until later, my dearest one."

Then, with the flick of his whip, Harry drove on while Kate turned into Harcourt. Today the duchess received Kate in a small library, a charming room, where a huge fire roared in the grate.

The duchess was clad in an outrageous robe of quilted satin, the light apple-green a ghastly color with her peculiar yellowish makeup. Her garish gold hair was piled up every which way on her head, with a variety of tortoise shell combs dangling from it, ready to fall if she moved her head an inch. The robe was fastened down the front with silver frogs, and where it fell open at the bottom, a turquoise petticoat clashed with it. Her slippers were pointed and curled up at the toes like the shoes worn in Eastern harems.

"Tea, my dear? So glad you dropped in. Gloomy day. Been trying to plan my next class for those unfortunate women in Whitechapel. You'll be going with me Tuesday?"

It was the last thing Kate wanted to do now that Harry was back. "I'm sorry, your grace, but I won't be able to go. Father isn't feeling well. Derek says he mustn't be upset. I think he might not approve of my continuing to go to the chapel to help you."

The duchess frowned but went on pouring tea. "Cress sandwich?" She waved toward a lovely Sèvres platter piled high with dainty sandwiches. "Always have a large tea on Sunday. Helps pass the time. Wimbley may drop by later."

Kate kept track of the time by glancing nonchalantly at the lovely ormolu clock on the mantel.

"Derek surprised me by taking on so when he found you in his clinic Friday." She gave Kate a shrewd look. "Derek courting you? Could do a lot worse, my dear."

"No, Derek is not courting me," Kate answered with some asperity. "Besides I think Father has his eye on Arthur Mansfield for me."

The duchess, who had just taken a swallow of tea,

nearly choked. "Good God!" she sputtered. "You must be joking."

"Actually, I am—but he does keep talking about the odious man. And we had dinner there New Year's Day, which was why we couldn't go to Scarlet Oaks for the party."

"Wondered why you weren't there. That young scamp Harry wasn't about either. Hoped you weren't off with him somewhere. Stay away from Harry, Kate. Bad blood there. Mother in a brothel in Manchester. Heard once that he went there with friends as a lark, found his own mother working in the place. Shocking experience for any young man. Tale might not be true. Mother gone so long, he'd probably not recognize her."

Kate was stunned at this story, which she'd never heard. She'd certainly not ask Harry about it. "How ghastly!"

"Letitia told me the story. She's prejudiced, of course. Angry when the old baronet, the boys' father, married that little chit of a nursemaid. Served him right when she ran off, Letitia thought."

"She doesn't like Harry because he's not her blood nephew. He's said that—" She wished she could snip off her tongue, for the duchess's blue eyes lighted up.

"Pretty friendly with young Harry, aren't you? Now, don't deny it. I've seen you with him. And heard a few rumors. Bad business, girl. Frederick should take you in hand."

Angry now that she'd allowed herself to be so maneuvered by the duchess, and afraid she'd be late for her tryst with Harry, who wasn't a bit like the old hag claimed, Kate made her excuses and left Harcourt. The rain had let up, and only a light drizzle was falling now.

Arriving at the lodge before her lover, Kate found the key, unlocked the door, lighted the lamps, and put a match to the fire, which caught with bright orange flames. Knowing that there would be little time for love today, she began undressing and was down to her shift when Harry arrived.

He caught her to him in a passionate embrace, teasing her mercilessly. "Couldn't wait for me. Stripped out of your gown like a French whore."

She tried to pull away from him, hurt at his words. "Is

that how you think of me, as a whore?" Kate thought of the drab women she'd met at Salvation Chapel and shuddered.

Instantly contrite, Harry said, "Cold, little Kate? I'll soon warm you."

Today they lay on the rug in front of the glowing fire, and Kate's response to Harry's skillful lovemaking matched the heat from the grate.

"It's been so long since I've loved you, Harry," she sighed, accepting his ardent body, arching her back to meet him in their rapturous union. Everything was blotted out for Kate—the rustic lodge, the fire, even the rug on which she lay, nude and eager. Only Harry existed, only the joining of their bodies. In his sermon that morning, the vicar had talked of one flesh. Kate knew what one flesh meant; she reveled in her knowledge. Passion swept them, and then they lay together, spent, caressing each other and murmuring their own private love words to each other.

All too soon Kate told Harry that she had to hurry home.

"But I want you again." His hand cupped her firm young breast, and he slid his lips down her throat, rousing her again to ardent desire.

"No, Harry, please don't," she moaned. "Father will be furious with me if I'm late. He's not well." Reluctantly she pulled away from his ardor. "Didn't you notice how bad his color was today?"

"I'm not the doctor in the family, Kate." He was annoyed that she was leaving him, and didn't try to hide it. "That's Derek's province, not mine. I just talked business with your father. I didn't take his pulse."

She leaned down and kissed him tenderly. "Don't be angry with me, dearest," she pleaded. "I'll be here tomorrow at the usual time."

"Maybe I won't be," Harry muttered darkly.

A frisson of terror swept over her. "Harry! You're not going away again? You just got back. I've missed you so—"

"Then stay awhile with me," he ordered.

"I can't," she wailed. "Father won't let me out for a week if I get home too late."

"Well, I'm sorry," he said coldly. "My business comes first, right now." Then he softened and planted a tender kiss on her pert little nose. "I'd rather your father locked you up for a week while I'm gone. Then no other man but me could have you."

"Does your business take you to the East End, Harry? The Duchess of Dorminster thought she saw you there."

Harry's hold on her tightened. "The old woman's daft. Besides, I leave the East End to my do-gooder brother. And let's not talk about him either. Let's make love instead!"

He pushed her down and threw his body across hers. Then slowly, deliberately, he kissed the tips of her breasts, making Kate's heart beat faster and faster.

She lay beneath him, feeling the passion rise in them both once again. Oh, why doesn't Harry marry me, she thought wildly, desperately. Then there'd be no partings. They'd make love whenever they wanted, constantly, for the rest of their lives.

CHAPTER 9

Saturday, January 9, 1888

Kate was furious with her father. Making such an engagement for her without even consulting her! It put her in the same class as Eastern women—chattel! The Duchess of Dorminster had explained it all to her one day.

"Oh, miss, you do look lovely," Vera said. "That coppery taffeta sets off your coloring to perfection."

The little maid in her dove-gray silk dress with white collar and cuffs, her ruffly cap set high on soft brown hair, twitched at the overskirt draped on a huge bustle. The under petticoat of dark brown silk hung in full folds, the color picked up in narrow ruching about the very low neckline of the gown. Tiny sleeves covered Kate's upper arms only, leaving her white shoulders bare.

"I wanted to wear the mauve." Kate felt like a rebellious child, thwarted at every turn.

"But, miss, for the opera! The mauve is an afternoon dress, all covered-up. You'll be the envy of all the women at Covent Garden tonight."

Ordinarily Kate would have been delighted to go to London to the opera, to wear such a delectably revealing gown, to be the center of attention. But to go with Arthur Mansfield distressed her. All this week she'd met Harry, made ardent love at their secret trysting place. She'd expected to meet him there this afternoon as usual. To her dismay, at breakfast that morning, her father had said

116

abruptly: "Mr. Mansfield wishes to take you to the opera in London tonight."

"I'm sure he does," she said drily, remembering those cold blue eyes that had stripped her naked.

"I have accepted his kind invitation for you."

Suddenly the country-cured ham on her plate threatened to gag her. "You've what?"

"I've sent him a message saying that you will be happy to dine with him and attend the opening of *Aida* at the Royal Opera House in Covent Garden. He apologizes for asking you to dine with him unchaperoned; but I feel you are quite safe with Mansfield. He's not some young Lothario but a steady, wealthy, older man who would make you a fine husband."

Kate took a deep breath, tried to control her temper. It wouldn't do any good to quarrel with her father about this. She'd try to reason with him.

"You know I don't care for Mr. Mansfield, Father."

She saw Kingsley stiffen as if he'd been doused with starch. "Kate, I have already told Mr. Mansfield that you would accompany him this evening. There will be no discussion."

"But I can't abide the man!"

"You've been reading too many of those trashy romantic novels. Sometimes I think that it was a mistake, educating you as well as I have. You haven't had sufficient training in filial obedience."

"Father, it's eighteen eighty-eight, not the Dark Ages. Young women·are people in their own right. You're treating me as if I were a—a slave!"

"Nonsense." His lips thinned, and she saw that they were that unhealthy blue again. "A young woman of your age knows nothing of life. Your head is filled with romantic notions. What do you know about the qualities of a good husband? Mansfield is interested in you, my dear, seriously. Although he has not yet formally asked for your hand, his intentions are plain to me. I feel it would be a suitable match."

"Suitable! Father, he's old!"

Her father laughed a mirthless laugh. "Old? No older than I. I assure you, my dear daughter, that I am far from being a doddering old man. In fact, of late I have thought it might have been a mistake not to remarry when your dear mother died all those years ago. It's not too late for that."

If he had dropped a bomb on the Oriental rug, Kate could not have been more stunned. First he planned to marry her off to that horrid Mansfield—now he talked of a marriage for himself.

"Have you picked out my stepmama?" Her voice was scathing.

"Not yet. But I would have no problem finding a wife. I have been told that I am not unattractive to the fair sex."

Far more attractive than Mansfield, she thought with despair.

"As it is a long carriage ride to London, and Mansfield does not wish to take you by train, he will call early in the afternoon for you. I expect you to be ready. Wear that new gown you had made—that copper-colored one. It is most becoming."

Kate had never known her father to be this way. She thought of crying, hoping her tears would melt his hard, cold heart; but there was something about his face that warned her not to try such tactics. She would have to give in this time, just as she'd given in about the New Year's dinner. This time—but not again. Kate was not going to allow her father to force her into marriage with Mansfield.

Her most urgent problem now was Harry. She was to have met him at their usual time in the lodge. Now, with this hateful engagement that her father had thrust upon her, there would be no time to have her tryst with her beloved. She had to let him know somehow. If she sent a message—no, that would never do. Someone at Scarlet Oaks might intercept it. The only thing she could do was to write him a note, explain the circumstances, and then ride with it this morning, leaving it at the lodge where Harry would find it when he went to meet her. Would he be furious? She hoped so! It might do Mr. Ravenshaw some good to know that there were other men interested in her. It might push him into a declaration of love himself.

"Take off this gown."

Vera, mouth open, stared at her.

"I said, take off this gown. I don't have to dress yet for the opera. Get my riding habit. Hurry up, Vera!"

"Miss! You're going riding now?"

"Do you want your ears boxed? Get me out of this gown."

Vera, so stunned by Kate's sudden display of temper that her fingers shook, quickly undid the gown down the back, and Kate stepped out of it impatiently. Soon she was in her dark green riding habit, thrusting her feet into the boots Vera held for her.

"If anyone wants to know where I am, you don't know. I'm going out for a short ride."

Then Kate hurried to the study, penned a short note to Harry, and tucked it into the pocket of her riding jacket. Making sure she'd not meet her father, Kate ran out to the stables and had her little mare saddled. Once out of sight of Fairlawn, she gave the horse her head and galloped along the road toward Scarlet Oaks, pulling cruelly at the bridle to turn the mare into the lane leading to the lodge. She didn't have time to unlock the door and leave the note inside. Instead, Kate put it under the urn where the key was hidden. Harry would be sure to find it when he got there later. Then she galloped the horse back to Fairlawn, knowing she had only a short time left in which to get ready for her trip to London.

Vera was waiting, with everything laid out ready.

"Oh, miss, Mr. Kingsley was inquiring for you just a while ago. I'm afraid I fibbed. I didn't tell him you'd gone riding. I said you were bathing. He impressed on me the importance of your being ready when Mr. Mansfield arrived." Then she added ingenuously, "He's very rich and important, isn't he, miss?"

Kate made a face. "And old. And horrid."

Vera murmured, "But he's taking you to the opera."

"I won't be bought, Vera."

"No, miss. Of course not. But we don't have much to say about who marries us, do we, miss?"

"I intend to have a lot to say about it. Vera, I can't abide the man. He's—he's oily and nasty. He's old enough to be my father."

"But so well-off." Vera's tone was wistful. "Oh, miss, no rich man's ever going to want me. I'll be lucky if I can marry the butcher's apprentice."

"If you love him, then you'll be luckier than I."

Kate was very bitter. She knew her father was pushing her toward marriage with Mansfield. It was all very well to be independent, to say she'd never marry a man she didn't love; but Kate could be very practical when necessary. She realized that a young woman had little to say in the choice of a husband. Marriages were not made in heaven, but in the drawing rooms of country homes or in the business offices of rich suitors.

Oh, Harry, she cried silently, *save me from Mansfield!*

Although she loathed her escort, Kate couldn't help but enjoy the opera. The Royal Opera House was aglitter with lights, and although it was not the season, there were still plenty of the aristocracy in their boxes, there to see and be seen. Mansfield had a box quite near the royal box.

"Will any of the royal family be here?" Kate asked him, willing to talk with him to glean any tidbits of gossip he might know.

"I'm not sure—wait, someone's coming into it now." He raised his opera glasses, and Kate followed suit.

"I do believe it is Prince Eddy," he said.

"The Prince of Wales's son?" She adjusted the focus of her glasses to bring the man's face into better view. He was not too tall, of slight build, with brown hair receding at the temples and a moustache with long, waxed ends. He was accompanied by a young man, clean-shaven, with his hair longer, in soft waves about his ears.

"Ah, yes. Prince Eddy it is," Mansfield affirmed. "And his friend from Cambridge, James Stephen."

There was something about the way that Mansfield said "friend" that made Kate look at him; but he made no further comment, so she could only wonder what he'd meant.

With the two men in the royal box, the orchestra struck up the strains of "God Save the Queen" and then went into the overture to *Aida*. Since Kate had not seen this opera previously, she was quickly caught up in the tragic plot.

At intermission, they joined the other well-dressed men and women in the promenade, sipping wine and chatting. Mansfield was acquainted with an astonishing number of people, and Kate began to feel important. Even though she loathed him, Kate had to admit that Mansfield obviously commanded much respect in many quarters. She told herself that it was only because he was rich. She reminded herself that he battened off the misery of the poor, that he was a slumlord of the worst kind; but she couldn't help being impressed with the number of lords and ladies who numbered Arthur Mansfield among their acquaintances.

They even had the opportunity to bow to Prince Eddy, although they did not actually meet him. Kate had never met a member of the royal family. She counted this as a smashing success, to be able to drop a low curtsy to the future Prince of Wales.

At the conclusion of Verdi's opera, Kate wiped away tears.

"Ah, you show such compassion—you are so tender hearted," Mansfield murmured; but she noticed that his eyes were not on her tear-streaked cheeks, but on her cleavage.

Opening her fan, a concoction of black net and lace, the sticks of painted and gilded blackwood, Kate carefully covered her bosom while pretending to fan herself.

"It's a bit stuffy," she murmured, laughing to herself at the look of disappointment on Mansfield's face, now that she was more modest, thanks to the art of the fan makers.

Mansfield, however, was not stupid. Leaning forward, he said, "What an interesting fan. Do those charming figures on the fan tell a story?"

It was an anecdotal fan, and Kate had to let him look at the delightful stylized milkmaid and her suitor, who went from rejection to embrace on the panels of the fan.

"Charming," Mansfield murmured, tipping the fan closer to him, once again baring the delectable creamy mounds of her bosom. He looked as if he'd like to eat her for dessert.

Kate wished now she'd brought along a gauze scarf, which she could have draped about her shoulders and bosom much the same way that ladies of the previous century had employed modesty bits. Normally, her father paid little attention to what she wore, paying the dressmaker's bills but letting Kate select her own wardrobe. It was just her bad luck that he remembered this particularly low-cut gown. Given her own choice, Kate would have worn the plainest, most covered-up dress she owned. She looked out over the crowd. She was dressed in the latest fashion, for although daytime wear covered a decent woman from chin to floor, with bare arms winning the most shocked looks from society, evening gowns were cut low, amply displaying good figures like Kate's. She wore no jewels; but many of the ladies there were covered with rubies, emeralds, and diamonds, so that they were as glittering as the crystal chandeliers in the opera house.

Kate was glad the opera was over, for now she could get back home. It would be very late. She did wish they were going home by train. There was something about the gleam in Mansfield's cold blue eyes that made Kate wary of the long carriage ride home to Essex with him.

"I thought we might have a bit of supper before we start the long journey home," Mansfield suggested as he helped Kate with her fitted velvet coat, letting his fingers trail over her bare shoulders as he slipped the garment around her.

Turning quickly to escape from his unwanted caress, Kate said, "Oh, it is much too late, I fear. Father has not been at all well lately. I felt very guilty leaving him there alone while I came away to enjoy myself. I feel I must return to Fairlawn promptly."

She saw the disappointment on his face and wondered just what kind of after-opera entertainment he'd planned. If he thought she'd go to bed with him, he was sadly mistaken. Kate had no intention of loving any man but Harry Ravenshaw. She didn't care what her father was planning —she would defy him, she'd run away from home, elope with Harry, before she'd marry another man.

Her worst fears about Mansfield were realized even before they were out of London. Feigning concern that Kate might be too cold, Mansfield tucked a rabbit skin robe about her, pressing against her thighs with eager hands. When she tried to pull away from him, he suggested, "We must sit close together, dear Kate, to keep each other warm."

Kate preferred freezing to feeling. Moving a little further into the corner of the seat, she said, "I often feel faint when I'm too closely confined, Mr. Mansfield."

"Please, dearest Kate, can't you call me Arthur?"

"Oh, sir, it would be most disrespectful of me to call a man of your age by your Christian name." There, that would put the old goat in his place.

"I assure you that I have very young thoughts about you," he said, refusing to be insulted. "You are the most delectable creature I have ever met. I intend to have you for my wife."

Kate was shocked at the baldness of his declaration. "Sir, you are too bold," she said coldly. "I am much too young to consider marriage."

"Twenty is not young at all." A little hard note crept into his voice, and for the first time, Kate felt afraid of this man. "You wouldn't want to become a dried-up spinster, would you?"

"Fie, Mr. Mansfield! Is that how you see me? As a frantic maiden who is desperate to get a husband? I find that most unkind of you, sir. I may seem immodest to say it, but I have noticed that most men look on me with some interest."

"I suppose you mean that young Ravenshaw pup! Oh, I know you've been seeing him. You needn't deny it. Does your father know? He might be most distressed if he thought his daughter was slipping away from the house to rendezvous with such a young rake as Harry."

Stunned that Mansfield knew her secret, Kate kept silent.

As if his knowledge granted him a kind of power over her, Mansfield boldly put his arm about Kate and pulled her close, turning her face to his roughly with his other hand. Before she realized what he was doing, he was kissing her with hot, passionate kisses that took her breath away. Frantically Kate pushed against him; but Mansfield was strong, and he was determined to have his way with her.

"Kate, my lovely Kate," he murmured, "I shall have you for my very own. Ah, you will learn to love me. I am older, experienced with women. You are young, untried, innocent. A woman such as you needs an older, lusty man to wake her fully. I know you don't even know what I'm talking about, but you shall know, my dear, you shall."

Frightened by the heat of his words, revolted by his kisses, Kate struck out at him blindly with her fist, hitting him squarely in the mouth. With a muttered oath, he released her.

His voice cold, he said, "That wasn't a clever thing to do, my girl. Not clever at all. You'll pay for that later. I intend for you to be my wife. Your father is in no position to refuse my suit. Once married to me, I shall train you in the ways I choose. Don't ever strike me again, I warn you."

She shivered. What did he mean about her father? What hold did Arthur Mansfield have over the owner of Fairlawn?

Determined, though, not to let him know how frightened she was, Kate said, forcing her voice to be calm and even, "I don't know what you are talking about, Mr. Mansfield. Once I tell my father about your outrageous conduct tonight, he'll take a horsewhip to you. Now, tell your coachman to whip up the horses. I want this disgusting journey to be over with as quickly as possible. Do not invite me to any more social functions, Mr. Mansfield. Nothing would induce me to accept another of your invitations. Poor Father, thinking that you are a gentleman, insisting that I accompany you to the opera. When I tell him of the indignities to which I have been subjected this evening, he'll have you drummed out of decent Essex society."

Mansfield laughed. "A pretty speech, my dear Kate. I like a woman full of fire. Taming you will be a delightful duty, I assure you. And you'll be mine. I always get what I want. Your father doesn't dare say no to me when I ask for your hand. I intend to make you my bride within the next few months. I'll allow you time to have a trousseau sewn, and there'll be time for the bans to be published in St. Michael-in-the-Dell. Then you'll be Mrs. Arthur Mansfield, my wife, mistress of Bassett Abbey, under my complete control. You'll learn obedience, humility, and you'll learn to satisfy me as a man, doing your wifely duty."

She was tempted to fling into his face the fact that she already knew how to be a woman, how to satisfy the most demanding of men—Harry Ravenshaw—but some inner caution made Kate hold her tongue. That was her own secret weapon, and it would do her little good if she let Mansfield know ahead of time what she would do to thwart his desires.

She refused to answer him, holding herself aloof, huddling into the corner of the carriage, pretending he wasn't there. Mansfield did not try to force his attentions on her again. He had issued his ultimatum. He was a man used to getting whatever he wanted by any means necessary. He even suspected something about Harry Ravenshaw, although obviously he had no idea that she had given herself totally to Harry. Very well, she would talk to Harry tomorrow when they met to make love. She would tell him that he must declare his intentions, ask Father for her hand in order to rescue her from the loathsome attentions of Arthur Mansfield.

After an interminable journey, the coach finally turned into the driveway of Fairlawn. To Kate's surprise, the house was lighted from top to bottom, with outside lamps lit also.

"Ah, I see that your father is waiting up for you."

"Good. I can't wait to tell him of your boorish behavior."

"I'll explain to him that—"

"You'll explain nothing. You won't be invited inside Fairlawn tonight, Mr. Mansfield. And I shall do my utmost to see that you never set foot inside it again."

She delivered her speech just as the coachman pulled up in front of the door to the Tudor house. The moment the coachman opened the door and set the steps, Kate alighted, swept up to the house without a backward glance, and pushed in past Vinton telling him tersely: "Close the door for the night, Vinton. Mr. Mansfield is not coming in."

Her father came out of the drawing room just in time to

hear her order to the butler. "Where's Mansfield?" he asked. "I'd assumed—"

"When I tell you what that odious man is like, you'll know why he isn't at my heels, Father. Oh, Father, how could you?" she cried, now that she was safe within the walls of Fairlawn once again. "He's horrible, Father, horrible. He tried to take my virtue away from me. I literally had to fight him off in the coach on the way home. He is no gentleman."

To Kate's consternation, her father glared at her. "What are you talking about? I've made it plain to you that you must be pleasant to Mansfield. Are you trying to ruin me?"

CHAPTER 10

Sunday, January 15, 1888

Kate flatly refused to go to church with her father. They'd had a terrible row when she came in from her trip to the opera with Mansfield last night. Her father was angry because she'd not invited Mansfield in for refreshments after the long drive from London. Kate was furious because her father wouldn't pay attention to her when she told of the liberties Mansfield had tried to take during the coach ride.

"Kate, you must be imagining things," her father said. "Arthur Mansfield has honorable intentions. He wants to marry you. He's said so. He is an eminently suitable husband for my only daughter."

"That lecherous old man! Father, how can you be so cruel? I thought you loved me."

"It is because of my love for you that I want you well provided for." He was cajoling now, trying to make her see reason.

"I don't want to marry a man old enough to be my father. I want a young man I can love."

"Love! What does an innocent young woman know of love? You read about romantic love in those trashy novels you smuggle into the house—oh, I know about them—but that's not love, Kate. It isn't for the establishing of a family. It is frivolous, tawdry, cheap. And it doesn't last. Marriage is forever."

127

Kate shuddered. "That's what scares me, Father. I shan't marry him." She said it firmly but quietly. Then she turned and left him to go to St. Michael's alone.

Kate couldn't wait to see Harry that afternoon. She had a huge Sunday dinner with her father, deftly steering the conversation away from her future. She kept urging more food on him, hoping that he would be so full that he'd take a nap later. This would give her a chance to slip out of the house unnoticed. Her father did retire to his own bedchamber after the meal and Kate quickly had Vera help her into her riding habit.

"You are going riding a lot these days, miss."

Did the little maid know anything? She did hope the servants weren't gossiping below stairs.

"I find the air invigorating." Kate said sharply, earning a subdued, "Yes, miss, of course," from Vera.

It was a cold day, but the weak winter sun managed to brighten the afternoon. Kate galloped along the road, anxious to talk to Harry and tell him of the dreadful fate her father had planned for her.

He was waiting when she got to the lodge, the fire was blazing hotly, and Kate went into his arms as if she'd not seen him for months.

"Your face is cold!" he exclaimed as he kissed her ardently.

"I've just come in from outdoors, silly. But you'll soon warm me up, won't you?" She shivered in anticipation of his lovemaking.

Swiftly he undressed her before the fire, then lifted her onto a velvet upholstered sofa he'd pulled close to the heat. Kate could scarcely wait for him to disrobe, she was so eager for his love. Reaching up her arms to Harry, she drew him down to cover her, embracing him with all the ardor of youth and love. She moaned with passion and matched his movements with her own, giving and receiving that most wonderful gift of all. Later, sated with loving, they lay in each other's arms and slept.

Kate woke moments before Harry did. Realizing that she must not stay too long, she caressed him until his gray eyes opened. Kissing him gently, she said, "I must talk to you, my dear. Something dreadful has happened."

"Kate, you're not—expecting a child, are you?"

"Oh, no. I wish I were. Then I could tell them, and that would put paid to all of their schemes."

Harry pulled her close to him, nuzzling her neck. "I don't want to talk about dreary things. I want to love you again before you go riding off home."

His merest touch set her on fire; but for once, Kate pulled away from his importuning lips, his skillful hands. "No, Harry. Not now. I have to talk to you about this."

"I could force you," he said jokingly, kissing her so roughly that he bruised her lips.

"Oh, Harry, you'll never have to force me," she breathed. "But please, dearest one, don't rouse me now. Truly, I must talk seriously with you."

Sulking, he flung himself up off the sofa, leaving her there alone. "Very well, what is it?" He snatched up his drawers and put them on, then finished dressing, not even looking at Kate.

Dismayed at his anger, she knew she must tell him anyway. "Father plans for me to marry that awful Arthur Mansfield."

Harry, still angry, didn't even turn around. "Does he, now? Well, he's picked a wealthy husband for you, Kate."

"Harry!" she wailed. "Don't you care?"

He looked at her over his shoulder and grinned an outrageous grin. "I'd have the best of all possible worlds—a rich man's wife as my lover."

Her eyes stung with unshed tears. Quickly she drew on her silk underthings, lacing her stays with shaking fingers.

"Tighter," Harry ordered, coming up behind her and pulling so hard on the laces that Kate gasped for breath. Then he slid his hands around her, cupping her breasts which were pushed high by the tightly laced stays. "Mine, all mine," he murmured. "Sure you can't stay longer, my dear one?" His hands moved enticingly, and she thought she would melt with desire.

Pulling his eager hands away from her bosom, she said crossly, "I'm very disappointed with you, Harry. I thought you'd have something constructive to suggest about Mansfield. Instead, you sound as if you want me to marry that old lecher."

"And you prefer young, handsome lechers, don't you?" His hand closed on her breast.

"If I had my riding crop in my hands, I'd beat you."

He grinned. "There are places in London where men pay for that privilege—but you wouldn't know about such things, would you, dear Kate?"

Crossly she said, "No, I wouldn't. Goodbye, Harry."

She flounced across the room, catching up her long riding skirt with one hand, reaching for the door with the other.

"Are you hurrying back to your prospective bridegroom?"

"Oh! You are insufferable. Harry Ravenshaw, I hate you. You're worse than my father."

Kate flung out of the lodge, hurrying to her horse, not waiting for Harry to lift her into the saddle. She was quite capable of getting on a horse by herself. She'd show him.

It was Harry who showed her though. He raced out of the lodge, caught at the mare's bridle, and then reached up for Kate, pulling her roughly from the saddle. His kiss was hard, ardent, "Kate, Kate, I was only teasing you. I have no intention of letting Mansfield marry you. You belong to me. But I do have some business dealings with him, dear. Right now I'd rather not have him fuming about anything, for some of his ire might rub off on me and ruin my business prospects. Remember, I have to work hard to get money. It was Derek who inherited everything from our father. So if you want to help me . . ."

"Oh, Harry, you know I'd do anything for you."

"Then be pleasant to Mansfield." Then he grinned and dropped a kiss on the end of her pretty little nose. "But keep your distance from him. I think he'd have his hands all over you if he had half a chance. Not that I can blame him," and he caressed her, causing her to shiver with pleasure.

"No one's hands but yours will ever touch my flesh," she promised. "Oh, Harry, must I be nice to him? He's so slimy—truly he is. And I feel he's undressing me with his eyes every time he looks at me."

"Just so long as he doesn't undress you with his hands!"

She sighed. "I wish you weren't doing business with Mansfield, Harry. He's a very unlovely character. The Duchess of Dorminster says he's the worst kind of slumlord."

"The Duchess of Dorminster inherited pots of money and a fine estate. She turns up her nose at everyone without a title or a fine house in the country. Listen to me, Kate. Mansfield came from nothing—but with his own hard work, his own shrewdness, his own skill, he's built himself a fortune whch is the envy of many of his titled neighbors. He owns Bassett Abbey, a real showplace. I admire a man who has enough gumption to fight the rotten system and beat it. And I intend for some of his business acumen to rub off on me. How else can I ever support a lovely creature such as you?"

"Very well, I'll try to be polite when I see him—but I hope that isn't very often. Although if father has his way, Mansfield will be underfoot constantly. I certainly don't want to steal time from you and spend it with Mansfield."

"But it won't hurt you to be friendly with him when he does come calling. A young woman should be anxious to help the man she loves. Keep him in a happy mood, and it could be to my benefit. It's the kind of thing a wife does to help her husband become a success. Listen, Kate, I may have to go away again. Chances are I'll not be able to warn you ahead of time."

All anger drained away. "But you've just gotten back, Harry! You can't go away again."

"Afraid I must, dearest Kate. Oh, I shall miss you. Come back inside with me," he coaxed, kissing her ear, sending waves of desire surging through her.

How she longed to acquiesce, but it was already getting dark. "I must get home immediately. Will you be here tomorrow, Harry?"

"I hope so. Ride over. If I can manage it, I'll see you in our little rendezvous."

"Doesn't Derek ever use the lodge? I keep having the feeling that someday I'll go rushing in and find that it's Derek there, not you."

"Derek's much too busy healing the sick and doing good."

"You don't like your brother, do you?"

"I hate him. He has everything, and I have nothing. All because he happens to be the older son. He has plenty, Kate, more than enough to keep himself comfortably and maintain Scarlet Oaks; but he has never once offered to settle a reasonable sum on me so that I could be independent of his largesse. That's why I'm working so hard to make my fortune without his help. Then, when I'm rich, I can spit in his face. Let him have Scarlet Oaks. I'll buy an even grander place for myself."

For us to live in, Kate thought happily. Then, with one last, lingering kiss, she let Harry give her a hand up into the saddle, and she rode home, galloping the horse all the way in order not to be too late. A carriage stood outside Fairlawn, and Kate recognized the driver. Mansfield was here. All of the pleasure of her interlude with Harry drained away when she saw that she'd have to go in, make herself agreeable to the man, pretend that the unpleasantness in the carriage last night hadn't happened. If Harry hadn't been so insistent, Kate would have gone directly to her room without letting her father know she'd come in; but if it would help her darling for her to be nice to Mansfield, then she'd do it. How pleased Father would be!

Rather than appear in her riding habit, Kate slipped in a side door and went up to her bedchamber using the servants' back stairs. Vera was there, her chubby face fearful.

"Oh, miss, wherever have you been? Your father has been sending Vinton up for you every five minutes for the past half hour. You have a caller. I have orders that you are to come down immediately."

"Quick then, help me change into something more suitable for greeting guests. The blue velvet, I think." It was high necked, long sleeved. Mansfield had seen quite enough of her flesh last night. She'd deny him that pleasure this afternoon.

"Shall I dress your hair longer, miss?"

Kate had her hair done up tight to her head, the dark

red fullness contained, pulled into a heavy knot at the crown.

"No, this is quite fancy enough." She'd be polite, but she wasn't going out of her way to be alluring to Mansfield. She didn't want to encourage the man. Kate still didn't quite see how her being nice to the man would help Harry; but he'd asked her to charm Mansfield, so she'd have to oblige. She couldn't deny Harry anything.

She swept into the small parlor where she heard voices. All smiles, oozing good nature, she walked over to Mansfield who was seated with her father at a small, marble-topped table, the heavy silverplated Georgian tea service in front of them.

Mansfield scrambled to his feet, setting down his Minton china teacup with a clatter that made Kate cringe inside. The Minton was their very best china.

"Ah, my dear Miss Kate, I had despaired of seeing you this afternoon. Your father said you'd gone out."

"Had I known you were coming . . ."

Her father, realizing that she intended to be affable, smiled indulgently on his wayward daughter, nodding his silent approval at her change of attitude from the stormy session this morning.

"I was just telling your father how delightful it was to have your company last night at the Italian opera."

Kate sat down on one of the ornately carved mahogany chairs. Her gown was just the color of the upholstery and the heavy drapes that hung from ceiling to floor. She poured tea for herself, and more for Mr. Mansfield while Vinton hovered unobstrusively in the background with a tray of tiny cress sandwiches and freshly baked tea cakes.

"I've been telling your father how lonely it is at Bassett Abbey with no wife to keep me company."

Kate wanted to scream at him, "Well, you'll not have me there to amuse you, you old lecher!" Instead, remembering Harry's admonition, she gave a docile smile which was so deliberately sweet that it was sickening.

"Bassett Abbey is a lovely home," she murmured. That was no lie. Kate would be quite happy to be mistress of such a showplace as the Abbey—if only Harry were the owner, not Mansfield.

"Kate, although perhaps I should not be the one to say this, would make a very suitable mistress of such an establishment," her father said a shade too eagerly.

What was happening to her today? Her father wanted to marry her off to Mansfield—and Harry jokingly said that it would suit him to perfection. They could keep on with their affair, she would meanwhile make Mansfield happy, and in doing this, she'd make life easier for Harry. Didn't the two men she loved most in the world care a fig for her feelings?

And Mansfield—today he was all polish and politeness. None of his highhanded ways such as he'd shown last night. Today he was all hints and delicacy. Of course she'd told him bluntly last night that she'd see to it he was never invited here to Fairlawn again—and now she sat pouring tea for him as if they were truly a courting couple. What Kate really wanted to do was to take up the heavy silver teapot and crack Mansfield over the head with it. But because she loved Harry so desperately, she sat and made polite conversation with him as if nothing untoward had happened on the trip back from London last night.

"I was just going to tell Kingsley, here, that I wondered at his letting you go to East London with the Duchess of Dorminster."

"Go where!"

Kate knew that tone. She was learning, these past few days, to beware of her father when he spoke that way.

There was a sly little smile on Mansfield's face. He'd not forgotten that Kate had hit him in the mouth last night with her fist. He was getting back at her now.

"The duchess is doing good works in Whitechapel. With your charming daughter's assistance. Surely you told your father, my dear Kate."

"He knows I've been going to London to help the duchess in her charitable work." But he didn't know where in London.

Her father was stiff and stilted. "You didn't mention just where in London that insane duchess was being helpful."

"Truly, Father, I didn't know myself, until she took me there the first time." Then, trying to ingratiate herself with her father, she added, "It's quite near to Derek Raven-shaw's clinic. We stopped to see him on Friday."

Mansfield cut in smoothly, "I fear Ravenshaw is doing more harm than good with his piecemeal medicine on Union Row. Those people are beyond help, and he knows it. He's just lining his pockets with their hard-earned pennies."

Incensed, Kate flared, "That's not true. Our cabbie told us that Derek's fees were very tiny—and that he was a fine physician."

Mansfield deliberately finished his cup of tea, patted his thin lips with the dainty linen napkin, and then said, "What would a hansom cab driver know of a physician's qualifications?"

"Ravenshaw has a good reputation," Kingsley put in. "I see him myself at times."

"Oh, I dare say he does some good," Mansfield admitted airily, "but there's talk about him and one of the notorious wh—pardon me, Miss Kate—one of the ladies of the street. I understand she once lived in this neighborhood—came from a decent enough family. A Monica Murphy."

"Old Paddy's daughter?" Obviously her father had heard none of the gossip about Monica. "Seems to me that at one time Derek Ravenshaw saw quite a bit of the Murphy girl. And she's—on the streets in Whitechapel?" Kingsley glanced at Kate to see if she understood what he and Mansfield were talking about.

"So I understand," Mansfield answered. "Truly, Kingsley, the East End is no fit place for such a lovely young woman as Kate."

"Monica has consumption," Kate cut in, remembering how the woman had coughed. "Derek's trying to help her."

"No help for consumption. She'll cough her lungs out."

Kate knew that Mansfield was right, but she didn't want to agree with him about anything. It was difficult to remember Harry's injunction when she was sitting across the tea table from Mansfield.

"We'll discuss this London charitable work later, Kate."

Knowing her father, Kate knew this probably meant he'd tell her she couldn't go back to Whitechapel with the duchess. In a way she didn't mind. It really was too awfully grubby there. She hadn't enjoyed it at all. The only reason she'd gone was to have an excuse not to see Mansfield. She'd much rather spend her afternoons in the lodge with Harry than with the scatty duchess doing good works on Whitechapel Road.

CHAPTER 11

Friday, January 20, 1888

"It's called a regard ring," Pam told Kate, showing off the bauble on the ring finger of her left hand.

Kate was green with envy, not only because it was a lovely piece of jewelry, but also because of what it signified.

"Is it because Alfie has great regard for you?"

"That's part of it—but notice the stones." She held the gem-encircled gold ring out to Kate. "See the arrangement of the stones around it? Ruby, emerald, garnet, amethyst, ruby, diamond. The first letters spell 'Regard.' Isn't that clever?"

"It's even more clever that you've gotten Alfie to propose. How did you do it, Pam?"

"I kept saying no when he wanted to take liberties. It works every time, Kate. Surely you know that. They all try to take advantage of an innocent young woman—but if you give in to their baser nature, all is lost. They want to have a good time with loose women—but they won't marry any but the purest virgins." Then, her voice suddenly sly, she asked, "You haven't allowed Harry to—you know."

"Pamela Oldham! What a wicked thing to ask me," Kate said, not having to put too much false indignation in her voice. She was truly indignant—that Pam had gotten engaged to Alfie, while she still was no nearer marriage

137

to Harry than she'd been when their affair first started. Kate knew all the rules. She'd broken them without a second thought, rapturously, madly. Without any concern for the future, Kate had fallen into bed with Harry. Had she forfeited his respect, made a terrible mistake? Was Harry ever going to marry her, make an honest woman of her, as they said?

"Will you be one of my bridal attendants, Kate? I want to have a huge wedding at St. Barnabas in Chelmsford. In June. That's such a romantic time for a wedding, I think. Father will have the bishop perform the ceremony, and then we'll have a lovely repast at Trinley. You will be in my wedding party, won't you? I'm importing all of the gowns from Paris."

Kate smiled at her friend's enthusiasm. "Well, how can I turn down an offer of a Parisian gown? Of course I'll be one of your attendants."

"As soon as my seamstress gets the pattern pictures, I'll ride over to Fairlawn and you can select your own color. We have to have all the measurements done by the end of the month in order to have ample time to get the gowns made and shipped." Then she asked, "Where have you been keeping yourself? I've scarcely seen you since the night of the Duchess of Dorminster's party on Christmas Eve."

"I've been busy. I'm helping the duchess with a reading class she has for women in East London." Then, lowering her voice to a conspiratorial level, she said, "They're harlots."

"Kate!" Pam was properly horrified. "Are they glamorous?"

Remembering the poor, sad women she'd seen at Salvation Chapel, Kate shook her head. "Oh, Pam, they're pitiful! Truly. They're old and ugly, dirty and diseased. They drink too much gin, and live in conditions you wouldn't believe."

"But in the French novels I read the courtesans are all beautiful, and are kept by princes or dukes or—"

"Not in East London, Pam. They are the dregs of society. Do you ever go visiting at the workhouse on Christmas?"

Pam's nose turned up and her mouth turned down. "Mother dragged me along for several years; but finally I rebelled. They're so—so—dreary!"

"The people in the local workhouse are a credit compared to the harlots of Whitechapel. And I saw Monica Murphy." She shuddered.

Pam's eyes lighted up. "Tell me! Is she really—one of those women? Alfie says it's true. But I can't always believe such tall tales. He says things just to tease me."

Kate sighed. "It's true, Pam. Monica has consumption. She coughs up blood." Pam made a moue. "The duchess tried to get her to come out to Essex—offered to take her in. But Monica just laughed and said it was too late for her. Derek Ravenshaw's taking care of her."

There was something in Kate's voice that alerted Pam. "I think he used to go around with Monica—before she went to London."

"So Mr. Mansfield said," was Kate's dry reply.

"And since when have you started quoting Mr. Mansfield? I thought you couldn't abide the man, Kate."

Kate glanced around the drawing room to make sure none of the servants were within earshot. "I can't stand him; but Father is trying to make a match for me."

"With Mansfield! Kate, you must be joking."

Bitterly Kate said, "How I wish I were. Father keeps telling me that Mansfield is such a good catch—wealthy, steady, with Bassett Abbey just waiting for a mistress."

"Well, I shouldn't mind presiding over Bassett Abbey—but not with old Mansfield in my bed. What will Harry say? You are still seeing Harry, aren't you?"

"Of course I'm still seeing him. But Father doesn't know."

"Tell Harry that your dear papa is going to put you on the marriage market, with Mansfield as the prospective buyer. That should jolt him into proposing."

Remembering all too well Harry's reaction to her sad tale of woe about Mansfield, Kate kept very silent. Pam, knowing her too well, gave her a shrewd look.

"What does Harry think about such a match?"

"I haven't mentioned it to him," Kate lied. "He'd be furious."

"Of course. That's the whole idea, Kate. Honestly, at times I think you aren't quite bright. Here's the most marvelous chance to force Harry's hand, make him think he'll lose you to Mansfield if he doesn't ask your father for your hand at once. Of course," she added slyly, "Harry's prospects aren't the greatest. A younger son. And Harry's not exactly cut out to earn a living. I suppose Derek gives him an allowance. You should have tried for Derek instead. He has the money! Maybe you would be better off with Mansfield. He's rolling in money."

"Pam, you're horrid. I'm not at all sure I want to be in your wedding party."

Realizing she'd gone too far, Pam said, trying to placate her best friend, "I'm only joking. Who wants to marry an old man when a young one is available? But I have heard, Kate, that Harry is sailing close to the wind on some of these stock ventures. I don't understand such things, but Alfie says that Harry may wind up in prison if he's not careful."

"Bosh!"

"Oh, Kate, we're going to have a house built in Chelmsford. A lovely house, with a tower, and a wide porch, and all kinds of decorations on the outside. Alfie has hired this marvelous architect. I know we'll eventually have to move into Yew House, when Alfie gets to be Earl of Morganton—but thank God his father is hale and hearty. I don't much like such an old-fashioned place. I'll have the most modern house in town—and Alfie is allowing me to furnish it as I choose."

Kate, green with envy, forced herself to smile at Pam. Sometimes she hated her friend's smugness. Life would always be kind to Pam. Her father was a baron and wealthy. Alfie was a viscount and would inherit the earldom from his father, who was also wealthy. Poor Harry had nothing except what he could make by using his wits. It was so unfair. And Derek, with both title and estate, didn't appreciate what he had. He didn't even bother to get married so that he could pass the title on to his son.

"I went to the Royal Opera House last Saturday," she said. Pam wasn't the only one who could boast. "For a performance of the Italian opera *Aida*. By Verdi."

"With Harry?"

"No. With Mr. Mansfield. Pam! I had to fight him off in the carriage! I could have lost my virtue, he was so inflamed with desire for me."

"I don't think I'd care to lose my virtue to Mansfield."

"Neither would I. Why do you think I keep telling my father that I have no intention of marrying Mansfield?"

"Has he really asked for your hand?" Kate nodded and sudden concern filled Pam's pretty face. "Surely your father isn't seriously considering arranging a marriage for you with that—that—"

Tears filled Kate's green eyes. "He is. Truly he is. Pam, I'm so worried. I think—I don't know, but—I think that Mr. Mansfield has some hold over Father."

"Oh, Kate, that's very dramatic," Pam scoffed.

"It's true. Why else would he keep insisting that I must be pleasant to the odious man?"

"Fathers can be such a bore. No doubt he sees only Mansfield's money, his position in the city, his beautiful home. He thinks it would be a great match for you."

"But he's as old as Father," Kate wailed.

Pam shrugged. "Lot's of girls marry older men, Kate. It's done all the time. The older ones have made their place in the world. There's no chance of hardship. I can see why a man would want such a husband for his only daughter. Particularly if he's—" She stopped short, clapped a long, slender hand over her mouth.

"Particularly if he's what, Pam?"

"Oh, Kate. Nothing."

"That's a lie, Pam. What were you about to say about my father?"

Pam sighed. "It's nothing much, Kate. I overheard my father talking with Lord Wimbley—something about a mortgage. Is Fairlawn mortgaged, do you know?"

"How would I know that? You don't think Father talks business with me, do you? Does your father discuss his affairs with you? Does he tell you how many kegs of brandy he imports?" There, that would remind Pam that her father, peer or not, was only a glorified tradesman.

"I'm sorry, Kate. I shouldn't have mentioned it to you. I'm sure it's nothing serious."

It bothered Kate though. If father had mortgaged Fairlawn, and Mansfield held the mortgage, it explained a lot. No wonder he was so anxious for her to be nice to the man. But marry him? Just to save their home? No sane father would ask that of his only daughter.

Then Pam chattered on about her wedding, discussing the kind of wedding gown she wanted to wear. Kate began to get worried. It was now late afternoon. If Pam didn't leave soon, she'd not have time to ride to the lodge to meet Harry. Maybe he had heard something of the rumor Pam had mentioned about a mortgage on Fairlawn. Could that be why Harry and her father were talking business recently? Perhaps Harry was putting Father onto some good investments. Kate was still very vague in her mind about what Harry actually did—she thought it had to do with stocks, or investments of some sort. That must be it. He was advising Father about his financial affairs. Lucky for Father that Harry was so knowledgeable about such things.

Now she understood her father's worried manner. If he had taken a mortgage on Fairlawn, no wonder he was concerned. Perhaps some of his investments had gone bad. She really knew so little about such things.

"Why don't you go to London with me next Monday to help me with some of my trousseau shopping, Kate?"

Kate was just ready to make some kind of excuse, not wanting to miss more time with Harry—drat, Pam, anyway; it was going to be much too late when she left to go to the lodge today—when Vinton came in.

"Yes, Vinton?"

"Sir Derek Ravenshaw, miss."

Oh, well, the afternoon was already ruined. "Show him in, Vinton."

Derek was all smiles when he joined the two young ladies.

"I was driving past on my way back from the Chelmsford Station, so I thought I'd drop by Fairlawn." He looked around, then lowered his voice. "Actually I hoped to see your father, Kate, strictly on a casual basis. I'm still worried about his health. Is he around?"

"I think he's in his study. I'll have Vinton tell him we're having tea here in the drawing room."

"You have the makings of a first-rate conspirator, Kate. That will do admirably. He'll think I've called to see his lovely daughter—and Pam, too, of course."

"Oh, I'm not available, Derek," Pam teased. "Alfie has asked me to marry him."

"My very best wishes, although I can scarcely say I'm surprised. You and Alfie have been keeping company since cradle days."

While they waited for Vinton to bring tea and inform her father that it was being served, Kate asked, trying to keep the eager note out of her voice, "How's Harry?"

"Gone again." It was terse to the point of curtness.

"Gone where?" Pam asked, giving Kate a chance to get over her disappointment.

Derek shrugged. "He never bothers to say. I just hope he's not getting himself into a pot of trouble. If he does, he needn't expect me to bail him out."

"Why, Derek, sometimes I think you don't love Harry like a proper brother."

"He's not awfully lovable," Derek answered.

"I find him quite nice," Kate said coolly, determined to defend Harry from such a vicious attack.

"Unfortunately, so do others, all too often to their sorrow. I feel I've failed with Harry. I've been too indulgent, and now he's gone completely off the tracks."

Indulgent! Kate could scarcely keep quiet. Horrid Derek kept Harry on such a tiny allowance that he could scarcely meet his tailor's bills. Fortunately, her father came in just then, so the subject of Harry was dropped.

When Derek was ready to leave, he signaled with a tiny movement of his head for Kate to see him out. "Make sure your father rests a lot, Kate, and has no worries. I'd tell him this myself, but he doesn't come to me professionally. I think he's avoided having a checkup because he knows he is not well—foolish, but all too many people do that. Just see that he lives as serene a life as possible."

"Thank you, Derek, I shall." She guessed she'd have to pretend a liking for Mansfield, at least until Father was feeling better. How boring.

Later, when Pam was leaving, Kate told her she'd love to go shopping on Monday. With Harry away again, she had nothing to occupy her days.

INTERLUDE 4

Sunday night, January 22, 1888

Good thing he was wearing the false beard tonight. He had to be careful. He could be recognized too easily.

A plan was forming in his mind. It combined his hatred of whores with his desire for revenge. If he could kill one of these vile women, leaving clues pointing to his hated rival, it would be wonderful. Yes! He'd do it. It would require careful planning, but he was quite able to initiate such a clever plan.

As he walked up Whitechapel, he could hear the sound of hymns being sung. Ah, Fiddler's beanpole wife was pumping out the music with great verve tonight. He wondered if she had as much energy in bed. Perhaps she thought that she was too religious for such sinful pastimes. Probably why old Fiddler chased whores up every dark alley in Whitechapel. Did he borrow from the collection plate to get coppers to pay his dirty women? Did he pray for their souls while he used their disease-ridden bodies?

The door of the chapel opened just as he came opposite it. The evening service was over, and a few dreary people left, clutching their ragged clothes about them to keep out the cold, raw night air. He recognized one figure, a woman almost as tall as the beanpole preacher who shook her hand as she left his chapel. Long Liz, they called her. Everyone knew Long Liz. He wondered if Fiddler had patronized her. Just the right size for him. Even taller than that long, skinny wife.

From a distance he trailed Liz, keeping to the shadows. He wouldn't be one of her clients. Not for him the grubby sex in one of the black cul de sacs along this way. Shouldn't be allowed to ply their trade in London. His fingers itched to close around her throat. His hand closed around the clasp knife he carried. How he longed to take his knife to her; but she turned into the corner grogshop, and he went on alone, plans fermenting in his head. He mustn't let passion catch him. Any murder he committed must be done carefully, so that he could shift the blame where he wanted it to lie. Patience. He must exercise patience. His time would come.

CHAPTER 12

Monday, January 23, 1888

Kate and Pam ate a late lunch at a confectioner's just off Bond Street, so weary from shopping that they sighed with relief when they sat down in the pleasant little shop. Soon revived by dainty chicken sandwiches, little cakes, and pots of steaming tea, they were ready to face the world again.

"More shopping?" Kate asked. She eyed all of Pam's purchases enviously: fine silk drawers trimmed with imported lace, exquisite petticoats, frilly corset covers, and the most daring stays guaranteed to give Pam a bosom, even if she wasn't so generously endowed as Kate. At least Kate could feel smug about that. She didn't need ruffles to make her dresses fit properly across the bust. And how Harry loved her firm, full, young breasts. She sighed. How long would he be gone this time? He'd not even said, hadn't left a note for her at the lodge, nothing. Well, she'd just have to fill her days with visits to Pam—perhaps even more do-good journeys to Whitechapel with the duchess, if she could go without her father's knowledge.

There was a mischievous gleam in Pam's gray eyes. "I have the most delicious idea, Kate. Let's go to that funny little chapel you've talked about. I'm dying to see this Ichabod Crane character you've described. Is he really such a lecher as those dreadful women say?"

Remembering the Reverend Mr. Fiddler's hot, mad eyes as they'd looked at her in that cold little assembly room,

Kate said, "I believe everything Monica said about him. And the others. I'd hate to have him for the vicar at St. Michael's. I don't know if I want to—"

"Oh, you're such a spoilsport, Kate. You tell me all about these adventures you have with the Mad Duchess; but if I want some of the fun, you demur. Come. I can scarcely go to the East End by myself."

Kate thought, Very well, let her see it for herself. "All right. Shall we take a hansom cab from here?"

"Heavens! That would take ages. Let's go on the Metro."

"Have you ridden the Metro, Pam?"

"Of course." Airily. "Lot's of times."

"But not to Whitechapel Station."

"Well, why would I have gone there? Oh, you are a timid soul today, Kate. Usually you're such fun, ready for anything."

"Salvation Chapel isn't awfully entertaining." Then, seeing the sullen look on Pam's patrician face, she acquiesced. "Oh, all right. We'll go. I've never gone to the East End underground. The duchess says it's such a dreary trip, she always insists on a cab from Paddington."

"She's an old fogey," Pam announced.

Once down under the streets in the dank, chilly tunnel, though, Pam had second thoughts. "It isn't very pleasant, is it, Kate?" She looked about apprehensively. The few people waiting on the platform were scarcely aristocratic. "Lower class," Pam whispered to Kate.

With some asperity, Kate told her, "This was your idea."

"Maybe a cab would be . . ." Her words were drowned out by the arrival of the train, the coke-burning steam engine noisy in the cut-and-cover tunnel. Pam picked up her skirts and got aboard, with Kate at her heels. The gas jets lighted the coach poorly, and it was smelly and close inside. By the time they had reached the Whitechapel Station, both young women were more than glad to leave the rattling, rough-riding contraption and climb up to the street level.

"How dreadful!" Pam exclaimed, holding a scented handkerchief to her delicate nostrils. "I'm glad I don't have to travel that way very often. It's nothing like the railroad in from Chelmsford."

Kate, not admitting this was her first trip by Metro, agreed wholeheartedly with her companion. No wonder the duchess insisted on a cab when they came to do their charitable work.

"Do we take a cab now to get to the chapel?"

Wickedly Kate pointed to one of the crowded, horse-drawn omnibuses jolting along Whitechapel Road. "We could go that way."

Pam just looked down her nose at Kate and scowled. "I have slummed quite enough for one day." As if riding the Metro had been Kate's idea, not her own.

"Father says that it is considered fast to ride in a hansom cab," Kate said slyly.

"Only if your companion is a gentleman." Then she giggled, "Or not a gentleman!" She waved down a cab, and she and Kate climbed in, arranging their skirts in the cramped space.

"Where to, miss?" the cabby asked through the little window in the roof.

Pam turned to Kate. "Where is this chapel?"

"Right up Whitechapel Road."

Pam started to give directions, then said, "Why not drive past Derek's famous clinic while we're here. Didn't you say you were there with the duchess?"

"We drove Monica there."

"Three of you crammed in a hansom?"

"And Monica none too clean, I can assure you. She smelled of sweat and cheap perfume."

"How revolting. She used to be rather attractive, for an older woman. Always a bit fast, of course. But she dressed well."

"Not now. And she's quite ill, Pam, with consumption."

They gave directions to the cabby to drive them along Union Row, then on to the Salvation Chapel. Pam peered avidly out of the cab windows, exclaiming at the poverty, filth, and degradation she saw all around her.

Kate sat and brooded about Harry and her father's attempt to marry her off to Mansfield. She wondered if the duchess really had seen Harry that day. He said he didn't go to the East End, but what if he was lying? Oh, well, at least it would be something to look forward to, even if

Harry was lying—a glimpse of her beloved, for whatever reason, would certainly cheer her. She began to brighten.

"Which are the fallen women?" Pam asked eagerly, turning to stare at some bedraggled women on a street corner outside a tavern. "How can you tell?"

"I don't know." Kate was feeling quite cross with Pam. She'd seen enough of the East End to realize the degradation of its teeming hordes. This trip smacked too much of the horrid practice of the last century when the members of the aristocracy took sightseeing trips on Sunday to see the poor mad patients in Bedlam. "If you see a woman approach a man and talk to him, she's probably one of the local whores."

Pam's eyebrows raised at Kate's use of the vulgar term. "There—is that one?" She caught Kate's sleeve and pointed to the entrance to a grubby little alleyway. A woman was talking with a man, her hand on his arm, and as they watched, she swayed toward him invitingly. "Oh, Kate, she's soliciting him, isn't—God! It's Monica Murphy!"

Just moments before Pam's words, Kate had realized that the woman in question was indeed Monica. It gave her a queasy feeling, not at all exciting or titillating.

"Yes, that's Monica." Then, noticing where they were, she added, "And Derek's clinic is just ahead, mid-block."

Pam tore her attention away from Monica and her customer who were entering the alleyway. "That broken-down building?" Shock was evident in her voice. "Derek works in there?"

"That's the place. And his patients fit the surroundings." Determined to make Pam feel terrible about this expedition, she asked, "What's wrong, Pam? You seem so interested in Derek, when you should think only of Alfie, your betrothed. You aren't in need of Derek's professional services, are you? You haven't allowed Alfie to take liberties, now that you're officially engaged? Could you be expecting? I don't know whether or not Derek does that kind of thing—you may have to go to a local granny woman."

Realizing what Kate was saying, Pam turned scarlet. "Kate Kingsley, what a rotten thing to say to me. You know perfectly well that Alfie and I—we haven't—I don't like that kind of joke, truly I don't." She reached up and rapped sharply on the roof of the cab. "Drive on to the Salvation Chapel."

"Don't want to be treated in the clinic?'

"Frankly, I'm beginning to regret coming here at all."

"I told you it wasn't pretty."

"Well, but I thought—"

"That it would be quaint? Different? Exciting? It isn't. It's grubby and ugly."

"How can Derek bear to come here two days a week and work with such—such—"

"I think he believes they are people, Pam, not some kind of low animals. Just as the duchess, crazy as she is, has real concern for them. I think neither can help here, but they try."

Pam would not be shamed by what Kate said. "I hope the chapel is more interesting than that dreary place Derek has."

Kate smiled inwardly. Wait until Pam saw the cold, bleak room in which Fiddler saved souls. This was the last time that Pam would ask to come here as a lark. Kate, for one, wasn't too eager to go to the chapel again. She hoped that the resident soul saver wasn't in evidence. There was something about the lean, cadaverous man that chilled the blood in her veins. Godly wasn't a word that aptly described Fiddler—godforsaken was more like it.

The cabby reined in his bony, sway-backed horse, and Pam leaned forward to look out.

"Why's he stopping here?"

"You told him to take us to Salvation Chapel."

"There's no church in sight. The cabby must be drunk."

The doors opened in front of them, controlled by the lever on the cabby's high perch, and Kate stepped down gingerly. Pam followed, protesting all the way.

"Where's the chapel?" she demanded, looking around crossly.

"Right in front of us." Kate picked her way across the garbage-littered pavement to the plain door of the chapel.

"This?" Pam's shocked tones gave Kate a feeling of satisfaction. Sometimes Pam was too smug for her to stomach.

"You were expecting St. Paul's? Or the Abbey?"

"Well, we might as well go in, now that we're here," Pam said, doubt in her voice. "It's so grubby!"

"It matches everything else in the East End." Kate opened the battered door and preceded Pam into the cold, gloomy room, holding up the skirt of her green bombazine gown to keep it from getting dusty. At first glance, the chapel was empty.

"There's no one here," Pam said, but Kate couldn't tell whether her friend was pleased or disappointed.

As if to give lie to her words, a sudden sound of loud voices came from somewhere at the back of the room, and nearby, someone cackled, startling both young women.

Peering into a corner, Kate saw that a woman was stretched out on one of the plain, hard benches. It was Molly, the fat prostitute she'd seen here before.

"Lissen 'em go at it, hammer 'n' tongs," the drab said, words slurred with gin. Laboriously she sat up, looked at them. "Oh, you're the gal comes wif the duchess. Who's that with you? Not her grace. Too young and fancy."

"It's Miss Oldham, Molly." Then, as the shouting in the next room got louder, "What's going on in there?" She thought she recognized Fiddler's voice.

"Preacher's wantin' a go wiv his wife, but she won't," Molly said bluntly, then laughed again. "Sez it's sinful, she do. Married to him, won't lay wiv him. So he pays me—or Long Liz—or Polly—or Annie—not particular, him."

Pam, as if drawn by a magnet, edged toward the door leading from the assembly room to the living quarters behind it. Kate, not wanting to get embroiled with the Reverend Mr. Fiddler, hissed, "Pam! Come back here!" but Pam paid no heed to her. Sure they'd be caught eavesdropping, Kate hurried after her friend, catching up with her just as she got to the door. "What are you doing? If he comes out here now, he'll catch us redhanded."

"Shh! I want to hear what they're saying." Her gray eyes were alight with mischief, and Kate was drawn into the game.

"It's my God-given right!" Fiddler was thundering, using what Kate thought of as his preaching voice.

"Evil! Corrupt! You're a man of God! Act like one!"

Kate recognized the acid tones of his wife, Abby.

"The Scripture says that God put Eve on earth for Adam!"

"St. Paul advocates celibacy," she countered.

"Don't quote Scripture to me to get out of your wifely duty!" he yelled angrily. "I married you. St. Paul says it is better to marry than to burn."

Her voice was bitter. "You think I don't know what you do? All of East London knows about you, Jonathan Fiddler. Whore chaser. Degenerate."

"If you performed your duties, I wouldn't have to resort to those lewd creatures. You drive me to it, Abby. You make me into a sinner."

"I pray for you night and day," she cried, her voice taking on a fanatical evangelism. "I get down on my knees and pray that your lust will be changed to spiritual exaltation. That you will forget the sins of the flesh, and think only of your own salvation!"

"Woman, you drive me toward madness!"

Then, while both Pam and Kate listened avidly, the door in front of them swung open, and Fiddler stood there, eyes blazing, confronting them.

"What are you doing here, snooping into things that don't concern you?" his wife asked, her face white with rage. She stood almost as tall as her husband, skinny and flat-chested, done up in a dress of navy blue, completely plain, without even a bit of white at the neck to relieve the severity of the cut and color. Her dull, dark brown hair was screwed up on top of her head in a knot so tight that it seemed to be pulling her face out of shape, and her cold blue eyes bulged as if they were going to pop out of her bony skull. "Where's the Duchess of Dorminster?" she demanded. "This isn't the day for her class."

Kate, terrified of the two evangelists, gulped and said in a tiny voice, "This is Miss Oldham. I'd been telling her about the class, and she wanted to see the chapel."

"I'll pray for your souls," Fiddler said, but there was lust in his mad eyes when he looked at the two women.

Mrs. Fiddler moved in front of him, as if to separate her husband from such temptations. "I think you should go," she said, her voice colder than the room. "This is no fit place for young women of quality. Are you unchaperoned?"

Kate quailed before the onslaught; but Pam lifted her patrician pose into the air and said, "We are adult women, Mrs. Fiddler. We've been to see Sir Derek Ravenshaw at his clinic." The lie tripped off her tongue easily. "Miss Kingsley mentioned the work she is doing with the Duchess of Dorminster, so I asked to see Salvation Chapel." She looked around and added scathingly, "A mean place. Come, Kate, I don't care to stay here a moment longer." She turned and swept out, with Kate at her heels.

The Reverend Mr. Fiddler wasn't about to let such delicious morsels out of his sight yet. By the time Kate had gotten to the door, Fiddler was beside her. As if to direct her through the doorway, his hand went around her shoulders, but his fingers slid under her arm and curled avidly about her breast.

"Mrs. Fiddler isn't feeling well," he murmured. "You must forgive her display of temper. I'm sure the dear duchess needn't hear of this little episode."

Worrying about his rent money, Kate thought cynically, sliding out of his grip. Monica was right. He had busy hands.

Pam turned to make sure that Kate was behind her, and saw her escaping from Fiddler's sly pawing.

"Come, Kate," she ordered haughtily. "Let's get away from that old lecher as fast as we can."

Kate scurried after her, to find that Pam was giggling.

"The look on his face when he heard himself called a lecher! If looks would kill, I'd be lying dead here on this filthy pavement. Ugh, what a horror. Kate, you're mad to go there to do anything. That man is a menace."

"I know. The duchess gets you trapped before you even see the noose on the snare—you know what she's like."

"Does she really think she can help women like that one who was sleeping off a drunk on the chapel bench? If so, she's madder than Mr. Fiddler." Then she said, curious, "Was that woman a prostitute?"

"Molly? Yes, she's one who comes to the class."

"What man in his right mind would want her. Are they all like that, Kate?"

"Pretty much."

"I thought that prostitutes were beautiful, glamorous types who were courted by dukes and princes, who set them up in posh establishments in Mayfair."

"I suppose some are." Kate had been thoroughly disillusioned when she'd made her first visit to Salvation Chapel with the duchess. "But the East End isn't like a French novel, Pam. It's dreadful. The women are drabs—even poor Monica. You scarcely recognized her."

"I'm sorry we came," Pam said. "Why didn't you tell me?"

"I tried to," Kate said drily. "You wouldn't listen."

"Well, let's find a cab and get back to the Metro. Is there a station closer than the one we came to?"

"I think maybe Aldgate East. But the duchess doesn't ride the underground."

As they rode along in the hansom, Pam laughed. "What a lover that beanpole preacher would be. He fits right into the locale. I saw him feeling your bosom."

"Made me want to strip off my corset cover and chemise and scrub myself," Kate told her. "He really is an awful creature. I think he's demented."

Pam nodded sagely. "It's associated with his kind of religion, you know. It's all so emotional. Add to it that dried-up stick of a wife who obviously isn't allowing him any husbandly privileges, and look what you get—a madman."

"I'd never treat my husband that way."

"Nor I Alfie." Then Pam shivered. "Oh, Kate, imagine. In just a few months I'll know what it is to be a married woman. Mama just makes vague references—tells me I must submit to my husband's carnal needs. I do hope it isn't too dreadful."

How Kate longed to reassure her friend; but she dared not give Pam even a hint of the raptures she had in store, for fear her friend would realize that she was no longer a virgin. She smiled smugly. How self-confident it made her feel, knowing that she could give such intense pleasure to the man she loved. Poor Pam, having to wait until summer to know wedded bliss.

Just as the cab drew up to the station, Kate got a glimpse of Monica Murphy talking to a loutish-looking sailor. She didn't mention it to Pam. Poor Monica. What had gone wrong for her? A little shiver went over her—someone walking on her grave. Monica's warning words came back to her. But Kate knew it wouldn't be that way with her. Harry loved her deeply, and soon they would be man and wife. It would be the fulfillment of all her dreams.

During the train ride back to Chelmsford, Pam asked, "What's happened to Harry? You haven't mentioned him once today, Kate. Is he less attentive than he's been?"

"Harry? Less attentive? Pam, you're joking." If she'd only seen them at the lodge the last time they met, with Harry so ardent that her very bones melted with passion, Pam wouldn't ask such nonsensical questions. "He's away on business this week."

Pam gave Kate a shrewd look. "Business? I heard the strangest story about Harry the other day. I was having tea with the Countess of Rothberry, when something was said about Harry. I forget how we got off on such a dull subject, but the talk turned to investments. The countess was saying that she was glad they hadn't listened to Harry Ravenshaw when he'd been trying to sell them shares in something or other. She'd heard they were forged certificates."

"What a wicked thing to say! Just because Harry's a younger son with no inheritance, whenever he tries to earn a decent living, people gossip about him. It makes me furious."

"I'm sure it's just the wacky old countess making up a story," Pam soothed. "Of course, Harry is a bit reckless at times—I'm not sure I'd want him to invest too much of my money."

"Pam, what a horrid thing you're saying. Harry's been your friend forever. I wonder what you say about me when my back is turned?"

Pam knew she'd gone too far with Kate, so she quickly changed the subject; but Kate wasn't easily mollified. She was very tired of having people pick on her darling Harry.

If only Derek weren't so tight-fisted, Harry wouldn't have to be constantly trying to earn some cash so that he could live well. She could learn to hate Derek Ravenshaw; Sir Derek, that was, baronet. And poor Harry was only Mr. Harry Ravenshaw until he died—unless Derek died before he produced an heir to the baronetcy.

CHAPTER 13

Saturday, February 11, 1888

Frantically Kate counted days on her calendar. Two weeks late—and this morning she'd felt very queasy when she got up. She had to see Harry, but he'd now been gone since the twentieth of January. Not a word. No note, no letter, no message from him at all. Derek didn't know where he was, nor did he care. She hoped Harry came back to Scarlet Oaks soon.

She smiled, a soft little smile that soothed her. A child. She and Harry were going to have a child. She was sure, even though it still was too early to be positive. Kate knew, though, and she couldn't wait to share the marvelous news with her beloved. What would he say when she told him he was going to be a father? A little shadow crossed her mind. Last time she'd been with him, after that terrible carriage ride from London with Mansfield, he'd seemed alarmed when he thought she might be expecting his child. Well, Harry had always been pretty footloose. Once he got used to the idea of paternity, once the two of them were properly married and settled in their own home, he'd calm down. Kate was in seventh heaven. How blissful to be carrying a child by the man you loved. How dreadful it must be for women married to men they didn't even like. If she had allowed her father to marry her off to Mansfield, this tiny scrap of life in her womb might be his, not Harry's. The very thought sickened her. Knowing she was pregnant put paid to any plans her father might have to give her in marriage to Mansfield. Kate was sure that Arthur Mansfield wouldn't be interested in a wife who was pregnant by some other man.

Now, however, the problem was to get hold of Harry, let him know her joyous news. She'd ride over to the lodge on the off chance that he was back. If he still was away, she supposed she could ask Derek how she could reach Harry by post; although she preferred the relationship to be kept on a low key until she and Harry had their plans settled.

Father would be furious. She'd not tell him about the baby. If she and Harry married quickly, she could always say that the babe arrived prematurely. There'd be gossip, of course. They even talked about poor Deborah Bostwick when she had that tiny, frail baby much too early, and it died. Anyone with sense knew it was not a full-term child. Very well, there might be a buzz of chatter for a time, but it would be quickly forgotten.

She called Vera in. "I'm going riding for a bit, Vera. The brown habit, I think." It was a bit looser. She'd noticed yesterday that the green riding outfit was already snug across the bosom, for with her pregnancy, her lovely, full breasts were swollen and tender. "Don't lace me quite so tightly," she cautioned her maid. "I want to be able to breathe when I'm riding." How soon would her sharp-eyed little maid notice her blossoming body, guess her secret?

It was a pleasant day, cold but clear, after the dreary days of rain and drizzle they'd had earlier in the week. Kate rode along, humming "Greensleeves" and hoping that her love would be at the lodge to greet her. It had been far too long since they had lain together before the fire, bodies joined in rapture. Kate wondered how the wives of sailors could stand being separated from their men for months on end. She burned with desire, longed for Harry's arms to hold her, for him to possess her completely.

As she turned off the road into the little lane leading to the hunting lodge, her mare put her ears forward and whickered. Another horse was somewhere near. Harry must be here, waiting for her. She urged her own mount forward, eager to be in his arms; but when they arrived at the lodge, Harry's big, rangy hunter wasn't tethered where he usually left it. There was a light shining from the front window, though, so he was here. Quickly she dismounted and tied the mare to the hitching ring on the mounting step beside the door of the small building. Picking up her long riding skirt, Kate ran up the steps and burst into the lodge crying, "Harry! Where are you?"

The room was empty, but she heard someone moving about in one of the small rooms that let off the lounge.

"Harry?" Her voice was hesitant, now. This wasn't like him at all. Why hadn't he rushed out to greet her the moment she called? Should she go into the other room? As she stood there, undecided, a figure appeared in the door to the lounge.

"Kate! I thought I heard someone come in." He seemed puzzled. "What are you doing here?"

It was a crushing disappointment. "Oh, Derek. It's you."

His mouth twisted in a wry smile, and he advanced toward her. "Your enthusiasm at seeing me almost overwhelms me, Kate."

"I'm sorry. I thought—" She stopped just in time. It would never do to say she thought he was Harry. "I saw a light on inside, and I took it upon myself to investigate. I thought the lodge was closed at this time of the year."

Did he believe her? She thought he was looking at her strangely.

All he said, though, was, "Thank you for your concern. I was looking for a hunting knife I seem to have misplaced. Now that you're here, I could light the fire and we could have a pleasant chat."

Kate had spent too many delirious hours in front of that fire with Harry. No, she didn't want to spoil this rendezvous by sharing it with Derek. She was desperate, though, to know when Harry would come home.

"Thanks, but I must ride back. I'm just out for a bit of air. I don't like to be away from Father too long."

"How is he, Kate? I wish he'd come to my surgery for a thorough check. His heart—well, he's not young." Then he added gallantly, "At least one member of the Kingsley family is bursting with good health. You are positively blooming, Kate."

"How kind of you to notice." Of course she was blooming. It was Harry's child within her that was making her look so lovely. Kate had never realized what it did to a woman, how wonderful it made her feel to be carrying the child of the man she loved. But she didn't want Derek to be paying too much attention to her now. As a doctor, he might guess her secret. She'd better leave before he noticed anything different in her, some subtle change a layman wouldn't be aware of, that might alert him to her pregnancy.

She turned to leave, then asked over her shoulder, trying to make it seem casual, "Is Harry still away on business? I haven't seen him around for weeks." It seemed months.

"Gone again." His tone was curt. "He was in last night, late, and then was gone by the time I breakfasted this morning."

"You don't—know where he's gone, do you? I wanted —I wanted to tell him I was to be an attendant at Pam's wedding. Possibly Alfie will want him to be best man."

"Harry doesn't keep me advised of his comings and goings. Kate, you've not been seeing a lot of Harry, have you?" He came close, put a cautionary hand on her arm. "Don't lose your heart to my brother, dear Kate. He will cause you naught but grief. Harry has a wild streak in him—he'll never let any woman, even one as lovely as you, tame him."

It annoyed Kate to hear him slander her beloved. "I think you do your younger brother an injustice, Derek. He's always been very kind to me." Kind! What a word for the effect Harry had on her—what he did to her—how he inflamed her senses, made her drunk with desire, giddy with passion, almost beside herself with love. And now this most precious gift he'd given her, a child.

Derek sighed. "Kate, Kate, I know Harry better than you do. He's been in and out of trouble for years. And I fear that—" He looked at her with concern.

"You fear what, Derek?" she challenged.

"Nothing, Kate. But don't let Harry charm you. Under that charm is a rather unreliable man."

"You think I haven't enough attraction to hold Harry if he should pursue me?"

At first he didn't answer. Then, his dark eyes so intense that it almost frightened her, he said hoarsely, "Kate, oh Kate, you could hold any man you chose. Except Harry. Kate, if ever you need a friend—if I can ever be of any service to you—you have only to ask."

Taken aback by this turn in their conversation, Kate only murmured, "How nice of you, Derek. I shall remember that."

"I mean it, Kate. Anything. Ask anything of me, and I will do everything in my power to give it to you."

Disturbed by his impassioned speech, Kate quickly took her leave. Derek held his hands for a step, and threw her into the saddle as deftly as Harry did.

"Remember, Kate. I'm here if you need me."

"Thank you, Derek. I'll remember."

As she cantered toward Fairlawn, she wished she had told him that the thing he could do that would please her most was to be more generous with Harry. Derek could well afford to settle a large sum on Harry, allow his brother to be independent. Instead he held the purse-strings so tightly that Harry had no chance at all. She shut her mind to the rumors Pam had heard that Harry was sailing too close to the wind these days, that he might wind up in prison. Pam was just being dramatic. She always had been catty. At times Kate wondered why she kept up their friendship, Pam so often said cutting things. Now, with her announced marriage to Alfie, she was unsufferably smug. Well, Kate would be wed before Pam. As soon as she got hold of Harry—she should have asked specifically for Harry's address. And what was this about Harry's being at Scarlet Oaks last night, yet leaving again before dawn? Why hadn't he gotten in touch with her? She'd have slipped out to see him, even at night. He could have driven by and picked her up in the tilbury. They could have had a heavenly reunion at the lodge. Instead she had to blunder on Derek there today.

Derek. Whatever had gotten into the man? He sounded like a suitor, not a friend.

When she rode up to the house, an all-too-familiar victoria was standing in the circular driveway by the front door. Arthur Mansfield was here again. He'd been haunting Fairlawn recently. Kate had been hard-pressed to be civil to him, not only for her father's sake, but also for Harry's, remembering his caution to be pleasant to the slumlord for business reasons. She wished she knew what business Harry had with such a one as Mansfield. No wonder Pam said there were rumors about Harry's business practices, if he was allied with her hated suitor.

As she went in, planning to go upstairs to change from her riding habit, Kate heard raised voices coming from Father's study. Knowing that it was bad for him to be so upset, she went to the door, gave a perfunctory tap, and went in without waiting for her father's call. The tableau which met her eyes was frightening. Kingsley and Mansfield faced each other across the large, leather-surfaced walnut desk. Her father was clutching his favorite inkwell, made from silver in the form of a Shand Mason horse-drawn fire engine. He looked ready to throw it at Mansfield, who leaned over the desk, supported by hands laid flat on the leather top.

"How dare you threaten to foreclose," her father raged. Today his color was very high, cheeks flushed a dull red; but even in the heat of argument, Kate saw the blue cast to his lips. She feared he might have a stroke.

Mansfield didn't shout. His voice was low, cold, and pitiless. "I threaten to foreclose, my dear Kingsley, because you owe me a packet of money which you can't produce. I gave you the alternative—marriage to your daughter. You've been putting me off on that, and Kate herself often is scarcely civil. So pay up. I've carried you too long already."

"I told you I'd get the money. I have to sell some shares—"

"Of the stock that young pup Ravenshaw sold you?"

Kate could see by the look on her father's face that Mansfield had hit the mark squarely.

"They're no good, Kingsley." Mansfield was inexorable, the voice of doom. "Forged. The scandal broke this morning. Word got out at the Exchange at closing bell yesterday. Those shares Harry peddled far and wide were clever forgeries. So if you're planning to pay me off with shares you bought from Ravenshaw, forget it."

The silver inkwell fell from nerveless fingers, and Kate saw her father's face twist with pain. He swayed, and she swept into the study to give him support. She put an arm about him and said, "Don't worry, Father, we'll manage somehow." She pulled the heavy desk chair closer. "Here, sit down," she coaxed. She didn't like the color of father's face at all. Now all the blood drained from it, leaving it gray as ashes.

Mansfield straightened up, then gave a little bow. "Ah, Miss Kate. I hoped to see you later."

"I wish you'd leave, Mr. Mansfield. Father is ill. I must send for Dr. Ravenshaw."

"No, no. I'm all right, Kate," her father said in a weak voice. "Leave us, my dear. I have more business to discuss with Mr. Mansfield."

"Not today. You are not well enough, Father, to talk business with anyone."

"There's such an easy solution to your father's troubles, my dear Kate," Mansfield cut in smoothly, forcefully. "I'm sure you heard what I said to him just before you came in. I want you for my wife. If you agree, then the mortgage will be canceled. The first act after we sign the register will be for me to burn the mortgage I hold on Fairlawn."

Kate was infuriated by his words. Her father had badgered her for weeks about this horrid man. Now he himself had the effrontery to blatantly push his suit when Father was ill. She drew herself up and said with all the dignity she could muster, "Mr. Mansfield, I will never consent to be your wife. I love another."

Her father made a little whimpering sound, and she turned hastily to see him clutching at his chest as if in pain.

"Kate, you'll kill me," he moaned. "Marry the man. It is the only way I can possibly save Fairlawn."

"You are listening to gossip from a common crook," she said. "Wait until Harry comes home before you believe what this man says. He wants to get his hands on Fairlawn—and on me. Well, he won't get either, Father. I dearly love Harry Ravenshaw. I'm going to bear his child."

She said the last defiantly, facing Mansfield. It gave her exquisite delight to see the chagrin on his face, then the rising tide of anger when he realized that she belonged to another, that she had given herself completely and fully to Harry Ravenshaw.

Mansfield had the last word though. He narrowed his cold blue eyes and hurled one word at her. "Whore!" Then he laughed, a blood-chilling sound in that tension-filled room. "A pretty pair you are, father and daughter, both taken in by the likes of clever Harry Ravenshaw, the biggest scamp in Essex County. Don't build any hopes on young Ravenshaw, Kingsley. He's gone. Scarpered. Fled the country ahead of the police. His righteous brother wouldn't make good on those forged stock certificates, so he had to leave or go to jail. So he won't be helping out either of you. You, sir, will lose Fairlawn, as I intend to start foreclosure proceedings immediately." Then he turned the full weight of his fury on Kate. "And you, my dear little slut. You'll bear Harry's bastard all alone. Surely you didn't think he would stand by you under these circumstances. And to think I wanted you for my wife— you, a common whore—to be mistress of Bassett Abbey, mother of my children! You'll wind up on the streets of East London along with Monica Murphy, soliciting sailors off the boats."

He turned and strode from the room. Kate was unaware of the venom of his final look at her, however, for at that moment she heard a horrible rattling sound and saw that her father was having some kind of seizure. She rang for Vinton and knelt beside the chair in which her father sprawled.

"Can't get my breath," he gasped. His lips were blue, his face mottled. His breath came in terrifying gulps. "Pain in my chest—terrible pain—terrib—" He slumped forward as Vinton hurried in.

The butler took one look and rushed across the room.

"Get him onto the floor, Miss Kate." Together they managed to get Kingsley out of the chair and stretched out on the Oriental rug.

"The doctor! Send for Dr. Ravenshaw immediately."

She knew from the look on Vinton's face, though, that

it was too late for the doctor, it was too late for anything in this world. Her father was dead.

By the time Derek got there, breathless from his mad dash of a ride, one of the footmen and a stableboy called in from outside had carried her father's body to his bedroom and placed it carefully on the bed.

"Push back the curtains, give him air," she cried.

"It's too late, Miss Kate," Vinton said sadly. "I've sent for Vera, Miss Kate. Let her take you to your room."

"No, no! Not until Derek gets here," she cried fiercely. "He'll do something for Father. You'll see. He's not dead."

When Derek rushed into the room, he found Kate kneeling beside her father's bed, clinging to the hand that was already chilling in death. It took him only a moment to see that Frederick Kingsley was past any help that he could give him.

Gently he lifted Kate to her feet. "He's dead, my dear. His heart has been bad for some time now. I'd hoped that with quiet he might last longer. What brought on this attack?"

The question loosed a torrent of wild weeping. Derek folded her in his arms, holding her tenderly, allowing her to cry until all her tears were gone.

"It's all my fault," she sobbed. "I killed him. I—he was having this terrible row with Mr. Mansfield—and then I told him—I said—" She broke down again.

Derek picked her up in strong arms and carried her out of the room of death into the hallway. There her little maid Vera was waiting anxiously, eyes wide and troubled under the frilly lace cap she wore.

"Where's Miss Kate's room?" Derek asked.

Vera scurried along the hall, with Derek at her heels. At her room he laid Kate down on the high bed with the white lace canopy, then motioned for the maid to leave them alone.

"You must rest, Kate," he said calmly. "Later, when you feel better, we'll talk. Right now I intend to give you a sleeping draught. Otherwise you'll not be able to get through the next few days. And Kate, remember what I said to you this afternoon. If I can help you in any way, all you have to do is to ask."

She had to know one thing, though, before she would allow Derek to give her the blessed sleeping potion which would take her, for a while, into oblivion.

"Mr. Mansfield said that Harry had forged the stock certificates he'd sold to Father. That's what made Father ill. He said Harry had—had run away, out of the country, to keep from going to jail. It's not so, is it, Derek?"

Then Derek knocked down the last bits of protective wall she had built around herself with the words, "I'm afraid it is. I'd hoped against hope that Kingsley hadn't listened to Harry's blandishments." Then, almost fearfully, he added, "Did your father lose much, Kate?"

"Much?" She laughed hysterically, so that Derek had to grip her shoulders, his fingers biting into her warm flesh, before she grew calm enough to answer. "He's lost everything, I guess. He had Fairlawn mortgaged to Mansfield—and that horrible man threatened to foreclose when I said I wouldn't marry him. Oh, Derek, what am I going to do?"

"Right now you're going to drink this medication and sleep. Don't worry your lovely head about Mr. Mansfield and mortgages. I told you I'd take care of you, Kate, and that's what I intend to do."

He motioned to the butler who stood at the doorway with Derek's black bag in his hands. "A bit of wine, Vinton. I'm going to give Miss Kate a sleeping potion."

"But I have so many things to do—the funeral."

"Later, Kate. Now you must sleep."

As she drifted into black velvet, Kate wondered muzzily what Derek would say if she told him about Harry's baby. Oh, Harry, Harry, she mourned silently, I need you so desperately. Why did you have to leave me now?

CHAPTER 14

Wednesday, February 15, 1888

The day of the funeral dawned bleak and cold. Since her father's death, Kate had been like an automaton, going through the motions of living without actually registering what was going on. Derek had called every day to make sure that she was all right. She had not told him that she was pregnant. Now she wished that she'd not told Mansfield either. It was an act of defiance that had cost her father his life. She was consumed with guilt, prostrate with grief. And always, looming dark and ugly on the horizon, was the fact that Mansfield held the mortgage on Fairlawn. He'd threatened to foreclose. Now that her father was dead, what would he do? Mansfield hadn't put in an appearance at the house, for which Kate was thankful; but he had sent an enormous wreath, ostentatious and common, with a brief note saying he was sorry that Kingsley was dead. Sorry! Kate knew it for a lie. At least, knowing she was carrying Harry's child, he no longer wanted to marry her.

Oh, where was Harry? Rumors had him in Ireland, on the Continent, even on board a ship bound for South America. So far Kate was numb, but she knew that soon the desperation of her situation would strike her. Where could she turn? Derek had offered to help her. Each day when he came to see her, he quietly reassured her.

"You aren't going to lose Fairlawn, Kate. Rest assured of that. I shall not let Arthur Mansfield wrest it from you."

She didn't know what Derek intended to do. She'd been too distraught to ask. There was something solid about him, though, something comforting, which helped to ease her mind. He must know that she'd been seeing Harry. Perhaps he suspected how much she cared for his younger brother. No doubt he saw her as part of the family, even though she had not mentioned the child.

Mr. Quillman, Father's solicitor, sent her a note asking if he could call on her after the funeral to discuss her father's affairs, and she had replied in the affirmative. Perhaps he would know of funds which she could use to pay Mansfield. If she lost Fairlawn, what would she do? Where would she turn? Her father was her only close relative, and now he was gone. All her life Kate had been cosseted, pampered, spoiled by her father. She'd never known a moment's want. If only Harry would return, she'd have no more worries; but he was gone without a trace. She'd had no word from him, no letter, nothing. At times during these days since her father died so suddenly, Kate had despaired. She loved Harry so desperately, and now, when she needed him, he was not here. Derek was being wonderfully kind, but he was a poor substitute for his younger brother.

Kate rose reluctantly. As she slid from the high bed, a wave of nausea swept over her, and she retched over the commode, miserable and weak. Vera came in and found her crouched on the floor and helped her back into bed.

"Oh, mies, it's been too much for you, your dear father dying so sudden like. Lie still for a bit. I'll bring you dry toast and sweet tea to settle your stomach."

Kate wondered how soon Vera would begin to suspect that her mistress was sick for the usual woman's reason. It had nothing to do with her father's death. Instead, it had to do with life—the tiny life developing within her.

Later, dressed for the funeral service in the only black dress she owned, a plain bombazine with high neck and leg-of-mutton sleeves, Kate pinned a black veil over her head. Derek had told her that he would come and escort her to the church. She went down to the parlor, where Father was lying so still and peaceful in his oak coffin, and knelt beside the bier briefly, but no prayers came to her

lips to comfort her. Her father's death placed a terrible
burden on her shoulders, and she was not accustomed
to bearing such loads. She rose, leaned over and kissed
her father's cold forehead one last time, then went into
the drawing room to wait for Derek. The undertakers
came and carried the coffin out to the hearse which was
drawn by four black horses. Derek presented himself,
solemn and watchful, a black armband on out of respect
for her father.

"Are you all right, Kate? I could give you a bit of
laudanum to soothe you—not enough to make you drowsy.
It would help you get through the funeral service."

"I'm all right." She took a deep, shuddering breath.
"I can't go through life taking drugs to help me over
bad times, Derek."

He gave her a shrewd, professional look. "Vera tells
me that you were nauseous this morning. Are you sure
you are up to the ceremonies? This has all been a terrible
shock to you, Kate. With no mother, no brothers or sisters
to turn to, no relatives, I think you may find you are
more deeply affected than you realize. I don't like for you
to be here alone after the service. Why don't you come
to Scarlet Oaks and stay for a few days?"

"No, there is much for me to do here. Mr. Quillman is
coming back here to the house after the service with me
to inform me about Father's business affairs."

"From what you tell me, they are in a disastrous state."

"I shall not let Mansfield have Fairlawn, Derek. And
I will not marry him either."

"Good God, I should hope not!"

"That's what he and Father were planning." Her voice
broke then, and she sobbed bitterly. Derek held her
gently and let her cry until she was calm.

"You aren't marrying Mansfield—and he's not going to
get Fairlawn from you. Trust me, Kate. Come now, it is
time to go to St. Michael's."

Kate survived the funeral. She stood in the drizzling
rain as her father's remains were consigned to the earth.
She endured the crowd of mourners who drove back to
Fairlawn for the repast that Vinton had laid out in the

main dining room. Finally, though, they had all gone except Derek and Mr. Quillman.

"Don't keep Miss Kingsley too long," Derek cautioned the lawyer. "It has been a very trying day for her."

"True, Doctor, but there are matters which I must lay before her immediately."

Kate took the solicitor into Father's study, and they sat there, Quillman behind the huge desk, while she had a side chair pulled up facing him.

"This is very painful for me, Miss Kingsley," Quillman said, fingering his ginger moustache and avoiding her eyes. He was a robust man of about forty, his hair still full and reddish, and he wore his black mourning suit with style. "Did you know that your father had mortgaged Fairlawn?"

"I just learned of it. He was quarreling with Mr. Mansfield when he died."

The solicitor raised his head and gave her one sharp look before burying his nose in the sheaf of papers he had laid out on the leather surface of the desk.

"Mr. Mansfield holds the mortgage. He came to see me yesterday. I'm sorry. He insists that he will foreclose."

"That threat killed my father." Her voice caught, and she had to stop for a moment before she could continue. "I was glad he did not come to the funeral. I might have had difficulty being civil to him."

The lawyer sighed. "He's a hard man, Miss Kingsley. A successful one, but hard. I explained your circumstances to him, and he said he was quite aware of your plight."

Indeed he was, she thought bitterly.

"Is there no money at all?" She hoped that somehow Quillman would wave a magic wand and discover funds which even her poor dead father hadn't known existed.

"I'm afraid your father invested very unwisely. I tried to warn him, indeed I was most vociferous in my pleadings. Even last year young Ravenshaw was engaged in some very shady undertakings. I cautioned your father, God rest his soul, not to buy any stock from the blackguard; but he didn't take my advice. Now everything is gone, and Fairlawn is mortgaged to the hilt."

Kate had known, of course, that this would be the case. No wonder Father had wanted her to marry Mansfield. If she had agreed, it would have averted his ruin. Now it was too late. And Harry was the cause of it all. This was the bitter cup she must drink. Harry had played her father false, and because of him, she now was in this dire plight. Yet, through it all, she still loved him with a consuming passion. It didn't matter to her what he'd done, she loved him.

"I know little of such affairs, but I do know that some of the furnishings here are valuable. The Georgian plate, some of the paintings—" At the look on Quillman's face, a pitying expression, she stopped. "Everything is mortgaged? The furniture? The silver?"

"I'm afraid so, Miss Kingsley. Your father lost ready cash last year; this year he began borrowing from Mansfield. He'd thought to recoup his losses with that stock. If it had been genuine, he might have managed to save Fairlawn. Unfortunately, forged shares benefit no one but the forger."

It was like a body blow to Kate. Harry a forger. Harry the cause of her troubles. Harry—the man she loved.

She took a deep breath, then asked the important question.

"How soon must I give up my home to that—that—"

There was a pained look on Quillman's face. "He was quite vindictive yesterday. I persuaded him, though, that it would look bad if he insisted on taking your home immediately. It would cause a lot of talk in the county."

"I dare say," she said drily. "How long, Mr. Quillman?"

"A month." He looked up and she once again saw pity in his eyes. "I wish it were longer."

Kate laughed, a short, bitter little sound. "It doesn't really matter, does it? A day, a week, a month—it's all the same. I lose my home and everything in it. Will he at least allow me the clothes on my back, or must I leave nude as Lady Godiva?"

"I'm sure he'll let you keep your personal belongings, Miss Kingsley," he muttered, flushing at her racy language.

Knowing Mansfield as she did, Kate wasn't at all sure that he'd leave her even a shift to cover her nakedness.

After Quillman left, she wandered over the house, touching a china plate here, a silver candlestick there. All gone. She didn't understand the intricacies of finance, but now she had to pay the price for her father's folly. She couldn't despise him though. He had tried to arrange her future for her. If only he had taken her into his confidence, they might have made more suitable plans. Too late, too late!

Very well, she would have no choice but to turn to Derek for the help he kept offering. In a flash of insight, Kate realized that there would be a price she'd have to pay for saving her home. Derek wasn't doing it because she loved his brother. Derek couldn't abide Harry. He'd refused to make good Harry's debts. If he'd settled the stock scandal, Father might yet be alive. Her mouth thinned with resentment. It realy boiled down to this: Harry's problems were a direct result of Derek's tight hand with his purse. If he'd not kept Harry constantly strapped for funds, her beloved would not have had to sail closer and ever closer to the wind to try to have money in his pocket. Now she'd have to give something, she didn't know what, to Derek as payment for his help.

Overtired from the funeral service, the guests, and the session with the solicitor, Kate climbed wearily to her bedchamber and rang for Vera.

"I think I'll disrobe and get ready to retire. I know, it's very early; but it has been a difficult day, Vera."

"Yes, miss. We're all so sorry for you, Miss Kate."

Kate was ready to burst into tears at the little maid's welcome sympathy. All too soon she'd have to tell Vera that she must seek another position. She'd wait though. Maybe, through some miracle that Derek might manage, she'd not have to do without a ladies' maid. If only Harry could return rich, without the cloud over him. Then they could pay off the mortgage and live happily ever after at Fairlawn.

When Kate was clad in a long, fine linen nightgown with hand embroidery at the neck and turned-back cuffs with lace to match the lace-edged capelets over long sleeves, she let Vera brush out her red hair and tie it back with a blue ribbon. Then she put on a wrapper of blue cashmere with jabot and frills of cream lace. A satin sash of dark blue draped to one side, the ends hanging to the pleated hem ruffle of the robe. She reclined on a chaise and let Vera rub her temples with cologne to relax her.

She had almost dozed off when there was a discreet tap at the door and Vera let in Vinton.

"A caller, Miss Kate. Most insistent." He offered a small silver tray with a calling card centered on it. The engraved card said simply: Arthur Mansfield, Esq.

"I can't see him. As you can see, I've retired for the night, Vinton."

The old butler hesitated. "Yes, Miss Kate, but he said it was most important that he see you today. He's—he's very persistent, miss."

Kate knew that she'd have to see him, much as she hated the idea. "Very well, tell him I'll be down directly. Show him into the small parlor. Tell him that I am very tired and can give him only a few minutes of my time."

Vera asked, "What shall you wear, Miss Kate?"

"Something easy. I'll not bother with stays, Vera. The mauve morning dress should do admirably." It was one of her most unbecoming gowns. Quite good enough for Mansfield.

Her unwelcome guest was standing in front of the fire when she went in.

"I find this most unkind of you," she said, moving to the attack the moment she was inside the parlor. "You know that my dear father was buried today."

"No use in waiting, Kate. I've come to a decision about you."

"Indeed! You may own this house, sir, but you don't own me. I find your words an affront."

He moved a step toward her, but she held her ground.

"As to owning you, that is exactly what I intend to do. I know what your situation is now." He smiled a smug, hateful smile. "You are destitute. You are pregnant by a cad who has left the country one jump ahead of the sheriff. I intend to have you for myself."

"You're mad. If this is why you've come, leave now." She drew herself up to her imperious best and stared him down. "I have no intention of marrying you."

He threw back his head and laughed then, laughed until Kate wanted to slap him. "Marry me! Oh, listen to the fancy talk from the elegant little whore. I have no intention of marrying you now, my pretty Kate. Marry Harry Ravenshaw's doxy? The slut who is carrying his child? I wanted you for my wife when I thought you were pure and innocent, a decent woman worthy of that honor. Now you are sullied, a fallen woman. I have my reputation to think of. No, I'm not suggesting marriage. I think a more suitable arrangement is for me to allow you to stay on here in Fairlawn as my mistress. I'm being very generous with you. You will not be humiliated by having a public foreclosure on your father's property. I will have it arranged discreetly. You can keep on the staff you have. I may even add more. There will be times when I shall prefer entertaining here, rather than at Bassett Abbey. Intimate parties, to entertain gentlemen with whom I do business. The type of party to which their wives will not be invited." He leered suggestively.

"What a rotten suggestion." Her voice dripped loathing, disgust. "Get out. Until the legal matters are settled, you don't own this house. And you never will. I have the money to pay off your mortgage."

There, she was committed. She only hoped that Derek would make good on his affirmations to her. If she had to be in debt to one man or the other, it would have to be Derek. Much as she was annoyed with him over his treatment of Harry, at least he was a decent person, not like the oily, revolting Mansfield.

At her words Mansfield's cold blue eyes narrowed. "Fancy words from a fancy woman. And where do you intend to get the sum you'd need to pay off your enormous debt to me? Go on the streets of Whitechapel? I assure you, Kate, those wretched creatures offer their bodies for pennies. It would take you the rest of your natural life to earn enough to buy me off."

"Get out. Get out of my house this instant!" Her voice raised hysterically.

Instead, Mansfield strode across the room and caught Kate in his arms, crushing her against his lustful body. "Mine. You're going to be mine—now. I won't wait another moment for you. I've wanted you from the moment I set eyes on you, and I intend to have you before I leave this house."

Kate knew real fear. There was a glazed look in Mansfield's blue eyes, a mindless quality that terrified her. Unless she could fight him off, or get help, Mansfield would rape her. She struggled valiantly; but he had caught her so that her arms were pinned, and she couldn't free her hands to beat at him or claw his face. She tried to kick him. Her skirt was so heavy and long that it protected his shins from the toes of her slippers. His kisses were so intense that she was left almost suffocated. Then, still immobilizing her body with one arm, which felt like an iron band around her, he began ripping at the high neckline of her dress, his fingers sliding between fabric and throat, and then getting a firm grip on the neck of the gown. With one mighty tug he tore the gown from neckline to waist with a ripping sound, baring her full bosom to his lips.

This had one saving feature. As he began to kiss her breasts and nuzzle them, it freed her mouth. There was no chance for her to get to the bellpull, but now she could scream. Somewhere far away she heard a bell ring and realized it was the front door of Fairlawn, but her immediate situation took all of her attention. Mansfield was now so aroused, so inflamed with lust, that he was trying to wrestle her to the floor to take her there, at once.

She opened her mouth to scream; but found that she could not make a sound, she was so frightened and overwrought from Mansfield's brutal attack. Again his hand ripped her gown, this time pulling it from her shoulders so that she was nude to the waist, for she had dressed hurriedly, having Vera leave off her stays and corset cover.

She fought him with a desperate strength, but Kate knew that without help, he would have his way with her, being so much stronger than she. Again she tried to cry out, and this time her voice did not betray her.

"Help!" she called. "Help me, someone!"

It was all she had time to scream, for he caught the back of her neck with his free hand and squeezed it cruelly, pressing her face against his waistcoat so harshly that she thought the imprint of the buttons would permanently mark her face.

"Be quiet, little whore!" he gasped. "This isn't new to you. Quit fighting me and give me the pleasure you've given young Ravenshaw."

Kate was afraid she was going to faint, her nose was held so tightly against his body. If she lost consciousness, she knew he would rape her before she recovered. All was lost.

Then there was a terrible, inarticulate cry of rage from somewhere near, and before she had a chance to know what was happening, Mansfield gave a horrible, gargling yell and let go of her so suddenly that she slumped to the floor in a heap.

Towering over her stood Derek Ravenshaw, his face flushed dark with rage. He had a strangle hold on Mansfield, pulling back the older man's head so that his already protuberant eyes seemed ready to pop from his head. With the pressure he was applying to Mansfield's windpipe, Kate feared that Mansfield would die of either suffocation or a broken neck.

She crawled across the floor and reached up, catching at Derek's arm. "No, Derek, don't kill him. He's not worth the grief his death would cause you."

At first Derek seemed not to hear her; but when she tugged sharply at his sleeve, he finally came to his senses and let go of Mansfield, who quickly scrabbled out of the reach of Derek's iron grip.

Mansfield stood backed up against the marble-topped table and massaged his bruised neck. The air in the little parlor was charged with tension, almost crackling with energy.

Derek picked Kate up from the floor and helped her pull her shredded gown about her to cover her naked breasts.

"Are you all right, Kate?" he asked, his voice hoarse with emotion.

"Yes." She didn't trust herself to utter more than that one confirming word.

"Get out of here, Mansfield," Derek ordered. "If you ever set foot on Fairlawn again, I swear I'll kill you."

Mansfield's face was mottled with suppressed emotion.

"This is my property," Mansfield said angrily. "I hold the mortgage."

"Which will be paid in full."

"And where is Kate going to find ten thousand pounds?" Mansfield sneered. "If she stayed on her back the rest of her natural life, she'd not earn that amount."

Kate heard Derek make a sound in his throat more like an animal growl than a human utterance. "Damn you, Mansfield—" His hands balled into fists, and he stepped toward the slumlord, menacing him.

Quickly Kate stepped between the two men. "Please, Derek, no fighting. Just tell him to leave."

"You heard the lady. Get out, and don't come back. Be thankful you're leaving with all your teeth still in your rotten mouth. You'll have a check to pay the mortgage in full by next Monday. Tell your solicitor to have all the papers drawn up, ready. Now, leave while I still have a rein on my temper."

Bested, Arthur Mansfield walked to the door, not hurrying; but Kate noticed that he kept watch on Derek out of the corner of his eye. He had the door to the drawing room open and had stepped out into the passageway, when he turned back, his face full of malice.

"Kate seems to have a liking for Ravenshaw men. She's carrying your no-good brother's child in her belly—now you will be sampling her charms. But remember this, Ravenshaw, she's just as much a whore as those drabs who frequent your ridiculous clinic on Union Row."

Derek was moving toward him, fists ready to give him a thorough trouncing; but Mansfield moved nimbly, slamming the door shut in Derek's face.

"Derek, let him go," Kate pleaded, reaction now setting in. She sank onto a walnut-framed loveseat padded with blue floral upholstery fabric and leaned forward, face in hands.

From across the room, Derek's voice was accusing. "Is what he said true, Kate? Are you pregnant?"

In a voice so still she could scarcely hear it herself, Kate answered, "It's true. When will Harry return, Derek?" She looked up at him, appalled to find his face closed, remote, cold. She could see the mortgage money flying away on the wings of eagles. Mansfield would fore-close, and she'd have to leave Fairlawn.

"I don't know anything about my rotten brother. Oh, Kate, how could you? So lovely, so desirable—and you let Harry—" He stopped as if it pained him to say more.

Defiantly she told Derek, "I love him."

"Well, he doesn't love you." The words were harsh as whip lashes. "Harry loves no one but himself. I suppose that was why Mansfield tried to force you—he thought that as you'd bedded Harry, you'd bed anyone. Is that how it is, Kate? Are you already on the same path as Monica Murphy?"

"What a rotten thing to say to me." She rose, holding her gown together as best she could, and moved toward the door with dignity. "I love Harry. He's the only man I've ever loved. I don't care whether you believe me or not."

He blocked her way, standing in front of the door.

"Please stand aside, Derek. I am very tired. This has been a terrible evening. I have a lot to think about. I must make plans to leave Fairlawn."

"Leave Fairlawn? Why? I told you I would pay off the mortgage."

"And what is your price, Derek? I thought you were doing it because I loved your brother—but then I remembered that you hate him, you always have. You've kept your hands on the money, keeping poor Harry so strapped that he has been pushed into these shady dealings. So if you are going to redeem Fairlawn, it will be for a price. What?"

His mouth hardened, his eyes were like black lumps of hard coal. "So I'm to blame for Harry's derelictions. I suppose I told him to get you pregnant and then abandon you."

"He hasn't abandoned me! He didn't know about the child. He had to leave to keep from going to prison." Her eyes filled with tears. "And what do you care about that? You could have shared your wealth with him, but did you? No! And you refused to make good on his stock, so that he had to flee or be jailed."

"He's a crook," Derek yelled at her. "He ruined your

father. He brought on the fatal heart attack. And you still love the rat? Kate, Kate, he's not interested in you except for one reason—lying with you. If you'd told him you were bearing his child, he'd have run to the ends of the earth to escape you."

"You don't know that! Harry is lovable, kind, wonderful. You're jealous that he's younger, more handsome—that he is popular with the women."

"I've never had any trouble finding women," Derek said drily.

"They just want your title or your money," Kate spat. "Now, tell me what price I'll have to pay in order to save Fairlawn."

"It's very simple. You have to become Mrs. Ravenshaw."

"I intend to, the minute Harry is able to come back."

"You deliberately misunderstand me, Kate. Don't provoke me too far. It hasn't been a very good day for me either. I shall pay off the mortgage. You will marry me. The child—the child will be raised as if it were my own, with full inheritance rights to the combined properties of Fairlawn and Scarlet Oaks, and the hereditary baronetcy."

Kate was stunned. Marry Derek? Never. She was Harry's.

"I can't marry you—I'm pledged to Harry."

He moved toward her, stopping just short of touching her. "Kate, listen to me, and listen carefully. Harry is gone. He's a rotter, and has always been from the moment he was born. He's been in other scrapes before, and I've bought off his creditors, kept him out of prison. The last time, I warned him that there'd be no more help from me. I tried to get him into some sort of work suitable to his talents—he's not stupid, just lazy. I sent him to medical school, but he didn't bother to study, so he was sent down. He's no good and never will be. He's gone; he's not coming back. You'll bear your child all alone—a bastard. I am offering you and the child my name. I will raise it to be my own child—this I promise you. But you have no choice. I will pay off Mansfield, and I will take care of you—but you are right—I have my price. You will be my wife."

"I don't love you, Derek."

"You don't now, but I don't care. I will teach you to love me, Kate, if you'll only give me the chance."

"I shall never love any man but Harry."

"Then ours will be a loveless marriage. But marriage it will be. You have no choice. Without my help, you are destitute. Mansfield will foreclose, and you will have no place to go—unless he plans to set you up here as his mistress." Her face gave her away. "Never! I won't let that slimy monster have you, Kate."

She was trapped and she knew it. Unless Harry returned soon, she had no choice. It was Mansfield's filthy offer or marriage to Derek. Kate knew that she'd have to accept the latter, although it angered and frustrated her to be forced into wedlock with Derek to save her home and her good name.

"Very well, Derek, I shall marry you. But I tell you now, I will never love you. And when Harry returns, I shall leave you and go with him."

He did not look overjoyed, but there was satisfaction on his face. "Very well. But I am not going to stay awake nights worrying about what I'll do when Harry returns to claim my bride. He's gone for good. Without money to pay off the people he swindled, he can't return." He walked to the bell pull and gave it a tug. "You must rest now, Kate. Would you like for me to give you a sleeping potion?"

"No."

"I will see you tomorrow, and we will plan the wedding. It will be done quickly and quietly, because of your condition. If anyone asks, I can say that it is because you are in mourning for your father."

Vinton came then, and Derek told him to see that his mistress's maid came to her here in the parlor. "Tell her to bring a robe, Vinton." When the butler had gone, Derek said, "Goodnight, dear Kate, until tomorrow."

He didn't try to kiss her when he left, for which she was glad.

CHAPTER 15

Monday, March 5, 1888

Kate's wedding day dawned bright and fair. Although it was only early March, there was a feel of spring in the air, a softness of breeze, a haze of green over the willows by the brook, that promised an end to winter soon. It should have been the happiest day of her life; but to Kate, it was the saddest, worse even than the day of her father's funeral three weeks ago. Instead of marrying her beloved Harry, she was tying herself for life to Derek. Kate knew she should be grateful to the baronet for rescuing her from a desperate situation; but all she felt was resentment that he had exacted such a price for keeping her out of the clutches of Arthur Mansfield.

Hoping against hope that somehow Harry would acquire the necessary cash to pay his debts and be able to return to Scarlet Oaks, Kate insisted on having a church wedding, although Derek recommended a quiet home wedding by special license because of her pregnancy.

"The sooner the better, Kate. As it is, there'll be talk. I can arrange things so that we can be married this week. The excuse for the type of ceremony will be, of course, your father's death."

She set her heels. "No. If I'm to be married to you, I shall do it properly. In St. Michael's. With the vicar publishing the banns for the prescribed three Sundays."

It gave Kate a brief moment of pleasure to see how annoyed Derek was at her words.

"You forget you are expecting a child," he said coldly. "The sooner the wedding takes place, the less talk there'll be when the baby arrives early."

"There will be talk either way. At least if we have a church wedding, they won't whisper that we hid away from our friends because we were ashamed. It's not as if I showed, Derek. No one will guess I'm with child."

She was adamant. Finally he capitulated; but he went immediately to the vicar and told him of the marriage, asking that the banns be published starting that first Sunday after the funeral, February eighteenth. It gave Kate too little time to wait for Harry's return. She had gone to church the three Sundays in a row, sitting with Derek, ignoring the stares of the surprised parishioners.

The Duchess of Dorminster had called on the Monday after the first calling of the banns.

"Glad to see you are using your head for something other than an ornament, Kate," the old woman said bluntly. "Derek's a good man. I was afraid you'd settled for the brother."

Kate kept silent, not trusting herself to answer.

"Wish you'd keep up the help you were giving me in Whitechapel," the duchess added.

"Derek doesn't approve of my going to the East End."

"I'll speak to him about that. No reason you can't do good works there just the same as he does."

"I—I would rather not go just now," Kate said. She was feeling worse every morning, and she had no desire to do good works feeling so queasy.

"Well, I suppose a funeral and a wedding on its heels can be time- and energy-consuming. But later, when you have a chance to settle down . . ."

Kate had to bite her lips to keep down hysterical laughter. What would the duchess do if she told her that later she'd be, literally, in no shape to work with the Whitechapel harlots?

I am just as much a whore as they, Kate thought. I have sold myself to Derek to escape from my problems. I have no right to judge Monica, Liz, and the others.

Pam had stopped by Fairlawn the week after the funeral, and Kate asked her to stand with her at the wedding.

Pam's gray eyes widened in shock. "What wedding? Has Harry——" She stopped short, knowing very well that Harry had absconded.

"I'm marrying Derek." Kate's voice was defiant, but she couldn't bring herself to look Pam in the eye when she told her.

"Derek! But, I thought——"

"There are good reasons why I'm doing this, Pam." She didn't dare tell even her best friend the truth.

"Derek is a better marriage bet than Arthur Mansfield," Pam said with surprising aplomb. "Probably he'll make a better husband than Harry would."

"Pam, that's cruel."

Pam put her arms about Kate. "It's true, Kate. I know you love Harry—but he is gone, and I doubt that he'll be returning to England. As he didn't take you with him, what can you do? You can't sit about forever, a spinster, waiting for Harry to send for you. No, you've done the wise thing. I don't know your financial situation now," she went on delicately, "but Derek is quite well-to-do.

He's ten thousand pounds poorer now, Kate thought bitterly. He's paid a pretty price for me, and I should be grateful. I'm not though. I resent being bought like a slave on the auction block. It is degrading. I shall always despise Derek for forcing me to marry him.

She put on a good face though. With so little time, she had practically no trousseau. It didn't matter. She still was in mourning for Father. She'd wear a white wedding gown, of course, although she was scarcely a virgin! But there'd be no balls or society affairs for months to come. All she'd soon need would be maternity gowns. She didn't tell Pam that she'd not be able to attend her in June. By then she'd be big as a barrel. Soon enough to break the news to Pam after the flurry about the wedding quieted down. Pam could think the child was Derek's, conceived immediately after the wedding. She might suspect—but with Kate legally wed, she probably would never mention any suspicions to her friend.

Mrs. Beadnell, a dressmaker from Chelmsford, came out to Fairlawn to sew Kate's wedding dress, a very plain style of heavy white satin trimmed with yards of Brussels lace. It had a high collar with lace edging, leg-of-mutton sleeves with lace insets and cuffs, and a large bustle with the overskirt draped high over it. The underskirt was of matching lace with a small train. On her head she pinned a small veil of the same white Brussels lace as that used on the gown, with a wreath of orange blossoms from the Duchess of Dorminster's conservatory to crown her russet hair.

Derek gave her a string of matched pearls, which had belonged to his mother, as a wedding gift, and she gave him a diamond stickpin for his cravat, the only bit of jewelry her father had left after selling off items one at a time for ready cash in the past year. Derek looked quite handsome in a morning coat, but Kate could only think how poorly he came off when compared with Harry.

Even until the carriage arrived to take her to the church, Kate kept hoping that Harry would appear miraculously and whisk her away with him. When, during the ceremony, the vicar asked if anyone knew of a reason why they should not be joined in holy matrimony, Kate wanted to cry out, "I don't love this man!" But she kept silent, repeated her vows, and accepted the plain gold wedding ring from Derek. The vicar pronounced them man and wife, and Derek kissed her for the first time, a chaste kiss, suitable for public viewing. She submitted to it, but did not return it. She thought Derek looked angry when they signed the register, but Kate didn't care.

The wedding breakfast was served at Fairlawn, although Derek had suggested having it at Scarlet Oaks.

"No, it should be at the bride's home, Derek." She was adamant. Kate wanted to put off her journey to Scarlet Oaks as Derek's wedded wife as long as she possibly could. There were few guests at the breakfast, which Vinton served in the main dining room. Pam and Alfie were there, as well as a Captain Coleridge, Derek's best man. The vicar and his wife; the Duchess of Dorminster, escorted by Lord Wimbley; and one or two others, including Derek's aunt, Lady Letitia Zangwill, made up the party. Cook had made a wedding cake with a tiny groom's cake on top, which Kate and Derek cut with Captain Coleridge's dress saber, and everyone toasted the couple with

champagne. Through it all Kate kept a social smile pasted
on her face until she felt that her cheek muscles might
freeze in that position. She saw Lady Zangwill peering
at her through her lorgnette throughout the breakfast. The
woman was a dried-up little witch with an indomitable
will. Kate knew instinctively that Lady Letitia didn't like
her, didn't trust her, and would be her sworn enemy at
Scarlet Oaks. She sat ensconced in a highbacked walnut
chair, allowing herself to be waited on.

Derek took Kate with him when Vinton carried a piece
of wedding cake to his aunt, and sat his new wife down
beside his elderly aunt.

"So, married at last," she said, looking at Kate with
distaste plain on her wrinkled face. "Didn't bring much
dowry with you, I understand."

Derek answered quickly, before Kate had a chance to
retort to this unfriendly remark, "I acquire Fairlawn,
Auntie. It joins my property, and increases my estate con-
siderably."

"What do you need with two houses in the country?"
the old woman persisted. She was dressed all in black,
wedding or no, still in mourning for her husband who had
died forty years earlier, when they had been married only
a few years.

Sweetly Kate said, "Perhaps Derek thinks you won't
enjoy having a new niece at Scarlet Oaks, and will prefer
to live here." There, let the old hag swallow that!

"I came to Scarlet Oaks when Derek was a young lad,
and that rascally Harry was a babe. It's my home, Kate."

The battle lines were drawn. Quickly Derek led Kate
to bid goodbye to the vicar and his elegant wife, who were
leaving.

"Please don't antagonize Aunt Letitia, Kate," Derek said
quietly. "She has a fearful temper, and she can be quite
spiteful when annoyed."

"She resents your having married me. Now I'm the mistress of Scarlet Oaks, and she is relegated to the position
of poor relation," Kate said with spirit. "No woman would
be good enough for you, according to your Aunt Letitia.
Very well, I shall try not to quarrel with her; but I give
you fair warning, Derek, neither shall I let her make a

door mat of me. You have chosen to force me into this marriage. Very well, then, I shall insist upon my prerogatives as mistress of Scarlet Oaks. Lady Letitia will have to come to terms with that fact." Then she turned a sweet smile on the vicar, accepted a kiss on the cheek from his wife, and thanked them for attending the breakfast.

Kate and Derek had not made firm plans concerning Fairlawn. He agreed to keep the house open, at least for the present, so that the staff would not be left without positions. Vera would, of course, come to Scarlet Oaks with her mistress as her personal maid. All else would be settled later.

The breakfast finally came to an end, and all the guests departed. Even Lady Letitia was sent on to Scarlet Oaks in a brougham. For the first time since their wedding, Kate and Derek were alone together.

Kate remained aloof. She was legally wed to Derek; but she felt no more his wife than she had before the vicar said the words over them and blessed the union. She was Harry's.

"Come, Kate, let's go home," Derek said eagerly.

"Home? I am home."

She saw the quick flash of annoyance on his handsome face, and inwardly she was happy, although she made sure that her emotions did not show on her face. She sensed an iron will in Derek, which it would be wise not to challenge too directly.

"You are now Lady Kate Ravenshaw of Scarlet Oaks. Do not forget it. I have married you to rescue you from an intolerable situation. In return, I expect certain things from you. You shall not dishonor my name, which is an old and honorable one, the baronetcy having originated in the early seventeenth century. I shall demand conduct of you befitting the name."

"Oh, you have surely bought me, Derek. I shall be your proper slave." She said it angrily.

"No, not slave, Kate. You are my wife, because I love you; I have loved you for a long time, and I have been determined that you would one day be my wife." She stood there, stunned, as he smiled complacently at her.

"So, as the admirable Mr. Shakespeare says, 'Kiss me, Kate.'"

He caught her to him and kissed her with an authority that stunned her senses. If it hadn't been for Harry, she might have found his kiss exciting; but Kate loved only his brother. Married she might be to Derek, tied to him for life, God help her; but she didn't have to pretend to enjoy it.

"Oh, Kate, Kate, I want you so desperately," he was murmuring, and his hand moved to her full breast for a more intimate embrace.

She didn't try to pull away from him, but mentally she retreated. It was obvious to Derek that she did not enjoy his caresses.

Angrily he said, "You're my wife, damn it, Kate. Act like one. It's not as if you were a virgin!"

She wanted to slap him. "That's just what Mansfield said to me when he tried to rape me," she spat. "He wanted to buy me from poor Father. You've bought me just as surely as he would have. You're alike, the two of you."

His face flushed with anger. "Don't ever again compare me with that filth," he said, his voice cold and harsh. "Never. I'll put up with some nonsense from you, Kate, because I love you. But I will not be compared with Mansfield."

She knew she'd gone too far, but Kate was too proud to apologize to her husband. She had her pride, too, and he must learn this if they were to have any kind of marriage. At least he no longer was holding and caressing her.

"Let us go to Scarlet Oaks, then," she said.

The carriage ride in the closed victoria was a silent one. She wore a short fur coat over her wedding gown, and she had removed the veil and orange blossom wreath so that she could put on a little matching hat of fur to keep out the cold March wind that had come up. The sun was now behind a bank of dark clouds. The wedding day, which had dawned so bright and fair, now more nearly matched Kate's bleak mood.

She had to feel a sense of pleasure, though, as they drove up to Scarlet Oaks through the long line of trees that gave the house its name. It was a graceful mansion built in the Queen Anne style, with wings on either side. The house was of mellow brick, almost entirely covered with ivy whose bare tendrils swayed in the rising March wind. The driveway made a circle in front of the house, and the carriage drew up before the front door. A footman in tan livery placed a dismounting stool for Kate and assisted her from the carriage. The whole staff lined the steps leading up to the front entrance. They bowed and curtsied as Kate started up the steps, and the butler, Parsons, murmured, "Welcome, Lady Ravenshaw."

At the door, to her chagrin, Derek swept her up into his arms and carried her over the threshold to the delight of the servants, who cheered lustily.

"Derek, put me down. I feel like a fool."

"Why should you? It's customary for the bride to be carried over the threshold. Custom started back in Roman times—and you know what a Roman heritage there is here in Britain."

Not only did he not put her down, he carried her up the grand staircase from the large entrance hall to the upper floor and into what was obviously his own bedchamber.

"I thought—won't I have a room of my own?" she asked, dismayed.

"This is the master bedchamber. I am the master. You are my wife." Finally, anger building again, he set her on her feet. "And there, dear wife, is our bed, which we will occupy together."

The bed was an old-fashioned one of black oak, with massive carved posts holding up a canopy not of fabric, but of ornately worked wood done in delicate cut-outs. The head of the bed was in squares, each one a shadow box with figures from mythological tales in bold relief. The wallpaper was contemporary, a dark red with a stylized floral pattern of gold on it. At the foot of the bed was a small lounge with a raised back of spool design, with caning. There was a fine white marble fireplace with mantelpiece, but it had been converted to burn gas rather than wood. The carpet was a darker red than the wallpaper, with a similar design worked all over, except for a border and fringe of solid gold. The bathroom was through a door covered with the same paper as the walls.

Derek rang for Vera, and ordered, "Your mistress should have some rest, Vera. It has been a tiring day for her. Please get her ready for bed." To Kate, he said quietly, "I'll be back shortly, when you are changed."

Feeling rebellious, and not at all interested in going to bed in the afternoon, Kate put off removing her wedding gown until she had examined the room and the adjoining bath.

Vera, peering over her shoulder, said, "Oh, miss, it is the fanciest bath I've ever seen!"

The little maid did not exaggerate. The tube was enclosed in carved oak, with a built-in shower bath as ornate as the pulpit of a cathedral. Behind the tub was a wall of tiles decorated with flowers and exotic birds in flight. The faucet over the wash basin was fully two feet high, of polished brass, pouring into a marble basin enclosed in the same ornately carved oak as the tub cover. The water closet pulled out from its cupboard on an ingenious arrangement of hinges. It, too, was completely encased in the oak which was found throughout the bath. The ceiling was beamed, the floor covered in large, octagonal tiles of blue and white.

"Sir Derek must be very rich to be able to afford this," Vera breathed in awe. "There's even a bath for the maids in the attics. But," she giggled, "our water closet is plain porcelain, not one with blue irises on it like this."

Finally, though, the marvels of the bathroom exhausted, Kate had to submit to Vera's ministrations. The wedding gown was carefully removed, the bustle, stays, and corset cover unfastened, and the shift and drawers shed.

"I think I shall have a bath," Kate announced. That would keep Derek waiting!

Vera drew her bath, made sure there were soft towels ready for her, and perfumed soap available, and then left Kate to her privacy. Luxuriating in the tub of hot water, Kate relaxed, happy for the first time that day. When there was a tap on the door, she called, "Come," thinking it would be her maid. To her surprise, she found that it was Derek, wearing a hooded bathrobe of blue-striped wool tied with a cord.

"Aren't you through with your bath yet, wife?" He picked up one of the towels and held it out to her.

Kate, meanwhile, had tried to cover her bare breasts with her arms, stunned that Derek had invaded her privacy in this fashion.

"If you'll leave, I'll get out of my tub," she said, tight-lipped and furious.

"I have no intention of leaving. You are my wife. And under the circumstances, such modesty is unwarranted."

She was appalled. She'd realized, of course, that he would expect her to be his wife in every sense of the word; but knowing this and being placed in the present situation were two different things. She felt that Derek was a stranger. To get out of the tub, to stand nude before him, went against the grain. If it were Harry—ah, but it wasn't Harry. Very well, he'd stand there, adamant, until the water in the tub was icy. She was quickly learning that her new husband had a stubborn streak as wide as his whole being. Kate reached for a towel, hoping to protect herself from his hot eyes; but he anticipated her, and took the towel himself, shaking it open.

"Come, my lovely Kate, I'll dry you and then I shall take you to bed."

"But it's not bedtime!" she protested.

"It is for us." Again that implacable tone that she now knew she must obey.

She stood there nude, her red hair tied up with a blue ribbon to keep it dry, while Derek patted her dry with a tender touch. Then, as she reached for the blue robe, he said, "You won't need that, Kate." He caught her up in his arms and carried her into the bedroom.

"Vera will—" she protested.

"Vera will not interrupt us." He laid her on the huge bed which Vera had turned down, apparently at his bidding. Then he threw off the robe he was wearing, and Kate found that he had nothing on under it, not even a nightshirt. His body was strong and muscular, heavier than Harry's by about a stone. There was something vital and very masculine about him, an animal something, which she'd not noticed when she was with Harry.

He joined her on the bed, and wooed her with skill and tenderness; but Kate loved only Harry, and she effectively turned off her senses, not allowing herself to be roused by his expert lovemaking. She submitted. That was all. When it was over, she turned away from him onto her side and pulled the bedclothes up over her to hide her nakedness.

"Kate, I love you very much," he said.

She didn't answer.

He sat up, then reached over and turned her roughly to face him. His face was angry, not joyous as it should have been.

"How much pleasure do you think I get from that when you make no response?" he demanded.

"I didn't guarantee you pleasure," she snapped. "I married you under protest. I don't love you, and you knew it from the very beginning. If I don't please you, you will just have to go elsewhere for satisfaction."

"I don't care to consort with whores," he said angrily. "I have a legal wife, and I expect more from her than submission."

"Then you are in for a bitter disappointment."

He caught her by the shoulders and pulled her up close to him, shaking her angrily. "If I hadn't married you, what would you have done? Become Arthur Mansfield's mistress? Gone on the streets? You're expecting a child, you need love and care. You would never get it from that rotten brother of mine; so I offered everything to you—Fairlawn, honorable marriage, love—and what do I get in return?"

"Me," she said bitterly. "You've already had me. You've satisfied your lust. What more do you expect of me? Surely you don't expect me to love you, after what you've done. You drove my dear Harry to a life of crime by being so stingy with him. If he'd not been strapped constantly, he'd not—"

"I don't want to hear another word from you about Harry. He's no good, he's always been that way. I've bought him out of scrapes for years, I've paid off serving girls and village wenches when he got them pregnant—

surely you don't think you're the only one, Kate! He has bastards scattered from Colchester to London."

"That's a lie!"

"No, God help me, it's the truth. And he'd not have married you either, my dearest one. Oh, why did you listen to him? Why didn't you see through his blandishments, his false promises?"

"I love him, Derek. I don't love you. And I never will."

"If I thought that—" He stopped, his voice unhappy. Then, softly he said, pleading, "I love you so much, Kate. I'd do anything on earth to make you happy. Won't you at least try to love me?"

"Love isn't something you command. I can't produce the emotion like a magician pulling a rabbit out of a hat. I already love one man desperately. I haven't enough love in my entire being to have any left over for you, Derek."

With a groan he caught her to him and covered her face with hot kisses, sliding his eager lips down her throat, just as Harry always did. He cupped one firm breast with his hand and kissed it passionately. To her horror, Kate found that her treacherous body was beginning to respond to his nearness, his maleness. Quickly she did what she'd done earlier, turned off her mind, detached her thoughts from her body which longed for love from her darling Harry. Again she submitted to Derek's demands, but she did not cooperate. By sheer strength of character, she managed not to let his ardent loving wake her woman's responses. That would be the final travesty, to lie here with Derek, wanting only Harry, yet responding to his older brother's skillful wooing.

Later, dressed in their robes, they had a wedding supper served to them in bed by a smiling Parsons and an underfootman, while Vera hovered in the background, eager to be part of this supposedly joyous occasion. At least in front of the servants, she veiled her antagonism toward her husband. Kate didn't want them gossiping about her belowstairs.

Sometime during the night, she woke to find that Derek wasn't in bed. Instead he sat at a small desk of bird's-eye maple fashioned in imitation-bamboo styling. He had lighted a small oil lamp which he had shielded with a fireplace screen he'd pulled up between the lamp and the bed so that the light wouldn't disturb Kate. She saw that he was writing in a book of some sort. What a curious thing to do in the middle of the night. While she watched, he blotted the page, then pulled open the desk drawer, put the book inside, and turned a brass key in the lock. Secrets! Then he blew out the lamp, cupping a hand about the top of the chimney. In a moment he was getting back into bed. Kate feigned sleep, even when he reached over and pulled her close to him. Eventually she did go back to sleep, only to dream of shadowy figures writing with ostrich plume pens in huge books of doom.

Journal entry. Tuesday, March 6, 1888. 2 A.M.

>   *My lovely Kate sleeps. Finally she is mine, completely, utterly. I have possessed her body, which I have burned to possess for such a long time.*
>   *If Harry were here, I might kill him for what he has done to her.*
>   *This should be the most joyous day of my life, but in truth I am bitterly disappointed. I knew that she was no virgin. I knew she carried Harry's child. But I did not expect her to lie there, unresponding, like a wax doll.*
>   *I shall teach her to love me, to respond to me as I know she has responded to Harry. If only the child she bears were my own. But I have promised her that I shall call it mine, and I must try to school myself to love it, to forget that it was conceived before I wed her. It will not be an easy task, for I am consumed with jealousy of my hated younger brother who despoiled my Kate, and I wish I did not have to be saddled with the fruit of his passion.*
>   *Kate, my darling Kate, I shall never cease striving to overcome your indifference, to make you respond to me in love just as you have responded to Harry. I live for that day.*

CHAPTER 16

Thursday, March 15, 1888

Kate lay in bed, not wanting to move, knowing that when she did she would be violently ill. She had begged Derek to give her some kind of medicine to stop her morning sickness; but he said that little was effective. "Drugging you with opiates isn't good for you or the baby, Kate. It will go away in a few more weeks, in all probability."

Vera tiptoed up to the bed. Seeing that her mistress was awake, she said softly, "I've brought you dry toast, milady. My mum says it is the best thing for—" She stopped short in confusion. "That is, you are so ill in the mornings, and I thought . . ."

Kate managed a wan smile. "You thought correctly, Vera. Dry toast. Just the thought of it makes me queasy— but I'm willing to try anything."

"Can't Sir Derek give you something?"

Kate started to shake her head, thought better of it, and closed her eyes. "He says not."

"The servants are all so excited about the baby, milady. They think it's grand. They all like Sir Derek, you know." Then she lowered her voice and leaned slightly toward the bed in a conspiratorial way. "And they're glad you'll soon be fully in charge of Scarlet Oaks. They all think Lady Letitia is a real dragon."

Later that morning, when she felt better and was up and about, Kate received an invitation to lunch with Lady Zangwill in her private apartment, which was in the other

wing of the house. In the ten days since the wedding ceremony, Lady Letitia had been scrupulously polite to Kate,
polite but distant. Kate knew that the old woman didn't
like her, probably seeing in the younger woman a threat
to her power at Scarlet Oaks. For years she had run the
house with an iron hand. Now she was no longer mistress,
but had been supplanted by a mere chit of a girl.

Kate dressed with meticulous care for the lunch. Derek
had persuaded her not to wear mourning for her father
in the house. "I don't want my wife going about looking
like an old witch," he said. "In public, bow to conven-
tion. At home, wear something bright and cheerful." Trying to please him at least this way to keep down friction,
Kate made no effort to have a complete new wardrobe
made in black and gray. Today she chose a morning dress
of soft lavender with tiny flowers printed on it. The neck
was high, with a ruffle at the top, and the long, full sleeves
had little capelets at the shoulders. Its lines were flowing,
the bustle small. Derek had given Vera orders not to lace
Kate up tightly in her stays.

"You women ruin yourselves by pinching in your
waists," he told Kate. "And yours is quite small enough
as it is. I can span it with my two hands," which he proceeded to do.

Ruefully she thought, He'll not be able to do that for
long.

Promptly at one, Kate tapped on the door of Lady Letitia's sitting room and was admitted by a maidservant in
gray alpaca with white mobcap and apron. The room was
jammed with as much furniture as could be crammed
into it, settees competing with loveseats, armchairs shoul-
dering out ottomans, while a plethora of marble-topped
occasional tables held her ladyship's enormous collection
of china dogs of all shapes and descriptions. There was
one maid who spent several hours daily dusting each ornament carefully. Lady Letitia was sitting in a huge chair
of carved mahogany and red plush, which dwarfed her.
A high footstool was in front of it, as her feet did not
touch the floor, she was so tiny. Tiny but mighty, Kate
thought.

"It was kind of you to invite me to lunch," she said punctiliously.

Her ladyship indicated a smaller, plain wooden chair, heavily carved, but with no padding on it.

"You may serve, now, Duncan," she told the maid who brought their light lunch and served it on a marble-topped table, which she first covered with an embroidered linen cloth.

As if the maid were a piece of furniture, deaf to boot, Lady Zangwill talked to Kate about the most intimate things.

"I hear that you are already with child."

No doubt everyone in Essex County knew by now, Kate thought with annoyance. She tried to keep her voice neutral, though, as she said, "Yes, that is true, Lady Letitia."

"You've been ill mornings." It was a statement, not a question, and Kate felt no obligation to reply. Instead, she sipped at her chicken broth. "Married only ten days, and sure of a baby already?" Lady Zangwill snorted in a most unladylike way. "Poppycock! Much too soon to be sure. And certainly too soon to be having morning sickness."

Angrily Kate snapped, "I would be happy not to be ill each morning, I assure you."

Seemingly changing tacks, the wizened old woman said, "Had six babies myself. First one a healthy boy. Unfortunately he contracted the typhoid fever and died on his second birthday."

"How sad for you," Kate said, genuinely sorry for her.

"All the others died at birth. Blue babies. God's will, I guess. Then my husband died, and I had no one—except Derek, when his mother passed on. And later, Harry." Then she gave Kate a sharp look. "You don't have morning sickness so soon. I know. Been through it six times."

Kate sighed. Nothing she could say would be right.

"Didn't wait for the parson, did you? I thought better of Derek. Didn't think he'd sleep with his wife before the preacher read the words. But you aren't just pregnant since the wedding, my dear. And everyone will know it sooner or later."

Kate laid down her soup spoon carefully, for her hands were trembling so that she feared it would hit the soup plate. "I find this conversation distasteful, Lady Letitia," she said, enunciating her words with great clarity.

"Do you, now? No doubt. No doubt. I heard a rumor some months ago that you were seeing Harry. I'd be inclined to think this baby in your womb is his, not Derek's." She looked at Kate with unconcealed venom. "Harry always was a terror, from the day he was born. His mother was no good. A nursemaid! Married to my brother! Unthinkable. It's just the sort of thing Harry'd do, get a girl with child and then disappear. Derek warned him the last time that it was just that—the last time he'd pay off a girl who was carrying one of Harry's bastards. But he's soft on you, Kate. I can see it in his face. Married you to save your good name."

With all the dignity she could muster, Kate said, "Derek married me because he loves me." Even as she said the words, Kate realized the ridiculousness of it all; she hated having Derek love her. But the old witch had set her teeth on edge. The fact that what she said was true didn't make it a whit more palatable.

"Derek won't love the child if it's Harry's." The old woman said it with relish. "You'll see. You'll rue the day you trapped Derek Ravenshaw into marrying you."

"Trapped—you have gone too far. If you'll excuse me, I shall leave you to your lunch."

Kate got up and walked out without a backward glance. Horrid old hag! How dare she say such things? And in front of Duncan. Kate was still seething when she went back to her bedchamber where, to her surprise, she found Derek.

"I thought you were off to surgery in Chelmsford."

"I had a call to make near here, so I stopped at home for lunch. I had hoped to eat with you; but Vera said that you were lunching with my aunt. Did you enjoy—"

"Enjoy! She's a wicked old woman, Derek. Today she went too far." Kate found she was shaking with rage.

"Calm yourself, Kate. It isn't good for you to get so worked up. What did Aunt Letitia do this time? You really mustn't let her provoke you. She does it just for that reason. Ignore her. Remember, she's no longer young. And she understandably resents having you here now as mistress of my home, when she's had that position for so long."

"Don't let her provoke me! Derek, do you know what she said, that miserable old witch? And don't pinch up your lips that way. I don't care if she is your aunt and took care of you after your mother died and Harry's mother left. She's terrible. She said—she told me that she'd heard I was expecting—"

"No doubt everyone in the house knows you're sick mornings."

"But she had the effrontery to say that it was too soon after the marriage for me to know—and too early in my pregnancy to be having morning sickness. Therefore, I was with child before the wedding. Then, the final slap: since you are so upright and pure, the child must belong to Harry. She'd heard gossip about me and Harry. All of this in front of Duncan!"

She saw that she finally had gotten through to Derek.

"Aunt Letitia has gone too far this time," he said. "I won't have you badgered, not now. It is not good for you."

"What will you say to her, Derek? I want to be with you when—"

"No. This is between my aunt and me, Kate. You stay out of it."

"Stay out of it! But I'm the one she insulted. And I want the satisfaction of seeing her face when you reprimand her. She was horrid to me, horrid. She said you'd married me only to protect my good name." Then she smiled smugly. "I told her that you married me because you loved me."

"I'm happy that you are so pleased with my love," he said drily. "If only you'd show some love in return, I might be more inclined to chastise my elderly aunt for her bad treatment of you. I shall tell her, of course, that she is not to say such things to you in front of the servants. It will cause all kinds of gossip belowstairs."

Kate resented his attitude. He was more concerned with appearances than with her discomfiture.

"I think that it isn't going to be pleasant, having your aunt here at Scarlet Oaks."

With a quick frown, Derek said, "This is her home,

Kate. She came here to take care of Harry and me when we were young. You certainly don't expect me to send her packing now?"

"Then tell her that I'm now mistress of Scarlet Oaks."

He left without a word. Kate wasn't sure she'd done the right thing. Maybe she'd pushed Derek too hard, but she couldn't live here if Lady Letitia continued to run the place. It wouldn't work. If Derek wanted her for a wife, then he must accord her first place at Scarlet Oaks.

She didn't expect to see her husband again, assuming that he would go directly to his surgery in Chelmsford once he had spoken with his aunt; but he stopped in after a short time, face like a storm cloud.

"Women! With you and Aunt Letitia, I'm caught between a rock and a hard place."

Kate just looked at him. It was his problem. Let him solve it.

"She says she is sorry she spoke harshly, Kate; but don't expect Aunt Letitia to apologize in so many words. She has her pride."

"And I have mine," Kate said haughtily.

"I know, I know. But I also know how my aunt operates. She'll never beg your forgiveness in words, but she'll do it in deeds. She'll be very friendly with you, as if nothing had happened. Please, Kate, when she makes that kind of overture to you, accept it as an unspoken apology."

"Oh, very well, if it means that much to you. But I find Lady Letitia hard to tolerate."

"She's old, Kate. Her life has been tragic. Show some tolerance for her."

Then he kissed her lightly and was off to Chelmsford.

Later that afternoon, just as he'd predicted, Lady Letitia approached Kate while she was reclining on a sofa in the library, reading one of Mr. Dickens's novels.

Walking to an ornate cabinet, Lady Letitia took a large volume from it. "I have an interesting album of photographs here," she said as if she and Kate were the best of friends. "Pictures of Derek when he was just a lad. I thought you'd be interested in seeing them."

Kate, remembering Derek's words, sat up on the sofa so that Lady Zangwill could sit beside her.

"That should be interesting. I can't think of Derek as anything but a man." She reached for the wine leather album. Maybe there'd be some pictures of Harry there too.

The older woman perched a pair of glasses on her bony nose, then began pointing out various pictures to Kate.

"That's Derek as a wee babe."

A lovely woman held a baby dressed in a long, lace-trimmed gown with a lace bonnet. It could have been any baby, Kate decided. She could see no look of Derek about it.

There was other pictures. Derek, still in skirts, playing with a black spaniel puppy. Derek, now in trousers, holding his father's hand, looking quite solemn. Even Derek on a pied pony. Further on, there was another woman holding another baby.

"Hortense, Harry's mother—with Harry, as a babe."

Kate could see the resemblance. Hortense had masses of wild, dark hair.

"Do you think that Derek's boyhood pictures bear any resemblance to him now?"

"Not much," Kate admitted. "If I didn't know who it was supposed to be, I'd never have guessed Derek."

The bony little hands, liver-spotted and wrinkled, turned more pages. "There's that brat Harry, when he was about three." He was playing with a ball.

"Now, that looks like him," Kate said, wanting to dwell on that photograph, endearing as it was. Harry was wearing a sailor suit, and his hair was a mass of black ringlets. There was that same smile that turned her bones to water even now. Oh, Harry, you were a charmer then as now, Kate thought.

There were other pictures of both brothers. As Derek grew older, he began to look more like he did now. Harry, even as a wee child, was easily recognized. Kate knew that she'd come back to this album again and again when Lady Letitia wasn't present with her eagle eyes, and feast her senses on the pictures of dear Harry.

"Do you embroider?" the elderly woman asked.

"A little. It has never been a favorite pastime."

"I have always enjoyed my needlework. I'm doing

covers for the seats of the dining room chairs. Needle-point."

"I'm sure they are lovely. You must show them to me sometime." Kate was trying her best to forget the horrid time at lunch, to be friends with Derek's aunt.

"My problem is getting floss. It is so hard for me to get out these days. There's a little shop in the village, and the woman carries a full line of embroidery supplies, but I so seldom can get there." She paused, then gave Kate a sidelong look with her beady eyes. "I don't suppose you'd be willing to shop for me, next time you take a drive to the village?"

"I'd be delighted to. In fact, I was thinking of going out later today. I get so restless, cooped up in the house."

"You're not riding, I hope?"

"Of course. Whyever shouldn't I? I ride all winter long."

"But, my dear—expecting! It isn't safe. Hasn't Derek told you that you mustn't go riding? He is most remiss."

"I've been riding all my life. I feel quite well, except in the morning when I first get up. I see no reason not to go riding, as it is good exercise and—" At the horrified look on Lady Letitia's face, Kate said firmly, "The idea that a pregnant woman must sit and lie about is very unscientific, and very old fashioned, Lady Letitia." Her tone brooked no argument. "Now, if you'll give me samples of the threads you need . . ."

Later, cantering along the lane that led to the village, Kate felt free, freer than she had since she'd married Derek. It was so good to get out. She passed the lodge and felt a pang of anguish. Oh, Harry! Lost forever. She still loved him so.

The shop was in the front room of a little thatched cottage. As Kate pushed open the door, a bell rang, and a buxom young woman, pretty in a harried sort of way, hurried in from the kitchen. Kate could hear a child whining inside.

"Yes, ma'am?"

Kate showed her the samples of floss to match. As the woman looked through a box full of skeins of every hue, a little boy of about three burst into the shop from the kitchen.

"Mama! I want my tea now!" he demanded.

"Hush, Harry, Mama's busy with the lady."

The child glared at Kate, his light gray eyes striking under his cap of soot-black curls. In that first shocking look at the child, Kate felt cold all over.

"Are you all right, ma'am?" the shopgirl asked anxiously. "If you are feeling poorly, I could take you into the kitchen to sit down."

The child stuck out his tongue at Kate, then tugged at his mother's dark blue skirt of linsey-woolsey.

"No, no. I'm all right, Mrs.—"

"It's Miss Gorman, ma'am." She said it quite unselfconsciously.

Embarrassed, yet unable to keep from asking, Kate looked at the child. "Your little boy?" Her voice was high and too bright.

"Yes, my Harry—the cross I must bear. Run along into the kitchen, Harry. I'll be in directly and fix your tea."

As if knowing that Kate was interested in him, the child lingered until Kate offered him a shiny penny, which he snatched and carried away.

"That's kind of you, ma'am." Miss Gorman sighed. "It's hard, raising a heller like that one without a pa for him."

"Is his father . . ." Kate paused delicately.

"Left me high and dry, miss, when he learned little Harry was on the way. Thank the good Lord that Sir Derek gave me enough to buy this shop. Otherwise, I don't know what I'd have done. My own pa threw me out when he found out about the baby. Ah, here's that color you want. Will that be all, ma'am?"

Kate paid, took the small package, and fled the shop. Oh, clever, clever Lady Letitia. She'd known about this little Harry. Sending Kate on such an innocent-sounding errand, in hopes that she'd see Harry's son. And it was Harry's son. The whole thing had been malevolently orchestrated—the picture album, the darling photo of Harry as a child, and then this shopping trip—so that Kate would see Miss Gorman's little boy.

And Derek had paid her off, just as he'd said. Would the child she carried in her womb look so achingly like Harry? She rode slowly back to Scarlet Oaks, tears streaming down her face. For the first time since she'd given herself to Harry, Kate felt cheap, soiled, degraded. She was no better than Miss Gorman. Derek had bought her off too.

INTERLUDE 5

Thursday, March 15, 1888. 9 P.M.

He found that he could hear the Fiddlers quarreling, for the window sash fit poorly; so he crouched outside, listening.

"God curse you, Abby!"

"Jonathan, don't blaspheme," came the waspish answer. "You must put lust behind you. To help you, I shall sleep here on this cot in the pantry. Knowing how you lust after the flesh, I must bar you forever from this chamber —for the good of your immortal soul."

"You're my wife, Abby. I'm entitled to lie with you. It is your duty."

"My duty is to God. Never again will I allow you to touch me in a carnal manner, Jonathan. It is sinful."

"I might as well have become a papist!" he raged. "They deny the flesh—how, I don't know. It is unnatural. God never meant for man to be unnatural, Abby. Man is a sinful creature who lusts after the flesh—but if he confesses, God forgives."

"God won't have to forgive what you don't do, Jonathan. From now on, our union is spiritual. We must forego the desires of the flesh."

"Desires! You never had any. Frigid. I've been cursed with a frigid wife."

He heard Fiddler storm out, so he followed the man at a safe distance. Did Fiddler sense that he was being fol-

205

lowed? The preacher kept glancing back over his shoulder, as if he felt he was under observation.

Then a hand reached out from an open doorway and plucked at Fiddler's sleeve.

He moved closer, well hidden in the throngs on the pavement. He could hear the whore solicit the so-called man of God.

"Want a bit of fun? Oh, it's the parson." Her voice was mocking. "Tuppence for you. Double if you pray over me." Then she added, "If you wants a bed, luv, it'll be eightpence at the lodging."

"Never mind a bed," Fiddler answered, voice hoarse with desire. "We'll just go around the side of the building here. No one will see us in the dark."

"Suit yourself, luv. Whatever you want, just so's you pay me. I have to earn enough for me own bed tonight."

As he watched Fiddler furtively follow the woman into the passageway, he was already composing a blackmail note in his mind. And could the parson play a role in the larger drama he was planning? Perhaps, perhaps. He must arrange it very carefully.

CHAPTER 17

Thursday, March 15, 1888

Kate retired very early. There had been a message from Derek saying that he was tied up with a difficult confinement in Chelmsford and would be home quite late. Kate dined with Lady Letitia, putting on a good face, not allowing that spiteful woman to know how distressed she was.

For all her tiny size, the elderly lady was a remarkable trencherwoman. She worked her way steadily through baked oysters, Dover sole, and then a large helping of duckling, all with suitable side dishes. Her wine glass was kept full by an alert footman assigned to her. Kate, who nibbled lightly at the sole, was constantly reminded by Lady Letitia, "Eat, Kate, eat! Remember, now you are eating for two."

Kate had not personally delivered the embroidery threads to Derek's aunt, not being able then to control her feelings sufficiently. She had sent them by one of the maids, pleading tiredness due to her condition. Now, after several hours, she had managed to compose herself. Harry had never pretended that Kate was the first woman in his life. He was lusty, healthy, and very masculine. It was to be expected that he had gratified his considerable sexual appetites somewhere. Kate managed to put the blame onto the unfortunate Miss Gorman. She had not had to gratify Harry's desires. The fact that she had a child was unfortunate; but Derek had bought her the shop, a considerable advantage to the woman, more than she could have hoped to have normally. Kate felt it was quite bad of Miss Gorman to have named the child Harry. No doubt he had been enticed by her charms in the first place.

Dinner had progressed to the crown of pork and the joint of mutton before Lady Letitia mentioned the errand to the village. Then, while the footman was heaping garden peas on her plate, she smiled sweetly at Kate and asked, "Did your ride to the village have any ill effects, my dear?"

"No, I feel quite good after riding." Horrid old hag. Trying to start something. Kate was determined not to play that game with Derek's aunt.

"I do thank you for running my little errand for me. Did Miss Gorman herself wait on you?"

Kate lied, smiling sweetly. "There was a young woman in the shop. I don't know her name."

"A young woman with a child?"

"I thought you said Miss Gorman. So how could she have a child, Lady Letitia?" Kate looked her right in her beady old eyes. A troublemaker, was Derek's dear auntie. Kate was going to have to do something about her, or life at Scarlet Oaks would soon become unbearable.

Lady Letitia, while inhaling a mound of food, seemed not to stop talking. "Kate, my dear, you are worldly enough to know about such things. Young women—of a certain class—often have children without benefit of marriage. As did our little shopkeeper." Then, avidly, "Did you see the child?"

Putting on a blank stare, Kate asked, "Child? What child?"

Lady Letitia bit viciously into a large bite of turnip before she answered. "The child, the child. Miss Gorman's little mistake."

"Oh, that child." Kate smiled sweetly, then took a small bit of mutton and chewed it thoroughly while her companion watched her avidly. "I do believe there was a child running about. A little girl? Or a boy. It's so hard to tell about children while the boys are still in skirts, isn't it?"

Lady Zangwill looked as if she might explode, but she didn't pursue the subject further. Kate didn't know if she thought she'd been bested or decided Kate hadn't realized the child was Harry's.

After dinner, her ladyship asked if Kate would like to play some cards, but Kate demurred. "As I'm expecting, I must get my rest," she said delicately. It was a game two could play, this business of her pregnancy.

The zest of besting Lady Letitia carried Kate for a while; but by the time the long evening was drawing to a close, with no Derek to talk with, Kate began to feel reaction setting in. No matter how many excuses she made for Harry, it still hurt dreadfully to see that little boy, so like her beloved, today. Miss Gorman hadn't named little Harry's father. Probably she assumed that everyone in the district knew that young Ravenshaw had fathered her child.

A hussy about it, Kate thought. Flaunting the fact, naming the boy for Harry as if he were legitimate.

Then she found that tears were streaming down her face. Her child could never be called Harry. She knew that Derek would be adamant about that. He'd pretend the child was his own, he'd put on a good face to the world, he'd protect Kate from the whispers, the sly smiles, the sniggers—but he'd never allow the child to bear Harry's name.

Vera, coming in just then, asked anxiously, "Oh, milady, are you feeling poorly? Is there anything—"

"I'm all right," Kate said brusquely, dashing away her tears with the back of her hand. She held up the book she'd been holding. "Just something sad in *David Copperfield*."

"Should you be reading sad things now, milady? It might be bad for the baby."

"Oh, Vera, that's just an old wives' tale."

"Yes, if you say so, milady." But the little maid looked doubtful.

If she only knew, Kate thought bitterly. My life is much more sorrowful than anything Mr. Dickens wrote. And as scandalous as a French novel.

"I think I shall retire early, Vera. I may lie in bed and read until Sir Derek arrives."

"Of course, milady. You need lots of rest now."

Kate thought she'd not be able to get to sleep. She was sure her mind would go around and around about Harry and Miss Gorman and the child. To her surprise, she fell asleep almost at once, with the lamp still burning beside her bed.

She dreamed. At first the dream was a happy one. She was with Harry once again, lying with him at the lodge in front of the fire. His lovemaking inflamed her, and soon she drew him to cover her, welcoming him with her eager body. Before she had reached the height of her rapture, though, she looked at him and discovered that it was Derek, not Harry, who was making love to her. She cried out in distress, and the dream ended with Kate unfulfilled. Then she was somewhere in a crowd, and a child clung to her skirts. He kept calling, "Dada, dada." Each time she looked down at him, he would be little Harry Gorman. She thought she saw Harry at the other side of the room; but when she tried to go to him, the child clung so stubbornly that she could make no progress. Then Harry disappeared, and Derek was there, saying, "Kate, Kate, what is wrong?"

She opened her eyes, dazed with sleep and the unpleasantness of the dream, to find that Derek was truly there, bending over her, saying the words she'd just dreamed. He was in his nightshirt of woolen flannel.

Sitting beside her on the bed, he gathered his wife into his arms, murmuring, "What is wrong, my dearest wife? You were moaning in your sleep as if you might be ill."

Shuddering, she remembered her dream, and the cause of it. Tears came; she couldn't stop them.

Derek held her gently and rocked her as if she were a tiny child. "Hush, dearest Kate, don't cry. Tell me what is wrong. If I can put it right, I will. I love you so much, my darling, that I can't stand it when you are unhappy."

"I had a horrid dream," she sobbed.

"Ah, but now you're awake, and know that it was nothing but a nightmare. No need for tears now."

"It's still here though," she cried. "Nothing's better. It's just as bad when I'm awake as when I'm asleep."

He held her more tightly, crushed to his chest, so that she could feel the thud of his heart under her cheek. It was very comforting to be held this way. When she'd been a tiny child and had dreamed awful things, her father would come to her room, take her up from her cot, and rock her just as Derek was doing now. It had calmed her then. Now was different. Her childhood nightmares had been only that. Her bad dreams now had their counterpart when she woke.

"What did you dream, Kate? Tell me. It will help to drive away the dream."

The words poured from her then—the dream, the child, Miss Gorman, Aunt Letitia, Harry—and she sobbed bitterly, crying for her lost innocence and her blighted love.

As she told of Lady Letitia's perfidy, she felt Derek's arms tense rock-hard, although he said nothing. When Kate was out of words, when all the bitterness, the anger, the anguish had been verbalized, she began weeping again, this time gently, the tears oozing from under the lids of her closed eyes. They ran down her cheeks and soaked the front of Derek's nightshirt.

"Poor baby, poor Kate," he crooned, still rocking her.

Then, slowly, she scarcely knew how it happened, their roles changed. It was no longer father and unhappy little daughter. The relationship became, subtly, man and woman. Derek no longer held her firmly but passively. Now his hands moved slowly, gently, but with increasing urgency, caressing her, molding her body to his. Somehow, she scarcely was aware of its happening, Kate's nightgown was gone, and Derek's nightshirt. They no longer sat on the bed, with Kate cradled in his arms, but they lay together, while his ardent hands explored her body as if he'd never lain with her before. In a way this was true; for now, as never before in their brief marriage, Kate found herself responding to his lovemaking. At first she wanted to be near him only to drive away the ugliness of the day, the disillusionment of learning about Harry's son, the knowledge that Miss Gorman had been Harry's love before she had even known him. Then something happened to their lovemaking, and Kate's passion was aroused as Derek's lips moved over her body, kissing her breasts, the insides of her wrists, the hollow in her throat, and the soft flesh of her thighs. Tonight she turned eagerly to him at last,

holding him close, yielding her body to him in total submission, sighing in rapture as he entered her. The sensuous
delight of the moment carried her higher and higher until,
in a cry of joy, she melted in that final, lovely moment of
love.

As they lay together afterward, as Derek caressed her
gently and murmured words of love, all of the distress of
the day had dissolved, leaving her relaxed and happy. Not
since the last time she'd been with Harry had Kate felt so
wonderful. Derek lay with his head cushioned on her
breast, and she traced the line of his jaw, the firm arching
of his brows, and ran her fingers through his coarse black
hair, an exciting sensation.

It seemed to excite Derek as much as it did Kate, for
soon he was ready for more love with his wife, and she
took him eagerly, this time slowly and lovingly, until their
excitement built to its explosion of sensation which left
her drained and content.

"Tonight was our honeymoon, beloved," Derek whispered as she fell asleep in his arms. "This is the moment
I've waited for, longed for, dreamed of. Now, finally, you
are truly and completely my wife.

And Kate fell asleep with no dreams to disturb her. She
woke some time later to find that she was alone in the
big bed. With a sense of *déjà vu* Kate realized that there
was a dim light on in the bedroom, as there had been on
her wedding night.

Sitting up, letting the covers fall from her, baring her
body to the waist, she called, "Derek?" As her eyes adjusted to the meager light, she saw that he was again
sitting at the little imitation-bamboo desk, writing as before. At her call, he looked around, startled; but the
fireplace screen he'd moved between the china lamp and
the bed cast a shadow on his face so she couldn't read her
husband's expression.

Again she said, "Derek? What are you doing up? What
time is it?"

Almost furtively he closed the book in which he'd been
writing and slid it into the desk drawer. Did he lock it as
he had that first night? She wasn't sure. The light was too
poor for good viewing.

"I'm sorry, my dear. I didn't mean to wake you." He blew out the lamp and made his way to the bed in the dark. Sliding in under the covers, he pulled Kate down beside him, his embrace loving, intimate. "But now that you're awake," he murmured, "I can think of more interesting things to do than to write in my journal."

Dying of curiosity, piqued by his way of hiding the book from her, Kate teased, "What were you writing about so secretly?"

"About you, my love," he whispered. "About how I love you, and how marvelous it is to have you respond to me when I caress you, hold you, make you mine. Oh, Kate," he groaned, "I have loved you so desperately for such a long time. And you disappointed me so much when we were wed. Tonight for the first time you loved me in return, and it has made my bed a heaven on earth."

"But to write about it in a diary!"

"Hush. I don't want to talk about it. Kiss me," he demanded hoarsely, pulling her close to him so that she felt his hard, muscular body the full length of her own softer flesh.

"No, I won't love you again until you tell me what you said. I want to read your diary."

She felt him tense, his muscles knotting.

"No one else can read my journal, Kate, not even you. It is a very personal, very private account, written only for me to see."

"What if I pick the lock when you're out," she teased. "Would you beat me, Derek?"

She felt him relax slightly at her joking tone.

"Remember what happened to Bluebeard's wife, Kate."

She laughed delightedly and offered her lips for his passionate kiss. For a moment she felt disloyalty to Harry —but Harry had deserted her, and Derek was here, so she loved him.

CHAPTER 18

Friday, March 16, 1888

It was a lovely March day, breezy but bright. From the window of the breakfast room, Kate could see the first yellow crocuses blooming in a sheltered spot in the garden. Truly, spring was almost here. She smiled softly at Derek as he worked his way through a huge plate of ham, eggs, and country sausages. It was his day at the clinic on Union Row, so he was up early to catch the train to London. This was the first morning since they had gotten married that Kate had joined him for breakfast. Usually she had a tray in bed long after he'd gone to his surgery in Chelmsford, or to London on clinic days. After last night, though, she wanted to be with him as he ate.

Her happiness was shattered by the arrival of Lady Letitia, who looked at Kate with surprise.

"Up early," she said. "Are you feeling better mornings?"

"Much better, thank you." It was hard for Kate to be civil to the old woman after yesterday's episode at the embroidery shop; but for Derek's sake, she must try.

A footman seated Lady Letitia, making sure there was a needlepoint-covered mahogany footstool for her feet. Then he heaped her plate with food, which she wolfed down, never stopping talking. Her eating habits had a kind of horrid fascination for Kate; it took the young woman's appetite to see the mountain of food the tiny woman consumed.

214

"Derek," Lady Letitia said, not missing a bite, "I am shocked at your lack of concern for your lovely wife."

Derek paused, fork halfway to his mouth, his face a study in shocked amazement. "Kate is very dear to me, Aunt Letitia." Was there a subtle warning there? "I have every concern for her, as you must surely know."

"But you know she is expecting. Yet you haven't told her that she must not go riding. She was out on horseback yesterday."

Annoyed, Kate said, "I went to the village to do an errand for you, Lady Letitia, if you recall."

"It wasn't necessary to ride, my dear." The tone was insufferably condescending. "You could have had one of the coachmen take you there in the victoria. Or you might even have taken out the tilbury yourself—although I do not think that is good either—driving your own gig when you are in your condition."

"I am perfectly healthy, as I told you yesterday. I am young and a good rider. It is quite safe." There, that would put the old witch in her place.

Lady Letitia was not used to being put down by her juniors. Turning back to her nephew, she said, "Derek, explain to this child the foolishness of her ways. You don't want your baby lost because its mother is willful and reckless."

Horrid woman. She knew perfectly well that the baby belonged to Harry, not Derek. She was pointing that out in her own inimitable nasty fashion. Kate felt rebellion boiling up in her even before Derek turned to her.

"I hadn't realized you still were riding, dear," he said. There was an implicit warning in his quiet words. Kate wasn't to keep secrets from him. "It isn't the best thing for you to be doing. Aunt Letitia is quite right in that."

Kate seethed. How dare he take his aunt's part instead of hers. She was his wife. He professed to love her to distraction; yet he humiliated her in front of this wicked old woman. It was too much.

"Am I to be a prisoner at Scarlet Oaks, not allowed to go out even for a breath of air?"

Derek frowned. Men didn't like to be drawn into intra-mural domestic squabbles between the women of the house. "I didn't say anything of the sort, Kate, and you know it. You are just acting childish."

It was the worst possible thing for Derek to say to her. Kate was infuriated. How dare he? How dare he say these things to her in front of his aunt? Kate looked at Lady Letitia, who was eating away as if nothing had happened. Then she looked up, just one quick glance at Kate; but the younger woman saw the triumph on the wrinkled old face. She'd won this round against Kate, the woman who had usurped her place as mistress of Scarlet Oaks.

Kate got up without another word and walked haughtily out of the breakfast room. After all Derek's words of love last night, she'd expected him to be on her side of any fuss with Lady Letitia. Well, she was wrong. Oh, how she longed for Harry to come back. She'd been wicked last night, letting Derek love her—enjoying every minute of passion in his arms. What would Harry think if he knew she'd been so unfaithful in spirit? She'd been forced into marriage with Derek. There'd been no other solution for her—with Harry's babe already growing inside her body, with Mansfield planning to start foreclosure proceedings unless she agreed to be his mistress. What else could she have done under those circumstances? But she didn't have to take pleasure from Derek as she had done last night. And see what the results were! He cared nothing for her, nothing.

She stormed up the main staircase, not bothering to rest a steadying hand on the beautifully carved balustrade. Kate skimmed up the stairs, holding up her negligee with both hands. If she fell, who would care? Certainly not Derek. Aunt Letitia would no doubt rejoice. And Harry? She didn't know where he was. Would she ever see him again?

Derek followed her upstairs, was on her heels as she turned into their bedchamber, and dismissed Vera with one curt movement of his head.

He caught Kate's arm and turned her to face him, holding her shoulders with fingers that bit into the flesh.

"You're hurting me," she said, voice icy.

He ignored her words, keeping his grip on her. "You

are acting like a spoiled little brat, Kate. I won't have such conduct from my wife."

"Indeed. Last night you seemed delighted with my conduct."

She saw his mouth harden in anger.

"Last night—last night I thought that finally you were willing to be a true wife to me, instead of a mere accommodation."

"Wife. I'm your wife, yet you take your aunt's part against me, you humiliate me in front of her—and I'm to say, 'Yes, Derek, husband, whatever she says is all right.' Well, I won't do it. She caused all my grief yesterday. She deliberately sent me to Miss Gorman's shop, hoping that I'd see Harry's child. She hates me, and you know it. She resents the fact that I'm young and loved, while she is old and despised. She doesn't want me to be mistress of Scarlet Oaks. She's going to make trouble for me every day that I live here—and if you take her part, I shall hate you."

He groaned and caught Kate to him in a smothering embrace.

"Oh, God, Kate, I love you so much. Don't be this way with me. I know that Aunt Letitia is old and crotchety; but see her side of things too. She's been here for so long. She hates to relinquish her hold on running the household. Remember, she was a mother to me for years."

"And she hates Harry. He told me, you know. She knows the child I carry belongs to Harry, not you. She'll be horrid to me every chance she has. Look how she stirred things up this morning with that nonsense about my riding."

"That's not nonsense, Kate. It isn't a good thing for you to go riding in your condition. I assumed you knew this already. I really must forbid you to go out on horseback while you are pregnant. If the horse should throw you—"

"You don't think much of my riding ability."

"Quit twisting my words, Kate. I am a doctor. I know more about such things than you do. Walks outdoors are good for you, at least for now. Riding in a carriage won't hurt you; but I don't want you riding again, nor careening about the countryside in a gig, driving yourself, until after this baby arrives."

She pulled away from his embrace, angry wth him for

placing such restrictions on her. He was an old fuddy-duddy. Why had she thought last night that he was exciting?

"Oh, go off to London and take care of your whores," she muttered. "See to Monica Murphy. Give her all the orders you like."

"You're very like her," he snapped, fury in his voice. "Neither of you will listen to a bit of common sense."

"So now you call me a whore." Her voice was stiff and formal with suppressed fury.

He lifted a hand toward her, a pleading hand; but Kate whirled away, turning her back on him.

"You know that isn't what I meant at all," he raged. "What did I ever do to deserve such a wife as you?"

Over her shoulder she snapped, "You bought me—remember? And you got just what you paid for."

Without another word he turned and stormed out of their room. Kate was delighted to so annoy him. Last night—she'd prefer to forget last night. She'd had the horrid dream, Derek had disturbed her with the light—oh, it didn't bear thinking about. Poor Harry, betrayed by everyone, even by her.

She prowled about the house all morning, snapping at the servants, finding fault, making a nuisance of herself. If she was mistress of Scarlet Oaks, then let the servants come to her for their orders, instead of going to Lady Letitia.

Shortly after lunch, which she ate from a tray in her room lest she encounter Lady Letitia in the dining room, there was a discreet tap at the door. Vera came back with a small silver tray with a letter on it.

"It's not post time," Kate said, reaching for what was obviously a piece of mail.

"Parsons said that this was delivered to you at Fairlawn, milady. It's from someone who doesn't know you're married. See, it's addressed to 'Miss Kate Kingsley' instead of Lady Ravenshaw. And, milady, it's foreign—from Ireland."

Ireland? She snatched the letter from the tray and ripped it open without waiting for Vera to bring her the Italian stiletto she used as an opener. Hands trembling, she read:

Dearest Kate,

How I miss you. My bed is lonely at night, and I long for your love. I hated having to leave England without seeing you, but I got in too deep with one of my business deals. If I'd been a lord—or rich—it would all have been taken care of. But Derek flatly refused to help me, so I had no choice but to flee. It was that or prison, and I do not think that I'd be able to live in prison. Do not despair though. I have a contact in England—I do not want to name him at this time, in case this letter should fall into unfriendly hands—who may be able to make all of my troubles disappear like a morning mist. In that case, I shall return to England. Watch for me. As soon as I can, I'll be at the lodge, waiting eagerly to hear the sound of your little mare's hooves, to see your lovely face, to hold you in my arms and make you mine once again. I may be back in England within the week; it may take longer. But I will soon be with you again, my adored one.

> With all my love,
> Harry

Harry! Harry was coming back! Joy surged through her; she wanted to dance about the bedchamber in celebration.

"Good news, milady?" Vera asked, obviously hoping that Kate would confide in her.

Caught up short, realizing that no one must know that she'd heard from Harry, Kate folded the letter, tucked it back into the envelope, and said, trying to be offhand about it, "Just a note from an old friend." Then, eagerly, "My dark green riding habit, Vera."

The little maid's eyes rounded to O's. "You're going riding again today, milady?" Diffidently she added, "Is it good for you, milady, to go riding when you are expecting?"

"I'm healthy as a horse, Vera, and you know it. Now, the riding habit."

Kate could see that her maid was reluctant; but she followed her mistress's orders and got out her riding clothes. As she adjusted the top hat and veil, Kate said, "If Lady

Zangwill should happen to want me, just say I've gone out. Don't say I've gone riding." At the hesitant look on Vera's face, Kate smiled and said, "I'm not asking you to lie, Vera. Just say, simply, that I've gone out. Don't embellish the story."

"Yes, milady." Then, confidentially, "The servants wish you had more to do with the running of Scarlet Oaks, milady. Lady Zangwill is a real Tartar." Her hand clapped over her mouth. "Oh, milady, forgive me."

Kate grinned engagingly. "Don't apologize for calling that old witch anything you like, Vera. I'd be happier if she were in the far reaches of Asia—or wherever Tartars come from! Now, help me with my boots. I want to get in a little ride before it rains again."

In case Lady Letitia was peeping out of the window, spying on her, Kate rode down the drive slowly, holding in the little mare, who was a bundle of energy. Once out of sight of the house, though, she gave the horse its head, and they went along the road at a full gallop. She couldn't wait to get to the hunting lodge. The letter had been written nearly ten days ago. By now Harry could be back in England, his financial problems solved, ready to take up with her where he'd left off. What was he going to say when he found that she was married to his hated brother? What would she do?

Kate had been in such a rush of delirious happiness since she opened the letter that she'd not thought this situation through. Now the full weight of it fell on her. She was married; What was worse, married to Derek. She couldn't imagine that Derek would quietly divorce her to allow her to be with Harry. Oh, God, why hadn't she waited just a little while? She should have had more faith in Harry. But it all had happened at once—Harry's disappearance, the news that the stock certificates were forged, Mansfield's threat to foreclose unless she married him, and her father's death. On top of it all was the stunning news that she was expecting Harry's child. It had been too much for her to handle alone. Derek had presented himself at just the one moment when she could have accepted his offer of marriage. Now she bitterly regretted it, as she regretted giving herself to him so willingly last night. She belonged to Harry. When he returned she didn't know what they would do. If he asked her to run away with him, she would do it, even though it meant that they would be ostracized. It didn't matter to Kate. All she wanted was to be with Harry again.

She pulled the little mare to a walk as she neared the lane into the lodge. Kate could have come in the back way from the stables, but she didn't want anyone at Scarlet Oaks to suspect that she was going to the hunting lodge. No doubt after all these years of running the house, Lady Letitia had spies among the servants. She'd know immediately if Kate went directly to the lodge, and she'd suspect the reason for it.

The building looked deserted when Kate rode up to it. No horse was hitched outside, and her own mount gave no indication that another horse was nearby. There wasn't a glimmer of light from the windows. Still, not wanting to risk missing Harry, realizing that he might still have to be in hiding until his affairs were satisfactorily settled, Kate dismounted and went to the door. It was locked, as she had expected. She tipped up the urn, found the key, and opened the door. Inside it was gloomy and cold, with no sign of life. She went through the rooms, looking for evidence of occupancy; but there was nothing. Harry wasn't here, and hadn't been here since the last time she'd met him. Well, it was too much to hope for to find him here today. It might be a week or more before he managed to get back to England. She'd ride out every day, keep a watch for him.

Locking the door behind her, she mounted the mare and started back toward the main road. There was a rustle in the underbrush, and something darted across the road in front of them. Kate couldn't see what it was—a weasel, perhaps, or a rat. The horse shied, catching her off guard, and reared onto its hind legs in fright. Not being prepared for such a reaction, Kate was thrown, falling badly. She fell face down across a rotting tree stump that caught her at the waist, doubling her over like a jackknife.

Kate let out a cry of pain and dismay. The fall winded her badly, and it took her a few moments before she was able to pick herself up. She felt queasy, due to the hard blow she had received from the tree stump. Fortunately, the mare was now standing, moving her hooves about in a nervous little dance. Bending over slightly to ease the pain in her abdomen, Kate managed to catch the reins so that the horse wouldn't bolt and leave her stranded. Then, slowly and painfully, she pulled herself up into the saddle, wincing with pain. For a moment she felt faint, and feared that she might fall again; but Kate clung to the saddlehorn until the weakness went away. Still not sure of herself, she held the mare to a walk all the way back to Scarlet Oaks. By the time she got home, she was feeling a bit better, although she still was quite sore where the tree stump had bruised her body.

Back in her bedchamber, she rang for Vera and ordered her to draw a hot bath. As the tub filled, Vera helped her to disrobe.

"Milady, you are all black and blue!" The maid was aghast at the bruising on Kate's abdomen. "What happened?"

"My horse threw me. Don't fuss about it—and please don't say anything to anyone else. I'm quite all right now, except for some sore muscles. I'll soak the soreness away in my bath."

"But milady—the baby—are you sure—"

"Oh, stop fussing, Vera. I'm fine. It's not the first time I've had a spill from a horse; nor the last, I dare say. Just help me into the tub, please. I don't want to take another spill in the bath. I'd probably fracture my skull. Homes are much more dangerous than the out-of-doors—you should know that. More people are injured indoors than out."

"Yes, milady, whatever you say." But Vera sounded doubtful.

The hot soak helped ease Kate's aches and pains, but her entire abdomen was beginning to discolor.

"Oh, milady, what will Sir Derek say?"

"I don't even want to think about that, Vera." Kate was quite apprehensive about Derek's reaction to her bruising. He'd given her strict orders to stay off her horse. When he discovered that she'd not only deliberately disobeyed him, but that she'd also taken a rather nasty fall, he'd be furious. "Maybe he'll be home so late from London that he won't see me tonight."

Vera just looked at her, a look that spoke volumes.

"Will you dress again for dinner, milady?"

"Do you know if there's been any word from Sir Derek? If he's going to be home to dinner, I want to dress and go down. Otherwise . . ."

"I'm sorry, milady, I don't know. I'll try to find out if you wish."

"Yes, do that. For now I'll just put on my robe and rest." She winced as Vera helped her from the tub.

"Let me go down to the kitchen and mix some embrocation of smelling salts, vinegar, and spirits, milady. It's not as good as Gebhard's Liniment; but cook told me that Sir Derek won't allow anyone else but himself to use the oil of vitriol that's one of the ingredients. My old gran knows the receipt, but she did warn that the vitriol could eat holes in my hand if I wasn't careful with it."

Kate looked at her with alarm. "I think the simple embrocation will be quite sufficient, thank you, Vera."

"I could apply a poultice."

"Perhaps at bedtime."

While Vera went to make the medication, Kate decided that it might be wise to eat dinner downstairs with Aunt Letitia, even if Derek was delayed at his clinic in London. Any sign of weakness on her part, and his aunt would pounce like a waiting cat, with Kate as the mouse. By the time she'd been treated with the rather pungent embrocation and had dressed, she was feeling a bit uncomfortable; but she was determined not to give Lady Letitia any excuse to criticize.

"I thought I saw you in your riding habit," the little termagant said, attacking during the soup course. "Derek told you that riding was ill advised."

"So he did," Kate agreed, determined not to fight with her critic. She changed the subject deftly. "I understand that Pamela Oldham's wedding will be the event of the season."

"Too bad you'll not be able to stand up with her."

"She asked me to and I accepted."

Lady Zangwill glanced at Kate's waistline. "By June, my dear, you'll scarcely be acceptable in a wedding party."

Kate kept forgetting this. What a bore not to be able to be a member of the wedding, wear a Paris gown, all because of loving Harry not wisely, but too well.

Her talk of Pam's wedding didn't divert Lady Zangwill for too long. Soon she returned to the attack, never stopping her eating. Tonight it made Kate a bit queasy to see the tiny woman devour so much food, from soup to fish to oysters to ham to a leg of mutton to potatoes to turnips to —too much! She wished she'd followed her first impulse and had her dinner on a tray in her room.

"Whatever will Derek say when he learns you went riding?"

Kate frowned at the busybody aunt. "There's no need for him to find out, is there?"

Self-righteously Lady Letitia said, "Surely you aren't going to lie to him—nor should you expect me to."

"Who said anything about lying, Lady Letitia? I just don't need to bring up the subject with him."

"That's deceitful, my girl! I think it is immoral for a married woman to have secrets from her husband."

Kate didn't bother to answer that. Derek had secrets from her. Probably his aunt would think that was perfectly all right. Anything Derek did met with her approval. If Kate did the same thing, it would be wrong.

Pursing her lips, Kate looked at Lady Letitia just as she was cramming a large bite of fatty pork into her voracious mouth. It quite turned Kate's stomach. Suddenly she felt ill. Muttering "Please excuse me," she rushed from the room, linen serviette clutched to her mouth, just hoping that she could make it to the bathroom before she became violently ill. As she hurried up the stairs, the pain struck, a vicious knifing that doubled her over. Kate clutched at the railing, afraid that she would fall and go tumbling down the stairs. Her head swam, and she thought that she was going to faint. Somehow she managed to pull herself up the rest of the stairs, and then she collapsed on the hall runner, awash with pain, trembling with nausea.

"Vera!" she called weakly. "Oh, please, somebody help me." Waves of agony radiated from her abdomen, turning her whole body into a thing of pain. Tears ran down her cheeks unheeded as she tried to get to her feet.

"Stay still!" It was a voice of command from somewhere outside her pain-filled being. "Don't try to get up. I'll have some of the footmen carry you to bed."

It was Lady Letitia who must have followed her, seeing that she was ill. Much as she disliked Derek's aunt, for this one time Kate was thankful that she had appeared when she did. In a half-fainting state, Kate was carried to her room and laid on the huge bed she shared with her husband. Then Lady Letitia sent out the footmen and gave brisk orders to Vera. Some of the sounds penetrated to Kate, some didn't. Her whole self was so suffused with pain that she was scarcely conscious of anything else. Quickly she was undressed and gotten into bed.

"What caused that bruising?" she heard Lady Letitia ask.

"I'd rather not say, milady."

"Don't you get impertinent with me, young woman. How did Lady Ravenshaw bruise herself? Tell me. It may have a bearing on what's happening to her now."

From the end of a long, long tunnel Kate heard Vera's words come and go in waves. ". . . horse threw . . . rotten stump . . . embrocation . . ."

And Lady Letitia's fierce reply, "It's going to take more than embrocation to help her now. Call Parsons. See if it's possible to get a message to Sir Derek. If not, call some other doctor—or get the local midwife."

The next hours or days or years—Kate didn't know how long she lay there suffering—were so pain-filled that she was unconscious as often as she was aware of her surroundings. At times when she was all too screamingly awake, Lady Letitia's wizened face hung over her. Or was it Vera, eyes wide with fright? Sometimes it seemed the woman's face was someone she didn't know. There was only one thing that Kate knew for certain. She had never felt such terrible pain in all her life until this moment.

And then Derek was there, his face a thundercloud.

Kate didn't want to look at him. She wanted to retreat into her private, pain-filled world to escape from his wild eyes. There was no escape, though, for the pain held her to her bed, went on unrelenting, forever.

Finally it was all over. She lay there, exhausted, and her eyes drooped closed. Someone was holding her hand—Derek? A strong arm lifted her shoulders, a glass touched her lips, and Derek commanded, "Drink this, Kate. It will make you sleep."

Obediently she swallowed the wine laced with laudanum. He eased her back onto her pillows. Then, before the drug did its work of sending her into oblivion, Kate asked muzzily, "Did I lose the baby?"

"Yes." Nothing else, just that one, terse word.

As she drifted off to sleep, Kate thought, I needn't have married Derek! I could have managed, somehow, if it hadn't been for Harry's baby. Now Harry's coming home —and I'm tied to his brother. Oh, why didn't I wait? Why didn't I have more faith in . . .

Journal entry. Saturday, March 17, 1888. 3 A.M.

I could have lost her! I get cold chills just thinking about it. That scene that greeted me when I got home at midnight—house ablaze with lights, strange carriage in front of the house, servants rushing about following Aunt Letitia's orders, the midwife—it was something out of Dante's hell.

Thank God Kate is a strong, healthy young woman. If only she doesn't get an infection or start hemorrhaging, she should be all right in a few weeks.

Horseback riding. When I forced Vera to tell me, I could have spanked my Kate. After I'd told her— but it is no use hurling recriminations at her. It's over with. She's been through the agony of a miscarriage, she's lost the baby—Harry's child.

And I'm glad! Not glad that she had the pain and the misery, but I'm glad that she won't have Harry's bastard. I know I promised her I'd accept it as if it were my own child, but I don't know if I could have done it, especially if the child looked as much like

*Harry as Miss Gorman's little boy does. A constant
reminder to me that Harry had Kate's love first—and,
I fear, still does. I am thankful that he is gone. Hopefully, he'll never come back. In time I hope to win
Kate's love—last night—God, that was wonderful!*

CHAPTER 19

Maundy Thursday, March 29, 1888

Kate fretted, "But it's so boring to stay in bed all day, Derek. I feel fine, now. Can't I get up today, at least for a little while?"

"Tomorrow, if you keep improving," he promised, "you may get up and sit in a chair. Or recline on the lounge, if you prefer."

"Could it be moved over by the window? Truly, Derek, I am sick to death of this bed. And I'm not ill at all."

"I'm the doctor," he reminded her firmly. "A miscarriage is a dangerous thing, Kate. You're very fortunate that you had no serious aftereffects. I want to keep it that way. I'll have two of the men move the little spool lounge over by the window, and tomorrow—not today, tomorrow—you may lie there for a while."

"Will you be going into London tomorrow?"

"I always go on Friday, Kate. You know that. Tuesdays and Fridays are my clinic days."

"But tomorrow's Good Friday, Derek. I assumed you'd stay home then."

"People are sick, no matter what the day, Kate. I'll try to keep my hours short tomorrow." He smiled down at her, and she had to smile in return.

Derek had been so good to her that she felt almost ashamed. He'd been furious at first when he learned that she'd gone riding against his express command. He loved her so much, though, he was so frightened for her, that he had forgiven her. Did he regret that she had miscarried? She didn't dare ask him point blank. Kate felt that Derek was glad she no longer carried Harry's baby; but he'd said nothing at all, expressing only heartfelt gratitude that she had survived the accident with no complications. As a doctor, he knew the danger she'd been in even more than she did.

Kate wasn't sure how she felt about losing Harry's child. She'd been so happy that she was going to be able to give him a baby; but when he left, everything had turned upside down for her. It was a horrid complication to be pregnant. What would he say when he learned that she'd been expecting his child—and lost it? Would he be angry with her, blame her for riding out in the chance hope of finding him at the lodge? Kate tried to close her mind to the fact that Harry had another child. She'd seen him. If she could believe Derek, it wasn't the only child Harry had fathered in the area. It grieved her to think of such a thing; yet he'd married none of those girls. He'd have married her, once he'd known about the baby. Kate was sure of this.

Now she was in a terrible dilemma. What was she to do when Harry got back? For all she knew, he might be here already. It was two weeks since she'd received his letter, the missive that had sent her out on horseback to see if he might already be waiting for her at the lodge. There'd been no further mail from him. Was it possible that Derek had intercepted other letters? Surely not. She was learning to read her husband rather well. Kate didn't think he'd be able to hide from her the fact that he knew Harry was corresponding with her. Could Harry be waiting at the lodge, wondering why she hadn't put in an appearance? If he came back to England before his debts were settled, he might have to hide for a time or risk being apprehended and put in jail. Kate knew that Harry would never survive in prison. He hadn't the temperament for confinement.

Unbidden, a thought came to her mind. Would Harry find marriage too confining for his free spirit? But why even think of marriage and Harry together? She was legally bound to Derek. If Harry wanted her, they would have to run away together, place themselves forever beyond the pale of society. She was willing to do this, she thought.

Perhaps, if Harry was successful in business, they could go to the Continent, live there in style. Such an irregular arrangement would go unnoticed in France.

How Kate wished that she could send a letter or note to Harry, but she had no idea where he was. If she weren't trapped in this wretched bed, she'd go to the lodge. If Harry hadn't returned, she could leave a message there for him. She might even leave a note at Fairlawn—although that might not be too wise. The servants would have to be told that it was to be given to Mr. Harry Ravenshaw should he come there looking for her. They might talk. Word could get back to Derek—or to his Aunt Letitia.

Ah, dear Aunt Letitia. The day after Kate miscarried, that redoubtable lady came in to see her, dismissed Vera without so much as a by-your-leave, and then proceeded to lecture her nephew's new wife.

"You are very fortunate to have lost that child, Kate. I know it belonged to Harry. Did Derek know? He must have—you were much too far along, unless you'd seduced him before the wedding. A wild type like you would stoop to anything."

Kate, weakened by her ordeal, wept at Lady Zangwill's harsh words.

"Crying will get you nowhere with me, my girl. I don't know why Derek married you—you're as surely a trollop as those poor, benighted women the Duchess of Dorminster works with in East London. But you're infinitely luckier than they. You managed to snare a fine young man to marry you—I'll never know how."

Tired of the abuse, Kate retorted, "Derek loves me."

"More fool he. But for his sake, I'm glad the child is gone. He deserves better than that—having to raise his own brother's bastard as his own. Oh, don't protest. I know the gossip. I know that child belonged to Harry."

"Please leave me," Kate said.

"You were glad enough to have me stand by and help you last night," the old lady snapped.

"I thank you for your assistance," Kate said through clenched teeth. "But now I must rest. Derek gave orders that I should be quiet, not upset myself. I'm sure he would not approve of your upsetting me, Lady Letitia."

Finally her enemy left; but she returned every day under the pretense of seeing how Kate was progressing. Each day she had some harsh words to say to her nephew's wife.

Today Kate was lucky. Very soon after Derek had gone to London, Parsons brought up a visitor who was more welcome than Lady Zangwill. It was the Duchess of Dorminster. Today the duchess wore a scarlet riding habit that clashed wildly with her bright yellow hair and her painted face. Her riding hat sported an ostrich plume dyed a bilious green. The effect was unsettling.

"Would have stopped by sooner, but I thought you didn't need company. Sorry to hear of your problem, Kate."

"It's kind of you to come by. I've been so bored."

The duchess looked at her with those shrewd blue eyes. "It's always a sad thing to lose a baby—particularly when you are newly married—but in your case, Kate, perhaps it was for the best. Now, now—don't be upset by my words. I'm a blunt old woman, my dear. That child wasn't Derek's."

"You've been talking to Lady Letitia," Kate said angrily. "She's spreading that story far and wide, I dare say."

"I know Letitia can be fair obnoxious, my dear. But I must give the Devil his due—she didn't mention such a thing to me. No, I've noticed things for months. I know you saw Harry on the sly. Remember, I warned you he was no good."

"He was pushed into whatever they say he did because Derek wouldn't give him enough money to live on!"

"Won't wash with me, Kate. I've known Harry since he was a little tad. No good. I told you that early on. You didn't listen. Well, now he's gone, and you should be glad." A shadow crossed her clown face. "Heard a rumor—heard someone was putting up the money so Harry could come back."

Kate was dying to know everything the duchess could tell her, but she didn't dare show interest. The duchess was much too astute for that.

Feigning disinterest, Kate said, "There are always rumors."

"Now, Kate, the thing for you to do is to get busy, once

you are up and around. I shall speak to Derek. Tell him I need you for my classes. Be a good thing for you—keep you in touch with what he's doing in his clinic. Hope he doesn't lose that building."

The duchess's rock-skipping conversational technique sometimes threw Kate for a loss. "What about his building?"

"Doesn't own it, you know—the house where he has his clinic. Trying to buy. I heard that Mansfield was after that entire block. Rotten man."

"Did you know that Father wanted me to marry Mansfield?"

"Heard a rumor." The duchess had ears at every door! "Frederick must have been balmy to suggest that creature."

Kate sighed. "He was very sick, much sicker than I realized. I blame myself somewhat for his death. He was desperately worried about money—"

"That scamp Harry took him for a lot, Kate."

Kate pretended she didn't hear that remark. "Mansfield held the mortgage on Fairlawn. He told Father that he'd not foreclose if I married him."

"Better off with Derek." Then, shrewdly, "Mansfield doesn't seem to have his filthy hands on your estate, Kate. Derek pay him off? Thought he might have. Bet Mansfield hates him for taking both you and Fairlawn from him. No wonder he's trying to buy that property from under Derek in Whitechapel."

"Derek hadn't mentioned that to me."

"Silly men think women don't know enough to manage a business. Forget that we're ruled by a woman—and ably."

The duchess waved away Kate's offer of refreshments. "Must be on my way. Will see you after Easter and arrange for you to go back to Salvation Chapel with me."

"How is the Reverend Mr. Fiddler?"

The duchess shook her head, setting the ostrich plume to waving. "The man is sick. And that silly woman of his won't sleep with him. I tell you, Kate, Abby will drive her husband around the bend. He hasn't far to go." The duchess smiled and swept out of Kate's bedchamber, leaving Kate aghast at her final words.

Kate couldn't imagine a woman not enjoying love. She recalled the one night when she and Derek had enjoyed each other's bodies in a healthy, happy, glorious fashion. That's what marriage should be, Kate knew; but how could she have a good marriage with Derek when she loved his brother? Much as she longed for Harry's return, she also dreaded it, for it presented so many complications. Would Derek allow Harry to live at Scarlet Oaks if his debts were settled? Who was the benefactor to whom Harry would be indebted? And the question she didn't dare ask herself—what would Harry do when he found that she was married to his brother? And what will I do? she asked herself. What will I do?

Determined to show an interest in Derek's work, Kate broached the subject of Mansfield at dinner that night. He'd given instructions to have dinner served in their room. He even lifted Kate from the bed and allowed her to sit in a chair at the small marble-topped table that Parsons set for them, covering it with an embroidered cloth of white linen. Kate was delighted to be out of bed, Derek seemed happy to find her so well, and wonder of wonders, he had not included his Aunt Letitia in their arrangements. The two of them were able to dine tête-à-tête.

"The Duchess of Dorminster called. Derek, she says that Mansfield is trying to take the clinic away from you."

"Trying—not succeeding," Derek said smugly. "I signed the final papers today. That building is mine. And as it sits squarely in the middle of the block, I've ruined Mansfield plans to buy up the entire row of houses and pack them even fuller than they now are with the destitute of the area. I might even buy the rest of the block myself, clean it up, try to turn it into a model row of decent housing. Perhaps I could, in time, convert one unit into a small hospital to serve that immediate area." Then his face darkened. "I don't know what to do about Monica Murphy, Kate. She gets worse daily. If only she'd let me help her."

"Did you used to go about with her, Derek?"

He gave her a strange look. "Who's been gossiping?"

"Well, I've heard it."

He nodded as if reluctant to make the admission. "A long time ago, Kate. When she and I were nineteen or twenty."

"Why didn't you marry her?" Kate asked. "At that time she must have been most attractive."

"She was; but there always was a wild streak in Monica, a reckless daring that I didn't think I could live with."

"Were you the man who started her on her road to ruin?"

"Kate! What a question to ask your husband!"

"Oh, Derek, don't be so stuffy. Everyone in the county knows that someone was the cause of her present condition."

"It wasn't I. Oh, all right, we made love a few times—but believe me, Kate, she was no virgin when I first had her. And I was only one in a long line of men who enjoyed her favors. I don't know what made her the way she was —but seeing her now grieves me. For what she once was— for what we were to each other, if only briefly, when we were young—I feel obliged to do everything I can for her. Which, God help me, is not much. Kate, do you have any idea how frustrating it is for a doctor to be powerless to cure a friend? But then much of my work on Union Row is frustrating. Sometimes—" She saw the muscles of his jaw knot, his hands double into fists. "Then to have to do constant battle with the likes of Mansfield—"

"Why don't you give it all up, Derek? Surely the tiny bit you do for those poor souls is negligible."

"If everyone thought that way, East London would be even worse than it is now."

Kate thought of the terrible things she'd seen there: pallid children in rags, scavenging in the garbage for a morsel to eat; a sea of white hands raised to bid for the spoiled meat and produce at the end of each market day; the whores, Monica included, selling themselves for a few pence just to earn the price of a night's lodging in a dirty, common bed. How could Whitechapel be any worse than it was now?

"The duchess wants me to go back to the chapel with

her, when I feel able. She insists that it will be good for me, take my mind off the child I just lost."

Derek's face was a thundercloud. "No. I will not have my wife in that place."

It annoyed Kate to be so ordered by Derek. She said nothing, but she decided that if the duchess asked again, she might well go back with her.

Instead of letting Derek know how she felt, she turned the subject into a joke by asking, "Do you think you do more good than that monument of rectitude, the Reverend Mr. Fiddler?"

Diverted, Derek laughed bitterly. "That man preaches hell and damnation to those poor sinners—and he is the biggest sinner of them all!"

"Monica told us that he patronizes the local women of the streets."

Derek shrugged. "Well, with a wife like that skinny prune he's married to, is it any wonder he wanders?" Then he reached over, took Kate's hand. "He's not lucky—I am. I miss you very much, dear wife. I wait impatiently for the day when we can resume our marital life."

Kate said nothing. What could she say? Harry was coming back and Derek might not have a wife for much longer.

CHAPTER 20

Sunday, April 1, 1888

Easter Sunday dawned bright and clear. There were crocuses blooming in the garden, and jonquils waved their golden trumpets in the light breeze.

"But I feel fine," Kate protested. "It's like being in prison, Derek. I've been cooped up here in our room for more than two weeks. How could it possibly hurt me to go downstairs, ride in a carriage to church, and sit there through the service?"

"It's out of the question, Kate, and I wish you'd quit complaining. If you'd stayed home when you were supposed to, you wouldn't be confined now."

It was the first time since the night of her miscarriage that he'd referred to the horseback ride that had ended so disastrously.

Kate sulked. It was so boring, just sitting here on the little lounge by the window. Derek did allow her to be out of bed now, but going downstairs was strictly forbidden.

Derek put his arms around her and promised, "If you're a good girl, I may let you go down to dinner this evening."

"Oh, very well." She said it with poor grace. Kate had never been sick before, and she found convalescence trying.

Derek went off to church, looking quite handsome; but he could never rival Harry in looks, Kate thought. She moped about the bedchamber, lamenting her decision to

236

marry Derek. She should have trusted Harry, waited for his return. The thought of facing a pregnancy without a husband had been too much for her, so she had succumbed to Derek's pressure. Now, having lost the child, she regretted her haste. Too late!

Thinking that she would send a note to Pamela Oldham, who might not even have heard about the miscarriage, Kate went to the little desk where Derek penned his nightly journal. A little imp whispered to Kate that maybe she could get the drawer unlocked, read what he put in that mysterious book. The lock defied her though. She tried a few keys she had in a little enameled chest on her sewing stand, but none of them fit. She even pulled a hairpin from her red hair and tried to pick the lock, with no success. Oh, well, it probably was dull reading anyway.

Then she heard a man's voice somewhere downstairs, and she thought it sounded like Derek. He'd been gone less than half an hour. Why had he come back? She went out into the hall and peeked down over the railing into the stairwell, keeping very quiet. If Derek had come home, he'd be angry to find her out of their room.

Then a man came in view, foreshortened by her position above him. Glossy black hair curled at the nape of his neck, broad shoulders filled a dark coat to perfection. He turned to ascend the stairs, and Kate saw his face for the first time. It was Harry! She tried to call out to him, but found that excitement had paralyzed her throat. She stood there, willing him to look up. As he started up the stairs, some sense, some tension in the air, caused him to raise his head. When his gray eyes met her green ones, he stopped dead on the stairs. Kate held out her arms to him.

"Kate!" He took the stairs two at a time, and she moved to meet him. They met at the top of the staircase, and Kate was caught in an embrace that was so hard she thought her ribs might crack.

Their lips met and a great swell of desire washed over Kate. Harry kissed her mouth, her throat, her eyelids.

"Kate, Kate. I was going to try to see you later today." Then, him arms still around her, Harry asked, "But what are you doing here at Scarlet Oaks?"

At that moment, Lady Letitia came sweeping down the hall from the wing where her suite was. Her black dress with its high collar and leg-of-mutton sleeves had a small train where the overskirt draped over the bustle and fell in long folds to brush the carpet. Beady eyes took in the scene at the head of the stairs.

"Harry! What are you doing here?" Then she gave Kate a look of pure hatred. "As if I need ask. I can see for myself what you're up to. How dare you come back here now to disrupt your brother's life. And you, Kate—a proper trollop you are, embracing Harry so brazenly. I can only be thankful that Derek isn't here to see this performance."

Drily Harry said, "What a charming welcome home, Aunt Letitia. Your regard for me is nigh overwhelming."

"Don't get sarcastic with me, Harry. Isn't it bad enough that you have disgraced the Ravenshaw name with your shady financial dealings? But to come back here, a hunted criminal, is too much. And to be passionately embracing Kate—disgusting." Then she turned her venom on Kate. "And what are you doing out here? You are supposed to be confined to your room. I suppose you don't care what happens to you—but unfortunately, Derek does. Did he give you permission to go gallivanting about the house?"

Harry, his arm still around Kate's waist, asked, "What nonsense is this, Auntie dear? What has Derek to say about Kate?"

Kate stiffened. Now it would all come out. She had hoped to break the news gently to Harry; but his Aunt Letitia couldn't wait to tell him the bad tidings.

"What has Derek to say about it? Everything. After all, Kate is his wife."

Harry laughed, that wild, reckless sound Kate loved to hear. "You're mad. I've suspected it for a long time, Aunt Letitia. All that hate in you has finally poisoned your brain. Derek's wife indeed." He turned Kate to him and deliberately kissed her full on the mouth, a long, slow, possessive kiss which left her weak and breathless.

"Shameless!" Lady Letitia hissed. "What an Easter gift for my dear nephew."

"If you'd gone to church like a good Christian, you'd

not have to suffer now," Harry said fliply. "Come, Kate, you must explain all my aunt's madness to me."

"You'll find out who is mad." The diminutive woman walked deliberately down the great staircase, not even deigning to touch the railing for support. Her back was ramrod stiff, her head regal.

"Now, Kate, what is all this nonsense?"

Kate felt faint. She had been in bed most of the past two weeks. That, combined with the intense emotional upheaval she'd just experienced, was too much for her.

"Harry, I feel ill," she said, leaning against him for support.

Immediately he scooped her up in his arms. "Which room are you using?"

"I'm—I'm in Derek's room."

He had started to walk down the hall, carrying her. Now Harry stopped short. "What did you just say, Kate?" His voice was dangerously quiet.

"I said that I'm in Derek's room." A sob burst from her throat, and she buried her face on Harry's shoulder. "It's true, Harry," she cried, tears blinding her. "I'm now Derek's wife."

"I don't believe it." He set her down on her feet. When she clung to him, weak and dizzy, Harry pushed her away, so that she tottered and would have fallen if she hadn't leaned against the wall. "What do you mean, you're Derek's wife? You belong to me, Kate. The kiss you gave me when I got here—that wasn't the kiss of a sister-in-law."

Kate buried her face in her hands and wept without restraint. Then everything began to spin about her, she felt herself slipping, and she fell into a dark, velvet-lined well.

When she regained consciousness, she lay on the bed she shared with Derek, and Vera was there, holding a crystal vial of smelling salts under her nose. Petulantly she pushed the maid's hand away.

"I dreamed—" Then she saw Harry standing beside the bed, his face a welter of emotions—anger, chagrin, annoyance—that paraded across his handsome features so that she seemed to see a multitude of Harrys, not just one. With a little moan she closed her eyes again.

"Sir, should we send for Sir Derek?" Vera asked him.

"What's wrong with her? I don't understand any of this," Harry fumed.

"It's all right, Vera. I feel better. You may go," Kate ordered. She had to get Harry by himself, explain the tragic situation to him as best she could.

Harry waited with his usual impatience until Vera had gone out, closing the door behind her. Then he approached the bed, towered over Kate, and demanded, "I want an explanation."

It all tumbled out in a jumble of words—the pregnancy, her father's financial failure due to the stock Harry had sold him, Mansfield's threatened foreclosure, and Derek's rescue. "He demanded marriage as his price for keeping me out of Mansfield's clutches."

"That's supposed to be a bargain? I'd rather have seen you married to Mansfield than to my brother. Tightwad Derek, keeper of the privy purse. You do realize, don't you, that it was Derek's highhanded ways that drove me into that phony stock deal?"

"But Harry, why did you have to sell that stock to my father? It ruined him—it killed him."

Harry sat down on the side of the bed and caught her hands in his own, sending a thrill through her that was almost more than she could bear. How she longed to be in his arms, to lie with him once again.

"Kate, darling Kate, don't paint me as a monster. I didn't ruin your father. He was in hock up to his eyebrows before he bought any stock from me. I tried to avoid him, truly I did, but he'd gotten wind of it and thought it sounded like the answer to all his problems. He begged to buy it. How could I dare tell him the shares were forged? All right, it was unfortunate that he bought from me, but he had already mortgaged Fairlawn to Mansfield. He couldn't have recouped his fortune, phony stock or not."

Kate wanted to believe him. The burden on her of knowing that Harry's shady dealings had helped kill her father had been enormous.

"Now I come back, free—thanks to the generosity of none other than Arthur Mansfield—"

"Harry, what do you mean?"

"He paid off my debts and greased a few wheels with the authorities. The charges against me have been dropped. I am a free man to live in England however and wherever I wish."

"Oh, Harry, how wonderful!"

"I asked Derek to do it for me. He refused. Ironic, isn't it? My own flesh and blood wouldn't help me, but the man everyone tries to paint as a villain would. Is it any wonder that I'd rather have found you married to Mansfield than to Derek?"

"But Mansfield wouldn't marry me once he knew about the baby." She remembered all too well that dreadful scene when he had announced she'd be his mistress and tried to rape her. When she told Harry, he laughed.

"The biggest blackguards of all are the ones who insist on virginal wives. Surely you know that, Kate."

"But it put me in the most awful position, Harry. When Derek promised that he'd raise your child as his own, grant it the inheritance—what could I do? I had no idea where you had gone, if you'd ever return. I was distraught when Father died. Mansfield was threatening me. I turned to Derek as my only salvation. I couldn't hope to have your child without assistance from someone!"

"So now my baby will be Derek's," Harry said bitterly. "Well, it's one way, I suppose, to get the inheritance for my son, if not for myself."

Kate was aghast. In all the turmoil, she'd not told Harry that she had lost the child.

"So when is my son due to be born, Kate?"

It was too much for her. She burst into tears. Immediately she was enfolded in Harry's arms, in an embrace that became increasingly intimate as the moments passed.

Fearful of what might happen, Kate pushed Harry away from her. "Harry—I—I lost the child. A little over two weeks ago, I went riding—I got your letter, and I thought maybe you'd already arrived in England, so I hurried to the lodge to see if you were there. Something frightened my mare. I was thrown—and I miscarried that night."

"Well, perhaps it was for the best, Kate. One less complication in an otherwise extremely complicated situation."

At that moment the ultimate complication burst through the door. It was Derek, livid with anger.

Inanely, Kate said, "Derek, I didn't expect you home so soon."

"Obviously." His smoldering look took in Kate and Harry—with Harry sitting on the bed, Kate enfolded in his arms. "Get out, Harry. Get out of here now, before I kill you!"

With surprising aplomb, Harry loosed his hold on Kate and stood up, making no move to leave the room.

"Why should I get out?" he asked, his voice calm, pleasant. "This is my home, too, you know. I've always lived here at Scarlet Oaks, and I intend to go right on living here, as long as it suits me."

"And cuckold me? Oh, no, Harry. Not this time. You've gone too far. I'll have the police here. There's still a warrant for your arrest."

Harry leaned indolently against the post of the bed. "Not any longer, Derek. My debts have all been paid. I'm a free man, to come and go as I choose. And I choose to live in England—in Essex County—in my lifelong home, Scarlet Oaks. As to your wife—well, if you can't hold her, that is your problem, Derek, not mine." He turned and smiled at Kate, a possessive, self-confident smile.

Kate feared that her husband might have a stroke of apoplexy, his face was so flushed with rage. Not wanting to be party to any more deaths, she said quickly, "Derek, nothing untoward has happened here. I swear it. Harry came home unexpectedly." That was only a half-truth, but she did not bother to tell him that she had been expecting Harry for several weeks. There were limits to her husband's credulity.

"I come in, find you in his arms, and you tell me—"

"Derek, I was weeping. I had just told him about losing the baby—his baby."

"Which you had planned to claim for your own, denying me even the right of fatherhood," Harry put in.

This was too much for Derek. "That's right. I had promised her that—I'd have promised Kate the moon in order to get her to marry me. I've always wanted her. You can't know what a bitter blow it was to me to find that you had seduced my lovely Kate. But you see, Harry, I have won in the end. She's my wife, not yours. And she will remain my wife. I will never let her go—never."

"That's for Kate to decide, not you." Harry's voice was icily calm, deadly.

"No, Kate has nothing to say in the matter. She made her decision when she agreed to marry me. Now she must stick to her bargain."

"Kate?" Harry held out a hand to her.

The time had finally come for Kate to make her choice. But it was a terrible decision to make. She wanted to go with Harry; she loved him. But Derek stood there glaring at them. Derek stood between them. She had married him and she owed him much. For some strange reason, Kate felt she couldn't betray Derek now.

"I can't go with you, Harry. Surely you understand that?" Her voice was imploring, her green eyes full of love.

It was a touching scene—but Derek spoiled it.

"See, Harry? When forced to make a decision, she chooses me. She's learned about you, dear brother. She's seen the son you gave little Miss Gorman. She knows what you're like."

"She loves me, Derek. It's a hollow victory you have."

"Get out! Get out of my house, and out of my sight!" Derek yelled, advancing on Harry with clenched fists.

Harry shrugged. "Very well, I'll leave for now. But take my word for it, Derek. Kate will be mine once again. She married you only for security, because she was trapped by circumstances which proved too much for her to bear alone. If I had been here—"

He smiled, bent over and kissed Kate deliberately—and then dodged Derek's fist, leaving the room before his brother could regain his balance to attack him.

Kate wished the earth would open and she could disappear. The situation was intolerable. Now that Harry had returned, what was she going to do? It was obvious that Derek did not intend to let her go without fighting to hold her.

CHAPTER 21

Sunday Evening, April 1, 1888

Derek had finally agreed to let Kate go down to the dining room for Easter Sunday dinner. He picked her up and carried her, cradling her in his arms like a child. He had not let her dress, telling her that her blue negligee was quite suitable for a family meal. "It will be just the three of us—you, Aunt Letitia, and me. Harry rode off somewhere."

"Will he come back, Derek?"

She felt his arms tighten with emotion. "Probably. He left his things here—the few he took with him when he fled one step ahead of the law."

Parsons had arranged a comfortable chair in the dining room, and Derek put Kate in it as carefully as if she were made of the finest Chinese porcelain. Lady Letitia had not yet put in an appearance, so Kate went on talking about Harry.

"Harry blames you for all his troubles, Derek. He told me, even before all the furor about the stock shares, that you refused to give him an adequate income. That's what led to his getting into financial trouble."

Derek pulled out one of the side chairs, turned it around, and straddled it, folding his arms over the back. "By now I'd think you'd have learned not to believe everything Harry says, Kate. He could have applied himself, gotten something to do, earned the money. Too lazy to work, he stole instead. It's as simple as that. I was willing to pay for his university education—finance him through medical school. He quit. He refused to study."

"But Derek, he hated medicine. He said it was awful, cutting up corpses." She shuddered delicately. "I can't blame him. It's gruesome."

"He had only to talk with me, Kate, tell me what field he preferred if he didn't want to be a doctor. He didn't want to study anything. All Harry has ever wanted is to have a good time, plenty of money to spend, no responsibilities. He'd have made you a rotten husband if he had married you."

"I could have changed him," Kate said.

"No woman ever changes the man she marries." It was Aunt Letitia, walking with the aid of a blackthorn stick. "Dampness gets into my bones sometimes," she said, sinking gratefully into the chair one of the underfootmen held for her. "Sit down, Derek, sit down—properly."

Without answering her, Derek took his place at the head of the table.

Frowning, Lady Letitia leaned forward. "Kate, you must speak to the housekeeper. That epergne needs a good polishing. You have to keep a tight rein in a large household, or the servants become lazy and slovenly." All this in front of Parsons and the footman who was helping serve.

"Kate's been ill, Aunt Letitia." For once he was taking his wife's part against his aunt. "When she feels well enough, you can instruct her in the proper running of Scarlet Oaks. It will take a lot of work from your shoulders."

Kate sat there, staring sullenly at the offending silver epergne, its four candles gleaming softly. The bottom bowl held bunches of purple and white grapes, artfully hanging over the fluted rim of the dish, while the top tray was filled with lemons and limes. To Kate the piece looked perfectly polished. It was only Lady Letitia's way of finding fault with her through the servants.

Parsons ladled a fish soup out of a Wedgwood tureen into matching soup plates, and while Lady Letitia inhaled her portion, she kept up a steady stream of comments. "I heard you speak of changing Harry if you had married him. Can't be done, Kate, with Harry or with any man. I hope you don't think you will be able to reform Derek."

"I'm sure I couldn't. I wouldn't try."

Derek looked up from his soup, a quizzical glance. "Do I have such terrible habits, Kate, that I need reforming?"

"I didn't say that." She spoke shortly. The day had been extremely upsetting.

"But you think I've been much too hard on Harry."

Lady Letitia gave a theatrical gasp. "Hard on him! One of the things wrong with Harry is that he's been spoiled from the moment he was born. My poor, dear brother, so distressed when that dreadful wife left him, lavished affection on Harry, doted on him, gave him everything he wanted. Always referred to him as that poor little motherless tike—as if Derek's dear mother hadn't died, leaving him." Her voice was indignant. Throughout the discourse, she worked her way through a large helping of baked turbot with parsley.

Kate, faced by such a large meal after she'd eaten rather lightly for two weeks, began to feel faintly ill. Derek, ever watchful, forever the physician, quickly noticed it.

"Don't you feel well, dear?"

"I don't seem to have much appetite."

"You're no longer eating for two," Lady Letitia said, sinking her teeth into a pheasant wing.

"I—please excuse me."

Derek was at her side instantly, gathering her up into his arms, carrying her from the paneled room.

"Will you be back, Derek?" his aunt called after him. "There's still the joint and the sweet."

"You must finish your dinner," Kate insisted. "I'll be quite all right. It's just that—watching your aunt eat all that food—"

He laughed, the first time he'd laughed since Harry had come home. "She does like her food. Yet she's as tiny as a sparrow."

"She uses up all that food for energy to be nasty."

"Kate, Kate, she's an old lady. Have some charity for her."

"She has none for me—nor for poor Harry. No wonder he's the way he is, having had her to raise him."

"Aunt Letitia raised me, too, Kate," he reminded her, carrying her into their room. "Do you want to lie on the bed or the lounge?"

"The lounge. Do go back to your dinner, Derek. You must be starving."

"I'll be back as soon as I finish. I'll have Parsons bring you up a cup of tea."

"Thank you, that would taste good."

"See, you aren't strong enough yet to go racing about." Derek must have done the racing, for he was back so quickly that Kate decided he'd taken lessons from his aunt in fast eating. While she drank tea, he sipped a glass of port.

"Are you going to force Harry to live elsewhere?"

"Kate, I really don't want him here, under the circumstances. With you at Scarlet Oaks—"

Indignantly she asked, "Don't you trust me, Derek?"

"It's Harry I don't trust," he said darkly. "I don't want to be cuckolded by my own brother, Kate."

"I promise you—"

He stopped her. "Don't promise anything, Kate. Harry has a way of getting around women. I'd rather you didn't promise me, than to break your word. I wish he'd stayed away. We could have had a good marriage . . ."

Kate sighed, closed her eyes, leaned back on the pillows. "You think our marriage won't succeed? If you believe that, at the first sign of trouble, then it probably won't, Derek. I don't love you. I never pretended to. But I'm grateful to you for rescuing me from an intolerable situation. The fact that the situation has now changed drastcially doesn't release me from my obligation to you."

He fell to his knees beside her, caught her in his arms. "Oh, Kate, I don't want you to feel obliged to stay with me. That is a crucifying concept to a man in love. I want you here because you want to be. I had hoped you would, in time, come to love me. That one lovely night—" He groaned, buried his face in her bosom. "Oh, Kate, Harry has spoiled everything for us. With him around, knowing that you love him—or that you think you do, which is just as bad—how can I hope that you'll try to care for me?"

"Poor Derek," she soothed, putting her arms about him,

holding him as gently as she would a child in need of comfort. "We've made an awful botch of three lives, haven't we? Well, we must make the best of it, I guess."

He drew away from her, not wanting pity, only love. "Do you still think that I should let Harry live here?"

"It's his home, Derek. It's the only home he's ever known. Where else would he go? Besides," she added in sudden wisdom, "if Harry's here, you can keep an eye on him."

Derek pulled a leather-covered ottoman over beside the lounge and sat beside Kate, but he did not even take her hand. Suspicion rife in his voice, he asked, "What does that mean?"

"Do you know who paid off Harry's debts, arranged for the charges against him to be dropped? Arthur Mansfield."

"Mansfield! What's his game? He and my brother are in league together, and you expect me to take Harry in? It would make as much sense as to take a viper into my bed."

She reached out, laid a pleading hand on Derek's. Kate thought he might pull away from her touch; but after one second when she felt his hand go rigid under her own, he relaxed, leaving her hand where it was.

"Derek, I don't know what Mansfield's game is; but he hates both of us. He expected to marry me—and when he found that I was pregnant, he then announced that he would have me as his mistress. From what he said, he expected me to preside over Fairlawn as if it were a high-class bordello. When you thwarted him by snatching me away, he hated you—and me. I feel that he's into some devious scheme that will harm you. You know that he's furious now that he can't have the building you occupy on Union Row. He knows you oppose him in everything he does, every rotten scheme his hateful mind concocts. I'd say he brought Harry into his camp deliberately, paying off his debts to put him under obligation. I love Harry." She said it simply, quietly; but she felt Derek wince. "You know that. Harry's not bad—I don't believe it. He's misguided—"

"Thanks to me," Derek said bitterly.

"Partly, yes. Don't glare at me, Derek. It is partly your fault. Think how it is from Harry's viewpoint just once.

Two sons—and one gets everything. He was raised to luxury, Derek, accustomed to having whatever he wanted. Suddenly he's penniless, dependent on you for everything."

"He could have learned to work for a living. I work, Kate, very hard."

"Yes, yes, I know. But Harry's not like you, Derek."

"That's the truest thing you've said yet."

"Derek, Derek, have a little charity in your heart for him. His mother abandoned him—"

"I was raised motherless too!"

"Ah, but your mother died, my dear. She didn't deliberately leave you behind when she decided she wanted out of her marriage. That's done something to Harry, warped him—oh, he puts on a good front. He pretends to be carefree, happy-go-lucky. But deep down, I think he is deeply troubled. Do you know that I've even heard he went to a brothel once, somewhere in England, and found his own mother there?"

"I think that's true."

"Can't you imagine what that would do to a man? Have you no pity in your soul at all, Derek? Or are you sorry only for those poor drabs in Whitechapel, while someone who needs your understanding gets a cold shoulder from you?"

"All right, all right, Harry can stay here—if he behaves himself. But if I find that he's sleeping with you—"

"Derek! I'm your wife, and I don't care to have you make such accusations. I don't suggest that you are carrying on an illicit relationship with Monica Murphy!"

"Good God, I should hope not!"

"Well, you once—"

"Kate, that was years ago. Are you going to turn out to be a jealous wife?" He asked it almost as if he hoped she would, for at least that would show she had some interest in him.

"I do hope that Lady Letitia doesn't try to make trouble when she learns that Harry will be here at Scarlet Oaks. She hates him, you know. That's another factor that shaped Harry's character—growing up with her as a substitute for the mother who didn't want him. His stepaunt. A woman who had concern only for you, because

250 RACHEL COSGROVE PAYES

you were her blood nephew. She is a wicked, conniving old woman, Derek. Can't you arrange for her to live elsewhere?"

"Kate!" He was properly horrified. "She spent years of her life caring for me. I can't toss her aside now as I would a worn garment. No, Aunt Letitia's home is here."

"She thinks I'm usurping her place, she hates Harry—can't you see what will happen? She's doing everything in her power to make life miserable for me, Derek. If you love me as much as you claim to, then you must consider such things."

"Give her time. She'll come around."

Kate doubted this very much; but she saw that she was not going to convince Derek that Aunt Letitia spelled potential disaster, so she said no more. Nagging wasn't the way to get a man to do what you wanted him to. But there were other ways, womanly ways, and Kate was determined to get her wishes, no matter what she had to do.

"Let's not quarrel, dearest husband," she said, leaning toward him, reaching up and caressing his cheek tenderly. "Give poor Harry one more chance. If he misbehaves, then send him away. I think you owe that much to him."

He swayed toward her and gathered her into his arms, and Kate tipped back her head so that her lips invited his passionate kiss. It was all for Harry, she told herself. She was doing this only for him.

INTERLUDE 6

Monday and Tuesday, April 2 and 3, 1888

The frustrations were building. He had to get out on the streets of East London again, allow his baser nature to hold sway. He walked for hours, finding himself in Limehouse, where gin battled with opium for the souls and bodies of the destitute.

At Fairance Street he saw a woman soliciting, a familiar face. He was sure she lived somewhere in the Whitechapel area. She'd come far afield tonight looking for customers.

Sidling up to her, he said, "Far from home, eh?"

She turned and peered at him. There was gin on her breath, and she smelled as if she'd never bathed in her life. She smiled at him, showing rotten teeth. Her hair straggled down from a battered bonnet, which might have been blue. It was so dirty the color no longer showed.

"Want a bit of fun, luv? Fivepence. That's all it costs you," she simpered. "A fine gent like you, fivepence is nothing. Or if you wants a bed, it'll be a few pence more. Whatever you like." There was no recognition in her eyes.

"What's your name?" he whispered.

"Emma, luv." She laughed drunkenly. "Emma Elizabeth Smith's me full name. Like it?"

"Smith's a common enough name," he said, adding with studied cruelty, "and you're a common enough whore."

Sensing that he wasn't going to pay her anything, she spat at him, so that he had to wipe the spittle from his coat. Then she picked up her tattered skirts, showing that

251

she wore men's heavy boots and striped stockings, and fled, afraid of what he might do to her. He didn't follow. Instead he continued his prowling, working his way toward Whitechapel.

It was getting late, but he couldn't settle down. He was opposite Salvation Chapel when he saw Fiddler hurrying along in the shadows as if the legions of hell pursued him. The glow from one gas lamp threw his long, skinny frame into silhouette just as he wiped his hands on something—there was a gleam of white—then tossed the kerchief, if it was that, into the dark entry to an alley. As he neared the entrance to the chapel, Fiddler slowed, stopped dead, looked about him.

Does he know I watch him? Probably not, the man thought.

Then Fiddler slipped into the chapel so quickly that if the watcher had not been alert, he'd have missed the black-clad figure as it slid through the door.

It was now nearly four A.M. As he passed the corner of Whitechapel Road and Osborne street, he looked down the long, poorly lit side street and saw a woman staggering along, moving away from him. There was something so peculiar about her walk that he turned into Osborne, lengthened his strides, and soon was close behind her. She walked as if something hurt her. Occasionally she would stop, lean against a grimy brick wall, then push herself upright and plod on. It was the whore he'd encountered earlier, Emma Smith. She seemed to have lost the woolen shoulder wrap she'd worn then. Once she stopped under a gaslight and turned to glance over her shoulder as if she'd heard him following. He slid into the black shadows of an overhanging roof and waited until she staggered away. It looked as if there might be blood on her face. His pulses raced at the sight. Again he followed; but when she reached a lodging house on George Street in Spitalsfield, she turned in at the doorway. He drifted past. Number 18. A common lodging house. He'd gone on down the street when he turned back at a sound behind him. Three people were coming out of the building Emma Smith had entered. He saw two men and the Smith woman. Again he followed the slow progress of the trio.

The men seemed to be holding the woman up, helping her along. He closed the distance between them and heard her voice.

". . . attacked me, they did. Robbed me."

One of the men, possibly the deputy of the lodging house, asked, "Where did you say this happened, Emma?"

"Osborne Street. Took the money I'd meant for my night's bed, they did." Then she swayed and would have fallen if the men had not supported her. At Whitechapel Road they turned left and made their way in the predawn hours of darkness. He heard Emma Smith protest, "Don't want to go in hospital."

Their destination was now established. Something had happened to Emma Smith. Probably she'd had a fight with someone, possibly another whore. He knew of Emma's reputation. She was a fighter when drunk. Losing interest in her, he ducked into the Whitechapel underground station and waited for a train.

As he sat huddled in the corner of one seat while the train rattled over the tracks, he remembered the blood on Emma Smith's face. There was something exciting about the sight of blood. He wished he could have been there when she was injured. To see blood let was even more exciting than sex. His hands curled unconsciously into claws. Whatever had happened to Emma Smith, she deserved.

He began to see how murder could be done in the East End with no fear of discovery or reprisal. No threat from the pitiful police force. Now, if he planned carefully, he could kill and then throw suspicion on his hated rival. What a fitting revenge!

CHAPTER 22

Friday, April 6, 1888

It was after dinner. For a brief time Lady Letitia joined them in the drawing room; but she soon tired of Harry's banter and Derek's short answers and retired. Kate was not sorry to see her go. This had been a trying week. Derek had relented and allowed Harry to stay on at Scarlet Oaks, but Kate was not sure that her idea had been a good one. There was an atmosphere of constant strain and antagonism whenever the two brothers were together. Derek watched Harry with suspicion bordering on paranoia, while Harry seemed to go out of his way to say and do things calculated to annoy the baronet. Kate was in the middle. Each man wanted her on his side. Harry openly tried to seduce her, which so far she had resisted. Derek worked to charm her when they were alone; but when Harry was with them, his feelings toward Kate seemed to change.

Harry now did something typical, trying to get a rise out of his brother. He picked up a copy of a newspaper which Derek had brought home with him from London.

"The Penny Illustrated Paper," he read aloud with much expression, "AND the *Illustrated Times.* What a high-quality paper you read, Derek." He leafed through the tabloid, snickering at bits in it. "All the scandal, all the murders, all the crime! No news but bad news. Have you seen this, Kate?" He proffered the paper to her, grinning hugely

when she shook her head. "Your lovely wife has better taste in literature than you do, brother."

"Your remarks do not amuse me."

Harry threw back his head and laughed uproariously. "Your remarks do not amuse me," he mimicked. "You are a stuffy, pompous ass, Derek."

Kate, seeing that Derek was ready to explode, cut in quickly, "Oh, I'll look at the paper, Harry. Here, give it to me."

"Never mind, Kate," her husband said, seething. "It is exactly what Harry says it is. But I bought it for a good reason."

"You can't understand the big words in a decent paper?" Harry suggested slyly.

"Hush, Harry!" she said, exasperated with both men. They bickered like children sometimes. Turning to her husband, she asked, trying to appear interested, "Why did you get the paper, dear?"

"There's a little crippled newsboy who sells it at the underground station. He needs the money."

"Oh, very altruistic, my dear brother. Well, as long as this is a charity endeavor, we should, perhaps, use the paper to edify ourselves." He opened the pages at random. "Ah, here's something. A death. Notice of a coroner's inquest to be held tomorrow on the death of one Emma Elizabeth Smith."

"Emma Smith! Here, let me see that." Derek snatched the paper from his brother's hands, quickly read the brief notice.

"A friend of yours, Derek?" Harry mocked. "You spend so much of your time in the East End, you must know most of those lovely characters." In an aside to Kate, he said, "Probably a woman of ill repute, to put it delicately."

"But a woman, Harry."

Kate could see that Derek was disturbed by the inquest notice. "Did you know her, Derek?"

"As a matter of fact, I was called in to London Hospital on Tuesday by a friend of mine who works there. To see this woman. It was an unusual case—so the poor thing died. Developed peritonitis, no doubt, from the wound."

"Wound? It's a rough neighborhood, Derek. I sometimes wonder that you aren't afraid to have that clinic on Union Row."

"They know I'm there to help them." His answer was terse, his tone annoyed.

Kate, curious now, asked, "What happened to her, Derek?"

"I'd rather not discuss it, Kate. It was very ugly."

"As no doubt the woman herself was."

"What did she do, get drunk and have a fight with another whore? Poaching on each other's territory, perhaps?" Harry sneered.

"The attack on Emma Smith was vicious—and sexual in nature," he said. "Let's change the subject."

"Away from sex? Priggish, Derek, decidedly priggish. How can you abide my prude of a brother, Kate? Once a woman has known a real man with real appetites, it must be boring to be tied to such a dull creature as my saintly older brother."

"Harry!" Derek's voice was cold, low, and deadly.

"Oh, Harry, I do wish you'd behave," Kate said. "It gives me a headache, hearing you two quarrel."

"You're the one who wanted him here," Derek reminded her bitterly. "Don't complain now, Kate." Then he smiled, a wicked, wolfish smile that chilled her. "Of course, the minute you decide that you're tired of listening to Harry's banalities, Kate, just tell me. I'll throw him out of Scarlet Oaks—this time for good."

"Kate isn't going to do that. She loves me, Derek. Or have you forgotten that interesting little fact?"

"Oh, stop it, stop it!" she snapped, furious with both of the men. "I'm going up to my room. I can't stand this bickering."

"I'll go with you," Derek said, giving Harry a smug, triumphant look.

"Oh, show your rights as a husband," Harry said, his voice airy but his gray eyes cold. "But remember, while you go off each day to your bloodletting and pill dispensing, I'm here with my lovely, loving Kate. Don't you wonder what goes on while you're in your surgery, Derek?"

"Nothing goes on! Harry, stop this nonsense this minute!" Kate ordered. She had no wish to see a display of

Derek's formidable temper. And she had no desire to have him more suspicious of Harry than he was already. She turned to her husband, put a placating hand on his arm. "Harry's only saying such dreadful things to annoy you, Derek. Don't pay any attention to him. Come, I'm tired. Let's retire."

Harry had the last word. As they left the drawing room, he called after them, "And don't you wonder what your wife's been doing to tire her out so?" Then he laughed suggestively.

In their bedchamber Derek exploded with rage. "You see what it's like with Harry here? Are you satisfied, Kate? You insisted that I let him live here at Scarlet Oaks —does he show any gratitude?"

"But he thinks of it as his right—this is his home, Derek, the only one he's ever known."

"Things are different now. You're here, as my wife. Kate—oh, Kate." He caught her to him, desperation in his voice. "I hate him, Kate. I hate him for what he did to you. I have pictures in my mind that I can't erase—ugly pictures of the two of you together in the kind of intimacy which only I should have from you. I wonder—"

"Rest assured, if I misbehave, your aunt will let you know." She let the bitterness stay in her voice. "What a delightful household we are. You—Harry—your Aunt Letitia—and I. I had never realized that this was the way marriage would be."

"Nor had I, Kate. Let's not fight between the two of us. Remember, I love you."

"Yet you are suspicious of me, Derek. No, don't deny it. I saw the look on your face when Harry joked about—"

"Joked! He says he shares your bed, and you expect me to pass off such a comment as a joke? What kind of man do you take me for, Kate?"

"A very jealous one. You know Harry says such things only to annoy you."

"And you think that's all right? You think that I should just ignore such remarks?"

"Harry shouldn't say them," she agreed reluctantly. "But you know what Harry's like."

He took his arms from around her and got up, pacing

about their bedchamber like a lion at the Royal Zoo. "You say I should know what Harry's like. Believe me, Kate, I know. If I know anything, it's that. He's a rotter—he's always been. It's *you* who needs to know what Harry is like."

"I know, I know." It disturbed her to have to defend Harry's actions; for truly, they had been uncalled for. "He has always felt second best, Derek. And he's not so different from other younger sons. You know as well as I do that Baron Aldershot's youngest boy has been in scrape after scrape—but his father pays his debts, gets him off. The Earl of Willington's younger son was arrested for some kind of swindle. The system is terrible. The oldest boy gets everything—the others, nothing."

"There's no other way to hold estates together, Kate. It takes a lot of money to run an establishment such as Scarlet Oaks. If the capital has to be divided up, the estate falls."

"Which is better," she asked bitterly, "no estate, or ruined lives?"

He stood over her, and she knew he was angry. "You are oversimplifying this, Kate, and you know it. Of course some younger sons go off the rails—but some oldest sons do too. Harry was given every chance to train himself so that he could be self-supporting. He chose not to do so. Why should I be required to support a grown man, one perfectly able to go out and earn a living if he tried? It isn't good for Harry for me to pay his way. Work develops character."

What could Kate say to that? She couldn't point at Derek and say, Look at you—you inherited wealth; because Derek worked very hard at his doctoring. He donated long, tiring hours ministering to the needs of those poor souls in Whitechapel. If only he and Harry weren't always at daggers' points. Wanting to change the subject away from Harry, she asked, "Tell me more about the woman who died, Derek. What did you mean, the wound was sexual in nature?"

"I—I don't think you want to know about it, Kate."

"Of course I do. Remember me, Derek? I'm your wife.

I am not exactly an innocent virgin," she added drily. "And now you've aroused my curiosity."

"Very well. But if it makes you ill, expect no help from me." He sat down again beside Kate. "This woman, Emma Smith, was one of the prostitutes in the area. She was attacked—now, her story is a bit odd in some respects. She claimed that she was attacked by four men and robbed. But at the hospital, the sister in charge of the ward thinks that for some reason, Emma Smith was lying. She felt that the injured woman was afraid to tell the truth. Or," and he shrugged, "she might well have been too drunk on cheap gin to know what happened. According to Smith, the attack took place on Osborne Street. That's a street off Whitechapel, near Fiddler's Salvation Chapel. Yet she walked home with this terrible injury. Home being George Street in Spitalfields, nearly a quarter of a mile from where she claimed the attack took place. She couldn't describe her assailants—or wouldn't. She lost a lot of blood from the injury, although none was found on the street where she claimed the attack took place. She'd stuffed her shawl between her legs to try to staunch the flow of blood. She had been stabbed in the vagina with something—not a knife—and badly injured. How she walked that distance and then, with the deputy and a fellow lodger from her lodging, to London Hospital, without collapsing is a mystery. When I saw her she was only semiconscious. She said nothing to me. I hadn't been informed of her death."

Kate shuddered. "Who would do such a terrible thing?"

"A madman. This worries me, Kate. If a madman is loose in that area, I don't know what may happen. The entire section is volatile, ready to explode. Men like Mansfield take advantage of the destitute and make their burden even greater."

"What of Mansfield? Is there anything he can do to get that building from you, Derek?"

"As long as I own it, there's nothing he can do. Unless I die, and he manages to induce my heirs to sell to him." He caught her hand. "If anything should happen to me, Kate, promise me that you won't let that building fall into the hands of that scoundrel."

This talk of death distressed her. "Nothing's going to

happen to you, Derek," she chided. "You're a young man, and healthy. Don't talk about such things. It upsets me."

He slid his arms about her, nuzzled her neck. "Does the thought of my death distress you, my dear? Does this mean that you have some regard for me, some measure of love?"

"I don't despise you, Derek. You know that. I'm grateful to you for what you've done for me."

"Grateful! How I hate that word, dearest Kate. I don't want gratitude from you, I want love. You gave your love freely to Harry—why not to me?"

Kate sighed, but she cradled his head on her breast. Poor Derek. What could she say to him? Did he expect her to love two different men at the same time? Wasn't it enough that she was his wife, that he could enjoy her body whenever he wished? And you enjoyed it, too, a little voice whispered in her mind. Don't deny it, Kate.

Now Derek's lips were on her throat, his kisses slow and gentle. Out of pity for him—or was it more than pity? —out of gratitude for what he'd done for her—or was it more than gratitude?—Kate relaxed and let her senses take over her body. She quit thinking. She tried to forget that Harry was somewhere in the house and allowed herself to respond to her husband's caresses. When his lips sought hers, she let her lips part, darted her tongue out to meet his. Slowly her passion built as Derek's skilled fingers undid the fastenings of her dress. He slipped the corset cover from her shoulders, and kissed the skin he'd bared. Kate, eager now for more love than this, unlaced her stays and tossed them aside with abandon. Then neither of them could get undressed quickly enough. The little lounge was surrounded by discarded garments. Derek gathered her up in his arms and carried her to their bed. Aching for him, Kate clung to him, arching her back to raise herself for his ultimate caress. The rhythm of their lovemaking reached a fever pitch, and Kate cried out as rapture swept over her, setting her whole being aflame.

As they lay in each other's arms, love spent, Kate realized something that was so startling, so alien to all her other thoughts, that she gasped.

"What's wrong, dear?" Derek asked drowsily.

"Nothing, Derek, nothing." She raised up on one elbow and looked down at her husband, his face strong, his smile a loving one. She leaned down and kissed him sweetly on the lips. Then she buried her face in the curve of his neck and murmured, "I just realized that I'm falling in love with you."

"Kate, oh, darling Kate." He caught her to him, and his kiss was not a gentle one. It was loving, passionate, demanding. And she responded to his demands with all of the fire of her young body.

CHAPTER 23

Friday, June 1, 1888

"Does Derek still keep his journal?"

"Has he always written in it?" Kate asked in return. She and Harry were having tea in one of the small parlors. French windows were open to take advantage of the June sunshine. In the garden the roses were a riot of red, yellow, and white, with bees buzzing about the fragrant blossoms. It was Friday, and Derek was in London tending to the sick in Whitechapel.

"I think he started keeping a journal in his teens," Harry said. "I was younger, of course, and not interested in writing anything. It was bad enough having to do my copybook for the tutor. I wasn't about to do any extra penmanship. But then Derek always was stodgy, a scholar, a nose-to-the-grindstone type."

Sometimes it annoyed Kate to hear Harry always put down Derek. In the weeks since Harry's return, she had grown closer to Derek, not further from him. If anyone would have told her she would come to love her husband, preferring him to her first love, Harry, she'd have laughed. Now she was learning the true depth of Derek's character —and in contrast, Harry seemed, at times, shallow. He was working though. Mansfield had taken him on as an associate. Kate wasn't sure what the business arrangements were; but Harry often had to go to London, particularly to the East End, to inspect properties owned by his mentor.

Derek was in a quandary about his brother's work. Glad as he was to have Harry gainfully employed at last, it was galling to know that this employment was with Arthur Mansfield; for he and Mansfield carried on a constant battle about conditions in East London. Mansfield wasn't the only slumlord who contributed to the woes of the poor; but he was the one Derek knew personally, he was the one who was trying to oust the young doctor from his Union Row clinic, so he was the target of all of Derek's efforts to eliminate the appalling conditions in the local housing.

"Harry, Derek isn't all that stodgy," Kate told her brother-in-law with some asperity. "He has many good qualities."

Those raven eyebrows raised quizzically. "Ah, do I hear the dulcet tones of the loving wife, dear Kate?" He moved closer to her, so that she felt engulfed by his maleness, the excitement that Harry always generated about him. As she couldn't escape, she tried to pretend that Harry's presence had no effect on her.

Before she realized what he was up to, Harry had his arm about her waist and his lips sought hers in a long, ardent kiss. It had been a long time since Harry had kissed her. She had avoided such situations since his return, not quite knowing what her reaction would be. As Derek's wife, Kate had honestly tried to be loyal to him, even though she thought when Harry first returned that she would perish from wanting him. As she began to love Derek, she had been less afraid to spend time alone with Harry, thinking that his attraction had lessened. Now, with his lips on hers, demanding a response, she found to her horror that he still could rouse her as he had from the beginning.

For an eternity she allowed herself to melt in his arms, to accept his kisses, to return them. Then a measure of sanity returned to her, and Kate pushed him away, twisting out of his intimate embrace.

"Harry, you mustn't!" she breathed, her voice hoarse with emotion. "It's wrong! I'm married to your brother."

"Married! You call it a marriage when he took advantage of your desperation to insist on a wedding ceremony?"

Harry moved toward her, but Kate retreated, putting a marble-topped table between them.

"I married him in good faith, Harry. I must honor my vows. Don't tempt me—please don't tempt me."

He laughed, his gray eyes aglitter with mischief. "Kate, you are the most innocent thing at times." Then, with his voice throbbing with intimacy, "And at other times, the complete wanton. Don't you know that the marriage vows were made to be broken? Everyone in society does it. Husbands have mistresses, wives take lovers. Everyone knows that the Prince of Wales is a womanizer. If it's good enough for royalty, it should be good enough for Lady Ravenshaw."

"Harry, that's wicked to say such things." Away from his close embrace, Kate had regained a measure of aplomb.

Harry smiled a slow, knowing smile. "You'll be back in my bed soon, Kate. You know you want me as much as I want you. If Derek is such a loving husband, why does he often spend such long hours away from you? I've heard him come in at two and three in the morning."

"He's a doctor. If someone has a baby, they don't necessarily time it to suit Derek."

"Ah, yes, the physician. What a clever excuse—I had a confinement to attend—a man was thrown from his horse and I had to set his broken leg—there's an epidemic of pox in Whitechapel, and I must stay there overnight. Kate, Kate, don't you sometimes wonder about Derek? Think of all those women he treats—how he sees their naked bodies—touches them in the most intimate places. Doesn't it bother you to think of what he must be doing with them? He treats the most degraded whores in the city. Do you think that they pay him in money? They pay him in kind, Kate. And you hold yourself away from my love for a man like that?"

"Hush, Harry! I don't even like you when you say such horrid things. Derek wouldn't do—"

"You think not? What does he write in that precious journal, Kate? Have you looked at it?"

"Of course not." Her voice was full of righteous indignation.

"He hasn't shown you what he writes?" Harry asked, voice sly, insinuating.

"A journal is a very private thing." The fact that she had wondered about what Derek wrote—the memory of trying to get the little desk open when her husband wasn't there, in order to peek inside his diary—made Kate's protest too vehement. Harry understood immediately.

"So you'd like to read all his secret thoughts?"

"Certainly not!"

"Come, come, dear Kate, remember it's Harry, your beloved Harry, you are trying to fool. Maybe you can deceive Derek this way, but then he has always been a bit dull. But don't try to convince me that you haven't tried to get your hands on that precious journal Derek keeps under lock and key."

"How do you know he locks it up?"

"I know Derek. Always secretive. Always has been—always will be. Is it in the little maple desk—the one carved to look bamboo?" He paused, looked closely at her, then smiled triumphantly. "Of course. Ah, Kate, your face gives you away every time." Again he moved toward her, stopping when she began to retreat. "Very well, Kate, I won't touch you. Obviously I still have the same effect on your luscious body that I used to have, or you wouldn't be so afraid to have me near you. I promise you something, dearest sister-in-law, you'll come to my bed again—and in the near future. I can see it in those lovely green eyes of yours. You'll get more and more tired of Derek's pomposity, more and more frustrated with his dullness, more and more eager for the kind of love we had together. Then you'll come to me."

"It won't happen, Harry." She almost told him that his brother was every bit as ardent and skilled a lover as he was; but something kept Kate's lips silent. She didn't want to discuss her marriage bed with Harry.

"Meanwhile," and his eyes sparkled, "I can do you a big favor, Kate. I can open that little desk where Derek keeps his journal." He grinned hugely. "I see by that open face that you are interested."

"It's a wicked, sly, deceitful thing to do, to read my husband's diary behind his back."

"But such good fun. And think, Kate, you'll finally know just exactly what Derek thinks of you. You'll learn whether or not you have rivals—if he's faithful to you, or if he warms other beds when you think that he is tending to his sick patients. Come, don't you want to know what he writes?"

She did. That was the terrible thing—Kate was dying of curiosity to know what it was that Derek penned so secretly.

"Haven't you ever asked him to see it?" Harry persisted.

"I did, once," she admitted. "But he joked and said that I should remember what happened to Bluebeard's curious wife."

"So you think Derek has a dark and secret side to his nature? That he's dangerous?"

"Harry! It was only a joke!"

Now his bantering manner was gone; he was deadly serious. "Do you really know your husband, Kate? I should think that remark alone would give you pause to think. Aren't you afraid of what might happen to you someday, married to a man who compares you to Bluebeard's wife?"

Kate shivered and turned away from Harry, not wanting to think about what he was suggesting.

"But enough of serious thoughts. Remember, Kate, if Derek should turn into a monster, the way Stevenson's hero, Dr. Jekyll, turned into Mr. Hyde, you can always flee to my bedchamber—and my bed. I'll protect you."

"Harry, sometimes I think you say such things just to annoy me. I'll have nightmares."

"Again I'll make my kind offer. If you have bad dreams, you may seek out my bed and I will comfort you."

Comfort! Unbidden, the memory of Harry in bed almost overwhelmed Kate. She had loved him so desperately —or so she had thought. Now—she didn't know what she felt now that she was married. Sometimes she thought she loved Derek. At other times—the emotion was tearing her apart.

"I can do something else for you, Kate." She heard the deviltry in his voice and turned warily. "I can open Derek's desk, get his journal out for you to read."

She was consumed with curiosity, but it irked her that Harry should realize this and take advantage of her frailty. Even as she protested, Kate knew that she would not be able to withstand Harry's tempting.

Ten minutes later, she stood with Derek's journal in her hands, the rich maroon leather smooth from years of handling. While Harry stood there smirking, Kate opened the diary at random at a date long before they were married. Her own name leaped up at her. *Kate was ravishing today . . . I shall have her. . . .* She hadn't realized that Derek had been interested in her even then. She read the page he'd written after the night they'd made passionate love and felt her face grow warm at the ardor of his words. Then she found the entry after she'd lost Harry's child. *I'm glad she won't have Harry's bastard . . . constant reminder . . . hope he'll never come back . . . last night— God, that was wonderful! . . .*

"What does old Derek say, Kate?" Harry asked. He held out his hand for the journal.

She couldn't let Harry read it, so she quickly closed the diary and tried to pass it off lightly. "Nothing exciting, I fear. All this effort to find out that he went to his clinic, or treated old Mrs. Fenwick's chill. Very dull reading. Let's put it back. I feel guilty prying, Harry, truly I do." She wished she had never consented to this invasion of Derek's privacy.

"Wonder if Derek stashed anything away in the secret drawer?" Harry mused. He reached in under the pigeonholes of the desk, released a catch, and the whole section swung forward. Kate, intrigued, had to go look.

"I've heard of secret drawers, but I've never seen one before." She watched avidly as Harry pulled out a shallow drawer. "Empty." What a disappointment.

Feeling guiltier by the moment, Kate urged Harry to close the secret drawer, put the journal back where it belonged, and lock the desk.

"You aren't cut out for clandestine activities of this sort," Harry teased. "Our meetings in the lodge—ah, that was a different matter." He looked pointedly at the big bed she shared with Derek. "We could enjoy a lovely interlude right now, Kate. You have only to say the word."

Afraid that she might yield to temptation, Kate said, "We shouldn't be here. Derek would be furious if he knew."

Harry caught her to him and kissed her before she could escape.

"But he'd never know, Kate."

"No, Harry. Let me go."

She wasn't sure whether she was glad or sorry when he obeyed her command. A bit chagrined, she opened the door into the hallway and went out with Harry at her heels. To her utter dismay, Lady Letitia was coming down the corridor, leaning heavily on her walking stick. Her eyebrows raised when she saw the two of them emerge from the bedchamber, but she said nothing.

Kate dreaded seeing Derek that evening, though, sure that his aunt had reported the incident. He said nothing until they had retired for the night. Then, before climbing into bed, he asked, "What was Harry doing in here today, Kate?"

She couldn't tell him the truth, that she and Harry had read his private journal. The first lie she thought of was, "A drawer stuck in my chest, and I asked him to open it for me. That's all, Derek."

His look was inscrutable. "You should have called for a servant. That's what they're paid to do."

"I know, but Harry was passing in the corridor, and . . ."

"Don't let it happen again, Kate."

Then he turned out the gas light and got into bed. Tonight his lovemaking had a desperate air to it, a kind of frantic hunger, which almost frightened her. She was slow to respond to him, which angered Derek.

"Did you make love to my brother today, Kate?" he demanded. "Did you?"

"Derek, I told you that nothing happened. Can't you believe me?"

"I want to," he groaned. "God knows I want to. But

when Aunt Letitia said she saw the two of you coming out of this room together—our room—I wanted to kill Harry—and you."

She remembered the words she'd read in the journal, words written in that bold, spiky handwriting that was so characteristically Derek's. Did he love her that much, that he'd rather have her dead than in Harry's bed? She soothed him in the only way she knew how, drawing him into her arms.

CHAPTER 24

Tuesday, June 19, 1888

In the breakfast room, with only Derek eating with her, Kate said, "I do wish you'd reconsider, Derek. I surely could be of some help in your clinic. I'm not a nurse. Not for a minute would I suggest helping you in that way—but I am just as able as that young woman you have working for you to usher patients in and out of your surgery."

"No!" The reply seemed to Kate to be more vehement than the occasion called for. "I've told you repeatedly, I do not think it is a suitable place for you, Kate. The degradation—the disease—I think it would tarnish you. When I come home to you, I want to feel that you are completely removed from such a sordid phase of my life."

"Then why don't you give up the clinic?"

"They need me on Union Row, Kate. Who else will tend to their ailments?"

"You let me go with the duchess—"

"Reluctantly!" He glowered at her. "You know I do it only to keep you away from the house when Harry is here."

"But if I helped out at the clinic, you could know exactly where I was and what I was doing," she said with sweet reasonableness.

"Kate, don't push me," Derek warned, "or I shall forbid you to go with the duchess ever again."

Spiritedly, she declared, "And I should go right ahead.

270

You may be married to me, Derek, but you don't own me. I'm your wife, not your slave."

"Bravo!" There was applause from the doorway, and Harry came in, debonair and handsome, his light eyes gleaming with mischief. "Declare your rights, Kate. Be an independent woman."

Derek glared at his brother, not even saying good morning. He quickly finished his breakfast, gave Kate a perfunctory kiss, and hurried away.

"Harry, I do wish you would stop trying to make trouble," Kate said, sighing. "Life is difficult enough without your constant needling."

"What was today's problem with my saintly brother?"

She shrugged, helping herself to more sausage, and didn't answer.

"Come, come, Kate. How can I help you if you don't tell me your troubles?" Harry chided.

Knowing he'd keep at her until she told, Kate said, "I wanted to help Derek in his clinic. He refused."

"As well he should. It's no fit place for you. Aren't you satisfied with playing lady bountiful with the scatty duchess?"

Kate laid down knife and fork deliberately. This was too much—a rebuff from Derek, now the same from Harry.

"Those women are beginning to realize that the duchess and I have only their good at heart. At first they scoffed. Now some of them, at least, are trying hard to learn to read. They know it may help them get employment other than prowling the streets, looking for men."

Harry shook his head. "Kate, Kate, my darling, gullible Kate. They get in out of the cold. And I dare say the duchess opens her purse to them. Doesn't she?"

"Well—sometimes she gives them a few pence—"

"Which they immediately take to the gin shops. They come to the classes only for the pennies. Surely you must know that by now. All right, the duchess is mad. If she wants to hand out coppers to the whores to keep them drunk, it's her money; but you should face reality, Kate. They can never escape their fate. If you saw them living as I see them—remember, I collect their rents now. I see the squalor, the misery. They live and die without hope. And all the duchess offers them is false hope. So they learn their letters. What job do you think those middle-aged, ugly, gin-ridden whores will get? What shopkeeper in his right mind would hire one of them, even if she could read?"

"I don't believe you, Harry," she said stubbornly. In her heart, Kate feared that Harry was right; but she was not going to admit this to him. "I've never seen their homes. I think you exaggerate."

"I'll prove to you that I'm right," Harry said. "Come with me today, make my rounds with me. You'll soon see that there is no hope for those benighted souls."

"Derek would be furious—"

"Derek needn't ever know. You can be home before he is. If you don't tell him—and I don't—how can he guess?"

"Your Aunt Letitia—"

"She isn't omniscient, Kate. We don't even have to leave the house together. I'll go on ahead. Meet me at the railroad station in Chelmsford in an hour."

Kate knew she should say no; but the fact that Derek had forbidden her to help at the clinic annoyed her. "All right—an hour."

She hurried upstairs and had Vera get out a traveling suit of cinnamon brown. "I'm going into the city to shop," she told Vera. If the maid chattered, it would all sound innocent. And perhaps she would go to a shop or two if she had time.

At the railroad station, Kate found that Harry was chatting with Lady Cynthia Farmington, a woman of Derek's age, quite a beauty. There was gossip that her older husband turned a blind eye when she sought younger male companionship—a polite word for saying that Cynthia took lovers where she found them.

Kate knew her slightly and didn't like her too well. But it seemed that she intended to join Harry and Kate for their journey to the East End.

"Harry tells me that you and the Duchess of Dorminster do good works in Whitechapel," Cynthia said. "I've been engaged in some charitable works in the East End, myself."

For some reason Kate couldn't fathom, Cynthia looked at Harry and smiled. He grinned in turn. It made Kate feel very unsure of herself. How naughty of Harry to make jokes with the beautiful blonde Cynthia and leave Kate out.

"I'm sure all of those people need help," Kate said. "I wanted to help Derek—he has a clinic for the poor on Union Row," she added.

"Yes, I know," murmured the lovely Lady Farmington, smoothing the royal blue velvet of her skirt with a slender, gloved hand.

"He thinks it not a suitable place for me to be."

Again that little look between Cynthia and Harry.

"I'm sure that Derek knows what is best for you," the older woman said.

Kate felt patronized and didn't like it. She was glad when they reached Paddington and Cynthia went off in a hansom cab by herself.

"Smug cat," Kate said. "And what was the secret you seemed to share with her?" she accused. "I was quite put out with you, Harry."

"Ignore Cynthia," he suggested. "Her bloom is fading, and she knows the blush of youth is still on your petals. She resents you because you are more attractive than she is."

Kate wasn't convinced, but Harry's subtle compliment made her feel better. The feeling didn't last too long. Once they reached the East End, she was plunged into poverty that her trips to Salvation Chapel hadn't prepared her for. They turned off Whitechapel Road onto Osborne, and from there to Finch. Then they left their cab and they began to walk the warren of streets off Finch, collecting rents.

"Lately they've gotten pretty ugly," he said. "I shouldn't have brought you here, Kate. If anything happens to you, Derek will kill me."

Lifting her skirts out of the mud and offal, Kate wished she'd had sense enough to stay at Scarlet Oaks today. The stench was sickening. There were ragged, white-faced children scrabbling in the garbage, putting morsels in their mouths. It turned her stomach to watch.

"Why don't their mothers watch them?" she asked.

"Too busy drinking or whoring or trying to make a few pennies in a shop—or sweeping in front of a tavern."

"They should be in school!"

"The kids? Schools cost money, Kate. They can't afford even a penny a day. And many of the children can get work in the sweatshops. Earn enough to feed themselves." He stopped, consulted his rent book, knocked on a sagging door.

"Oo's there?" came a cracked voice.

"Rent man."

There was an audible groan. No one opened the door. Harry pounded harder with his fist. "Open up! I know you are there." Kate was surprised at the hard note in his voice. He turned to her, murmured, "Think I'm a fool, do they? If they don't come to the door, think I'll go away? Not likely." Again he beat on the door.

Finally Kate heard a scraping sound, and the door was opened a few inches. A woman, obviously ill, looked out. "Everyone's sick 'ere," she said, then coughed. "Can't you come back next week?"

"Rent's not been paid for a month," Harry said, consulting the book. "Pay now or out on the street you go."

A pale, scrawny hand slid out through the crack in the door, clutched at Harry's arm. He pulled away with distaste.

"Please, mister, everyone's sick," she sobbed. "Gertie's so still, I think—"

Horrified, repelled by the poverty and the stink, yet drawn by the misery, wanting to do something to help, Kate stepped forward and pushed open the door. Inside the dark, cold room the stench was appalling. There were children everywhere. In all, she thought she counted seven, the oldest no more than nine or ten. In the corner, on a filthy cot, lay a child of three. Kate picked her way through the coughing, crying little ones until she was beside the cot. One hand on the child's forehead was enough. The little girl was dead. Turning back to the mother, Kate said angrily, "Why didn't you have the doctor?"

"No money, lady. Doctors cost money."

She went back outside, said urgently, "Harry, we have

to get Derek. There's a dead child in there, and all the rest of them are sick."

"He can't do anything for them. And my job is to evict them. They're long overdue on the rent. I've let them go now until Mansfield has threatened to fire me if I didn't do my duty."

"Duty! Harry Ravenshaw, I'm ashamed of you. They are ill—including the mother. And you want to throw them out onto the streets?"

"They can go to the workhouse, Kate. That's what the workhouses are for."

"How can that woman work when she has a room full of sick children?"

Harry refused to go with her, though, to the clinic. Kate, furious with him, hurried back to Whitechapel Road. Hailing a hansom cab, she had him drive her to Union Row; but as the cab turned in at one corner, she saw Derek run out of the clinic, black bag in hand, and leap into a waiting cab. Then the cabby whipped up the horse and they went careening off toward Mulberry. Her own cabby tried to catch up with Derek's, but lost the other cab in the maze of streets.

"Sorry, ma'am. It were the doctor. He's probably off to help someone sick. Good man, for all he's a baronet."

Not knowing what to do next, Kate had the cab take her back to where she had left Harry. As they turned onto Osborne, she noticed a little crippled boy, rude crutch under one arm, with a bundle of newspapers under the other. Probably the one from whom Derek bought that dreadful penny paper. As the cab slowed for the next corner, she saw a familiar figure come out of a building and approach the newsboy. It was Arthur Mansfield, no doubt making sure his investments were paying him well. He tossed a penny to the boy and took the proffered paper. The boy, hampered with papers and crutch, was not able to catch the penny. The last sight Kate had of him as the cab went down the sidestreet the lad was on his knees in the mud, scrabbling for the coin.

"Sure you want out here, ma'am?" the cabby asked in disapproving tones. "Rough neighborhood. Not proper for a lady likes of you."

"It's all right. I'm meeting a friend." She paid the man and picked her way back to the house where she'd left Harry. To her dismay, a constable was ordering the removal of a roughly tied bundle from the premises. The sick children were huddled on the filthy street, the woman stood crying hopelessly, and Harry was no place to be seen.

Kate fumbled with her beaded drawstring bag to see if she had some money for the woman. The constable, seeing her and rightly interpreting her plans, hurried over, murmuring, "Don't show money around here, ma'am. You might be killed for a few pennies."

"But that woman—I want to help her—"

The woman, seeing Kate, let out a shriek. "Come back to see me driven from me home, have you, wicked rich bitch. I curse you! I spit on you!"

She lunged toward Kate, who fell back, stunned by the ferocity of the woman's onslaught.

"Please, lady, get out of here," the constable urged. "I can't guarantee your safety if you stay."

Sick at heart, determined to do something for the poor, wretched woman, Kate pressed some shillings into the officer's hand, told him to get the family a place for the night, and then fled back to the relative safety of Whitechapel Road.

Harry was gone about his business, Derek was away from his clinic, and Kate was frightened to stay in the area alone. Flagging a cab, she had him take her to Paddington Station.

CHAPTER 25

Friday, July 13, 1888

"I've not seen Monica Murphy of late," the Duchess of Dorminster told Kate as their hansom cab rattled along Whitechapel Road. "I think she is deliberately avoiding me when I come to the East End."

"I guess she still is on the streets," Kate said.

"I know—improbable as it sounds. Remember the last time we saw her? Sick. Coughing up her lungs. What kind of man would want to be with that?"

"Poor Monica. I haven't mentioned her to Derek lately." In truth, Kate hadn't even thought of Monica Murphy. She had enough on her mind just surviving at Scarlet Oaks. In the weeks since Aunt Letitia had caught Harry leaving her bedchamber, Derek had become increasingly jealous. No matter how many times Kate protested her innocence, no matter how she gave of herself when they made love, Derek still harbored his suspicions of his brother and his wife. Just that in itself was beginning to affect her responses to him in bed. Kate now knew that she truly loved her husband, that what she had felt for Harry was mere infatuation. She regretted giving herself to the dashing younger man, but that was all in the past. Harry kept hinting—often quite openly—that he still would like to share her bed; but Kate ignored all of his pleading. She wished now that she had not insisted on having Harry live at Scarlet Oaks. Derek had been right. The tensions were building, and Kate feared that they might reach explosive proportions in the near future.

The duchess, uncanny in her ability to sense entangled situations, asked quietly, "Is everything all right between you and Derek, my dear?"

It wasn't meant as prying. Kate knew that the duchess was a true friend, genuinely interested in her welfare.

"I've learned to love him, your grace."

The raddled old face was transformed by that beautiful smile. "Good girl. Derek's a fine man. But," shrewdly, "isn't it trying to have Harry there at Scarlet Oaks?"

"Yes, it is. And Lady Letitia doesn't improve things by constantly harping on that fact." In a burst of confidence, needing to talk to someone about their troubled lives, Kate added, "She fuels Derek's jealousy by telling him lies. The slightest innocent thing—she can find me chatting with Harry in the library—and she has us in bed together."

"Derek was a fool to let Harry stay on."

Kate sighed. "That was my fault. I thought it unfair to force Harry out. Scarlet Oaks has always been his home."

"And now he repays Derek's kindness by trying to undercut him on all occasions. Working for Mansfield! Appalling. Mansfield is trying to buy up all of East London. The fact that Derek is holding out—and encouraging others to do likewise—infuriates Mansfield. A wicked man when opposed."

"Derek and Harry argue endlessly about his working for Mansfield. Harry's final argument each time is that Derek insisted that he get a job—and he has."

By now the cab had brought them to the Salvation Chapel. Six weeks ago Kate would have sworn she'd never again set foot in Fiddler's church, but the situation at home had changed all that. Although Derek was desperately opposed to her coming to the East End with the duchess, he finally decided that it was one way to get her away from Scarlet Oaks when he, too, was away. This lessened her chances of sinning with Harry.

Kate had begun to feel that she might be doing genuine good at the chapel school. Some of her pupils could actually read now from a primer, an amazing accomplishment.

"Something's brewing here at the chapel," the duchess said as the cabby pulled out of the traffic and drew up in front of the grimy little building. "Abby's scared, Fiddler's getting scattier by the day."

"Mrs. Fiddler scared? I find her impossibly formidable. I can't imagine anything that might frighten her."

"I'm much older than you, Kate, more experienced. Under Abby's stern façade, there's terror. I can feel it."

Today they were a bit early for the classes, so the duchess marched through to the drab, crowded living quarters behind the chapel, knocking imperiously on the door. At first there was no answer, only a waiting silence. Again the duchess rapped. This time a voice called, "Who is it?"

"The Duchess of Dorminster." She could be imperious on occasion, yet surprisingly gentle when compassion counted.

In a moment the door opened, showing Abby Fiddler, eyes red from weeping. It surprised Kate to see any emotion in this cold, stern, fanatically religious woman.

"Abby, what's wrong?" The duchess sailed into the tiny sitting room and turned to confront her hostess. "What's bothering you?"

"Nothing."

"Don't lie to me." It was a tone to put dread into the soul of even the most hardy. "I know something is tearing you apart. Is it your husband?"

Abby Fiddler's long, bony face crumpled. She sank onto a horsehair settee, buried her face in her large, capable hands, and sobbed.

"Put the kettle on for tea, Kate."

When Kate came from the minuscule kitchen, she found the duchess sitting with a comforting arm around Mrs. Fiddler's shoulders. "You must tell me, Abby. I may be able to help."

"No one can help him, not even God," sobbed the distraught woman. "No one!"

"Come, Abby, where's your faith?" The duchess's tone was bracing. "You don't know who can help. Tell me what's gone so badly wrong here. Is your husband mad?"

Kate gasped at the brutal bluntness of the question, but it seemed to help Mrs. Fiddler to recover her calm.

"I'm not sure, your grace." She was as blunt as her questioner. "Someone thinks he's done something terrible." She reached into a pocket of her black dress and drew out a crumpled letter.

The duchess took the soiled sheet of paper, smoothed

it out, and peered at it through pince-nez worn pinned to the front of her gown. "Blackmail. An anonymous letter. This is wicked, Abby."

"Jonathan doesn't know that I have found him out."

The duchess made a moue of disgust. "Sounds lurid. But nothing specific. *I know. I saw. The blood will come on your head. Leave ten pounds*—Has he paid this villain?"

"I think so." Abby sounded distracted. "Money has been missing from the collection, I think." She sobbed. "Robbing God to pay a criminal."

"Do you have any idea what it is Mr. Fiddler is supposed to have done?"

Abby shook her head too quickly, and Kate was sure she was lying.

"Make us a pot of tea, Kate, that's a good girl," the duchess insisted, getting Kate out of the room briefly.

When she came back in, tea pot and cups on a tin tray, the duchess was saying, "This woman, Emma Smith. I don't think I knew her. Did she come here?"

"Not to your classes. She was just one more prostitute, plying her trade, luring my Jonathan into sin."

"Abby, you must assume some of the blame for that." Tact was not the duchess's forte today. "Deny a man his marital rights, he'll go elsewhere."

"It's sinful!" Abby's voice was shrill. "He should renounce temptations of the flesh."

"Poppycock! But you say he's been more withdrawn, more inclined to rant and rave since this Smith woman's death?"

"I remember that," Kate said. "Derek was called in to look at her in London Hospital."

"Got what she deserved," Abby Fiddler said with spite. "Wicked—they're all wicked. Jonathan and I are fighting a losing battle against the Devil, trying to save them."

"That may well be," the duchess said drily. "But surely you don't think your husband killed this woman?"

"Why else would he pay?"

"Perhaps he's afraid too, Abby." Her voice softened. "He might think he'll be discovered in his whoring—foolish man. Everyone knows about him. Tell him not to pay."

"I dare not mention it to him. He doesn't realize that I know."

"You should go to the police."

"I can't do that! They'll find out how he sins with the whores!"

The Duchess of Dorminster urged Mrs. Fiddler to talk with her husband, or to consult a doctor on his behalf. "Then take him to Sir Derek Ravenshaw's clinic on Union Row," she suggested. "Let him tell you if your husband is too sick to be allowed to roam. But never pay a black-mailer—it will be the beginning of a long list of demands."

Finally Mrs. Fiddler promised to think about it. That was all the assurance she would give.

"Whoever is sending those notes must be desperate for money," Kate said.

"Not necessarily, my girl. He could just be a mischief maker. "See,"—she took the crumpled letter from Mrs. Fiddler—"he has used letters and words cut from a cheap newspaper. The newsprint is of the poorest quality."

Kate remembered the penny paper Derek had brought home, the one in which Emma Smith's inquest was noted. But then, it was a common enough newspaper in this area. Anyone could have composed the blackmail letter.

Then the clock on the mantelpiece struck the hour, and the duchess exclaimed, "My class! Come, Kate. We must see to our pupils." She patted Mrs. Fiddler's hand and wished her well.

This was not to be one of the duchess's better days though. Not a single pupil showed up for the reading class. She shook her head ruefully, so that her yellow hair threatened to fall down around her painted face. "Silly women. They could do so much better for themselves if only they'd learn to read, get decent jobs, quit drinking gin and whoring."

"They'll never stop, your grace," Kate said, sighing. Just when she thought she was accomplishing something with the women—this. It made her work seem so futile.

"Sometimes I think you're right, Kate. Well, shall we go back to Essex now? No point in staying here, unless you have some shopping you wish to do."

"I suppose I could go to the clinic and wait for Derek."

"I'll drop you at Union Row."

"Derek may be annoyed with me. He doesn't like for me to go to the clinic. He's not awfully happy about my coming here with you—"

"I dare say." Her voice was dry. "Then I shall get on home. Come along, we'll get a cab outside. I do hope that Fiddler hasn't gotten himself into a horrible mess," she went on once they closed the door of Salvation Chapel behind them. The duchess waved imperiously to a passing cab, and the cabby pulled over to pick them up. "Union Row," she ordered. Once he'd worked the lever to close the doors of their cab, she went on, "I read about the Smith woman. Pretty gruesome."

"Derek said it was sexual in nature." It bothered Kate to remember this.

"No doubt. And there's also no doubt that Jonathan Fiddler has sex on his mind all of the time. Religious fanatics do tend that way, I think. Or else they go to the other extreme, as that silly Abby has done. Don't know why women get married if they don't intend to give their husbands what they want. Stupid."

It all was very sordid. A dreadful murder, a mad parson, blackmail.

The little door in the roof of the cab opened, and the cabby said, "Union Row, milady. Where do you want to stop?"

As Kate went up the steps to Derek's clinic, an elderly man and woman came out.

"Best to wait, Samuel," the woman was saying. "Doctor will be back—the lady said so."

"Hurts too much to set on a chair," the grizzled old man protested. "Oughta be here when I'm sick, he ought."

Oh, dear, was Derek out? She'd go in, though, ask that young woman he hired when she could expect him to return. Kate pulled her skirts to one side to make room for the old couple who came hobbling down to the street, then went into Derek's waiting room. She was halfway across the small, dark room when Kate realized that the young woman behind the table, the guardian of the inner sanctum, was not the woman she had seen here the time she had visited the clinic. Instead, smiling smugly at her, sat

Cynthia Farmington, dressed in an elegant but very plain white shirtwaist over the blue skirt.

"Kate!" She didn't even stand to greet Derek's wife. "What brings you here?"

It was all Kate could do to answer. She was determined that Cynthia would never know of the surge of jealousy that swept over her when she found the blonde beauty in Derek's clinic. "Is he out?" she asked, keeping her voice light.

"I'm afraid so. He was called to London Hospital for a consultation."

"You don't know when he'll be back?"

"No, I'm afraid I don't. Doctor's hours, you know."

Seething inwardly, yet maintaining a surface aplomb, Kate smiled at the triumphant Cynthia, then said, "There's no point in my waiting, then. Don't bother to tell Derek I dropped by. He has so much on his mind. I'll just go along to Paddington and go on home."

"Of course." The two words spoke volumes. Cynthia knew that she had bested Derek's wife and she let Kate know it.

Nose high, Kate swept out of the grubby waiting room. How dare he! How dare her husband let Cynthia Farmington help him in the clinic, yet forbid her, his own wife, to do the same. Kate was furious. Wait until he got home. She'd tell Derek a thing or two.

Furious, she was even angrier when she found that there wasn't a cab in sight on Union Row. She had to go along to Mulberry Street before she could hail an empty hansom. She told him to take her to Paddington Station. When she consulted the departure board, Kate found that she would have to wait for a train to Essex. She went into the tea room and ordered a pot of tea to pass time while waiting for her train. She was just pouring a cup when she heard her name.

"Kate! I thought you were doing good works today."

It was Harry, all smiles.

"No one came to the class, so the duchess went home. Derek wasn't at the clinic—he was on a call to London Hospital—so I decided to go on home." Not for the life of her would Kate mention that Cynthia Farmington had been helping at Derek's clinic.

Harry beckoned to a serving girl and gave his order for tea. Then, smiling that insouciant, outrageous smile, he said, "Plenty of time for us to go for a pleasant ride in a hansom cab, Kate. We could even find a small, discreet hotel and spend several happy hours there."

"Harry, I do wish you'd stop talking that way. You know I always say no. I'm now a happily married woman."

He dropped his bantering air, reached over, and caught her hand before she could escape him. "Are you truly happy, Kate? Lately I've sensed tension between you and Derek. He's a troubled man, and that leads to a troubled marriage. You should have waited for me, Kate, had more faith in me."

She snatched her hand away from him. "Wait for you! I'd not had a word from you. Father died as a result of your financial scheming—you'd gotten me pregnant— Mansfield threatened to foreclose if I didn't become his mistress—and you think I should have waited for you!"

"But I didn't know any of this," he said, all sweet reasonableness. "I came back as soon as I possibly could. If Derek had his way, I'd still be exiled in Ireland, with a price on my head, unable to return to my home. Mansfield made it possible for me to come back—gave me a job. I think you make the man out as too much of an ogre, Kate. He recognizes you for what you are: a voluptuous, passionate woman. You should be glad that men find you so attractive."

"I don't want to attract him," she said, lips thinned with anger. "He's slimy. How can you bear to work with him?"

"I am learning a lot, Kate. I am finding out how to make pots of money legally—how to gain power, financial and political. Mansfield is the man to know."

"Well, he won't best Derek," she said spitefully. "And eventually Derek will destroy him."

"My, my, you have a very destructive husband, Lady Ravenshaw."

In her vehement attack on Mansfield, Kate had not noticed that someone had come to stand by their table. Looking up she was mortified to find that it was Arthur Mansfield himself, smiling his sly smile.

"Is your beloved older brother truly such a fiend?" he asked Harry.

"I think so." Kate gasped with anger. "But you must forgive Kate. She's married to the man, so she feels honor bound to protect his good name and reputation." Then, gesturing to an empty chair at their table, Harry asked, "Won't you join us, Mansfield?"

Kate scowled at Harry, but Mansfield had already sat down with them. If she got up and left, it would cause a scene in public, which she wanted to avoid. She sat there, pretending that Mansfield was nonexistent.

He, though, chatted away as if they were the best of friends. "You'll be pleased to know, Kate, that your lover, Harry, is doing splendidly in my company. I predict great things for him."

She sat like a stone statue, ignoring him. She couldn't turn off her ears though. She heard all his sly remarks, his insinuations that she and Harry were carrying on an illicit affair. Harry did nothing to allay Mansfield's suspicions. Finally, in desperation, Kate turned on Mansfield. "Sir, I find your remarks in poor taste. I am a respectable married woman having tea with her brother-in-law."

"And what of the poor child you lost—Harry's babe?"

It was the last straw. With dignity she rose to leave the men to themselves. As she did so, Derek entered the tea room with the lovely Lady Farmington on his arm. He seemed stunned to find Kate there with his brother and Mr. Mansfield. Cynthia smiled her sweetest at Kate, causing her to consider mayhem at the least against the statuesque beauty. "Ah, you have come to save your charming wife from your lecherous brother, and you have brought the delectable Lady Farmington with you." Smiling smugly, Mansfield added, "I assure you, Sir Derek, that your wife and your brother were most circumspect in this public place. No holding of hands, no stolen kisses. If they touched knees, it was safely hidden by the table."

"By God, Mansfield, I'll beat you to a pulp!"

Kate, terrified, grabbed Derek's arm and pulled him

from the table. "Don't pay any attention to him," she pleaded. "He's just trying to make trouble." She tugged at his arm, trying to drag him from the tea room. People were beginning to look at them to see what was going on. "Please, Derek. Everyone's looking at us. Let's go, or we'll miss our train."

"But Derek promised me a cup of tea," Cynthia said, not letting go of Derek's other arm. She pouted prettily.

"Most ungentlemanly of you, Ravenshaw," Mansfield said, voice low but carrying. "Refusing tea to so lovely a creature as the Lady Farmington. And you came here too early. You wouldn't have found your wife and your brother if you'd arrived here after their train left for Chelmsford. Would he, Harry?"

Kate felt Derek tense, but she kept pulling at him. "Don't listen to him, he's rotten. It was quite by accident that I met Harry here."

Cynthia laughed, a tinkly sound, trilling daintily.

"I don't like accidents of that kind," Derek stormed. He did pull his arm away from Cynthia's grasp though. "I thought you were safely with the duchess, and I find you in a public place with my brother, who wants to cuckold me, and the man who is trying to ruin me financially. And you don't want me to pay any attention to it?"

"And *you* come in with Cynthia, who is helping you at your clinic, after you forbade me to work there," Kate said, voice frigid. "I was here alone, having a cup of tea while I waited for my train, when Harry came in and sat with me. Mansfield just got here a few minutes ago. He was so insulting that I got up to leave, as you saw when you arrived."

"Why didn't you get up and leave when Harry joined you?"

"Oh, honestly, Derek, your jealousy is almost more than I can bear. Nothing happened. We sat and drank tea together. What if I asked you what Cynthia is doing here with you, holding onto your arm as if she owns you?" She turned to her rival, spat, "Does your husband allow you to be so familiar with married men in public?"

Cynthia only smiled, a pitying smile. Derek, though, was livid with rage.

"I suppose I'm to think that Harry didn't try to get you to go to bed with him. I know what's on his mind. He's had you in the past, and he intends to have you again—or is he enjoying your love now, Kate?"

"Hush! Do you want dear Cynthia to know all of our private business?" Kate was exasperated and let Derek know it.

"That's right, I mustn't let anyone know that my wife is sleeping with my brother." His voice was low and savage.

"Derek, that isn't true. I swear it to you. If you believe it, then ask Harry to leave Scarlet Oaks."

"Oh, dear," Cynthia said in mock dismay, "the train for Chelmsford is in—I shall have to leave now and miss the grand finale of this fascinating domestic brawl." She laid a hand on Derek's arm, swayed toward him in an intimate manner. "Do let me know how it all comes out, Derek."

Then, before Derek had a chance to answer, Lady Farmington swept out of the tea room.

"Cat!" Kate said furiously.

Then Mansfield, dropping some coins on the tea table, said, "Come along, Harry. We'll ride to Chelmsford together, talk business. I think that Kate and Derek may want to be alone." He chuckled. Kate felt like picking up the tea pot and hitting him with it.

Derek found them an empty compartment on the train, then continued his accusations. "Send Harry away, you now suggest. You can always go out and meet him, can't you, answerable to no one, now you're lady Ravenshaw? Aunt Letitia was right. You will bring dishonor onto the name, you and Harry."

"I hate it when you say horrid, untrue things to me, Derek. Don't do this to our marriage." She touched his hand lightly, but he pulled away, angering her. "If you aren't careful, Derek, you and your dear Aunt Letitia will push me right back into Harry's arms."

"It wouldn't require much of a push."

"What a nasty thing to say to your wife."

"What do you expect me to say? Do you want me to give my blessing to your affair with Harry?"

Through clenched teeth she said slowly, "There is no affair with Harry. Since I married you, I have not looked at another man, let alone gone to bed with one. If you do not believe me, then what can I do or say? You'll make yourself sick if you keep up with this irrational, jealous behavior."

"Ah, so now I'm irrational. Will that be your excuse? Your husband is mad, so you turn to his brother for love? It won't work, Kate. I won't have you and Harry playing behind my back. I warn you I can be violent when angry."

She shuddered. "There's no need for violence. Send Harry away—but don't turn away from me. I love you, Derek."

"Do you? I wish I could believe that, Kate. But I find it more and more difficult as the days go by. It's tearing me to pieces, wondering what is going on at Scarlet Oaks while I'm at Chelmsford or in London. And today, when I thought you would be safely chaperoned by the Duchess of Dorminster, I find you with Harry—and that rotten Mansfield."

Their quarrel was not settled by bedtime. Kate had Vera dress her in her most alluring nightgown, one shockingly sheer, of the finest Egyptian cotton, the neckline cut low to show the swell of her bosom, the arms bared. When Derek came into the room, she purposely stood between him and the lighted lamp so that her body would be silhoutted enticingly; but he scarcely looked at her. Collecting his nightshirt, robe and slippers, he said curtly, "I'll sleep in another room tonight."

Kate cried herself to sleep. What had happened to her marriage? She had come to love her husband—and now he rejected her. He was so jealous of Harry that he seemed almost mad at times. Bitterly she regretted urging Derek to allow his brother to live here with them. Now it was too late. Even if Harry moved elsewhere, Derek would be sure she was meeting him clandestinely, giving her body to him, laughing at her husband behind his back.

What could she do to prove her love to Derek and win him back? Was she going to lose him to the glamorous Cynthia Farmington?

INTERLUDE 7

Tuesday, August 7, 1888

He had heard it striking midnight when he first observed the woman with two soldiers. Her name was Martha something—Turner?—Tabram? She was one of the Whitechapel regulars.

The frustrations of the past weeks began to pile up, and he focused all of his pent-up feelings on the dirty whore. She wore a draggled skirt of some dark material, so soiled that he couldn't tell what color it had once been. Her coat was short and fitted, her hat a shabby bonnet of felt tied under her chin with a tattered ribbon. She and the two soldiers went from one grogshop to another, until finally they were so drunk that they had to support each other to keep from falling down in the street.

He had the bayonet concealed up the sleeve of his coat. Tonight was the night he planned to do murder, seeing that the blame was laid elsewhere. He'd picked up the latest blackmail payment from under the brick at the side of the Salvation Chapel, pocketing the money gladly. He'd hoped that his blackmail victim would kill again; but apparently he was too afrad to do further murder. Very well, he'd do his own killing from now on. His plans were well made.

Now he discovered that Martha had staggered out of the dingy grogshop without her two soldiers. She moved

290 RACHEL COSGROVE PAYES

off along Whitechapel Road, calling out lewd greetings to the men she met. Quickly he followed her, stalking her as carefully as he'd stalk a deer. He caught up with her as she passed Toynbee Hall. Hearing his footsteps, she stopped, swayed slightly, then turned to greet him.

"Wanna woman? Do it for fourpence." The odor of gin was so strong it almost nauseated him.

"Do you have a room nearby?" he asked.

"Don' need a room. We can go in the George Yard—I knows how to get inside the buildings. Come on," she wheedled.

He was revolted by her rotten teeth, her filth, her whoring. "Very well, but inside, out of sight."

She staggered off down the street and he followed, making sure that no one saw them together. She turned in a small, dark, malodorous passageway, and he was already slipping the bayonet from his sleeve into his hand. Pushing at a door that hung crookedly on its hinges, she sidled into the brick building, with him right behind her.

"Need a match," she mumbled. "Can't see."

He struck a match and saw the stairs ahead of them. "Up there," he directed.

She stumbled up to the landing with him at her heels. "Les do it here." She turned to him and hauled up her skirts.

He stabbed her repeatedly with the bayonet, reveling in the feel of cold steel severing her wicked flesh. Time after time his arm flashed forward and the sharp point of the bayonet pierced her body. Finally, his frenzy abating, he took stock of the situation.

Lighting another match, he examined his clothing for bloodstains. He'd worn a dark brown suit, so that they did not show up too clearly. With the butchers and slaughterhouses in this area, no one would notice if he had some blood on his clothing.

He left the woman crumpled on the landing and fled the building, exiting with caution to make sure that no one saw him in the vicinity of the George Yard. Then he hurried to the Aldgate East underground station. By the time another drunken prostitute took a client into the George Yard at three A. M. and found the body of Martha

Tabram, he was miles away from the site, his soul purged by the letting of blood.

The beauty of the crime was the misleading clues he could plant, pointing away from himself—but toward the man he hated.

CHAPTER 26

Tuesday, August 7, 1888

Kate had spent a miserable day. She'd called on Pamela, now the Viscountess Cabot, in the lovely new home Alfie had built for them. It was marvelously contemporary, the outside a mass of porches, towers, and ornate carving set in a large park of trees.

"There's nothing wrong between you and Derek, is there?" Pam had asked quite bluntly once she'd shown Kate over the entire house. They were now sitting in the parlor on a carved, overstuffed settee with tea things on a rolling teacart.

"Of course not," Kate said too quickly. Not for the world would she tell Pam—tell anyone—that Derek was no longer sharing her bed, having moved to a room of his own. Kate was getting desperate at his lack of love. She was tense and moody, prone to sudden bursts of anger at poor Vera and the other servants. The fact that Harry kept at her to go to bed with him did nothing to allay her frustrations. "Why do you ask such a silly question, Pam?"

Hateful Pam, so smug as always, sitting her in her dream house, now a titled lady, her husband a rich and influential peer of the realm.

"Oh—I heard a bit of gossip about Derek and Lady Farmington. I'm sure it's exaggerated—you know how these stories start."

"Yes, I know." Kate kept her voice sugary sweet, hating her friend at the same time. Trust Pam to suggest that

Derek was having an affair with Cynthia Farmington. She was the talk of Essex county, with her succession of lovers. Her husband, the baron, was twenty years her senior and from all the gossip, he was impotent. She found her pleasure wherever she could. Being a beautiful, full-blown woman with rich golden hair and wicked eyes, her body a mass of curvaceous flesh, Cynthia had no trouble finding men to warm her bed. But Derek!

"I'm glad it's just a rumor," Pam went on. "There's been a bit of talk in our set, now that Harry's back. Everyone knows you went with him before his troubles." She paused, frowned briefly, and asked, "Is he in business with Arthur Mansfield, Kate? Alfie told me some big story about real estate maneuvering in East London—but my head is a sieve when it comes to business. Why anyone would want property there is beyond me. Remember that dreadful day when you and I went to the grubby little chapel and met that scarecrow madman of a parson—what was his name?"

"Fiddler."

"Oh, yes. Had his hands all over you, as I recall." She tittered. "Oh, most men are like him if they have half a chance. But I wouldn't buy property in that neighborhood."

"Derek says that men like Mansfield are getting rich by taking advantage of the poor in East London. I've been going with the duchess again to help with her reading classes."

"I thought Derek didn't approve of your going there."

"Well, he has changed his mind somewhat." He'd changed his mind about his wife, to her sorrow, but Kate didn't say that. Pam was an awful gossip. If Kate even hinted that things were not as they should be between her husband and herself, Pam would have the story all over Chelmsford by tomorrow.

She didn't stay long. It did not make her feel kindly toward Pam to learn of Derek's affair—and affair Kate was sure it was. As lusty a man as her husband was, since he wasn't visiting her bed, he'd be in some other one. And all because he thought she was sleeping with Harry. How unfair! Didn't Derek realize that this kind of treatment might well send a wife into the arms of another man?

Driving home in the tilbury, Kate made up her mind that she would try to settle her differences with Derek. He was scrupulously polite to her in front of others. She doubted if Harry or Lady Letitia knew they were sleeping apart—no, the old she-dragon probably did know. Derek's aunt still ran Scarlet Oaks, no matter how Kate had tried to wrest control of the household from her. Probably the servants all kept her informed of what went on. They had to know that Derek was occupying another room. Vera had not said anything, but the girl wasn't stupid. She knew that her mistress was sleeping alone in the huge bed that was made for two.

This was Derek's day at the Union Row clinic. Kate hoped that he'd not be late. Sometimes he didn't even get home from London in time for dinner. Since he'd chosen to sleep away from her, he often was late arriving home. Kate had wondered if he had a woman. Now, thanks to Pam's gossiping tongue, she knew the worst.

Derek didn't get there in time for dinner, and Harry was nowhere to be seen. Had Kate known ahead of time that neither man would eat with her, she'd have had her dinner on a tray in her room. As it was, she and Lady Letitia dined alone.

As she stuffed herself with food, Derek's aunt asked, "Is that a new gown, Kate? Cut rather low, isn't it?"

"It's a dinner gown, all the fashion—and this is dinner."

"Well, don't bend forward, or you may find your bosom is exposed."

Kate, proud of her full breasts, ignored Lady Letitia. The old woman was just jealous of Kate's charms.

"Trying to lure Harry into your bed, I suppose, with such a brazen gown. Or keep him there. I dare say, now that you've driven poor Derek from his marriage bed, forcing him to sleep apart from you, there's nothing to stop you from having Harry with you whenever you wish."

"That's a wicked lie!"

"Indeed! Call me a liar, will you? You can't pretend that Derek is sharing your bed. I know where the poor man sleeps."

"Yes, I'm sure you have all of the servants spying for you, Lady Letitia. If you are so concerned about where

Derek sleeps, then I suggest that you discuss it with him, not with me. If anyone has driven him to that other room, it is you, with your insinuations and lies about what goes on between Harry and me. You are ruining my marriage, Lady Zangwill. I hope it makes you happy."

They were only into the main course of the meal, with a roast of sirloin, fresh country ham, and a stuffed duck. Kate didn't stay to finish. She rose with what dignity she could muster and swept out of the room, head high. Behind her she could hear comments from Lady Letitia about bad manners, but she didn't care. It took away her appetite to eat with Derek's aunt, especially when he wasn't here to act as a buffer between them.

Back in her bedchamber, Kate tugged angrily at the bell-pull, waiting impatiently for Vera to come help her out of the green satin gown which had so incensed Lady Letitia. It was a beautiful dress, a bit formal for eating at home, of course; but Kate had chosen it with care, hoping to find Derek's eyes on her. The décolletage was daring, cut so low that almost her entire bosom showed. She'd had Vera lace her so tightly she could scarcely force down a bite of food, just to show off that magnificent bosom to her husband, hoping the sight would rouse him, make him desire her once again. Instead, he probably was romping with Cynthia Farmington, wicked slut. If Harry were here this evening, Kate might just show Derek that it was a game two could play. As he was accusing her of going to bed with his brother, she might as well have the pleasure of it. Sleeping alone wasn't what Kate wanted. She longed for Derek to hold her in his arms, to caress her, to make passionate love to her. They were married. It was heartless of him to leave her alone, to go find his pleasure with someone like Cynthia.

Kate turned eagerly when she heard someone at the door, but it was only Vera, still chewing a bite of food.

"I thought you'd never get here," Kate snapped at the maid. "Where were you?"

"I'm sorry, milady. I thought you were at dinner, so I went to the kitchen to eat my meal. I didn't dream you'd be ready for me so soon."

"I wasn't hungry. Get me undressed, Vera. I'm laced much too tightly. I can scarcely breathe."

Silently Vera undid her gown and unlaced the stays, never suggesting that it was Kate herself who'd insisted that they be pulled up so tightly. Her mistress was cross more often than not these days. Sir Derek didn't sleep in here with her—everyone in the house knew this. It made her sad that her mistress and master were having problems. Everyone thought they made such a handsome, loving couple.

"Draw me a bath, Vera. And put in some of that French perfume." It was Derek's favorite scent. Kate intended to wait up for him tonight if she had to sit until dawn. They had to settle their differences. She couldn't go on this way, loving him, yet being rejected by the man who had claimed to love her so desperately.

Later, clad in a diaphanous gown of pale green chiffon, she pulled on a silk wrapper of a darker shade of green and let Vera brush out her red hair until it hung about her shoulders in gleaming strands. Finally she dismissed Vera and lay on her bed, reading, with one ear listening for Derek's steps. It struck midnight, and she had not heard him come in. Kate slid her feet into embroidered satin slippers and hurried to the room he now used, thinking that she must have missed hearing him. She tapped on the door, then stood there, heart in mouth, afflicted with stagefright, as she heard steps inside coming toward her.

Her disappointment was complete when she found that it was Tolliver, Derek's valet. "Isn't Sir Derek home yet?" she asked, sorry she'd come to the room, mortified that the servants should know she was pursuing her husband so blatantly.

"I'm sorry, milady, but he is not yet back from London. He told me that he might be quite late. I was not to wait up past midnight. I was just going to my room when you knocked."

"Very well, Tolliver. That's all."

Sadly she went back to her own room, the room that had been Derek's, which she had shared with him until recently. Once in the safety of the bedchamber, she sobbed bitterly. Whatever was she to do? She loved Derek, and she thought he still loved her; but he was so jealous of Harry that he was acting almost insane.

Kate flung herself across the big, lonely bed, determined to wait until Derek came home and then confront him. Finally she slept, her slumbers disturbed by vague dreams. She woke with a start to find that the sky was paling with early dawn. What had waked her? Then she heard the footsteps in the hall. It must be Derek, home at last. Catching up her negligee, she threw it around her shoulders, not bothering to put her arms into the sleeves. By the time she got out into the hall, there was no one in sight. Hurrying to the door of Derek's room, she stood listening. Yes, someone was moving about inside. She tapped, then opened the door before he could answer.

Derek was there, undressing. He hadn't called Tolliver to help him.

"Kate! What do you want at this hour?"

She walked to him, arms outstretched, pleading. She had no pride where Derek was concerned. She only wanted his love, she needed him so much.

"Derek, what's happened to you? I thought you loved me, and now you avoid me as if I had some dreadful disease. I love you. Don't you understand that? I long for you. Please come back to your room again—sleep with me —love me."

She saw hunger in his face, desire; so she let the robe slip from her shoulders and moved to him clad only in the sheer nightgown. She thought he was going to take her in his arms, crush her to him, make love to her. Instead, just as she could touch him, he turned away from her.

"Can't Harry satisfy you, Kate?"

"Oh, What a horrid thing to say. You know I have not been to bed with Harry since I married you."

"I don't know anything of the kind. I find you in compromising situations—Aunt Letitia sees the two of you coming out of the bedroom—how stupid do you think I am?"

"Derek, please, look at me," she begged. "I love you, only you. I thought I loved Harry, I was swept away by his good looks, his charm. I didn't love you when I married you. I resented you then—but I have learned to love you since that. What can I do to prove my love to you?"

"Nothing. I won't be made a fool of, Kate. Go to bed."

Anger flared in her at being so summarily rejected. "I suppose you aren't interested in me because you've been to bed with that trollop, Cynthia Farmington."

"I have no intention of being a monk. Chastity doesn't interest me."

He neither denied nor confirmed the rumor about his affair, but Kate knew that the story was true. Hurt, angry, she left her husband and walked, disconsolate, back toward her lonely room. As she neared the door, she heard someone coming up the stairs. Who would be prowling about at this hour? It was too early for the servants to be abroad.

Then, before she had time to go into her bedchamber, she saw Harry by the dim glow of a tiny gas light that burned all night in the hall.

"Up late or up early, Kate?" he asked. There was an air of excitement about him, a tension, which she could not ignore. "Ah, you look ravishing in that outfit. But then you look ravishing in any outfit—and even more lovely in nothing at all."

Before she could protest, he caught her in his arms and kissed her with a wild passion. First she struggled to free herself from his embrace; but he only held her more firmly, kissed her more ardently. Starved for love for too long, Kate found herself responding to his proximity, his maleness, so that soon she was kissing him with as much passion as he had kissed her.

"Kate, don't do this to me if you don't intend to take me to bed with you," he said hoarsely, his fingers tangled in her russet hair, which hung like silk about her shoulders.

For answer she reached behind her, found the doorknob, and opened the door.

Harry caught her up and carried her into the room she had shared with his brother, kicking the door shut behind him. "I don't know where your loving husband is, nor do I care," he said, burying his face in the soft flesh of her throat. "I've waited for you for much too long, Kate." He laid her on the bed and ordered, "Get out of that robe and nightgown, or I'll tear them off of you." His fingers trembled as he undressed himself.

It had been a long time since Kate had submitted to Harry. In that time she had come to truly love his brother. Now, rejected by Derek, she turned with all her woman's passion to Harry again, thrilling at his caresses, moaning softly as his lips found her breast.

"I want you now, Kate. Don't make me wait."

"Now, Harry, now," she whispered, opening her thighs to welcome him.

There was a wildness to their lovemaking that night that was like nothing she had experienced before, either with Harry or with her husband. Harry seemed almost in a frenzy, and it affected her also. It was sheer sensuality, with no thought of tenderness, no words of love. It was wild and animal, almost impersonal in its intensity, mounting and mounting until the blazing rapture of their climax left Kate almost fainting.

Then she realized that it was getting light outside. Soon the servants would be up.

"You mustn't stay here with me, Harry," she whispered. "We have to be very discreet, or Derek might find out."

Harry laughed. "He already thinks you warm my bed, dear sister-in-law. How could finding out that you do make any difference?"

It was true. That's what hurt Kate so badly, what had driven her into Harry's arms. It was the knowledge that she had been a good and faithful wife to Derek, that she had come to love him dearly—but that he believed sincerely that she was sleeping with Harry behind his back. And horrid Lady Letitia augmented this belief with her insinuations of immorality between Kate and Harry.

Very well. He thought she was a trollop, she'd act like one. Maybe it was Harry she loved. Now she was so mixed up in her own mind, so unsure of her own emotions, that Kate scarcely knew what to think. That she had enjoyed loving Harry again was obvious; but if she hadn't been so rejected by Derek, this episode would never have happened.

"Go back to your own room, Harry," she begged once again.

"Your wish is my command. But I will come back again —and again—and again, dear Kate. I can't get enough of you."

CHAPTER 27

Saturday, September 1, 1888

Kate was coming to hate dinner at Scarlet Oaks if both
Harry and Derek were at home. The cross currents, the
veiled remarks, the bitterness, were terrible. She felt increasingly tense, unhappy; and the fact that Lady Letitia
invariably sided with Derek did nothng to relieve the strain.

She and Harry were still involved with each other. She
wasn't sure whether or not Derek realized this, for he had
assumed from the beginning that she was sleeping with his
brother. He made no overtures to her, did not seek her
out, did not join her in her lonely bed. Kate still loved
him, she thought. It was difficult, though, to love a man
who rejected you. Harry was always willing to share her
bed. Sometimes she thought it would be better if they ran
away together. Once she'd hinted this to Harry, but he
pretended that he didn't understand what she was suggesting. Kate said no more of eloping. She couldn't bear it if
Harry, too, decided that he was no longer interested in her.

At times she wondered how this all would end. Was
Derek ever going to be her husband again? Things couldn't
go on like this indefinitely.

Tonight Harry introduced a gruesome subject during the
soup. Aunt Letitia tried to silence him, but he kept right
on talking.

"Horrible murder that took place in Whitechapel yesterday. Another of your patients, Derek?"

301

Derek just glared at him, but his Aunt Letitia took up Harry's flung gauntlet.

"Why do you think a dead woman might have been one of Derek's patients? You can bring up the most distasteful dinner subjects, Harry." Her mouth pursed with dislike.

"Ah, Aunt Letitia, we must keep track of what goes on, mustn't we? Here's a poor whore slain and ripped apart. And Derek has lots of patients who qualify as whores, don't you, Derek, old man? I can't, for the life of me, see what your fascination is with the filthy creatures."

"Must we discuss this now, Harry?"

"But Derek, you are the one who brings home that penny dreadful newspaper. That's where I read all of the lurid details of this murder. A woman known as Polly Nicholls. Listen to the description of her wardrobe." He pulled the paper from his pocket and read: "She wore a reddish-brown ulster, a brown linsey frock, and black, ribbed wool stockings."

"Those women can't buy Bond Street wardrobes, Harry." Kate was annoyed with him. She didn't want to listen to talk of such a lurid murder and said so.

"Kate's quite right, Harry." For once Lady Letitia sided with her. "This is not a fit topic for discussion with ladies."

"But we all know each other so intimately," he said, smiling slyly at Derek. "And it will be the talk of London, mark my words. A mutilation murder—women will be afraid to walk the streets at night. They'll think a madman is on the loose. This is the third murder of a Whitechapel prostitute this year. Maybe someone is trying to rid the city of its vice."

"That's scarcely the way to do it," Derek said angrily. "These women are forced into such sordid lives by their poverty. And it's men like Mansfield—and you, Harry, now that you are his errand boy—who make their plight worse."

Kate saw Harry flush red with anger when Derek referred to him as Mansfield's errand boy. One of these nights, the two men would goad each other into violent action.

"At least I haven't an abnormal interest in these whores, as you seem to have, Derek."

"What does that mean?"

"You seem eager to treat them. Do they allow you intimacies in the sacred inner sanctum of your Union Row clinic? Is that how they pay you—in kind?"

"From a womanizer like you, that is a vile suggestion, Harry." Lady Letitia was so incensed that she actually stopped eating from the haunch of venison she'd been attacking in order to castigate her stepnephew. "But you don't need to go to London to find a woman, do you?"

Kate was appalled at the implication—knowing it was true didn't make it any more palatable.

"I suppose that Derek likes a change from the lovely, accommodating Cynthia," Harry suggested.

"That's enough!" Derek thundered. "If you can't keep a civil tongue in your head, then leave the table. Get out of Scarlet Oaks."

"Not so hasty, dear brother. How can I desert your lovely, lonely wife? She needs a friend so desperately these days. You are so seldom here."

"Hush, Harry!" Kate was afraid Harry would push him too far.

"Very well, then, we can go back to discussing the nice, neat murder of Polly Nicholls. You didn't tell us, Derek. Did you know her?"

Grudgingly, Derek said, "As a matter of fact, I did."

"One less patient, old man. But I dare say there are plenty more where she came from. East London is filthy with whores."

"I deplore the use of that word in polite company."

"Sorry, Aunt Letitia. I shall try to remember to use some euphemism in the future. Although a whore is a whore."

"That's enough, Harry." Derek's tone brooked no defiance. And for once Harry took the hint and changed the subject.

Later the four of them played whist in the small drawing room. As they sat around the inlaid gaming table, Harry asked, his voice innocent, "How's Monica Murphy, Derek?"

"Not well."

"Pam told me that some man has set up an apartment for Monica," Kate said, thinking they were now on a safe subject. "Remembering how she looked the last time I saw her . . ."

"Consumption, I understand," Lady Letitia said. Her gossip sources were usually impeccable.

"Yes, unfortunately. I feel helpless, for there's little I can do for her, except try to keep her comfortable."

"The Duchess of Dorminster tried to get her to come back to Essex—offered her a place to stay—but Monica said it was too late for that."

Derek sighed. "Too true."

"But a man has paid her rent? How exciting," Harry said, mischief in his sparkling gray eyes. "I do hope he provides her with soap. If she's like most of the other wh—sorry, Aunt Letitia," he said with exaggerated politeness, "women of the streets, she's a filthy pig you can smell from ten feet away."

"You seem uncommonly familiar with the East London drabs," Derek jibed. "Do you spend your off hours there prowling the sordid streets, spying on the wretched people who live there?"

Harry's face flushed with anger. "I work there—just as you do."

"Unfortunately, you work for Mansfield."

"He's a rich and powerful man, dear brother. And don't think that just because you managed to buy that miserable building which houses your clinic that you'll be able to stay there forever. Mansfield wants that block—and what he wants, he gets."

"Not always," Kate said coldly.

"Well, of course I'm glad he didn't get you. I dare say that Arthur Mansfield would be a difficult man to cuckold."

The implication was so blatant that Kate winced. Derek gave her a scathing look, and she wished she could shrivel up and disappear.

"You'll come to no good end, working for that man," Aunt Letitia warned him. "He's a crook, Harry. And if you work for him, you'll be an even bigger crook than you are now."

"Ah, well!" His tone was flippant, calculated to anger his elderly aunt. "If you must be a crook, be a good one!"

"Play your cards, Harry," Derek ordered, "and keep your mouth shut for a while."

The evening was not a success. Lady Letitia finally retired, leaving the three of them together. Kate decided that she couldn't take more of the bickering between the two brothers, so she, too, went to her bedchamber. She had just left her bath when she heard someone moving about in the bedroom. As Vera had gone to get her some hot wine to soothe her, she assumed that it was Harry. Usually he waited until the house had settled down before approaching her. Even he knew that he must use a little discretion in his affair with Kate.

Pulling on her nightgown, a demure white cotton with sleeves and ruffles at neck and hem, she went into her room. Kate was stunned to find that it was Derek there, not Harry. He was sitting at his desk, writing in his journal.

"Who has a key to this desk, Kate?" His tone accused, but he didn't look at her. He kept his eyes on the maroon leather book in which he wrote.

"You have—why?"

"Someone's been into my desk—this diary was put back the wrong way." Now he turned, suddenly, confronting her.

"I—I have no key, Derek."

"I suppose Harry has—or that he has learned to pick locks. No doubt his crooked friends know lots of tricks."

Kate saw this as a chance to ingratiate herself with her estranged husband. "As a matter of fact, Harry did open the desk one day. He wanted to show me the secret drawer in it."

"Why? There's nothing in that drawer. I'd almost forgotten it was there. Trust Harry to remember something like that."

"That's what he was doing the day your aunt saw us come out of here, Derek. Nothing else. You accused me falsely, and it hurt me badly. Is there nothing I can do to win back your trust?"

He turned away from her, and Kate's heart fell. Derek

deliberately blotted what he had written in his journal, closed the leather-bound volume, and then locked it away. "Although why bother, if Harry has access to it," he muttered. Then he stood up and came to Kate, standing close to her but not touching her. "Trust you? Oh, Kate, if only I could! You're my wife, and I love you desperately—but no man wants to share the woman he loves with someone else."

She was treading on very shaky ground now. The day in question, when Harry had found the diary, they had not been sleeping together. If she could make Derek believe that this still was the truth—she'd stay away from Harry, refuse him her body, if only Derek would come back to her and love her.

Kate closed the tiny distance between them, putting her hands on his shoulders, turning her face up to him, inviting him to kiss her.

"I love you, Derek—only you. Can't you believe that?"

"But Harry—"

"—means nothing to me now. I swear it." She let her hands slide around his neck and pressed her eager body to him. "Come back to our room, my dear," she begged, "and love me once again."

With a sound almost like a groan, he caught her to him, nearly crushing her with his powerful arms. He kissed her passionately, his tongue seeking hers. Then he buried his face in her hair, murmuring, "Kate, my beloved, my darling. I've died a thousand deaths away from you."

"And it was all needless," she said softly, again offering her lips to him. "Come to bed, dear."

"Help me undress," he commanded as he slipped her gown high and caressed her body with hungry hands.

They lay on the bed she had been sharing with Harry, but there was no thought in Kate's mind of anything or anyone but her husband. It had been so long—too long—and she surrendered herself to him completely as the sweet, maddening sensations swept over her body, eliciting such a response from her that it was overwhelming.

Later, still in his arms, she whispered, "Will you go back to Cynthia Farmington, Derek? If you do, I won't be responsible for my actions. I'm a very jealous woman, Derek."

"Love me the way you just did, and I'll never look at another woman, my darling," he promised.

While they lay there, entwined in each others arms, there was a light tapping on the door.

"Kate? Are you awake, love?"

She died a thousand deaths. It was Harry, coming to join her in Derek's bed.

With a cry of rage, Derek pulled away from her encircling arms, swearing, "I'll kill him!"

"No, no! Derek, stay here!" she begged, reaching for him, clinging to him, to keep him from making good his threat.

Harry, obviously hearing the two of them, had sense enough to leave. When Derek did pull away from her and opened the door, the corridor was empty.

No emptier than his face. He turned on her, his face full of loathing in the dim light from the one gaslight he had left on for their lovemaking.

"So you haven't been sleeping with Harry? Ah, Kate, what a clever little liar you are. And I thought—"

He snatched up his clothes, dressed quickly, and left her without a backward glance. Kate lay in bed and sobbed herself to sleep.

INTERLUDE 8

Saturday, September 8, 1888. 5:25 A.M.

He had prowled the streets of East London since midnight, growing increasingly tense as the hours passed. It had been little more than a week since he'd killed and mutilated Polly Nicholls, but already the thrill of it had faded, leaving him restless and unhappy. Tonight he'd worn another disguise, powdering his hair a bit to make it look gray, wearing the shabby brown suit he'd bought from a barrow. His brown deerstalker hat was pulled well down over his forehead, hiding his eyes.

Now, on Hanbury Street, only about half a mile from Buck's Row where he'd killed the other whore, he saw a woman leaning against the dirty brick of a common lodging house.

When he came up to her, she smiled at him. " 'ello, 'andsome," she said. Her pudgy face was dirty, and strands of greasy hair made a fringe on her forehead. "Name's Annie."

He stopped to chat with her for a moment until a woman hurried past them. Then he asked her, "Will you?"

"Yes. We can go through this passage. There's a yard back there we can use."

She led him through the dark, noisome passage, through a side door, and into a small yard paved with stones forced crooked by grass growing between them. There was a high wooden fence separating the yard from the next one.

308

He moved close to her, raised his hands, and pressed her chin up and back, cutting off her air. In a moment she slumped unconscious to the ground. He laid her out neatly, then drew his knife and slashed her throat with two savage strokes. To keep the blood off his suit, he'd pulled on a leather slaughterman's apron he found hanging on the fence. Then he pulled up her skirts and proceeded methodically to disembowel her corpse, laying the intestines over her right shoulder, and flaps of abdominal skin over the left.

The bloodletting was soothing. After the first frenzy was over, he realized that it was not safe to stay here too long. The clock at the brewer's had struck half after five as the woman had solicited him. Soon people in this lodging house might well be up and about. He slit open the pocket she carried under her skirt and found that all she possessed was a comb, a paper case, and a bit of muslin. He laid these by the body. Next he pulled off two rings she wore, found some pennies and two new farthings in a pocket of her coat, and laid them at her feet. He also found a twist of paper containing two pills. These he put at the head.

Then he took off the leather apron, rinsed it under the water tap in the yard, made sure his hands were clean of blood, threw down the apron, and left the way he had come. He was in luck. No one saw him enter or leave the common lodging house. As he left he saw that the house number was 29. Satisfied with his night's work, he left the district.

CHAPTER 28

Tuesday, September 11, 1888

"And where do you think you're going, all dressed to go out?" Derek asked at breakfast.

"It's my day at Salvation Chapel," Kate reminded him.

"Are you out of your mind?" His voice was cold, harsh. Since that dreadful night more than a week ago, he had not sought out Kate, but slept alone as he had done previously. No matter how she'd tried to explain Harry's coming to her door, it was not enough to convince Derek that she was his and his alone.

"Now what?" she snapped, wearying of this deadly game they played. What was marriage for, if all it meant was quarrels over everything, with no love to leaven the trouble?

"Kate, several women have been murdered in the past fortnight in the East End. A madman is loose in Whitechapel. Don't you read the newspapers? And you expect to go into the midst of all that today?"

"The duchess is going."

"I shall advise her to stay home and be safe."

Kate laughed at that idea. She couldn't imagine that the Duchess of Dorminster would pay any attention to Derek.

"I'm sure that the duchess will go as usual, and she will expect me to go with her to help her."

"No." Just that one word, a flat order.

Kate bridled. "What right have you to order me about?"

"I am your husband. Or have you conveniently forgotten that fact?"

"Then why don't you act like a husband instead of a jailor?" she demanded, near tears. "You ignore me, you sleep apart from me; yet you give me orders—do this—don't do that. What kind of a marriage do we have, Derek?"

"The kind you have made," he hurled back at her.

"Then why concern yourself about me, if you have no love for me?" she demanded. "I'd think you wouldn't care where I went, what I did. If this madman killed me, then you'd be rid of me."

For a moment he closed his eyes, and Kate felt a pang of distress at having said such cruel things to him. Derek looked so tired. He'd been staying out late—his excuse: his medical practice. She thought he just didn't want to come home to her. Her anguish was terrible, but no attempts on her part to reconcile their differences seemed to reach him.

"Kate, don't push me too hard," Derek said, still not looking at her. "I can't take too much more of this."

"Then end it!" she pleaded. "Believe me when I tell you that there's nothing between Harry and me."

There was the sound of clapping from the door. To her dismay, Kate saw that Harry stood there, face sardonic, applauding her words as if she were an actress on the stage.

"Well said, dear sister-in-law." He turned to Derek. "Your heart must be made of stone—that is, if you have a heart, Derek. Surely Kate's words would melt even a stone. And I should let her go wherever she chooses if she were my wife."

"She's not your wife!" Derek shouted.

"Not in name."

"Harry, that's enough!" Kate snapped, furious with him for making trouble when she had trouble enough without him.

"Remember, Derek," Harry said, going to the sideboard and lifting the silver covers from the dishes to see what was for breakfast, "if Kate stays here, she'll be safe. I shall be here to look after her."

"Not going to London to run errands for your master?"

Derek asked, tone nasty. "No poor souls to evict today? No exorbitant rents to collect for Mansfield?"

Harry helped himself to kippers and eggs. "Jealous. Always jealous of my success. You'll still be a plodding, stodgy doctor, treating the dregs in the East End because you couldn't hope to be a successful doctor in Mayfair, when I am rich and powerful in the city. Mansfield will be a force to reckon with in London—in all of England. And he'll carry me to the top with him." He sat down beside Kate, ignoring Derek's scowl. "You really chose the wrong brother, Kate. You'd have a much more spectacular future with me."

"I have no future with you, Harry," she said sadly.

He just smiled at her. "Time will tell, Kate. But I think Derek is right about one thing. East London is not a safe place for you these days. This madman who is ridding the city of its whores by rather drastic means—he might not understand that you are a decent, upright, married lady and have you for his next victim. Don't tempt him, Kate— although I must admit that you are a very tempting morsel. Remember, when you get tired of sleeping alone and want a real man in your bed once again, I am always ready and willing to oblige."

"By God, Harry, some day I'll kill you." It was spoken softly, but with such venom that Kate was terrified. Her husband was white with fury.

"Derek, you know that Harry is only saying these horrid things to make you angry. Don't pay any attention to him."

"She's right, Derek." Harry grinned engagingly. "Go off to London happy and at ease, knowing that Kate is safe here—as safe at Scarlet Oaks as she would be in Whitechapel." He gave a little, secret smile. "Safer, probably. Kate, have you heard the latest rumors about the bloody murders in East London? They think that it may be a doctor who is doing them. The latest case—the woman was mutilated by someone who knew just what he was doing—knew just where to make the cuts. Beware of any doctor who practices in the East End of London."

Derek got up, threw down his napkin, and stalked out of the room without a further word.

"Harry, you can be dreadful at times," Kate scolded.

BRIDE OF FURY 313

She hurried out after her husband, hoping to be able to right some of the things Harry had done.

"I'm surprised that you didn't stay in the dining room with your lover." He was pulling on his raincoat. His black doctor's bag was on a walnut table in the vestibule.

"He's not my lover, Derek," she said, trying to control her anger.

"Or so the lady says." Harry had followed them and stood there, smug and handsome.

"Harry, go away!" she begged.

"I just wanted to be sure that Derek was properly outfitted for the day," Harry said, voice full of reasonableness. "We don't want him to catch a chill in the damp autumn air, do we? Where is your hat, Derek?"

Kate caught up Derek's bowler and handed it to him.

"Oh, you're not wearing your deerstalker hat? Tired of imitating Conan Doyle's hero—the detective chappie? Now there's an idea for the penny dreadful paper you bring home for Kate to read. Get that fictional detective— Holmes?—to find the mad killer of Whitechapel."

Because Harry was there, Kate took perverse pleasure in twining her arms about Derek's neck and kissing him goodbye. She could feel him tense. At first he did not return her kiss, but finally he put one arm about her and pulled her close. It was the first time he had kissed her since that awful night when Harry had come to her room.

Then he was gone. She watched the victoria drive off down the road, the gray matched team tossing their heads in the soft fall rain.

"Give up, Kate," Harry said softly. He had moved silently so that he now stood directly behind her. "Come back to me. I appreciate your talents so much more than Derek does."

Annoyed with Harry for provoking her husband to anger, she said coldly, "There are many times when I regret begging Derek to let you stay here at Scarlet Oaks. You seem to enjoy making life miserable for me, Harry."

"Or wonderful—it's your choice, Kate. Come to bed with me. You'll not feel miserable for long, I guarantee."

"I'm married!"

"That hasn't been bothering you much."

"It was a dreadful mistake on my part to take up with you again. Do leave me alone, Harry."

"But I want you. And I intend to have you, Kate. You know that Derek isn't enough man for you. You need me in your bed, not that old stick-in-the-mud. A warm, passionate woman wants an equally warm, passionate man—me."

So it was going to be that kind of day. Just then the Duchess of Dorminster's carriage drove up to the door. Kate made a lightning decision. Derek had told her it wasn't safe for her to go to East London, but she knew that it was even less safe for her to stay here today with Harry. Perhaps she'd get home before Derek did, and if Harry would only keep quiet, Derek need never know she'd defied his orders again.

The duchess was full of the account of the murder.

"Derek forbade me to go to the chapel. I don't know what he'll say when he finds I've disobeyed."

"I scarcely think the madman will attack the two of us in broad daylight," the duchess observed drily. "Besides, all the women who've been murdered recently in Whitechapel have been prostitutes. We don't qualify, my dear."

"Harry said—" She stopped short, appalled at what she had almost said.

The duchess eyed her shrewdly. "And what does the dashing Harry say about the murders?"

"Is there a rumor that a doctor committed this heinous crime? Because of the—the dissecting?"

"That's one theory. But any butcher could do as well. And that area is rife with butcher shops and slaughterhouses." Then those bright blue eyes widened momentarily. "You don't mean that he's suggesting that Derek—"

"Oh, no, no! Harry didn't say any such thing." Kate heard her own voice, shrill and vehement, protesting too much.

The duchess sighed and shook her head, threatening to lose the scarlet bonnet with ostrich plumes which perched on top of her mountain of yellow hair. "Harry always has been a troublemaker, Kate. Now—don't go protecting him, defending his mischiefs. I know Harry Ravenshaw."

"He does pick and pick at Derek."

"That husband of yours ought to throw the young scamp out. It can't be pleasant for you, constant tension between the two brothers."

"It's terrible. And Lady Letitia fuels the fire by always siding with Derek against Harry."

"So I suppose you think you have to take Harry's part?"

Kate didn't answer, for the duchess's perception was too close to the mark for comfort.

At Paddington they got a hansom cab and rattled along to Salvation Chapel. Even from the cab they sensed that things were different in the East End. People hurried along the streets as if afraid to be outdoors for long. The women kept glancing back over their shoulders to make sure they weren't being followed.

"Bad business, that murder. Has the whole area on edge. Can't you feel the tension, Kate? This section could explode if there's another killing."

"Another? Do you think there will be?" Kate asked fearfully.

"It could happen. These things often go in series."

They had now reached the Salvation Chapel. As they went to the door, Kate said, "I hope that the Reverend Mr. Fiddler isn't here today."

They opened the scarred door and stepped into the gloom of the chapel. As Kate's eyes adjusted to the dim light, she saw a horrifying sight. The duchess saw it at the same moment, for Kate heard her give a little gasp.

"It's—" Kate whimpered, unable to tear her eyes from the swinging, slowly turning figure hanging from one of the crossbeams.

"Get a constable! I'll see if Abby is—"

Kate fled the place, not sure she wasn't going to be sick. On the street she cried, "Where's a constable? We need the police!"

"What's wrong? Not another knifing?" a passing laborer asked. "Has the madman struck again?"

"No, no—suicide," she managed to say.

Then there was the shrill whistle of a police constable, and a familiar, uniformed figure came pushing through the throng.

"Inside," Kate whispered. "It's the parson—hanged."

Soon the duchess came out, her face pale under the paint. "God help him. He confessed to murdering some poor whore. Or I think he did. The note he left is incoherent. I guess his mind finally snapped."

"Is Mrs. Fiddler—"

"Not here. Perhaps out marketing. I gave the police our names, told them we knew nothing. Come, Kate, we'd better get away from here. There'll be a field day once the papers hear of this."

"Did he—did he kill that poor Annie Chapman?"

"Don't know. Probably. Or maybe he only thought he did. Mental. I've known it for some time. Sometimes people confess to crimes they didn't commit, just to get attention. But he'd been blackmailed about some killing."

"Then if he's the killer, everyone can relax," Kate said, drawing a deep breath. "It's terrible for his wife, but at least women can walk the streets of Whitechapel now without being afraid of having their throats cut."

CHAPTER 29

Friday, September 28, 1888

"Isn't Harry with you?" Alfie asked as he greeted Kate and Derek. The occasion was a dinner party in the new Cabot home in Chelmsford.

"Harry?"

Kate could hear the suppressed anger in her husband's voice, but she thought he probably concealed it well from others. It was just that of late she'd learned more and more of Derek's temper. The situation at Scarlet Oaks deteriorated daily. Occasionally Derek sought her bed; usually he slept apart from her. At times she gave in to Harry's importuning and took him into her lonely bed, although she knew that it was Derek she truly loved.

"You mean old Harry isn't coming?" Alfie asked. He turned to call to Pam, who looked glowing in a daringly lowcut gown of heavy scarlet taffeta. "One short at table, love. Harry isn't here."

"Is he ill?" Pam asked, coming forward to kiss Kate and offer her cheek to Derek.

"I didn't even know he was invited," Kate told her. "He never mentioned it to me."

"A man short. How dreadful. And how wretched of Harry not to let me know." Pam was very annoyed. It would ruin her seating plan.

Derek and Kate went into the huge living room to find the Duchess of Dorminster, Lord Wimbley, and the lovely Lady Cynthia Farmington, obviously unescorted. Kate seethed inwardly. How dare Pam do this to her?

Cynthia, striking as always in deep blue velvet cut with simple but revealing lines, her golden hair dressed with a large pompadour, moved languidly toward them.

"Kate, dear, how charming you look." Her tone said it all. Kate, in emerald-green satin, looked lovely in a more spectacular fashion. Beside the elegant Cynthia, she felt young and gauche. "And Derek. I haven't seen you lately, you naughty man." She tapped him playfully on one cheek with her lace-and-ivory fan. "He's such good company," she said to Kate, making her seethe with anger.

Derek was charming to Cynthia, which further infuriated Kate. It was with delight that she noticed, in a few minutes, that Harry had arrived, looking very elegant in his dress suit.

"If you two will excuse me," she murmured, "I must see Harry." She turned a brilliant smile on Derek, pleased to see that familiar flash of anger in his dark eyes. If flirtation was what Cynthia intended, Kate would show her how it should be done.

"Naughty Harry," she said loudly enough that her husband could hear her, "you nearly gave Pam heart failure. She thought she'd be short a man, and poor Cynthia would have no partner."

Harry took in the scene with one glance, bowed with charm to Kate, and tucked her hand in his arm. "Now Cynthia can have dull Derek to amuse her, while we younger folk have fun."

If ever she thought she loved Harry, it was then; for Cynthia heard his cruel jibe, and flushed an ugly red, while Derek looked ready to commit murder.

The evening rapidly became disastrous. Derek, enraged at Kate's coquetry, devoted himself to Lady Farmington. At dinner, served at an enormous round table in the paneled dining room, Kate and Harry were paired, and Derek was with Cynthia, Pam's own little mischief-making scheme.

Somehow, during the soup course, as Kate sipped bisque while Harry had the oxtail, the subject of the Whitechapel murders came up.

"Solved with the death of poor Fiddler," the duchess said. "Why all this further hue and cry in the papers?"

"Eh?" asked Lord Wimbley, resplendent in a lavender coat of satin with a purple waistcoat embroidered with gold thread. He wore the customary knee breeches, and his shoes had gold buckles. His wig tonight was a small, powdered bagwig.

"The authorities aren't at all satisfied that Fiddler did those murders," Derek said. "One, maybe. They aren't sure. The man was mad as a hatter. I think the murders worked on his already overtaxed brain, causing him to hang himself."

"Then the blackmail was a goad too," Kate said.

"He was a dirty old man," Pam giggled. "Remember how he had his hands all over you that day we went slumming, Kate?"

Derek looked daggers at his wife, and she hated Pam for mentioning it.

"Perhaps he found me more attractive than you," Kate said with honeyed tones, only to find that it gave Cynthia an ideal opening.

"I'm not sure I'd find it complimentary to be pawed by a crazy parson," she said, a smug smile on her peaches-and-cream face. Then she turned and smiled up at Derek.

"Oh!" Wimbley put in, nodding sagely.

"Fiddler was sick, and his wife did nothing to help him," the duchess cut in. "But why do the police think it wasn't he who did the other killings?"

"They've gotten letters—and the newspapers have too," Harry said. "From the man who says he is the killer." He leaned forward slightly, ignoring the deviled whitebait the footman had just served him. "Crazy letters—but clever too. He threatens other killings. And the letters have come since Fiddler hanged himself. The fellow is signing himself Jack the Ripper."

"Ah!" Again Wimbley nodded.

"Gruesome!" Pam said, catching up her wineglass and sipping it as if she felt faint. "Do you think there will be more of those horrid women killed, Harry?"

"Who knows? The man is mad, obviously. He might

kill again. There are all sorts of stories circulating about
him."

"Heard he was royalty," Alfie said. "All kinds of tales
in the House of Lords. They say that several letters have
been sent to the police and the papers. Most of them are
crank notes, of course. Happens every time a crime is
committed. People want to confess—or send letters—nuts,
all of them."

"Oh!" Wimbley said.

"That was the trouble with the Reverend Mr. Fiddler.
He could have done one or more of the killings—or he
might have told people he did. Sad case."

"They also suspect a doctor," Harry cut in. "Are you
guilty, Derek?"

Derek dropped his fork, which rattled against his plate.
"Sometimes, Harry, your jokes are not funny."

Kate died a thousand deaths. It was bad enough when
this kind of thing went on at home—but out in company!

"Aren't you worried to be with Derek, Cynthia?" Harry
asked, turning from Kate at the very last moment of his
question.

Derek flushed with rage, Cynthia smiled coyly, and Kate
wanted to hit Harry across the knuckles with her knife.

"Saw something in the paper about the notes," the
duchess cut in quickly to avert open warfare between the
Ravenshaws. "The notes they get are in a disguised handwriting—or so the authorities think."

"I thought it was impossible to disguise handwriting,"
Lady Cynthia said.

"Anyone clever enough can do it," Harry assured her.

"I don't want to go near London," Pam said breathlessly. "When I think back on that day you and I went to
Whitechapel, Kate, I shudder. We might have been killed."

"We weren't," Kate said sharply. All this talk bothered
her. Hints that a doctor might be the killer—when Derek
was a doctor who worked in that area. Talk of deerstalker hats. Suggestions that the killer was really someone
of high birth, who went into the slums to do his terrible
work—it made her uneasy. The fact that Derek had been
under such a terrible strain of late, that their marriage was
disintegrating, made her terror even more real. Was it pos-

sible to be married to a madman and not know it? Abby
Fiddler had known that her husband was erratic. Determined to keep such thoughts down, Kate devoted herself
to the entrees the butler was offering, choosing quenelles
of rabbit instead of the lobster cutlets, although she noticed that Lord Wimbley took a helping of each.

"I don't think the police are doing everything they
should do to catch this monster," Alfie said. "A lot of
politics going on there, you know. And jurisdictional problems. Is it the Metropolitan Police or the City of London
force?"

"My husband says that the police are protecting someone in one of the best families," Cynthia told them.
"There's all sorts of speculation as to who it might be."
She lowered her voice suggestively. "There's talk of a
ring of—feminine type men—you understand? And that
some sons of the very best families—royalty even—belong.
They hate women, you know. They might be involved."

"It's all just horrid guesses," Kate said hotly. "People
will be ruined, their lives shattered, by such loose talk.
Next they'll say it's a woman who is doing the murders."

Fortunately the servants brought in the removes at that
moment, and the guests, in choosing between quarter of
spring lamb or capon with ham, were distracted from the
murders.

During the game course, though, Pam asked Derek, "Is
Monica Murphy still in Whitechapel? You do know her,
don't you, Derek?" Her gray eyes were avid with curiosity,
and Kate hated her hostess for bringing up such a subject.

"Of course I know her," Derek said, "as do you—and
everyone else here. As to where she is, she is in the East
End—very ill with consumption."

"I heard some man had set her up in a flat," Harry
said.

"She has a room in the building where I have my clinic." Derek's words fell like stones on Kate's ears. So it
was true. Derek had given her a place to live. Harry had
been right, Derek was keeping Monica.

The duchess dispelled such illusions promptly though.
"I'm paying her rent, Harry. I won't allow you to throw
mud on your brother. I arranged for her to stay there.

Pay Derek regularly. Poor girl, health bad. Won't live long, I dare say."

For once in his life Harry Ravenshaw had nothing to say.

The dinner finally ended and Derek said to Pam, "It's been a lovely evening, but Kate and I must be getting home."

Mischievous Pam asked, "Who'll escort Cynthia to Bard Hall?"

Derek just smiled. "Ask Harry. He's your extra man."

Kate loved him then, with such a fierce love that she could scarcely contain herself. In the carriage going home, she asked, "Why didn't you tell me about Monica when Harry brought it up at home?"

"I wouldn't give him that satisfaction, Kate." His voice was hard. "It was none of Harry's business, my arrangements with the duchess about Monica."

All the way home, Derek sat with his arm around Kate, and for the first time in weeks, she felt at peace with him and with herself. That night in bed, Derek was passionate and loving, and Kate reveled in his love, giving of herself with abandon, reaching heights of rapture she had not known were attainable. Later, lying in each other's arms, he whispered, "Oh, Kate, beloved, be mine—only mine. At times I think I'll go mad when I believe that Harry has you."

"If you love me, you don't have to worry about Harry," she told him, kissing him sweetly and holding him close. "That's all I want, Derek. Your love. When you stay apart from me, I can't bear it."

Then he made love to her again, slowly, gently, and she fell asleep in his arms. Sometime later Kate woke to find the bed empty. Derek was at his desk, writing in his journal. Sleepily she watched him close the book, put it away, and lock the desk. This time the screen was not placed quite the same way as usual to keep the light from her eyes. She could see his hand go under the desk, and then come away. What was he doing? Then she realized that somewhere under the desk was where Derek left the key.

CHAPTER 30

Thursday, November 8, 1888

Kate and Derek slept late; when they finally dressed and went down, Harry wasn't about. Kate wondered if he had spent the night with the fair Cynthia, but she didn't mention it to Derek. Things were too good between them at the moment. She thought any question about Lady Farmington might be misconstrued by her husband.

Derek went out to his Chelmsford surgery for a few hours in the afternoon, but he was back in time for dinner with Kate and Lady Letitia.

"What news of those terrible crimes in Whitechapel, Derek?" his aunt asked. "A woman isn't safe these days in London. The police are useless." She cut a large bite of roast pork and chewed it vigorously. "I think Warren should be relieved of his duties. He's done nothing to catch this madman."

"Don't blame the poor fellow entirely, Aunt Letitia." Derek sipped claret, then went on. "He has a terrible problem on his hands. The streets of East London are like a rabbit warren. They are dark, poorly lit, and there aren't enough constables to patrol them. Someone could commit murder with a constable only a few hundred feet away and never be seen. As to the madman—if he is that—he could be anyone. He may be a normal, law-abiding citizen most of the time, until this apparent blood lust hits him. Then he's a beast."

"There's been talk that a well-dressed man has been

seen talking with those unfortunate women before they were slashed."

Kate wished that Lady Letitia would stop talking about the murders. When Harry had brought up the subject at dinner, his aunt had been most annoyed with him. Now she was talking nonstop about the horrors herself.

"Aunt Letitia, there are plenty of well-dressed, well-bred men who walk about the East End. It's the thing to do these days. The men even learn the Cockney slang and use it as a kind of code."

Avidly she asked, "Is it true that Prince Eddy goes there?"

Derek shrugged. "I haven't seen him."

"I dare say he'd go incognito," his aunt said. "It would look bad for the queen if her grandson was caught in such low surroundings." Then, directing her attention to Kate while the footman served her raspberry ice, she said, "I do hope you have given up that foolishness of doing good works in Whitechapel, my dear. I know the duchess has taken you there; but it is bad business now, with a killer on the loose."

Kate shuddered. "My last trip there was completely horrible." She still had nightmares in which Fiddler's body twisted and turned at the end of the rope from the beam in Salvation Chapel. "I don't want to go there ever again. Frankly, I don't think that the duchess and I did any good at all. The women would come occasionally to a class, but no one attended regularly."

Lady Letitia shrugged and bit into a juicy pear, which she selected from the assortment on the silver epergne in the center of the table. "But enough of such dreary talk," she said, as if it had not been her idea to discuss the murders. "I think it would be nice if Kate played for us on the piano. I received a shipment of new music in the mail yesterday. I'd like to hear some of it."

Kate wasn't too interested in entertaining Derek's aunt, but she acquiesced rather than cause bad feelings. There were enough tensions at Scarlet Oaks without making more.

They adjourned to the music room, Derek taking his port with him. Kate sat at the lovely, square, rosewood piano and Derek stood behind her, turning the pages while she played. She was very conscious of his presence. After last night, Kate wanted nothing more than to go up to their bed together. If she could cut short this musical treat for Aunt Letitia, she and Derek could retire for the night.

Just then Parsons came in and caught Derek's eye.

"Begging your pardon, sir, there's a message just been brought by hand." He had a small silver tray with a letter on it, which he brought to Derek.

Kate saw the worry on her husband's face. "What can it be?" she asked. Her first thought was that something had happened to Harry—a carriage accident, perhaps—and then she realized that it would be the authorities who would notify him of that.

Quickly Derek slit the envelope with the Italian stiletto that Parsons had provided as a letter opener. He drew out the note, glanced at it, and sighed.

"Sorry, Kate, I have to go to London immediately."

"London! But it's ten o'clock, Derek."

"I can get the last train if I hurry. Have the groom get the light carriage ready at once, Parsons."

"One of your destitute patients?" Aunt Letitia asked, voice acid.

"As a matter of fact, it's Monica Murphy."

A wave of jealousy struck Kate, making her giddy with its intensity. She remembered all of Harry's insinuations. More sharply than she intended, Kate said, "I don't see why you have to go clear to London at night to see about her." Her lips were tight with displeasure. "Surely there are other doctors in the East End. This is ridiculous, Derek."

"Kate's right. You'll ruin your own health, traipsing about at night this way," his aunt said with authority.

Derek wasn't to be dissuaded. "She's my patient, and she's having a crisis. I left word with a neighbor woman that I was to be notified if she got worse. Don't wait up for me, Kate. I'll probably be there all night."

"Take me with you," she begged, not wanting him to see Monica alone. It was a silly fear, the jealousy was probably uncalled for. Kate remembered how sick Monica was when she saw her in Whitechapel. By now her condition must have deteriorated even more, in spite of the care she'd gotten from Derek. Yet she did feel jealous and wanted to go with him.

"Out of the question, Kate." Her husband's voice was curt. "East London at night is no place for you, not with this madman about."

"But I'd be with you."

"I have to take care of Monica. She's very ill—I don't want you in contact with her, Kate. It isn't safe. I don't want you contracting consumption, God knows."

"And you don't know when you'll be home?"

"I'll be back at the first possible moment," he promised. "Come now, I must get my instrument bag."

They went upstairs together, and once in the privacy of their bedchamber, Derek caught her to him and kissed her until she was weak with desire.

"Stay here," she begged. "Don't go off and leave me."

"I wish I could," he murmured, his face buried in her hair. "But when a patient is desperately ill, a doctor must put aside personal desires. I must go now, dearest. Go to bed and dream of me."

He put on his topcoat, took a black bowler from the wardrobe and set it on his head at a jaunty angle.

"Whatever happened to that deerstalker cap you had?" Kate asked.

"I seem to have lost it." He was quite casual about it.

Then he kissed her again, a quick caress, and was gone.

Kate rang for Vera and got ready for bed, but she was too restless to sleep. She decided she would read for a while, but the new Dickens novel failed to hold her attention. She wished that they'd been out when the note came. Maybe he'd not have gone to London if he had received it later. But she thought he probably would have. Derek was, at times, all too conscientious about his work. Unless this was an excuse to get out, away from her. Could it have been a prearranged signal from Cynthia? Was he lying to her?

She wondered if Derek had written anything about the luscious Lady Farmington in his journal. Well, she'd never know. Harry had opened the desk, but she didn't know how to pick locks. Then Kate remembered watching Derek's hand go under the desk. Curiosity got the better of her. Slipping out of bed, she pulled on her blue robe, put on the harem slippers with embroidery that she liked, and walked to the maple desk. For a while she just stood there, looking at it, reluctant to invade her husband's privacy this way. Then she lit the lamp on the desk, lifting the chimney until the match caught the wick. Then, with sudden resolution, she felt under the desk, finding a little recess, touching the brass key. Committed now, she unlocked the desk and opened the drawer where Derek kept his journal. Taking out the leather-bound book, she sat there with it closed for a few minutes, getting up the courage to read it.

She turned to the entry of the last time they had made love. Reading her husband's words caused a wave of desire to sweep over her. He loved her. There could be no question in her mind after reading the entry. She leafed back through several pages, looking for Cynthia Farmington's name, but she didn't see it. Perhaps all her fears were unfounded. Derek loved her. It was just Harry who kept making trouble. Kate decided that she'd talk to Derek about his brother, tell him that for the sake of their marriage, Harry must live elsewhere.

Ashamed of herself now, sorry she had looked into the diary, Kate put it back in the drawer where she'd found it. She started to close the desk when she remembered the little secret drawer Harry had shown her. Wondering if she could open it, she reached in under the section of pigeonholes and felt around for the catch. Her fingers touched a small raised knob of wood. Pushing it, she found that it released the latch and the pigeonholes swung forward, revealing the drawer. Idly she pulled it open, expecting it to be empty, as before. To her surprise she found that a small copybook with gray-marbled board covers lay in the shallow space. Frowning, puzzled, she took it out. This hadn't been here the other time when Harry had opened the secret drawer to show her.

There was nothing written on the cover of the book, the space under THIS BOOK BELONGS TO being empty. She leafed through it and found that portions of it were filled with writing, some of it Derek's distinctive spiky hand she knew so well. Other places the writing seemed to deteriorate into a sloppy, illiterate kind of penmanship. There were even sections of block printing.

Curious now, she turned back to the beginning to read what her husband had written in this secretive volume.

Tuesday, August 7, she read. *She fell down, all bloody. It excited me even more than sex does.* Further on there were bits of sentences in a different handwriting. *A prostitute of high repute, the Harlot of Jeru . . .* then the writing ran downhill into scribbles. Kate's heart thudded and she felt faint. What was the meaning of this? It looked like the ramblings of a madman.

"No," she whispered. "Oh, no!"

She slammed the copybook shut and thrust it back into its secret hiding place. As if it might burn her, she pushed the pigeonhole section back in place, then slammed the desk and locked it.

Kate paced the floor of the bedchamber, wringing her hands. It couldn't be what it sounded like. It couldn't. Derek wasn't mad. Derek couldn't possibly be involved in those ugly killings in Whitechapel. He was a doctor, dedicated to giving life, not snuffing it out. Tonight he'd made that long journey into London just to take care of poor Monica. The Duchess of Dorminster approved of Derek—that should be enough for anyone. The duchess was no fool.

She shook as if with ague. Kate went to her bed—their bed, when Derek chose to share it with her—climbed in under the cover, still wearing her robe, and huddled there, eyes squeezed shut to try to blot out the ugliness she'd just read. It didn't help. Eyes open, eyes closed, Kate could still see that terrible writing—as if done by the hands of different men. Was that the answer? Was Derek like the man in Stevenson's story, sometimes the good Dr. Jekyll, sometimes the evil Mr. Hyde? She pulled the covers over her head, but it didn't shut out the horrid wondering. Derek had been under such a strain lately. Their marriage was rocky, Harry kept jabbing at him, Mansfield battled with him in the East End. Had it all made his mind crack?

Tears came and she sobbed helplessly. She loved Derek so much. Was she the cause of his problems? Oh, God, don't let him be the terrifying Jack the Ripper, she prayed frantically. She couldn't bear that. She remembered how tender he could be when he made love to her, how passionate, how loving. And how demanding. She also remembered how short-tempered he'd been of late, his almost pathological jealousy of Harry, his distrust of her—some of it well-founded.

"My fault," she whispered, although there was no one there to hear her confession. "All my fault. I deceived him, I went to bed with Harry, and it has turned his mind."

She sobbed despairngly, huddled there, head covered. Finally, after hearing the little gilt clock on the mantel strike three, Kate dozed off into a troubled sleep.

She woke with a scream, hands feeling for her through the coverlet. Fighting blindly, she cried, "No, no, I'll never tell. I promise, I promise! Just don't kill me too."

Then the covers were pulled away from her head roughly, and standing over her, face a study in emotions, was Derek.

"Kate, wake up! You're having a nightmare!"

She wasn't sure whether she slept or was awake. "What time is it?" she whispered, still in the grip of the terrible dream.

"Nearly six. It'll be getting light soon. Why did you go to bed with the lamp still burning?"

"Lamp?" Then she remembered. She had lighted the lamp on Derek's desk so that she could read the—her mind shied away from thoughts of the two journals. Maybe that had been part of the dream. Maybe there wasn't a second diary in his desk, one with wild, mad things in it. She smiled tremulously, sure that was the explanation. She'd dreamed all of that sequence about finding the second journal. "I planned to wait up for you, Derek. I got chilly, so I crawled under the covers—and I guess I went to sleep." She shuddered. "I had a ghastly dream."

"I heard you screaming and talking about killing."

"Too much chatter about those awful Ripper murders in East London," she said, subdued. Then, realizing that he still wore what he'd had on when he left for London, she asked, "Are you just getting home?"

"Yes. It was a long night." Weariness was in his voice, and his face was lined and gray with fatigue.

"Let me ring for Tolliver. He can help you undress, and bring you something to eat."

"No, I don't want to wake him. And I'm not hungry for food—only for you, Kate."

She reached up loving arms for him, and drew him down to the bed beside her. "Here, let me be your valet," she offered, undoing the buttons of his coat and waistcoat. She helped him out of them, then started to unbutton his shirt when she noticed something brown on the cuff of his white shirt. "You've gotten something on your shirt sleeve. It looks like—" She stopped short, terror washing over her like a tidal wave. It looked like blood.

"Oh, that's probably blood," Derek said, quite matter-of-factly. "Poor Monica, she had a bad night. She hemorrhaged once, and I dare say I got blood on me then. Probably some on my suit too. I'll have Tolliver sponge it with cold water tomorrow—today, I guess it is. Oh, Kate, I'm so glad to be back home with you. It's been a long night."

When he joined her in bed, he didn't make love to her. He put his arms about her and fell asleep, exhausted.

She lay there, clinging to him, troubled. It was such a logical explanation for the stains on his clothing. She herself had seen Monica spit up blood weeks ago.

But the dream—or was it reality, the secret journal?—plagued her. She loved Derek deeply, but she was afraid of him. Was he innocent? Had she dreamed the diary? Or was Derek the dreaded Jack the Ripper?

CHAPTER 31

Friday, November 9, 1888

Harry had been gone for several days. He did this now and again, never saying where he had been when he returned to Scarlet Oaks. Now that her marriage with Derek was on an even keel, Kate paid little attention to Harry's comings and goings. She was happier when he was away; but as the tensions at home had lessened, she didn't insist that Derek ask Harry to leave.

She had just left the kitchen after settling the day's menu with the cook when Harry suddenly came stamping in, his boots muddy from the heavy November rains which had made a quagmire of the roads. As he threw off his wet top coat and put his top hat on the rack, Kate sensed a wild excitement in him which she hadn't noticed for weeks.

"Ah, my delectable sister-in-law," he cried, catching her up and swinging her around. As he set her dizzily on her feet, he kissed her soundly.

"Harry! Stop!" she said crossly.

"Ah, Kate, the time was when you'd beg me not to stop!"

She just glared at him, not dignifying what he said with any reply.

"And where is my dear older brother?"

"It's Friday," she reminded him. "You know he goes to his clinic every Friday."

"And what about yesterday?" he asked slyly. "Where was Derek last night, Kate?"

"If it's any of your business, he was taking care of Monica Murphy."

Harry shrugged, smiled. "Or so he told you."

"Harry, I don't like your innuendoes, your insinuations. You've behaved yourself rather well for weeks. What's gotten into you this morning?"

He looked around, then caught her hand and drew her into the library. "So the servants can't hear us," he explained.

"What's so private that we must discuss it in secret?"

"There was another Ripper killing in the East End last night," he told her. "Another whore was slashed."

Kate felt a sickening sensation in her middle. She thought she might faint. Immediately Harry's arm was around her, supporting her.

"Are you all right, Kate?"

Determined not to let what he said upset her, she pulled away from him and said, "I'm perfectly all right. I do wish you'd keep your hands off me, Harry."

"My, my. The time was—"

"That time is long since gone," she snapped.

"But why should you be so upset at the murder of an unknown whore in Whitechapel, Kate?" He looked intently at her, his light gray eyes aglitter. "Are you worried that Derek wasn't where he said? Do you think he might have been up to something much bloodier and nastier in London?"

"That's an abominable thing to say about your own brother."

"Kate, get your head out of the sand. Stop being an ostrich," Harry said, voice low, pleading. "Surely you've seen how Derek has changed over the last few months— he's turned tense, sullen, angry. He explodes at the least thing. He snaps at you—at me—even at Aunt Letitia. He goes off to that rotten clinic of his twice a week, or so he says. It puts him squarely in the middle of the East End, which is a cesspool. You've been there with the duchess. You can't think it is healthy for Derek to be there, week after week, associating with those low classes, seeing their filth and degradation. I worry about you, dear

Kate." He reached out, touched her cheek gently, his fingers caressing. "I don't want something horrible to happen to you. We've been too close, you mean too much to me. Can't you see that Derek is ill?"

Kate felt sick at heart. "It's been so nice this past month—no murders—no troubles. Derek and I—it's . . ." Tears came then, and she didn't try to check them. She loved Derek so much. Why did Harry have to spoil everything?

"I know what you're thinking. Your face is so easy to read," he said softly. "But Kate, I'm only trying to get you to face the bitter truth. There are so many things pointing toward Derek. The consensus that the Ripper is a doctor—the fact that Derek is always away when these things happen."

"You're away lots of times too," she said, hitting back, trying to hurt him as much as he'd hurt her. "Maybe you're the Ripper."

He laughed. "Somehow, I can't imagine that they'd believe such a story. A man who had to drop out of medical school because he couldn't bear to dissect a cadaver—how could I be the Ripper?"

"You're just making all this up," she said. "It's circumstantial evidence. Happenstance."

"I wonder if Derek writes about the murders in that precious journal of his?"

Kate's hand was against her mouth, her eyes wide with horror. The secret diary. The one Harry didn't know about.

"Do you think we have a right to look into his journal, under the circumstances?"

"No! That's wicked. I won't listen to another word from you, Harry." Kate caught up the skirt of her pale blue print morning dress and fled from him, running upstairs into her bedchamber, locking the door behind her lest Harry follow her.

The diary. The awful, secret, copybook volume she'd found in the hidden drawer. What should she do about it? Should she say something to Derek about it, demand an explanation? But if she did, he'd know she'd been prying, that she'd gained access to his desk, invaded his privacy. Like Bluebeard's wife.

She stared with horror at the imitation bamboo desk with its damning secret journal. There was no logical explanation for its presence there. The other journal she knew about. Derek had never made a secret of it, although he acted as if he didn't want her to read what he'd written in it. What she had read surreptitiously was nothing to alarm her. It was very personal, intimate, and sometimes it involved their married life together—but there was nothing to frighten her in that writing.

But that other horrid diary with the strange bits of writing in different hands. What could it mean? Now Harry's suspicions were added to her own, fueling the fire. Another Ripper murder after things had quieted down. Kate had been lulled by the respite. Now it hit her harder than ever. Derek had once possessed a deerstalker hat—he told her he had lost it. He was a doctor. He was familiar with the Whitechapel area and knew most of the prostitutes who had been so brutally slaughtered. And he had been strange these past weeks, moody, prone to fits of anger. And last night he'd come home covered with blood. . . . Oh, God, what was she going to do?

Finally she decided to go riding, even though it was a cold, raw day. Maybe the brisk air would clear her brain, give her some insight into the best plan to follow with Derek.

She went to the bellpull and rang for Vera. When her maid came, she had to knock. Kate had forgotten about locking her door to keep Harry out of the room.

"Are you all right, milady?" Vera asked anxiously.

"Yes, yes, just a headache. I think I'll go riding for a while, to see if the fresh air will make me feel better."

"You'd better wear your warmest petticoat under your riding habit, milady. It is very cold out."

Clad in her warmest habit, a dark green wool serge, Kate tied a length of heavy veiling over the riding hat for added warmth. When she rode out from Scarlet Oaks, she had no destination in mind; but she decided that she'd ride to Harcourt to see the Duchess of Dorminster. Maybe that wise woman could help set her mind at rest.

Over cups of tea in the rose salon, Kate unburdened her heart to the duchess. When she mentioned the strange diary, the duchess exclaimed, "That doesn't sound like Derek at all!"

"I know. But he's been very—upset—of late. And now there's been another murder—"

"Another! I thought all that was over," exclaimed the duchess.

Kate shook her head. "Harry heard that another woman was killed by this Jack the Ripper."

Shrewdly the old woman looked at her. "And where was Derek while this went on?"

"He was called out to see Monica Murphy; she'd had a very bad night."

The duchess leaned toward her, patted her hand. "Then you needn't worry. He can prove where he was."

But Kate did worry, and it showed. Derek had gone off for many hours—long enough to treat Monica *and more* . . .

"Would you like for me to come back to Scarlet Oaks with you and look at this strange journal you found?"

"Only if we can do it without Derek's knowing we've pried."

"We'll ride over—and if he's there, we'll let it go until some other time," the duchess suggested. "I'll go in my victoria. It's not a good day for my old bones to tackle horseback."

Kate was impatient to get to their room, for she never knew just when Derek would come home on Fridays. He hadn't arrived when she and the duchess got to Scarlet Oaks. Parsons said he'd had no word when to expect Sir Derek.

"It should be safe, then," Kate said; but she made sure to lock the bedroom door so that Derek couldn't walk in on them unexpectedly. She hurried to the desk, unlocked it with the concealed key. "I suppose you think it's terrible of me to have peeked."

The duchess replied, "We do what we must Kate."

Then Kate worked the secret latch to get at the hidden drawer. It opened at a touch. Kate was stunned to find that the drawer was empty. No copybook lay there.

"It's gone!"

"Kate, are you sure it was there? You didn't imagine this, did you? You've been under something of a strain yourself these past days, wondering if Derek is this dreadful Ripper."

"It was here! I swear it. An ordinary copybook, the kind schoolboys use. And it was full of these odd bits and pieces of writing—some in Derek's very distinctive handwriting, others in other hands. An incoherent kind of record."

"When did you see it?"

"Saturday night—Sunday morning—after we had dinner at Pam's. Derek was called to London—Monica had a crisis. I was upset, and I admit it, I pried."

"Have you seen that book since then?"

"I haven't looked. I had nightmares about it—Derek woke me when he came in, I had my head under the covers, and I was terrified."

The duchess smiled then. "Kate, it's simple. You dreamed about that book. It was a nightmare. And it seemed so real that you thought it had actually happened."

"Just a dream? Is that possible?"

"Of course. Put it out of your mind, child. You'll make yourself ill—and wreck a good marriage—if you don't forget about it. You know that Derek is a good man, a loving husband. Do you honestly think that he could be this dastardly murderer, a man who kills and mutilates women?"

"No, not when you put it that way."

"Then my advice to you is to forget it. You've been through a bad time, my dear. You and Derek both have been under tension. If you'll listen to an old, foolish woman, send Harry packing. He's caused enough trouble for a lifetime. Forget all this other nonsense."

It made Kate feel so much better, and she embraced the duchess in her relief. After the old woman had gone back to Harcourt, though, Kate had second thoughts. She was positive she had read that secret journal, held the copybook in her hands. It couldn't have been a dream. If it wasn't a dream, then it had to be reality, a reality that she was loath to accept.

INTERLUDE 9

Friday, November 16, 1888

He saw her turn onto Whitechapel from Union Street. She was gasping for breath. Obviously she should have been in bed, not out soliciting. She had to stop and lean against a dirty brick wall until she had the strength to go on. She called out to a few men who passed her, but her voice was so weak that they didn't pay any attention to her.

He moved toward her, recognizing Monica Murphy, a Monica fallen so low that he could see no remnants of her former beauty in her raddled face. The fever spots on her cheeks told him she was far gone with consumption. When he approached her from behind, she turned quickly, no recognition in her eyes. Then something happened, and he saw realization dawning on Monica's face.

"What are you doing here in that get-up?" she asked, amused. "A false beard?" She reached up, caught the VanDyke in her hand, and tugged, pulling it loose on one edge.

"Stop it, Monica," he said angrily.

"But I don't understand," she insisted. "In disguise? Why are you walking the streets of Whitechapel this way?"

"The Prince of Wales walks these streets incognito."

She scoffed, "And you put yourself on a level with royalty?"

By now he had an arm around her waist. "Come along, Monica, we must talk," he said. "I'll buy you a gin."

He saw her eyes light up at the promise of gin. She went with him willingly.

CHAPTER 32

Friday, November 30, 1888

As Kate rode in to London on the train, the bundle on the rack over her head, she thought of the last terrible two weeks, the days that had set her on this final journey. She had to know. It was no good anymore. Derek was a stranger, Harry was edgy as a cat before a thunderstorm. London was seething with emotion. The newspapers were full of nothing but the Ripper killings. Everyone was in the grip of this reign of terror. Until the madman was caught, no woman was safe in London.

Monica Murphy's death had been the final straw. When Derek came home that Saturday morning, after having been away all night, Kate had taken one look at him and her soul was plunged into terror. He was haunted. His face was gray with fatigue, his eyes glittered with a kind of madness, his hands shook when he took off his topcoat.

Kate had gone to him, but her heart was heavy with dread. Putting her arms about him, she said, "What happened? I waited up for you until long after midnight." She could feel him tremble. "Derek, you're ill!"

"Sick at heart, Kate." A terrible sob tore at his throat.

"Oh, my dear, what is it?" she said, frightened. This wasn't the Derek she knew, the strong, calm, resourceful man she loved.

"I don't want to talk about it," he murmured, pulling away from her, heading toward the staircase.

There was the rattle of the front door, and Harry came

in, muffled up so that his scarf covered the bottom of his
face. Only his eyes showed, those light gray eyes. There
was a wildness about him that set the place crackling with
tension.

"Did he tell you?" Harry asked Kate, pulling the woolen
scarf from his face. His words were to her, but his eyes
were intent on his brother.

Derek turned, almost as a stag might when ringed by
the death of staghounds. "I didn't see you on the train,
Harry."

"I was there. You got away from me at the station. I
hired a cab to bring me home." Then, again, he asked,
"Did Derek tell you, Kate?"

"Tell me what?" She stood between them, not sure
what was happening. At Harry's repeated question, she
saw Derek wince almost as if the words were physical
blows.

"The Ripper has struck again!"

"Oh, no." It was almost a whimper. She thought she
might faint, she was so frightened.

"Another whore, this one killed in her room."

"Harry, I don't want to hear about it," Kate said. She
moved toward her husband, worried sick at the look on
his face. He was deathly pale, and he flung out a hand to
the newel post, as if he needed some support to keep
from collapsing.

"But I thought you'd be vitally interested, Kate, since
the latest victim is someone you know."

Horrified, she looked from one man to the other. Harry
and Derek were staring at each other now as if she weren't
there. A kind of contest of wills seemed to progress.

"Who—who died?" She had to know. She suspected—
but she had to be sure.

Derek answered her, not Harry. "It was Monica, Kate.
She was murdered in her room up over the clinic."

Kate walked slowly toward her husband, then sank
down on the bottom step and buried her face in her hands.
Monica. The woman who had been Derek's lover so many
years ago. Poor, dying Monica—murdered by that madman.

"How did you know about her, Harry?"

"It's all over London. Do you think that the police can keep another Ripper murder quiet, Derek? Bad for you, right? Woman you've given a room to—right there in the heart of the murder district. A whore."

Kate raised her head, angered at Harry's words.

"Don't call her that, Harry."

He shrugged. "Very well, a woman of the streets, if the word 'whore' offends your sensibilities, Kate. You know what she was. And now she's dead by the butcher's knife."

Derek turned and went up the stairs slowly, an old man's gait. After a moment, Kate got up and followed him. At the top of the stairs she stopped and looked down. Harry was standing at the foot of the stairs, looking up. It reminded her of that day all those months ago when Harry came back from Ireland and found that she was Derek's wife.

"Take care, Kate," he said now softly; but his voice carried well, and she heard the words all too clearly.

She turned her back on him and hurried after Derek. He was sitting at his desk, his head cushioned on his arms. Not sure what she should do, Kate approached him slowly, reached out a hand, touched his head. The feel of his thick black hair was exciting, as it always was, and she swayed toward him.

"Was it very bad, Derek?"

He groaned. "You can't know how horrible, Kate." She felt him shudder. Then he turned and caught her to him, burying his face in her bosom, shaking as if he had ague. Her arms went around him, and she laid her face on his head, aching for him yet afraid of him in some undefined way.

"Come, Derek, you are exhausted. You must get some rest," she said as if he were a sick child.

"Rest! God, will I ever be able to rest again? They took me up to her room. I'm a doctor—it's not supposed to affect a physician, the sight of blood, of that pitiful, mutilated body." She felt the shudder run through him. "Horrible, Kate. What a ghastly end for Monica."

"Let me call Tolliver, have him help you to bed," she

begged him, but he clung to her and said he didn't want his valet to see him this way.

In desperation, Kate helped him get ready for bed. Then he asked her to get in bed with him, so she undressed and slid into the high bed beside him.

His lovemaking was wild and desperate, as if he wanted to forget everything in loving her. He was almost frightening in his demands on her; but she kept reminding herself that he was her husband and she loved him dearly. She gave and gave until he was satisfied. Then he fell into a deep sleep in her arms.

Derek wasn't himself, though, and his manner affected the entire household. Aunt Letitia sent for Kate and demanded to know what Kate had done to poor Derek to put him into such a state. Angered that the blame for his manner be put onto her, Kate was short with Lady Zangwill, which did nothing to make the atmosphere at Scarlet Oaks more peaceful.

On Monday Derek went back into London, telling Kate that he must give evidence at the inquest. He'd scarcely gotten out the front door when Harry was beside her.

"You do know, don't you, Kate? You know what Derek has done?"

"I don't know what you're talking about, and I won't listen to any of your insinuations, Harry. Leave me alone."

"I'm only trying to help you, Kate. Derek is beyond help. Don't you realize that? How can you be so blind?"

"Stop it! Stop it!" she cried, running up the stairs, stumbling at the top, nearly falling. Anything to get away from Harry's voice, from the words that ate into her mind.

In her room, the door locked to keep him out, she paced the floor. The desk drew her. It was there that Derek had sat when he came in on Saturday morning after Monica's death. If she hadn't followed him into the room, would he have sat there, writing in his journal, perhaps putting on paper the things he couldn't say aloud?

Reluctantly, drawn to it by some compulsion she could not deny, Kate sat before the maple desk, traced the bamboo carving in it, then felt under it for the key. She turned it in the lock but sat without opening the desk for minutes while the gilt clock ticked loudly in the silent room. Finally she opened the desk and took out Derek's journal. She opened it only to find that he had made no entries in it since Monica's death. She put it away and was going to close the desk when she thought of the secret drawer. It would be empty—had there ever been a copybook in it? —but even as she thought this, her hand was groping for the latch to release the pigeonhole compartments. With trembling hands she pulled out the secret drawer. There, lying like an adder in wait for her, was the secret diary.

"No," she whispered, "no"; but words didn't make it disappear.

She took the book from the drawer and sat looking at it, afraid to open the pages, compelled to look at what was written on the lined paper. Finally she began to leaf through the diary. It was the same book she had seen before. The early pages were in Derek's distinctive bold spiky hand. Then the writing deteriorated. It seemed to be done by a variety of men. The spelling was bad, the grammar atrocious; a schoolboy could do better. One isolated fragment caught her eye. Printed in a juvenile manner were the words, *The Juwes are not the men* . . . The letters of *men* were scrawled down across the page. On another page were lines of doggerel, *Eight little whores, with no hope of heaven, Gladstone may save one, then there'll be seven.* Further along in the book was the date, *September 8,* and the name *Dark Annie.* In parentheses after this were the words, *Siffey or Sievey.* She recalled that the victim, Annie Chapman, had gone by the name of the man she lived with.

There were entries, she thought, since the other time when she'd found the diary. With fearful fingers she found the final word written. Only a name: *Monica.* Heavily underscored.

Kate did not return the book to the secret drawer. Instead she hid it in her own chest of drawers under a stack of lacy corset covers. If she wanted to show the book to anyone, she was determined this time to know where it was.

It was the beginning of the end. That night in bed, something about her manner told Derek more than she wanted him to know. Fingers painful on her bare shoulders, he demanded, "What is it, Kate? What do you believe about me? Has Harry's filth finally poisoned you against me?"

"No, of course not, Derek," she insisted—after the tiniest of hesitations. It was enough. With an oath Derek left their bed, gathered up his clothes, and flew out of the room. He had not approached her since then. Often he was gone by the time she got up.

Finally, early in the week, Kate made her desperate plan. She told Derek that she was going to visit a cousin in Manchester for a few days. He seemed almost relieved that she would be away. Then she made a trip to London, ostensibly to shop for the brief vacation. She shopped—from second-hand clothing barrows near the underground station, smuggling her purchases back to Scarlet Oaks under legitimate purchases she made on Bond Street. She washed the clothing in secret and looked up addresses of rooming houses in *The Penny Illustrated Paper*, which Derek still brought home from the East End.

Now she was ready, determined to find out once and for all if Derek was Jack the Ripper. She would take a room in the East End, dress like a common whore, and prowl the streets, hoping to lure the dreaded Ripper to her. Until she saw his face, knew whether or not he was her beloved Derek, she could have no peace.

CHAPTER 33

Friday, November 30, 1888

Kate left the dreary room on Finster Lane, locking it behind her and hanging the key around her neck on a narrow ribbon. Outside, the air was raw, with the first wisps of fog curling opaque tendrils around the gas streetlamp. She walked the streets of Whitechapel until the fog descended, blotting out everything. It was then that she first heard the footsteps behind her. When she heard the furtive sounds following her, she panicked. Terrified, Kate kept moving, but she had no way of knowing if she was actually headed toward the buildings along the street. Then she stumbled over a step leading into a building, and she fell heavily to her knees, crying out from pain. There was a rush of footsteps and a voice saying, "Whore!" Hands came out of the fog, imprisoning Kate in a grasp of iron.

"Whore, whore, whore!" he hissed. "You'll join the others."

The words echoed in Kate's ears. Dear God, how she knew that voice! She'd heard it in anger, she'd heard it in love. All of her suspicions, all her nightmares and terrors, were realized at that moment. Derek was Jack the Ripper, and she was slated to be his next victim. Part of her died then, with the knowledge that her beloved was a brutal, mad killer, a mutilator of helpless women. She wanted to die too. But when he held her more tightly against her struggles, even though she thought she couldn't live now with the awful knowledge she had, Kate fought instinctively. When she lashed out behind her with the sharp edge of the heel of her heavy shoe, her assailant eased his grip momentarily, giving her a chance to wrench her head away from his hand. She managed to cry out twice, "Help! Help!" before the Ripper gave her no further chance. His powerful hand was around her throat, thumb digging in under one ear. The pressure increased and Kate felt herself falling, the fog closing in on her inexorably. Just before she lost consciousness, Kate felt the cold steel of something sharp at her throat.

She came back from some far-off place, a place of terror, of nightmare, of fog and fear. She was lying in bed—but such a hard bed it was. Her fingers felt for the sheets, but touched what felt like wet stone.

Then a light shone directly in her face, so that even with closed eyes, it bothered her. Moving her head from side to side she moaned, "No, no!"

"Kate! Oh, my God, Kate!"

It was Derek's sweet voice, full of worry. Why was Derek worried? Derek. Something about Derek—fear clutched at her throat, cutting off her voice. Her eyes opened and there, in the strange glow, Derek's face hung, disembodied.

Memory poured back over her, and with it mounting terror. Derek was still there—Derek, her beloved Derek, was the madman Jack the Ripper, and he was going to kill her too.

Uncontrollably, a scream filled her throat, burst from her lips. "Don't kill me, Derek!" she begged, trying to roll away from him on the wet, cold pavement.

His hand came out of the fog then and caught her shoulders. His face was a mask of dismay, of sorrow.

"Kate, Kate, what are you saying?"

"Don't pretend," she begged. "I can't stand any more pretense. Go ahead and kill me. Why didn't you finish me off? Why prolong the agony, Derek? If you are going to slit my throat, do it now."

A groan escaped his throat, and Kate heard another voice. She suddenly realized that someone else was standing there in the fog with the two of them, someone holding a bull's-eye lantern. Dimly she saw the blue of his trousers—a constable.

"Out of her head, sir," the man was saying to Derek. "Scared most to death. We got to her just in time."

"Thank God!" Derek said, catching her to him in a fierce embrace.

Kate struggled against her husband, terror filling her. "Let me go! Let me go!" Pulling away from Derek, she scrambled to her knees, caught at the coat of the policeman, begged him, "Don't listen to him! He tried to kill me! I heard his voice—I knew him."

"Not the doctor, ma'am," the constable said, his face coming down toward her, a good face, middle-aged, with a bushy ginger moustache drooping over his mouth. "Twarn't the doctor, ma'am. He's been with me for the past half hour, searching for the Ripper."

Derek reached down, picked her up, held her tenderly.

" 'Twas the Ripper, ma'am, who attacked you. We heard your cry for help and got here just in time." He shone the lantern to one side, and a long, sharp knife picked up the glint of light on its polished blade. "Dropped his knife when we approached and tried to apprehend him. Hear the whistles? They're after him now."

Kate realized she'd been hearing some commotion all of the time since she'd regained consciousness. It was shouts and the sound of police whistles, diminishing in the distance.

"No more talk, now, until I get my wife to my clinic and get some brandy into her. She's had a terrible shock."

"Of course, Doctor. Lor! Imagine! Your own lady wife almost one of the Ripper's victims."

Kate, held tight in her husband's loving arms, felt the shudder run through him, the little inarticulate sound he made, music to her ears. It wasn't Derek, after all, who was the Ripper.

With the constable to lead the way, Derek took her to the clinic where he made her lie on a sofa and sip brandy. He had brandy, too, and she saw that his hands were trembling.

"We'll be here for at least an hour before we get the

train for Chelmsford," Derek told the constable. "Would you let me know what happens. . . ."

"Of course, sir. I'll let you know who the villain is once we've caught him. This time I think he'll not escape."

When they were alone, Kate quietly went to pieces. Derek gathered her in his arms and held her, not talking, just being there with her, giving her strength. When finally she had recovered somewhat, she asked him, "Can you forgive me, Derek, for believing that you could be the Ripper?"

"Harry filled your head with nonsense."

"But I should have known it was false!" she cried. "I did—until I found that awful secret diary."

"Reading my journal again, Kate?" he chided gently.

"No, not the one you write in regularly—not the leather-bound volume. The other one."

"What other one? The one in my desk is the only one I own, Kate."

Then she told him about the copybook with its incoherent bits and pieces, its damning evidence. She told him how it had disappeared when she brought the Duchess of Dorminster to their room to read it, only to find the secret drawer empty, the copybook gone.

"Then it reappeared after Monica's death. Oh, Derek, I was terrified. It sounded—it sounded mad! Where could it have come from?"

"Harry. He always was clever with a pen. You, of all people, should know that, Kate. Your father lost Fairlawn because Harry forged those stocks."

"Of course! But during these last few weeks—you came home with blood on your clothes after one murder—you seemed so distraught—"

"How would you feel if your wife thought you were Jack the Ripper?" he asked, voice dry.

"Please forgive me! I'm so sorry. I loved you so much, and I was so scared! Harry kept hinting horrid things—he—he kept it all in my mind."

"Poor Harry." Derek's face was bleak. "You do realize, don't you, that he's the one who attacked you—he's the Ripper."

"Harry? It was Harry?" She had difficulty taking it in. "But—he kept hinting to me that you were the one." Then she nodded, comprehending. "Your voices are so alike. That's why, when he attacked me—spoke to me—I thought it was you."

"I feel it must be, at least in part, my fault that Harry turned out this way."

"No—don't blame yourself, Derek. Oh, I know, I took Harry's part for a long time. I said you were to blame for not giving him all the money he wanted. Now I realize that he'd never have been different even if he could have had all he wanted."

"He wanted it *all*, Kate. If he could have me blamed as Jack the Ripper, then I'd be executed—and he'd be heir to Scarlet Oaks, the baronetcy—even you!"

"No, never to me, Derek, never to me. What I felt for Harry wasn't true love. When I came to love you, I realized that."

He kissed her, a long, slow, passionate kiss that sent her senses reeling.

"Oh, Derek, I thought I'd lost you," she murmured.

Then he asked, "But what were you doing there on Greenfield Street—and in these awful clothes? You're dressed like—like—"

"A whore." She told him, simply, what her desperate plan had been. "I had to know, one way or the other, Derek. I was being torn apart. I loved you so much—and yet all of Harry's clever machinations made the finger of guilt point to you. I knew I couldn't live if you were Jack the Ripper. So I came here tonight to try to lure the killer—to get a look at his face—to know the truth, even if it killed me."

"And it nearly did. I—oh, Kate, if we'd been a minute late—"

"How did you happen to be there?"

"I'd become suspicious of Harry these last few days. There were little things—the fact that he knew about Monica's death made me very suspicious, for I did not think anyone but the police and I knew about her that night. She was not killed on the street, but in her room.

How could he have known? And he seemed always to be away from Scarlet Oaks when the murders occurred."

Kate laughed shakily. "That's one of the things he said about you. Did he deliberately choose times when he knew that you, too, were not at home?"

"Probably. It sounds as if he began laying the false clues pointing to me months ago." His voice sounded desolate. "It is terrible to know your own brother hates you so much."

"I wonder what Arthur Mansfield will do when he learns about Harry?"

"I hope he never finds out. Is it terrible, Kate, for me to wish our family name needn't be stained by this horrible affair? To hope that somehow Harry's name won't be known?"

"No, dear, of course not." Yet Kate didn't see how the dreadful story could be suppressed.

"Hopefully, this will help in my campaign to oust Mansfield and his ilk from the East End. He is to blame for so much of the degradation here. I only hope that I can be instrumental in destroying his power. With the tremendous feeling rampant about the Ripper, it certainly won't do Mansfield any good when decent people learn that such slumlords make crimes of this kind inevitable. East London is a breeding place for all kinds of evil."

Just then there was a discreet knock on the door of Derek's clinic. It was the moustached constable who had helped to save Kate's life.

"Any word, Constable?" Derek asked.

Kate felt her throat constrict. It still was difficult for her to absorb the dreadful truth about Harry—Harry, who had been her first love—handsome, wasteful, reckless Harry, who had given her pleasure and pain, love and hate.

"I'm sorry, doctor," the constable said, obviously ill at ease. "They chased him clear to the river. When he saw he couldn't escape, he leaped into the Thames. They put a boat in as quickly as they could—but what with the fog, and the fact that the tide's going out—it was no use."

"His body?" Derek asked fearfully.

"Not recovered, sir. Nor is it likely to be. They'll look

for it, of course—but with the tide on the ebb, it'll be carried out to sea, and chances are it will never be found."

Kate sobbed quietly for Harry; but it was best this way. Now no one need ever know that Harry Ravenshaw was the monster known as Jack the Ripper.

"What a waste," Derek murmured, "What a tragic waste."

The constable left them then, and Derek said, "Let's go home, Kate—let's go home."

THREE STUNNING HISTORICAL ROMANCES BY ANDREA LAYTON

_____ 16489   *SO WILD A RAPTURE* $1.95

On the eve of the French Revolution, Juliette is enticed against her will by a passionate liaison with a wealthy baron that sweeps her from the heights of ecstasy to the depths of shame.

_____ 16455   *LOVE'S GENTLE FUGITIVE* $1.95

A runaway to the New World, beautiful Elizabeth Bartlett tries to escape her secret past. But soon she surrenders her heart—and her destiny—to the passionate stranger who could choose to love or betray her.

_____ 16532   *MIDNIGHT FIRES* $2.25

Caught between her Loyalist lover and a lusty American rebel, Carolyn Salford flees the backwoods for the safety of the city in this exciting tale of Revolution-torn America. A thrilling sequel to *Love's Gentle Fugitive*.

PLAYBOY PRESS PAPERBACKS
Book Mailing Service
P.O. Box 690 Rockville Centre, New York 11570

NAME_____

ADDRESS_____

CITY_____STATE_____ZIP_____

Please enclose 50¢ for postage and handling if one book is ordered; 25¢ for each additional book. $1.50 maximum postage and handling charge. No cash, CODs or stamps. Send check or money order.

Total amount enclosed: $_____